A War by Diplomacy:

At Home and At Sea

1804

by

John G. Cragg

A War by Diplomacy: At Home and At Sea – 1804

Copyright © 2017, 2020

Dedicated to

*My most encouraging
and helpful critic*

Olga Browzin Cragg

Preface

This is a work of fiction. It follows on from the first two volumes in this series, *A New War: at Home and at Sea, 1803* and *A Continuing War: at Home and at Sea, 1803-4*. They are available at Amazon.com and other Amazon sites by searching for my name or the title. The present tale takes place in 1804. A great many things have changed in the more than two centuries that have elapsed since that date, including items and phrases that may be unfamiliar to many readers. To help those who are curious, a glossary is provided at the end of the book. Items that appear in the glossary are flagged on their first appearance in the text by a * as in, for example, taffrail*.

Contents

Chapter I

Captain Sir Richard Giles rode his horse up a gentle slope to turn just in front of his house, Dipton Hall. He had been home from the sea for more than three weeks, but he continued to take great pleasure just at being on his estate. Before him lay the newly designed grounds of his property, still a vista being created so that he could only imagine the finished look. The slope in front of him had been planted with grass seed. It had sprouted nicely and was already up almost an inch. The new lawn was dotted with raised patches of earth where flower beds would go, and it was bordered with wide swaths of rich-looking earth that eventually would be perennial borders. The slope ended in a muddy area where a stone wall was being constructed that would eventually surround a pond through which would flow the stream. The water was now diverted around the area in an artificially made new stream bed, which made a further scar on the landscape. Beyond the stream, the land sloped upwards towards another construction-site where an open, circular Grecian temple was being built.

The view gave him great satisfaction, even in its present unfinished state. Only a few weeks before, it had been a well-tended area of landscaping where shrubs and trees hid the view that was now exposed. His wife Daphne had conceived the new layout. Together with his man-of-business and prize agent, Mr. Edwards, she had also organized the extensive work-crew and contracted with specialists to get the work undertaken. Behind Giles, a stone terrace was taking shape. New doorways to the house were being built coming from narrow and not very useful rooms in the house. There would be no need for glass doors in the French fashion. Daphne thought such doors would make it much more difficult to keep warm and draft-free the large drawing-room, which would have the best view of the newly reconstructed grounds.

After pausing for several moments, Giles continued around the house to its facade. To the side of the house, some distance away, he could see the new stables taking shape. Beyond them was a paddock holding several horses, the start of his stud farm. At the portico of the Hall, he was about to dismount when he noticed Daphne's horse being led by a groom towards the stables. She must have just returned and would be upstairs changing. He thought it might be better to wait a while before he entered. Daphne's long-time lady's maid, Elsie, had recently left her service to run the inn whose lease she and her husband, Carstairs, had just assumed.

Elsie had wanted to understand all aspects of her new responsibilities before her baby was born and her husband returned to the war. Unfortunately, Daphne's transition to a new lady's maid had not gone entirely smoothly. She was accustomed to Elsie's ways and Elsie to hers. She was impatient with her new maid, Betsey, not automatically understanding what she liked or how she thought things should be done. Betsey had her weaknesses, but also areas where she was superior to Elsie. It would just take a while for the two to get used to each other. It didn't help that the discomfort from the later stages of Daphne's pregnancy often left his wife uncharacteristically irritable. Giles reckoned that it would be wise for him to wait a while before seeing his wife. He figured that she would be happier to see him after she had completely changed out of her riding apparel. A drink at the Dipton Arms would admirably fill the time.

Giles found that the new landlord of the Dipton Arms was equally eager to escape his wife for a spell. Right from the start, Elsie's pregnancy had not gone very easily, and now she was suffering from swollen ankles and a sore back. Carstairs sometimes had the feeling that he could never do anything right. Despite their vast difference in rank, the two old friends settled down with two pints of ale to recount the latest neighborhood gossip. In particular, Giles enjoyed hearing about the minor doings in his area, and, just as when they were at sea, he knew that Carstairs would bring to his attention any source of dissatisfaction among the tenants or neighbors that might require his attention.

Back at the front door, Giles did dismount, ignoring a slight twinge in his knee as his right leg took his weight. The injury was no longer preventing him from doing anything he wished. The slight discomfort did remind him that he should be getting word any day about the repairs to his frigate, *Impetuous*. No doubt, he would have to return soon to his duty. But for now, all was well, and he could enjoy his home without feeling rushed to get away.

Giles tossed his reins to a waiting groom and strode to his front door, not even noticing the imposing portico that graced his manor nor how its harmonious placing enhanced the whole structure. Thrusting the door open, he found Steves, the butler, standing with a silver platter containing a letter. Giles took it and was scanning it as he mounted the stairs to his wife's dressing room.

"At last!" he exclaimed as he entered

"What is it?" Daphne asked, looking up at him. As always, her heart leapt to see the man she loved. He was quite tall and thin without being in any way willowy. His straight blond hair was brushed back, with only one wayward lock sliding forward to gently adhere to his forehead. His face was weather-beaten and lined by the countless hours he had spent on deck in all weathers, while his habitual expression, whose lines also were etched in his countenance, were ones of mild pleasure at life. His most striking feature was his clear blue eyes.

"I have finally heard from the Admiralty. They want to see me at ten o'clock on Thursday – three days from now, so there is no rush," Giles replied. "Odd, though."

"What is odd?"

"That they are not in a great hurry. Usually, when the Admiralty summons someone, they seem to want him the day before yesterday. I don't have to leave right away. Would you like to come with me to London?"

Daphne rose from her chair to face him. She was slim and of above-average height with her nose almost on a level with Giles's chin. Her chestnut hair was in slight disarray since Betsey had not finished brushing it to bring out its full luster. Her face was tanned more than was fashionable, a fact that didn't bother her. Her red lips were slightly open in a smile that revealed her straight, white teeth. Her warm brown eyes glinted with intelligence.

"Oh, Richard, yes! I have never been there. My father has always tried to avoid the city. Maybe I can see some of the sights while you are at the Admiralty, and do some shopping. I'll take Betsey so it will all be proper. She is not annoying me quite so much as she did before, are you, Betsey?"

"I hope not, my lady," replied the servant though her tone suggested that she was not sure that this was more than the calm before another storm.

"Thank heavens for that," Giles said optimistically, "and in London, we can do some other things together, I hope. Perhaps we could go to the Opera or see a play while we are there."

"Oh, this is exciting. Thank you, Richard." Quite ignoring the presence of her lady's maid, Daphne stepped right into Giles's arms to give him a kiss, which soon turned into a long embrace.

"I'll have to get ready," said Daphne as she reluctantly stepped back. "Betsey, look out what clothes might be suitable for London, and I'll decide later, so you can be sure that they are all ready to go. And everything else that I will need. And you will need to get everything ready for yourself too, since, of course, you are coming with me. I don't imagine that you have ever been to London before, have you?"

"No, my lady."

"Then, we can explore together when Captain Giles is occupied."

That was a most unusual invitation coming from her mistress, but then, Betsey reflected, there was nothing very usual about Lady Giles.

Giles went to his own dressing room to get changed. There he found Ralph, the footman who was acting as his valet, ready to help dress his master.

"Ralph, I see you have already laid out my clothes. I can dress myself. I want you to go to the inn and tell Carstairs that I need to see him immediately."

Giles had almost finished dressing when Carstairs, now in his role of coxswain rather than as innkeeper and pal, appeared.

"Carstairs, I need you to ride to London, starting tonight. Go to Nerot's Hotel in King Street in St. James's and reserve rooms for Lady Giles and myself. If they are full, and if they are still full after you've slipped the desk man half a crown, ask what other hotels might have rooms. Maybe Lothian's Hotel in Albemarle Street. Here," Giles stepped to his dresser to extract a few coins from his purse, "this should be enough to cover your expenses. We will be arriving sometime late on Wednesday afternoon. Meet us at Nerot's, even if you can't get rooms there, to tell us where to go."

"Aye, aye, sir."

Carstairs was about to leave when Daphne entered.

"Wait a minute, Carstairs. Richard, are you sending him to London to arrange our accommodation?"

"Yes, my love."

"I think we should take Lady Marianne and the girls with us. They are rather stranded here, and it might do some good in the way of knocking off some of the girls' rough edges. Make Catherine more interesting to possible suitors. Lady Marianne too."

"I think that you are just being kind, Daphne, if truth be told. And I have noticed that you are mellowing towards them. All right, if that is what you really want. Carstairs, we will need more rooms, obviously. Better raise that tip to a crown. And ask the hotel to book us a box at Covent Garden if they are doing an Opera, or The Haymarket if they are not, or a play if that also isn't possible. A play, too, for another night. I forgot to tell you, but we might as well book the rooms until Sunday."

"Richard, that is very sweet of you."

"I don't know about that. I am still surprised that you want to include the others, but you're right. It is the proper thing to do. If I do have to rush off to my ship, you can, I know, manage on your own. Now, we had better go down and tell the others about our plans."

"You know, Richard," said Daphne, "on the way to London, we can continue with the French lessons. We never seem to have enough time here."

Giles had learned that it would be highly convenient if he understood French. When he was in Chatham during his last assignment, he had obtained some material that might help in that direction. It included a dictionary and a grammar book as well as a couple of books in French. He had struggled valiantly by himself on his last cruise and had made some headway on being able to translate French into English but had no real understanding about how any of the French passages over which he was laboring should be pronounced. He had, of course, told Daphne about his efforts. She was reasonably fluent in the language, having had a French governess for a while, though she had never actually used her knowledge in France or with French-speaking guests. She had suggested to Giles when he returned home with an injured knee that they spend an hour a day on her teaching him French. It was hard work, certainly, but he was already making some noticeable progress.

Two afternoons later, the coaches carrying the party from Dipton pulled up to Nerot's Hotel. A footman gave Daphne a hand to help her descend from the lead carriage. She was followed by Giles. Carstairs was on hand to help them to their rooms and to make sure that Betsey and the servants working on Lady Marianne and her daughters knew where their duties would be fulfilled.

"The hotel has secured a box for you tonight at the Haymarket Theatre, Captain," Carstairs reported, "and another one the following night. The other theatres royal are closed for the summer. And I've arranged for a private dining room this afternoon with roast beef as the main dish. I hope that is all right."

"Very good, Carstairs. Do you know what is being performed at the theatre?"

"Tonight it is *Artaxerxes*, sir, by a Mr. Arne, and tomorrow the play is *Pizarro*, by Mr. Sheridan," Carstairs read from a note-card.

Daphne and Giles started ascending the curved staircase that was one of the features of Nerot's Hotel, a carved staircase in the fashion of the time of the Restoration. Its panels featured allegorical paintings of Greek gods and goddesses.

"Look at that nymph, Daphne," commanded Giles.

"I see it. What makes it worth remarking?"

"It depicts Daphne, being chased by Apollo."

"Does it? Poor Daphne. I am so much luckier to have you rather than Apollo if that is how he looked."

"Poor Apollo. His Daphne does not bear comparison with mine!"

After changing and eating dinner, they all went downstairs to their carriages. It was not a long trip to the theatre, but the streets were thronged, and the crowds became thicker as they approached the Theatre Royal in Haymarket. It must have been very stressful for their coachman, Daphne thought, as she heard him shouting from the box. He didn't encounter crowds like this at Dipton, or even at Ameschester, the nearest real town to Dipton. She noticed a large number of garishly dressed women in the crowd, rather vulgar-looking with painted faces. It was clear that they were not chaperoned.

"Who are those women, Richard?" she asked. "Why are they in the street?"

"They are … are… are ladies of the night, my dear."

"Do you mean whores?" Daphne had read Shakespeare, and her father had never hesitated to explain what strange words and phrases meant. "They do not look at all attractive. I can't see why men would be interested in them. Have you ever used a whore?"

"Ugh … ugh … Oh, look, do you see the children selling nosegays*? London is very malodorous."

Daphne left the subject. Giles had revealed the answer by his response, and she would wait for a better time to pursue the matter.

At the theatre, attendants maintained a passage so that those alighting from carriages would not have to push through the crowd to enter the theatre. Giles's party was shown to their box, a good one, Daphne realized, quite close to the royal box with a full view of the stage. Daphne, Giles, and Lady Marianne sat on chairs at the railing of the box while Catherine and Lydia Crocker sat behind them. Servants brought refreshments before the performance began. Daphne, looking around, realized that they were lucky not to have seats on the benches in the main part of the theatre or in the gallery above them. The gallery was filled with raucous patrons who seemed to toss orange peels and apple cores down on the people on the main floor. Some loud thumping induced some reduction in the noise from the audience, and the orchestra launched into the overture.

Daphne was fascinated. She had never been in a theatre before, though she had seen some plays put on in the assembly rooms at Ameschester, and she had never heard a proper orchestra. When the singing started, she realized how much more exalted was the technique and expression relative to the singing of guests and hosts that entertained them at home. She was also delighted that the opera was in English, though it was not always easy to make out the words. She had been afraid that the words would be in Italian and so be totally incomprehensible to her. She was annoyed that many in the audience did not remain silent so that a constant murmur underlay the music.

Giles's party stayed in their box at intermission, though Daphne noticed that a great many other people left their boxes. Some people entered boxes where they had not been during the performance. Going to the opera seemed to be quite a social occasion. No sooner had she noticed this than there was a knock on their own box's door, and two men entered. Giles obviously recognized them and welcomed them warmly before introducing the two naval captains whom he had known as lieutenants in the West Indies, Captain Bolton and Captain Greenway. Both were delighted to be introduced to Daphne and the others, and Captain Greenway kept Daphne amused and interested by discussing the performance. He seemed to know a lot about opera and music as well as being up on the latest gossip about the performers. Captain Bolton spent some time sharing naval gossip with Giles before turning his attention to Lady Marianne's daughters. He and Catherine struck up a conversation about painting, and he was astounded that she had never seen any of the great paintings, even though she was quite knowledgeable about them from sketches and comments in magazines. Captain Greenway slipped away when it was clear that the performance was about to resume, but Captain Bolton remained, and he and Catherine continued talking until a very pointed look from Daphne indicated to them that they should be quiet while the performers were singing.

When the curtain had fallen for the final time, and everyone was about to leave, Captain Bolton suggested that he would be happy to show the ladies the paintings at the Royal Academy the following day while Giles was at the Admiralty. Daphne begged off, wanting very much to explore the shops in London, but Lady Marianne, sensing that a budding romance might be possible, accepted with enthusiasm, quite silencing Lydia who did not want to go, but who could hardly be left on her own unchaperoned.

The crowds had thinned while they were in the theater, but many people were still on the streets. Daphne noted that there were more raffish-looking gentlemen than earlier, and few respectable-looking women, and those few were dressed in very poor-looking clothes. The women flaunting themselves were more prominent than ever. They reminded Daphne of her unanswered question. She took up the subject again when she and Giles were alone in their room.

"You never did answer my question," she began. "You just changed the subject to nosegays."

"Yes, I didn't answer your question. I rather hoped that you would forget it."

"Well?" Daphne pressed.

"I did just once. That is, have a whore. It was at my father's instigation and Ashton's, my older half-brother. It happened just before I joined my first ship as a midshipman. They said it would make a man of me and … and … and prevent me from becoming a…a… a bum boy. I didn't want to, really, but they told me not to be a sissy and, well, they made me. They took me to a brothel – rather a good one, I imagine – it was actually quite near here. My father selected a woman for me."

"What happened?"

"Do you really want to know?"

"Yes. I don't want there to be any secrets between us."

"Ugh … well…ugh … she took me to a room and … ugh … she took my member out of my trousers and …"

"And?"

"And she … ugh … she got me hard. And she lay down on the bed and pulled me into her. It didn't last very long. In fact, I had to wait sometime downstairs until my father and Ashton had finished."

"That was your only time with a doxy?"

"Yes. I hated it, to tell the truth. I was embarrassed and scared. I hated that my father made me do it and that I didn't know how to say no or how to talk to the woman and explain that I wasn't comfortable about it. I have never forgiven him. It wasn't even any good. I reckoned my hand could do a much better job, so that is what I used afterward instead of hiring a — a strumpet."

Daphne decided that it was wise not to pursue that last remark, lest she have to confess her own secret discoveries concerning how her own hand could be used in ways she suspected were inappropriate. She didn't want that to be material for discussion – that was certain!

14

Chapter II

Giles was several minutes early for his appointment at the Admiralty. Nevertheless, he was shown to the First Lord's room immediately. There had been a change of government since he had last been at the Admiralty, and now the First Lord was his old acquaintance, Sir David McDougall. Sir David greeted him and waved him to a chair. The Second Secretary was also on hand.

"Good to see you again, Captain Giles. I trust that your leg has recovered."

"Yes, sir."

"Now about your ship, *Impetuous*. She has been condemned and will be broken up."

"I am surprised, Sir David. My latest news from the Chatham Dockyard was that repairs had been delayed but that she would be ready soon."

"Aye, well, that was my doing. A ruse to keep your crew together."

"I don't understand, sir."

"Aye, well, I knew that I had a delicate matter for you, and I didn't want you to have to waste time training a raw crew when your new ship is ready."

"New ship?"

"Aye. A frigate. Thirty-six. Twenty-four pounders. Plus those eighteen-pounder bow-chasers that you like.

Being built at Stewart's Yard at Butler's Hard. I believe you know him."

"Yes, sir. My previous ship, *Patroclus*, was built by him, and his son is one of my midshipmen."

"This ship will be called '*Glaucus*.' I don't know where we get these names."

"It is the name of a Greek sea god, Sir David," announced the Second Secretary.

"I know. It is also the name of a sea-slug. I hope the ship is named after the first meaning and not the second."

'Yes, my lord. I didn't know about that other meaning."

"You should have since the name has been given to the disgusting creature by someone on one of the Navy's discovery voyages. Anyway, Captain Giles, like it or not, your ship is called '*Glaucus*.' She should be ready to sail in three weeks' time. Your crew and officers are being transported from Chatham and should already be at Butler's Hard or will arrive there shortly.

"Now, about your duties. You are going to St. Petersburg. With a special ambassador, a fellow called Sir Walcott Lainey, pompous fool in my view, but capable of doing the job we want. He has no knowledge of what we really have in mind, nor does he have the imagination to realize what that is likely to be. As near to spy-proof as we can get, especially as we rather hope that the details of his ostensible mission will be leaked to the French. He will be offering the Tsar rather lower support than we are already committed to. The hope is that the Tsar will appear to be so infuriated with that sum and with the ambassador who you will be taking to Russia that he will publically and angrily declare that he is refusing all aid from us. To strengthen that belief among spies in St. Petersburg, our ambassador will now seem to be an unsympathetic person, so the Tsar might well get angry with him as well and so appear to reduce the strength of our alliance with him.

"It is all sham. Directed mainly at Prussia. Prussia is likely to be the first target if Bonaparte decides to go east again. But if the Prussians think that Russia is about to attack them, they might try to form an alliance with Bonaparte to attack Russia or Austria. We certainly do not want there to be any such alliance, since if Bonaparte feels safer on his eastern flank, he may devote even more troops to trying to invade us. The plan strikes me as being a bit too complicated to be successful. It's based on too many hypotheses about how others will react. I doubt that it will work, but that is the reasoning of the people who are supposed to know diplomacy, and we just have to try to implement this scheme

"The special ambassador will be joining you at Butler's Hard in three weeks' time. He thinks going there is for secrecy, though the news that he has a mission that he thinks is of paramount importance will be well known to French agents long before he leaves London. He is the type who thinks that all gentlemen are inherently honorable and that servants do not have ears. Neither is true and certainly not in the circles in which he mingles. I am sure that he would be unable to resist boasting about anything that he thinks might enhance his status so we can be sure that every spy in London will know about his mission and its purpose, as *he* sees it, long before he joins you.

"Sir Walcott is sure to bring far too much luggage, and you may have to tell him that discretion should mean that he should appear more businesslike and less like a fashion plate. You might suggest that less baggage is better than more for purposes of appearing unremarkable and efficient. He will certainly stand out, but we don't want to overdo it. He most assuredly is not efficient. In the same vein, he should not have too great an entourage. You can tell him that he can only have two servants, as he has already been informed. Threaten to press any extra servants if he protests. I am sure you can always use extra crew members, so actually do it. He doesn't have nearly as much influence as he thinks he has.

"Sir Walcott's apparent mission is to persuade the Russians to support us and build up their army, largely at our expense. There is nothing much to it. It will all be in a letter he delivers and is a straightforward bribe. You may wonder why we don't use our regular ambassador, Lord Malthampton."

"Yes, sir."

"Aye, well, the cover story is that he is too much in love with the Russians, particularly with the Tsar, Alexander. We will be supposed not to fully trust Malthampton, for he thinks we were wrong to resist Russian expansion into Turkish areas. He's a bit like Sir William Hamilton at Naples, though without the flamboyant wife. In fact, he has already negotiated a very important secret treaty whose existence we would prefer Prussia and France not to be aware of.

"Now, for your own role. I want you to keep your ears and eyes open. We need to know more about the state of the Russian navy. That is your real mission. You will be in Kronstadt undoubtedly, and will likely be moored at their naval dockyard when you get to St. Petersburg. You are sure to be entertained by Russian officers. They will be curious about you, especially as your exploits will not be unknown to them. We know that many Russian officers follow the Naval Gazette. You don't speak French, do you?"

"No, sir."

"Pity. It is the language of the court in St. Petersburg. But quite a few of their officers, I am told, do speak some English. Presume that anything you say will get back to the French. So make us sound very well-prepared to deal with the French fleet and with any invasion. Don't be blatant about it. An 'unintentional' hint often carries more weight than a straight-forward boast about our strengths. Remember that. For that reason, make sure you don't tell the real state of our defenses to anyone, no matter how friendly they seem. We would rather have the French think we are stronger than we are. If you want, you can even boast about how we sent a lot of misinformation by that turncoat captain; what was his name? Oh, yes, Hoxley. Aye, mention him in connection with our hope that the French would try to invade prematurely and so be beaten – I know, that is another fiction.

"Now, the second and crucial part of your own mission. This is an offer for you to deliver to the Russian Minister of the Navy, Count Smirnov, in person. You will have a letter to him, but it is only an introduction. The message is to be transmitted orally. You are to offer a subsidy of £50,000 per annum, to be paid secretly, though only as long as Russia continues to be a member of the coalition against Napoleon. There will also be a payment of £5,000 for the Count himself for arranging for this.

Luckily, the Count is not a particularly rich man and has some expensive tastes. The principal payment is in addition to the subsidy for the army that we are already paying to keep Russia neutral. It has nothing to do with Sir Walcott's false offer. The reality is that we are already shoring up the coalition, and you will be offering new money to strengthen their naval commitment, which is somewhat lacking.

"There are some additional terms that you are to propose to the minister, and this is the part that we especially do not want to put down on paper because of repercussions elsewhere if it is known to what we are committing ourselves. First, if Russia allies herself with France, we will deal with the Russian fleet the way we dealt with the Danes at Copenhagen, that is, attack them in their home anchorage and wipe them out. You will also promise that if Sweden should join the French, we will destroy their fleet, in the same way as we did the Danes, provided, and only provided, that Russia enters the war on our side. Otherwise, we will leave the naval side alone. Well, that is, in summary, what you are to do. Secretary Newsome, of course, has your written orders. However, we should go over your real mission more carefully, since none of it will be written down, except for the letter indicating that you speak for us."

The next half-hour was spent with Sir David elaborating on the messages and with Giles and the Second Secretary trying to anticipate whatever questions the Russian minister might raise. When they had run through all the possibilities that they could anticipate, and it was quite clear that Giles had by memory all the important details of his mission, he raised an issue that had been bothering him.

"Sir David, how am I to communicate with Count Smirnov. I don't speak Russian or French."

"Aye. A good point. The Count is believed to speak English quite fluently. If he doesn't, you could use your lieutenant who is fluent in the French language, Lieutenant Hendricks, I believe. Newsome here has your commission and orders, don't you Newsome?"

"Yes, Sir David," responded the Second Secretary.

"Then add to them that Captain Giles is to press any servants that Sir Walcott seeks to bring with him above two. You can tell Sir Walcott that it is for discretion, but that, once enrolled, the men will remain in the navy when you return. That should put him in his place, without you, Captain Giles, appearing to be petty.

"Oh, and, Captain Giles, no taking of prizes and avoid clashes with the Danes and the Swedes. In fact, only engage a French ship if there is no alternative."

"Aye, aye, sir."

"Good! Are those orders ready? Good day, Captain Giles. We are counting on you to perform your duties in accord with the highest standards of the Service."

Giles found himself on the pavement outside the Admiralty without really being aware of how the transition from the First Lord's room had been effected. He had been thinking more about how Sir David seemed to have every detail at his fingertips, even to which of Giles's lieutenants was fluent in French, rather than about his new ship and where his orders were sending him. He didn't have to rush away to his ship now, and Daphne would probably be away from the hotel all day. He would go to his club in Pall Mall and see if he could find someone with whom to have luncheon.

Giles was sitting in the lobby of the hotel, reading a newspaper, when Daphne returned in the afternoon. "I have had such a wonderful time, Richard! You cannot believe the stores there are in London. I bought so much fabric for dresses, both for now and for after the baby. I am sure that I have spent all your money, and you will be deeply in debt."

"I doubt that, my dear."

"Have the others returned? I suppose there is a bit of a rush to get changed and to eat dinner and still get to the theatre."

"There is a bit. Ah, here they are now."

Lady Marianne was just coming through the hotel's doors, followed by Lydia and Catherine with Captain Bolton bringing up the rear. Lady Marianne looked tired but willing to endure still more in a good cause, Lydia clearly looked bad-tempered, while Catherine, quite uncharacteristically, was happy and excited.

"Aunt Daphne, Uncle Richard," Catherine greeted the couple. "Captain Bolton is wonderfully knowledgeable about paintings and painters. The day wasn't nearly long enough."

"I am glad you had a good time, Catherine. It was very good of you to show them the paintings, Captain Bolton," Daphne responded.

"Not at all, Lady Giles. The pleasure was all mine."

"Uncle Richard, did you say you have a box at the theatre tonight?" asked Catherine.

"Yes, I do."

"Could Captain Bolton come with us, would there be room?"

"Yes. Bolton, we would all be delighted to have you join us, and for dinner too."

"It is very good of you, Giles, to invite me, but I won't have time to change."

Daphne looked him up and down critically.

"I think you look very elegant, Captain Bolton. Richard, you will go in your day clothes too, won't you? So that Captain Bolton will not feel out of place."

"Of course, I will. That quite solves the problem, doesn't it, Bolton?"

With that matter settled, the ladies went to change, with firm orders not to dawdle, and the two captains retired to the lounge to catch up with each other's doings over a glass of sherry.

Giles broke his news to the whole company at dinner. Daphne was the first to speak, "Richard, that is very good news. A new frigate. When do you have to join her?"

"Not for a couple of weeks, more or less, but I would like to go down tomorrow to Butler's Hard, just to see that everything is in order. Would you like to come?"

"I would love to. But what about the others?"

"They can return to Dipton tomorrow, just as we planned."

"Oh, Uncle Richard, can't we stay another day?" asked Lydia. "I haven't seen anything very much of London. I want to shop. Especially with my wedding coming up soon."

"I will be happy to accompany the ladies again tomorrow," interposed Captain Bolton.

"I don't want to see any more pictures," declared Lydia. "I will just go shopping alone."

"Oh, no, you won't," responded Lady Marianne, "even if you are betrothed."

"I promise no more pictures. There are many other things to do in London, and we could spend as much of the day as you want on any of them," Captain Bolton said, clarifying his offer.

All three agreed, so it was settled.

The sun was easing towards the horizon when Butler's Hard came into sight the next day. Anchored in the river was a new frigate, no doubt *Glaucus*. Giles stopped the coach to look at her and to point out some distinguishing features to Daphne, most of which she did not actually appreciate. They then went on to the inn where they intended to spend the night. However, even as they were getting out of the coach, a small, well-dressed man, not young and with an air of authority, came running up.

"Captain Giles, welcome to Butler's Hard. I suspected that you would be here soon when your crew arrived. It is a pleasure to have you here."

"Thank you, Mr. Stewart. Daphne, may I present Mr. Stewart, who is the man who is building *Glaucus*. He is also the father of Midshipman Stewart, whom you met at our wedding and also on *Impetuous*. Mr. Stewart, my wife, Lady Giles."

"Lady Giles, I have heard about you from my son. He almost worships you. Both of you, actually. I thought it must be you when I saw a private coach arriving."

"You don't have many coaches here, Mr. Stewart?"

"No, my lady, very few. I thought I would just come to see if it was you, Captain Giles. Now, you cannot stay at the inn, especially not with Lady Giles accompanying you."

"Why ever not?"

"It's a pretty rough and ready sort of place. Not really suitable for ladies. Anyway, Mrs. Stewart and I want you to stay with us. Ship-building has been very good to me, and we have a large house. Quite comfortable, if I do say so myself. I am sure you would be much happier with us than at the inn. And both Mrs. Stewart and young Daniel would be devastated if we weren't able to provide you with our best hospitality."

"Thank you, Mr. Stewart," Giles replied. "We will be honored to accept your generous offer. I shouldn't be surprised by your welcome, though I was certainly not expecting it. Midshipman Stewart is a very well-brought-up young man."

Mr. Stewart directed the coachman to a large, stone house built in the current fashion, the home of a prosperous business-owner who did not feel the need to ape the aristocracy. Although there was a butler, who opened the door, Mrs. Stewart was in the entryway to welcome them warmly and show them to their rooms. She was a large, unpretentious woman who spoke with a pronounced Wiltshire accent. She seemed to be somewhat awed by her guests.

Dinner was a hearty meal, with several removes* excellently prepared and presented. Much of the conversation was about ships and the war. Mr. Stewart's yard had all the work they could handle building for the navy, and describing this activity inevitably led the conversation to the war and the Navy's role in it. Mrs. Stewart was not much interested in the general threats that Napoleon presented but was very concerned about its implications for her son, Daniel, Giles's midshipman. She was inordinately proud of him and his service in Giles's ships, but she was clearly worried about the hazards that attended service in a ship-of-war in a time of conflict. Giles could do little to set her mind at ease on the latter topic, though he did let drop that he would not be surprised if the next cruise provided little fighting. He did praise the young man's progress, adding enough detail that it was clear that he was monitoring the lad's development and not just giving *pro forma* replies to an anxious parent.

The conversation inevitably turned to the new frigate. Daphne asked about the Captain's cabin.

"That will be one of the features of the ship," Mr. Stewart replied. "*Glaucus* has a splendid stern window. I was warned that she might be required to transport very distinguished people, so I have made the area so that it can accommodate two versions of the cabin. One is for Captain Giles when there is no special passenger and another in which there are two sleeping cabins and day cabins with a special adjoining dining area that can be used by both. The layout will cramp the wardroom* a bit, but not nearly as much as when an extra guest has to be accommodated in the wardroom, and the officers have to put up with the complaints of the visitors who are not used to the Spartan arrangements of a ship of war. The arrangement will also prevent situations where the captain feels he has to give up his own cabin to some visiting dignitary.

"But how can you have two different cabins on the same ship?" Daphne inquired.

"It's easy," replied Mr. Stewart. "The cabin partitions in a ship-of-war are all temporary. In fact, they are removed and stowed below when the crew is ordered to 'clear for action.' *Glaucus* just has two different sets of partitions. Daniel tells me that Captain Giles always clears for action at daybreak, so his passenger will have to get up at dawn, like it or not."

"We will be supplying two hanging cots, two tables and two chairs for the cabins, and a table that can seat ten and the corresponding number of chairs for the dining area, and a serving table. They are all pretty plain, I am afraid. Many captains get their own furniture, and they even put a rug on the floor to make it less utilitarian, but that is up to them, not to the shipbuilders nor to the Admiralty."

The following morning, Giles and Daphne were rowed out to the new frigate. It was evident that a substantial amount of carpentry was still to be done. Giles's crew had already arrived and settled in and were now speeding matters by helping with the rigging tasks that would normally be done by the yard, as well as doing as much of the fitting out that was usually left to a ship's crew as they could while the ship was still being built.

Daphne was welcomed on board enthusiastically by the officers and crew. Most of them had already seen her on a couple of occasions and definitely approved their captain's choice of a wife. Lead by Mr. Stewart, Giles and Daphne were given a tour of the main features of the ship, and the builder was very keen to show Daphne how the Captain's cabin could take on different configurations, even though doing so caused a good deal of confusion and interruption of other tasks. What Daphne most noticed was that *Glaucus* smelled much more pleasantly than had Giles's previous ship, *Impetuous*.

When the general tour was over, Giles wanted to go over every part of the ship in detail with some of his petty officers. Daphne announced that she would like to return to the shore to see Mrs. Stewart's garden, which, she said, contained some unusual features. She had learned about them when the ladies were waiting for the gentlemen to finish their wine after dinner. Giles was surprised because she hadn't mentioned this interest earlier but had no objection. When he glanced ashore a bit later, he was puzzled to see Daphne going into the shipyard's office with Mr. Stewart rather than walking directly to Mrs. Stewart's house.

When they met before dinner later in the day, Giles had completely forgotten about Daphne's strange behavior.

This may have been because she had a new proposal to put to him.

"Richard, do you remember that we were supposed to have two full days in London."

"Yes, of course, though we came down here instead on the second day."

"I would still like to have the second day to shop and sight-see in London."

"Shopping again? Can I afford it?"

"Of course you can. Don't be silly. Can we do it? Or do you still need to be here?"

"No. And I don't suppose that the work at Dipton will be ruined if we are away an extra couple of days."

"So, we can go to London tomorrow?"

"Yes, indeed. It should be entertaining. We can stay at the same hotel. I am sure that I can find much to do while you are about your business."

30

Chapter III

"Captain Giles," the desk-man at Nerot's Hotel greeted him as he and Daphne arrived from Butler's Hard. "It is good to have you with us again. This note was delivered for you a few minutes ago, in the hope that you might be returning this evening."

The note was from Sir David McDougall. It read:

Captain Giles, I do not know if you are still in town. If you are, and if it is convenient, I invite you and Lady Giles to a reception at the home of Viscount Ducksworth in Chaverly Square. Any time after eight. Sir Walcott Lainey will be in attendance, and it would be a good idea for you to meet him before your trip begins.

"Daphne, we have been invited to a reception at the home of some viscount or other this evening. Something about meeting that fellow I am supposed to take to St. Petersburg. Would you like to attend?"

"Yes, I would – very much. You know that I have never been in a London house – or in one that is owned by a viscount. I had no idea that I was marrying such an important man. But I don't have anything to wear."

"Nonsense, what you wore to the Opera will do very nicely, I would think."

"I suppose so. After all, we will be going to see what London Society is like, not to dazzle Society with my own looks."

"Oh, you'll do that, my dear, and not because of your clothes."

The carriage delivered Daphne and Giles to a brilliantly lit, large house in a square that Giles said was in Mayfair. Footmen helped them from the carriage, and they followed some earlier arrivals through the front door, where they gave their names to some sort of servant. In turn, he led them to the door of a very large room where he bellowed their names at the groups of people gathered there. Just as Giles was wondering what he should do next, for he had spotted no one he knew and had no idea of what Viscount Ducksworth might look like, Sir David detached himself from a group and greeted them warmly, seeking, in particular, an introduction to Daphne. She suspected that he had a roving eye, but she had no intention of flirting with him to advance Giles's career, something that rumor said happened quite frequently in these circles.

Sir David led them over to a man who was standing alone, gazing off into space. He turned as Sir David announced, "Sir Walcott, may I introduce Captain and Lady Giles." The person addressed was a tall, red-faced man with straw-colored hair tied in a queue. His most prominent feature was a slightly pursed mouth with a jutting lower lip suggesting a man whose habitual state was being aggressively displeased with everything. He was expensively and rather foppishly dressed.

"Ah," he said, "you are the man who is supposed to take me to St. Petersburg. I hope you know your business. In my experience, most of you fellows do not seem to know what they are doing. You are, of course, under my orders, you understand."

Giles was wondering how to respond to this falsehood when Sir David intervened. "Sir Walcott, you know that is not the case. *Glaucus* will sail under Admiralty orders, and Captain Giles has been instructed to convey you to St. Petersburg and to bring you back when your business is concluded or appears to be completely stalled, in any case before winter sets in. He has also been instructed to avoid conflict, if it is possible in his judgment, because you are aboard. Allow me a few moments with him to make sure that he understands his orders."

Sir David took Giles by the elbow and led him to one side where the others could not hear him. Sir Walcott turned to Daphne to continue his complaints.

"Stuff and nonsense, Lady Giles. I will have my orders obeyed, of course, no matter what that place-holder McDougall says. I do hope that your husband at least knows -- what do they say? – starboard from...ah... t'otherside. I imagine that you will be coming with us and cluttering up the boat with women's things."

"Why, no, Sir Walcott, I will not. I have important matters to attend to in England."

"Just as well. Quite the country mouse, are you? I should have guessed from your clothes."

"These old rags. We only received Sir David's invitation at the last minute. Some mistake at the hotel, I suppose. I had already sent my other evening clothes on ahead to Dipton Hall. That is Captain Sir Richard's estate, you know. Anyway," said Daphne, with sudden inspiration, "accommodations are very Spartan on Captain Sir Richard's ship. We were just down in Wiltshire inspecting her yesterday. Very plain accommodations, I am afraid, with only very crude furniture made by the shipbuilder. That is the way it is in the Navy. Of course, passengers may bring their own furniture, though it has to be suitable for the unusual lines of a ship, and specially made so that it will remain steady when the ship is not."

"You seem to be very knowledgeable, Lady Giles."

"I am indeed. Yes! I spoke to the chief shipbuilder while we were at Butler's Hard. He said that the best place to get such furniture is Siddon's in Duke Street, here in London. He highly recommended that establishment, said it was better than anything in Portsmouth. They may well have the measurements for *Glaucus*."

"I really do think that the Navy should have provided me with adequate accommodations on the ship. It is a remarkably inefficient service. I don't see how these Admiralty flunkies can expect me to undertake an important mission if they do not make sure that my quarters are fitted out in the very best taste. What you describe may be good enough for your husband, but not for me. Siddon's, you say?"

"Yes, Sir Walcott, Siddon's in Duke Street. Just down from Piccadilly, I believe."

"Good. I shall have to make arrangements, I suppose. I shall also have to speak to Sir David. In very firm terms. Ah, here he is now."

Sir Walcott drew Sir David aside, and from his agitated manner, which contrasted with Sir David's curt responses, he did not seem to be getting his way. Giles and Daphne were left on their own, but not for long.

"Richard," a large, stately woman addressed him. "I didn't expect you to be in town. Almost no one is. I hear you have been doing great things! And this must be your wife. You are a beauty, my dear, and so wise not to swathe yourself in the gaudy nonsense that Lady Hamilton inspired. But I get ahead of myself. Do introduce us properly, Richard."

"Yes, Aunt Gillian. Lady and Lord Struthers, may I present my wife, Daphne. Lady Struthers is my mother's sister, and they are very close. When I was growing up, Lord and Lady Struthers were very good to me. Uncle Geoffrey gave me my first pony and helped me to ride him."

. "He was a real hellion at that age, but we are very fond of him," Lord Struthers remarked. "So glad to hear from Clara that he married well, and not just for money. I hope we may get to know you better soon."

The two couples chatted for a while, Giles's aunt drawing Daphne into explaining the changes they were making to Dipton Hall. However, after ten minutes, Lady Struthers spotted someone across the room to whom she 'absolutely *had* to talk.' Giles and Daphne were marooned among the groups of chattering, elegantly dressed people, and Daphne started to feel very uncomfortable, especially as Sir Walcott's remark and the kind words of Lady Struthers made her aware that Giles had not been the most informed source for information on what clothes would be appropriate.

"I would like to leave, if you would, Daphne," Giles announced. Daphne was more than happy to agree. She had no objection to an early night at the hotel.

Next morning, at breakfast, Daphne announced, "Richard, I want to go shopping on my own this morning, with Betsey, of course. Then I would like to have lunch here with you, and then you can show me all the sights."

"Hardly all the sights, my dear. There are too many."

"Well then, the ones you like best."

Giles was a bit surprised that Daphne had not tried to get him to join the shopping expedition. However, he would be quite happy to spend the time on his own. He would like to visit Hatchard's new bookstore in Piccadilly and possibly also find some music for his violin or, even better, some piano and violin music that Daphne and he could work on while he was away. Besides, it would be a rare pleasure for him to visit a coffee shop to read the newspapers, a delight in which he could readily indulge himself. He could anticipate being happily engaged for the morning on his own.

Giles was just leaving Hatchard's when he saw Daphne and Betsey farther down the street emerging from a shop. They turned down Duke Street almost at once. He suspected that the store was Fortnum and Mason's, which was also his own next stop. He had heard from captains who were richer than he that this particular emporium was the best place to order superior cabin supplies. At the time he had learned about the shop, such extravagance was well beyond his purse. It was only for the well-off, which he had not been, but now he was. Furthermore, he had never liked the idea of his having much better food than his officers, so he had found that getting his cabin supplies in the port from which he was leaving was quite satisfactory. However, with Sir Walcott sharing the captain's quarters with him, he supposed he should get some high-end delicacies. He reflected that he was indeed now among those richer captains who could afford to satisfy their tastes with the best provisions.

Giles entered the long-established institution for supplying the needs of gentlemen, especially officers in the military. The attendant who assisted him was very knowledgeable about what supplies gentlemen particularly liked to order. He soon found himself choosing various preserved fruits and biscuits, smoked hams and beef, and several cheeses. Giles had soon put together a large order, which he reckoned would provide enough special items for the dinners he would have with Sir Walcott and his own officers. When he was ready to complete the order, the clerk looked up in surprise when he heard the name of the customer and where the goods were to be delivered.

"Captain Giles. Lady Giles visited us earlier in the morning. She also placed a large order to be delivered to *Glaucus*."

"Well," thought Giles, "that explains the mysterious shopping excursion that Daphne insisted on taking by herself."

"Did she buy the same items?" he asked.

"In many cases, yes," declared the shop-attendant, "though sometimes in the very best quality, rather than the more ordinary ones you chose. Yours are, of course, perfectly adequate and very popular with many of my captains. And Lady Giles ordered somewhat larger quantities."

"Then remove those items from my order that overlap hers. Keep the other things that are only in my order. Make sure the packaging of the two orders is separate, so it will be clear which order is which."

"Yes, sir. And send the account to Mr. Edwards?"

"Yes, do so."

Giles's next stop was a coffee shop. He sat with his cup, reading a newspaper, but found he could not concentrate on it. How thoughtful it was of Daphne to think of his comfort, even when he himself only remembered to visit Fortnum and Mason's because of the unfortunate shipmate he was about to endure. She would have enjoyed this coffee house, he was sure, but, of course, women were banned from such establishments. How he was going to miss her while he was away! Some Navy captains did take their wives with them on voyages, even in wartime, but he could hardly ask Daphne to accompany him when she was pregnant. Also, she would become bored on shipboard with nothing useful to do. She got great pleasure out of managing their estate and her father's one. The wives who went to sea were probably much less active on shore, and, he suspected, in most cases, it was frugality on the part of the captain, rather than a reluctance to be separated from their mates, that drove their decision to take their wives with them. How he wished this war would end: in truth, he would rather be with Daphne at Dipton than sailing to St. Petersburg.

Giles came out of his reverie to realize that he had little more time before he was supposed to meet Daphne. His newspaper remained largely unread, but it did not matter. He had better things to do. He did arrive at Nerot's Hotel with time to spare, and, while waiting, he inquired about concerts that evening. Daphne would enjoy one, he thought. He was in luck; there would be a concert in the Hanover Square Rooms that night, starting at 8 o'clock.

Daphne and Giles did not tarry over lunch. He suggested that they walk to Westminster to see the Abbey and Houses of Parliament. They did so, going through St. James's Park before turning off to see the Abbey. Giles then took Daphne by the other sights of Westminster to the river near Westminster Bridge, where he arranged for a boat to take them downstream as far as the Tower of London and then bring them back. Some of the best views of the metropolis were to be had from the water, Giles maintained.

The concert took place in the Hanover Square Rooms. Unlike the Opera, where the audience kept talking throughout the performance, absolute silence was the rule, even though people were sitting on benches with open backs, and remarks on the performances would have been easy. Daphne had never heard playing of such refinement, skill, and feeling. She was particularly amazed at the proficiency of the pianist whose fingers flew through the fast movements of a Mozart concerto, finding the keys apparently effortlessly, as he seemed to be racing towards the finish in perfect accord with the orchestra.

"Richard," Daphne announced the next morning as their carriage was passing Hyde Park at the start of their return to Dipton, "London has been much more exciting than I expected. My father never wanted to visit it, saying that he expected that it was just a big, noisy, crowded, dirty city, like Birmingham, only worse. It is crowded and noisy, but there are so many exciting things to see and do. I hope that we can come back sometime."

"I am sure that we will, Daphne, and often."

As the coach rolled towards Dipton, they started to reminisce about the trip. There were no conclusions, except that the difference between the professional players and the amateurs whose performances were their standard musical fare was immense, but maybe, with more practice, they could improve their own music-making. They switched to Daphne's giving Giles some more instruction in French, but their concentration lagged. Hanging over them was the impending separation. After their second stop to rest the horses and to get some refreshment at a posting inn, they lapsed into silence. Daphne's thoughts took a darker turn. Would Giles miss the more glittering, exciting life in London? Would he regret marrying a woman whose whole experience had been in the country, and not even in the grand estates of the nobility where all the best people gathered? She had caught snatches of the repartees that enlivened the reception they attended. Would Giles miss that back and forth of witty, empty conversation when all she offered was plain and often practical thoughts? More importantly, would he miss rubbing elbows with powerful men like Sir David McDougall, which would be a feature if he had chosen a city life? Was it only a whim that had made him interested in farming enough to want to get a country estate? Would that interest fade, and with it the attraction of the down-to-earth, unexciting woman he had married?

After a while, however, Daphne shrugged these thoughts aside. She did not have much more time with him before he had to leave. She shouldn't spoil any of it worrying about what Giles might be thinking or feeling sometime in the future. Society was not all glamor and wit. It had people like Sir Walcott Lainey, as well. Richard was certainly eager to get on with the improvements to Dipton

Hall and the establishment of the stud farm. If he were to lose interest, well, she would just cross that bridge when she came to it. Anticipating it in advance would do no good.

Giles broke into her thoughts at that point. "Daphne, I am so glad that you came with me on this trip," he declared. "I had to go to London, and then see my ship, but I expected no pleasure from it. I have enjoyed having you with me. It has been a very special time. But for longer periods, I far prefer Dipton. There is so much to enjoy where we live! I wonder how the work is progressing. I can't wait to see how everything has developed. And how the stud farm is coming along."

"Richard, we have only been away six nights. None of our improvements are going to progress very much in a week. But you are right; we will want to find out just what has been accomplished."

Daphne found that she was more than happy to be home when the carriage finally pulled up before Dipton Hall. The London trip had been wonderful, but her real life was here, and she would not have it any other way.

IV

Several days after getting home from the London trip, Giles was conferring with Mr. Griffiths, his stable-master, about opportunities that might arise while he was voyaging to St. Petersburg. There had not, in fact, been much to discuss, but the two had happily adapted the meeting to talking about blood-lines, famous horses, and likely prospects for the next racing season. They both knew the importance of keeping in mind the goal of breeding first-class, all-around hunters, but the glamor of winning steeplechases or just jump races, without respect to whether the horse could follow the hunt well, kept nagging at them, and their dreams even extended to the highly risky and rarely lucrative business of raising champion flat-track racehorses. The conversation led nowhere on this occasion, but both men enjoyed it nevertheless. Giles rather reluctantly broke off the conversation and returned to the Hall as the afternoon drew on towards the time for dinner.

"What is this letter, Steves?" he demanded as he entered through the front door to find his butler standing with a letter, which had a black border around it, on a silver server,

"A letter from the Countess, Captain Giles. It was delivered a few moments ago."

"I see."

Giles broke the seal and straightened out the paper. "Where is Lady Giles?"

"Upstairs, sir. She returned only a few moments before you did."

"And Lady Marianne and her daughters."

"In the small drawing-room."

"I must change and see Lady Giles. Please ask the others to stay where they are. This news affects us all."

"Yes, sir." Though there was no way of telling it from the butler's demeanor, Giles knew that Steves was bursting with curiosity about the substance of the message.

"Viscount Ashton is dead, Steves. Some sort of riding accident."

"My condolences, sir. I shall arrange for the house to go into mourning immediately." Steves seemed completely unaffected by the news though he had seen Viscount Ashton many times at his father's London house where the butler had formerly been employed.

"Yes. I suppose that is necessary, even though my brother and I were far from being close."

"Yes, sir, I believe that it is required. He was also Lady Marianne's brother, of course."

"You are right. Carry on, Steves."

Giles proceeded up the staircase with a spring in his step. If he was grieving for his eldest half-brother, it certainly didn't show in his actions. Upstairs, he went directly to his wife's dressing room. Before doing anything else, he gave Daphne a kiss, which was fully reciprocated.

"I have just received some bad news," Giles started.

"Oh! No! Not about the pond, I hope."

"Nothing like that, my dear. It is my brother, Ashton. He's dead. I just had a letter from my mother."

"When did it happen?"

"Let's see… three days ago, in London. According to my mother, he fell off his horse and broke his neck. Apparently, he had been drinking and gambling all night and went for an early morning ride on Rotten Row. That is where the accident occurred."

"You weren't close to him, were you?"

"No. Ashton was a lot older than me. I don't even remember him living at Ashbury Abbey when I was growing up. Later, when I saw him at my father's house in London, I did not like him at all. I will feel like a fraud pretending to mourn him."

"I expect that we will all have to go into mourning, even though I have never met him."

"I'm afraid so, at least until he is buried. I will have to go to the funeral, I think."

"Yes. I will go too, of course. Where and when is it, do you know?"

"It's six days from today. At Ashbury Abbey. My mother says, 'That should give even your father time to get here from Norfolk.' Apparently, Ashton's solicitor in London is arranging to have the body transported to Ashbury."

"I hope that I will finally meet your father. He didn't come to our wedding, and I have never been invited to Ashbury Abbey."

"You have not missed much. He is a devious, unfeeling, old fellow. And that's when he is in a good mood."

"Have you told Lady Marianne?"

"No, though Steves knows about it. I wanted to tell you first. I should change and go down and tell them."

"I'll come with you. Betsey and I are almost finished."

Daphne and Giles entered the small drawing-room a few minutes later. The afternoon sun had moved around to bathe the room in a warm glow, and its rays nicely illuminated Lady Marianne and her daughters, who were seated near the window, as if they were in a Dutch painting. Giles went over to them and announced.

"Marianne, I am afraid that our brother, Ashton, is dead."

"Oh. Good riddance!"

"Don't say that."

"Why not? He never did anything for me when I was in trouble, and he was just a bully when we were growing up. How did he die?"

Giles gave once again the information he had received from his mother.

"I expect that we will have to go to the funeral, though I don't know why. It won't change our father, you know. But he is my brother, and we did grow up together. Hard to get that out of my mind. There are a lot of memories, and some of them are good."

"Mother," asked Catherine Crocker, Lady Marianne's older daughter, "Do we have to go too?"

"Yes, Catherine, and we'll all have to go into mourning. He was your uncle."

"But we never saw him, ever," said Catherine's sister, Lydia. "I don't want to go into mourning. And I don't want to go to the funeral. Going into mourning will most definitely interfere with my plans to marry Mr. Dimster."

"That cannot be helped. It would be an awful scandal if you didn't attend the funeral and go into mourning. It might completely turn your Mr. Dimster's parents against you, and they are supposed to provide his allowance.

"Yes," said Daphne, "I am afraid that we all must do it. But maybe, if Captain Giles permits, we can shorten the period of mourning to a minimum."

Giles laughed, "As far as I am concerned, you can forget about the mourning as soon as the funeral is over and we are back here. Lydia, your aunt and I have caused enough raised eyebrows in this region that another cause for shocked gossip will surprise no one. Sir Thomas and Lady Dimster are not likely to hold it against you personally."

At that moment, Steves appeared to announce, "Lord David Giles."

Giles's brother, who was the vicar of Dipton, followed the butler into the drawing-room. "Richard, Marianne, have you heard the news about Aston?"

"Yes, we have."

"Mother wrote to me. She wants me to take the funeral service. I've checked, and I can do that, though it would be a good idea to give the rector at Ashbury a fee. Mother can't tolerate the man, nor can I. I checked the rules, and I can officiate without him as long as I have his permission."

"Then we can all go to Ashbury together," said Giles. "It will require at least two coaches, and you can take Lady Marianne and the girls in yours."

"Do I surmise that you are no more saddened by the death of Viscount Ashton than any of the others here, David? And will you stay for dinner?" Daphne asked.

"Yes, to both questions, Daphne. No, I scarcely knew him, and I did not like what I saw. I am not surprised that he fell off his horse while drunk and broke his neck. I believe that he was always drunk."

"Mother didn't actually say that, did she?" asked Giles.

"No, I inferred the details from her saying that it had occurred early in the morning on Rotten Row."

The following day was a frantic bustle for the servants trying to get ready for their employer's trip to Ashbury Abbey. Steves already had them wearing black armbands or caps. Now they had to get ready black gowns and veils for the ladies and black coats and trousers and cravats for the gentlemen. Giles and Daphne dashed about the estates giving last-minute orders, mostly superfluous, for the time they would be away. The other ladies were subjected to several fittings for their black clothes. They had all assembled in the small drawing-room when Steves came in with another black-bordered letter from the Countess.

Giles started to read the missive and gasped, "I'll be …"

"What is it, Richard?" demanded Daphne.

"My other brother – step-brother – Thomas has been killed … in a duel … the day after Ashton died… Mother says that they will both be buried at the same time."

"How very odd," exclaimed Daphne. "Were they in London together?"

"No. Mother says Thomas was with his regiment in Hampshire."

"Aren't duels outlawed?"

"They are, but they still happen," Giles answered her. "I don't suppose that it really affects us. It will just be one funeral."

"Yes, it will, Ashton." declared Lady Marianne.

"What?"

"You are now Viscount Ashton and the oldest living son of the Earl of Camshire."

"I guess that I am unless our father can stop me taking the title. It is the custom, I think, but not automatic."

"I don't think even he could stop it. And you must be his heir now."

"What a thought! Do you imagine there is anything to inherit except his debts?"

"Most of his properties are covered by entails* and they will be yours."

"I suppose. Well, I certainly do not need them nor his title."

This conversation was broken off when Steves announced dinner. It was not till later, when they were in their bedroom, that Daphne returned to the subject.

"Are you really Viscount Aston now, Richard?"

"I imagine so."

"And are you going to inherit Ashbury Abbey?"

"Yes. Someday, I think, and the earldom too. I hope you will enjoy being a countess."

"I don't see why I should. I am completely happy now. Can't you get out of it?"

"I don't see how."

"Does that mean we have to live at Ashbury Abbey?"

"Not unless you want to. Dipton Hall, especially when we have finished our improvements, is a much nicer place. It certainly has everything that I would want that Ashbury Abbey has, and better too. But we are getting way ahead of ourselves. We don't need to think about any of that right now."

"I suppose not. I am eager to see Ashbury Abbey. You know your mother has never asked me to visit? I thought that I had got her to like me."

"You have. If she had her doubts about you, I know you completely won her over at Christmas. She took me aside before she was leaving and said, 'You know, Richard, you are very lucky to have Daphne.' I think she is embarrassed by the fact that my father never visits Ashbury and that the Abbey is not being properly kept up. That is likely why she has never invited you."

"I have never met your father, either."

"You may not now. I would not be surprised if he does not bother to attend his own sons' funerals. It is just unfortunate for me that they didn't decide to die a couple of weeks later. I would have been at sea."

"And left me to manage this trip all by myself! Thank heavens your ship wasn't ready sooner!"

Chapter IV

Several days after getting home from the London trip, Giles was conferring with Mr. Griffiths, his stable-master, about opportunities that might arise while he was voyaging to St. Petersburg. There had not, in fact, been much to discuss, but the two had happily adapted the meeting to talking about blood-lines, famous horses, and likely prospects for the next racing season. They both knew the importance of keeping in mind the goal of breeding first-class, all-around hunters, but the glamor of winning steeplechases or just jump races, without respect to whether the horse could follow the hunt well, kept nagging at them, and their dreams even extended to the highly risky and rarely lucrative business of raising champion flat-track racehorses. The conversation led nowhere on this occasion, but both men enjoyed it nevertheless. Giles rather reluctantly broke off the conversation and returned to the Hall as the afternoon drew on towards the time for dinner.

"What is this letter, Steves?" he demanded as he entered through the front door to find his butler standing with a letter, which had a black border around it, on a silver server,

"A letter from the Countess, Captain Giles. It was delivered a few moments ago."

"I see."

Giles broke the seal and straightened out the paper. "Where is Lady Giles?"

"Upstairs, sir. She returned only a few moments before you did."

"And Lady Marianne and her daughters."

"In the small drawing-room."

"I must change and see Lady Giles. Please ask the others to stay where they are. This news affects us all."

"Yes, sir." Though there was no way of telling it from the butler's demeanor, Giles knew that Steves was bursting with curiosity about the substance of the message.

"Viscount Ashton is dead, Steves. Some sort of riding accident."

"My condolences, sir. I shall arrange for the house to go into mourning immediately." Steves seemed completely unaffected by the news though he had seen Viscount Ashton many times at his father's London house where the butler had formerly been employed.

"Yes. I suppose that is necessary, even though my brother and I were far from being close."

"Yes, sir, I believe that it is required. He was also Lady Marianne's brother, of course."

"You are right. Carry on, Steves."

Giles proceeded up the staircase with a spring in his step. If he was grieving for his eldest half-brother, it certainly didn't show in his actions. Upstairs, he went directly to his wife's dressing room. Before doing anything else, he gave Daphne a kiss, which was fully reciprocated.

"I have just received some bad news," Giles started.

"Oh! No! Not about the pond, I hope."

"Nothing like that, my dear. It is my brother, Ashton. He's dead. I just had a letter from my mother."

"When did it happen?"

"Let's see… three days ago, in London. According to my mother, he fell off his horse and broke his neck. Apparently, he had been drinking and gambling all night and went for an early morning ride on Rotten Row. That is where the accident occurred."

"You weren't close to him, were you?"

"No. Ashton was a lot older than me. I don't even remember him living at Ashbury Abbey when I was growing up. Later, when I saw him at my father's house in London, I did not like him at all. I will feel like a fraud pretending to mourn him."

"I expect that we will all have to go into mourning, even though I have never met him."

"I'm afraid so, at least until he is buried. I will have to go to the funeral, I think."

"Yes. I will go too, of course. Where and when is it, do you know?"

"It's six days from today. At Ashbury Abbey. My mother says, 'That should give even your father time to get here from Norfolk.' Apparently, Ashton's solicitor in London is arranging to have the body transported to Ashbury."

"I hope that I will finally meet your father. He didn't come to our wedding, and I have never been invited to Ashbury Abbey."

"You have not missed much. He is a devious, unfeeling, old fellow. And that's when he is in a good mood."

"Have you told Lady Marianne?"

"No, though Steves knows about it. I wanted to tell you first. I should change and go down and tell them."

"I'll come with you. Betsey and I are almost finished."

Daphne and Giles entered the small drawing-room a few minutes later. The afternoon sun had moved around to bathe the room in a warm glow, and its rays nicely illuminated Lady Marianne and her daughters, who were seated near the window, as if they were in a Dutch painting. Giles went over to them and announced.

"Marianne, I am afraid that our brother, Ashton, is dead."

"Oh. Good riddance!"

"Don't say that."

"Why not? He never did anything for me when I was in trouble, and he was just a bully when we were growing up. How did he die?"

Giles gave once again the information he had received from his mother.

"I expect that we will have to go to the funeral, though I don't know why. It won't change our father, you know. But he is my brother, and we did grow up together. Hard to get that out of my mind. There are a lot of memories, and some of them are good."

"Mother," asked Catherine Crocker, Lady Marianne's older daughter, "Do we have to go too?"

"Yes, Catherine, and we'll all have to go into mourning. He was your uncle."

"But we never saw him, ever," said Catherine's sister, Lydia. "I don't want to go into mourning. And I don't want to go to the funeral. Going into mourning will most definitely interfere with my plans to marry Mr. Dimster."

"That cannot be helped. It would be an awful scandal if you didn't attend the funeral and go into mourning. It might completely turn your Mr. Dimster's parents against you, and they are supposed to provide his allowance.

"Yes," said Daphne, "I am afraid that we all must do it. But maybe, if Captain Giles permits, we can shorten the period of mourning to a minimum."

Giles laughed, "As far as I am concerned, you can forget about the mourning as soon as the funeral is over and we are back here. Lydia, your aunt and I have caused enough raised eyebrows in this region that another cause for shocked gossip will surprise no one. Sir Thomas and Lady Dimster are not likely to hold it against you personally."

At that moment, Steves appeared to announce, "Lord David Giles."

Giles's brother, who was the vicar of Dipton, followed the butler into the drawing-room. "Richard, Marianne, have you heard the news about Aston?"

"Yes, we have."

"Mother wrote to me. She wants me to take the funeral service. I've checked, and I can do that, though it would be a good idea to give the rector at Ashbury a fee. Mother can't tolerate the man, nor can I. I checked the rules, and I can officiate without him as long as I have his permission."

"Then we can all go to Ashbury together," said Giles. "It will require at least two coaches, and you can take Lady Marianne and the girls in yours."

"Do I surmise that you are no more saddened by the death of Viscount Ashton than any of the others here, David? And will you stay for dinner?" Daphne asked.

"Yes, to both questions, Daphne. No, I scarcely knew him, and I did not like what I saw. I am not surprised that he fell off his horse while drunk and broke his neck. I believe that he was always drunk."

"Mother didn't actually say that, did she?" asked Giles.

"No, I inferred the details from her saying that it had occurred early in the morning on Rotten Row."

The following day was a frantic bustle for the servants trying to get ready for their employer's trip to Ashbury Abbey. Steves already had them wearing black armbands or caps. Now they had to get ready black gowns and veils for the ladies and black coats and trousers and cravats for the gentlemen. Giles and Daphne dashed about the estates giving last-minute orders, mostly superfluous, for the time they would be away. The other ladies were subjected to several fittings for their black clothes. They had all assembled in the small drawing-room when Steves came in with another black-bordered letter from the Countess.

Giles started to read the missive and gasped, "I'll be …"

"What is it, Richard?" demanded Daphne.

"My other brother – step-brother – Thomas has been killed … in a duel … the day after Ashton died… Mother says that they will both be buried at the same time."

"How very odd," exclaimed Daphne. "Were they in London together?"

"No. Mother says Thomas was with his regiment in Hampshire."

"Aren't duels outlawed?"

"They are, but they still happen," Giles answered her. "I don't suppose that it really affects us. It will just be one funeral."

"Yes, it will, Ashton." declared Lady Marianne.

"What?"

"You are now Viscount Ashton and the oldest living son of the Earl of Camshire."

"I guess that I am unless our father can stop me taking the title. It is the custom, I think, but not automatic."

"I don't think even he could stop it. And you must be his heir now."

"What a thought! Do you imagine there is anything to inherit except his debts?"

"Most of his properties are covered by entails* and they will be yours."

"I suppose. Well, I certainly do not need them nor his title."

This conversation was broken off when Steves announced dinner. It was not till later, when they were in their bedroom, that Daphne returned to the subject.

"Are you really Viscount Aston now, Richard?"

"I imagine so."

"And are you going to inherit Ashbury Abbey?"

"Yes. Someday, I think, and the earldom too. I hope you will enjoy being a countess."

"I don't see why I should. I am completely happy now. Can't you get out of it?"

"I don't see how."

"Does that mean we have to live at Ashbury Abbey?"

"Not unless you want to. Dipton Hall, especially when we have finished our improvements, is a much nicer place. It certainly has everything that I would want that Ashbury Abbey has, and better too. But we are getting way ahead of ourselves. We don't need to think about any of that right now."

"I suppose not. I am eager to see Ashbury Abbey. You know your mother has never asked me to visit? I thought that I had got her to like me."

"You have. If she had her doubts about you, I know you completely won her over at Christmas. She took me aside before she was leaving and said, 'You know, Richard, you are very lucky to have Daphne.' I think she is embarrassed by the fact that my father never visits Ashbury and that the Abbey is not being properly kept up. That is likely why she has never invited you."

"I have never met your father, either."

"You may not now. I would not be surprised if he does not bother to attend his own sons' funerals. It is just unfortunate for me that they didn't decide to die a couple of weeks later. I would have been at sea."

"And left me to manage this trip all by myself! Thank heavens your ship wasn't ready sooner!"

Chapter V

Giles ordered the coachman to stop at the top of a small rise. He helped Daphne to alight so that she could enjoy the view. The following coach also stopped, and Lord David, Lady Marianne, and her two daughters got out. Before them lay a shallow valley with a stream meandering through it. Right before them in the valley was a country mansion. It had a large medieval hall close to the stream with a small brick block on one end, which was followed by a stable block. At the other end of the hall, a larger stone block ran inland at right angles to the hall. A road, which seemed to be following the stream, looped around the house. To the right of the stable-block side of the grounds, a small village huddled about the road and extended down to the stream. Beyond the stable-block, almost on the road, was a large church built in the late gothic style. The church seemed to be all sparkling glass and featured a square tower with pinnacle adornments. To one side of the church, there was a graveyard surrounded by a low stone fence. Beyond the road, fields spread out, with here and there a farmstead. A drive from the road ran up the front of the stone house. It then turned to parallel the hall and finally ended in a large, circular, graveled area at the stable block.

"What a beautiful sight," enthused Catherine Crocker, "I would love to draw it."

"Not now, certainly, Catherine," said her mother, who little appreciated the view since she had grown up in the house that lay before them and had few nostalgic feelings about her former home.

"The house seems to have a very strange layout," commented Daphne.

"It certainly has," replied Giles. "It was originally a small castle with a wall and a moat and a hall. In the time of Henry VI, the knight who held it must have done terrible things in France while he was becoming rich. He left his castle and a lot of money to found an abbey, whose chief job seems to have been to pray for his soul. Most of the money went to building a magnificent chapel just outside the castle walls. It is now the parish church that you can see beyond the house. It is quite out of proportion for what the parish needs.

"The first Earl of Camshire was one of William the Conqueror's henchmen, but his descendants never prospered consistently. They had a genius for backing the wrong side in the medieval disputes. Their traditional seat, which was in Norfolk, was confiscated by Henry VII when the Earl of that time died on Bosworth Field supporting Richard III. His grandson caught the eye of Henry VIII and became some sort of fixer for him. The King did not restore the family holdings to his follower, probably because they had been given to someone who was even more useful to the monarch. However, when the monasteries were dissolved, he did give Ashbury Abbey to our ancestor. The Earl in King Charles's time continued the family pattern of backing the wrong side, but, at the Restoration, his son had the property restored to him, and because of services to the King became quite rich. What the services were is unknown, but they are rumored to have been something quite improper. That earl had the old walls torn down, the moat filled in, and built the residence you see to the right of the hall. The building to the left is the kitchen block, which dates to the time it was a castle, and the stables are a conversion of some other building that was inside the walls.

The next earls continued to maintain and improve the property, but my father has let it deteriorate.

"We used to have a crypt or tomb or something where the original earls had their castle, but, for some reason that I don't understand, my great grandfather discontinued the practice of burying our family members there, and now the churchyard here suffices.

"What a lecture! I don't know what came over me. We really should get on."

The carriages took them in a long loop to the manor house, on the way crossing a bridge over the river, which had not been visible from the viewpoint. As they were crossing the bridge, Giles remarked, "Do you see that old mill over there? I spent a lot of time fishing in the millpond when I was a boy." It was the only landmark he pointed out. It seemed to Daphne that he was sinking deeper and deeper into gloom as they neared the Abbey.

When they arrived at the house, it was evident that it was in mourning. Black crepe draped the portico, and the doors were dotted with black cloth rosettes. The front door opened as the carriage drew to a halt, and a footman came forward to open the door. Behind him, a butler stood at attention. Daphne alighted first, followed by Giles, who then took the lead.

"Georgeson," he greeted the butler. "It's a long time since I last saw you."

"Yes, my lord," was the reply. "Welcome home, even for such a sad occasion."

"Thank you. This is my wife, Lady Giles."

The rest of the party had stepped from their coach as this exchange was taking place.

"I don't know if you knew Lady Marianne, Georgeson," Giles continued.

"No, my lord, she had left Ashbury Abbey before I took up my position here."

"Well then, this is she. And her daughters, Miss Crocker and Miss Lydia Crocker. Is the Earl at home?"

"No, sir. We are not even certain that he will be attending the funeral. The Countess is in the drawing-room. I will announce you."

The butler led the way, threw open a door, and announced, "Viscount Ashton, my lady, and Lady Ashton, Lord David, Lady Marianne, Miss Crocker, and Miss Lydia Crocker."

The Countess rose from the armchair in which she had been sitting. The gentlemen bowed, the ladies curtsied, and the Countess herself responded with a slight curtsey.

"Richard, I am so glad that you have come. I wasn't sure that you would. It seems so strange to have you announced as Viscount Ashton. Daphne! Let me welcome you to Ashbury Abbey. And David and Marianne. It is a sad occasion, but at least we are all gathered together. I don't know whether the Earl will come or not."

"Are any of Ashton's friends coming, mother," asked Giles.

"Not that I know of. Or Thomas's, though a Captain Gregg arrived this morning to represent his regiment. He is away somewhere but should be back for tea and dinner."

The conversation turned first to the deaths of the two brothers. Nothing more was known about Ashton's accident. He was riding alone, following a night of drinking and gambling, with substantial losses, his solicitor had reported. Details about Thomas's duel remained unknown. The bodies had already arrived at Ashbury, and all was ready for the funeral the next day.

"I am afraid, David, that Mr. Medcraft, the rector, insists on conducting the service. I imagine he expects a big fee from the Earl, in which case he is in for a surprise."

"That is fine by me, Mother," responded Lord David. "I had no desire to officiate."

The group conversation then broke up. The countess singled out Daphne, and their discussion turned to the gardens, with Lady Camshire regretting that her plantings looked rather woebegone relative to what she had seen at Dipton. "I don't have the people, you know, to keep the beds properly in order or to tidy up the shrubs," she explained. The others talked about what they remembered of their childhoods at the Abbey and about their secret places and forbidden activities. The two girls listened spellbound; it was a side of their mother that they had never seen, and they stored up her stories for use when next she tried to discipline them.

Sometime later, they were joined by Captain Gregg.

"What a beautiful village you have here, Lady Camshire," he enthused after being introduced to the others. "The well-cover is most picturesque, and, of course, the church is outstanding. Good pub, too, the Camshire Arms!"

Before more comments could be made, Georgeson announced dinner. It would be held in a small dining room, not in the hall, which was only used for very large gatherings. The discussion of Amesbury continued through much of the meal, providing a convenient way to avoid thinking about the reason they were all together. Captain Gregg turned out to be not only interested in the details of Amesbury and its Abbey but also to have a fund of knowledge about the typical construction of castles and houses from different periods and even of the dwellings of the less fortunate. They did not tarry over the meal, however, and soon the Countess led the ladies away. When the three men had gathered at one end of the table and had poured glasses of port, Captain Gregg took the lead.

"I am glad that I am able to see you, Viscount Ashton, and you, Lord David, before your father arrives."

"If he arrives," muttered Lord David.

"Quite. You may not know, Viscount Ashton, that your brother very much admired you."

"Please call me 'Captain Giles', Captain Gregg. I don't use my titles among military men. No, I was not aware of that. I am afraid that I have seen very little of Thomas in the past ten years."

"Oh, yes, he followed your career eagerly and was always reciting the more important features of it in the mess. Rather enviously, I must confess. He would say, 'Look at what my brother Richard has done. Been in another fight and will get a great deal of prize money. I would never guess that he had it in him. If my idiot of a father had let me go to sea instead of buying me a commission, that could have been me. I am afraid that your brother was rather abrasive, not the most popular man in the mess by any means, but that is beside the point.

"My colonel asked me to represent the Regiment at the funeral, not only out of respect for a comrade, but also to talk to you."

"Yes?"

"You may not know it, but Captain Giles – oh what confusion all these similar names can cause – our Captain Giles, made you his heir. Not that there is much to inherit, because there are some unpaid bills and other debts, I know, and Tom was not one to save money. There are also some delicate matters that have to be attended to…"

"Yes, spit it out, man."

"Yes. Ah, my colonel wants you to come to the regimental headquarters, in Laidsburg, you know. It's in Hampshire. To see about straightening things out."

"I don't know if I can. I have to join my ship shortly. Couldn't my man of business handle whatever there is to do?"

"My colonel foresaw that might be your wish. He strongly suggested that it would be best if you could at least see what the situation is yourself."

"Then, I suppose that I must. I have already had a note from my brother Ashton's solicitor that he has some matters that would be best handled in person, especially as my personal response would be needed quickly. It's all very mysterious. What in the world did my brothers get up to, I wonder. I'll come, if at all possible, but, if I cannot, then you will have to make do with Mr. Edwards, my prize agent."

A noise broke out at that point coming from the Abbey's entranceway. A moment later, the door to the dining room was flung open, and in marched the Earl of Camshire. The three men rose to their feet.

"There you all are, guzzling my port, I see. And you, Richard — or do you think I should call you Sir Richard? — trying to take my place before I'm dead. Well, you will just have to wait! If it weren't for the entail, you would never get any of this," declared the Earl. "Georgeson, get me some food and some proper wine. But a new glass first. Hurry, man."

The Earl sat in the place which Giles vacated and poured himself a full glass of port. As the others resumed their seats, he kept up his monologue.

"I would have been here earlier if my damn horse had not lost a shoe near Braxleford. The fool of a blacksmith there had let his fire go out, so it took a long time to get the horse shod again. The inn there is atrocious. Made me a Welsh rarebit that I could hardly eat. Had the ugliest barmaid you ever saw. Certainly not good enough to make me stay the night, so I came on here. Their sack* was good, at least after the third bumper*."

The Earl paused to down his glass of port before pouring another one and continuing with a sneer, "Well, Viscount Ashton, so you are now my heir as well as

Ashton's. Not that it will do you much good. Of course, it's all entailed, but we have both borrowed against the income as much as we can, and your mother is due a third of the income in any case. You just didn't think about how you were cutting off your own nose when you got all prim and proper about Captain Hoxley and stopped his privateering, did you? A quiet word with him would have lined your own pocket and kept my money coming from the venture."

Giles had recently exposed the man being referred to by the Earl as a pirate and a traitor.

"Father, the man was a pirate."

"Didn't matter. He was paying me good money, you sanctimonious turd."

"And you, David," he continued turning to his other son. "Just as stupid as your brother. Taking a country living and not even getting a curate, I hear. That is no way to become a bishop! Bishops' emoluments are big, and they have any number of other ways to use their position and influence to make more. While you, you just sit around giving sermons."

Giles rose to his feet. "Father, since you cannot keep a civil tongue in your head, I am joining the ladies. I imagine the others are too."

Lord David and Captain Gregg immediately rose to their feet and joined Giles, leaving their glasses unfinished.

"I must apologize for my father, Captain Gregg," Giles said loudly before they reached the door. "I am afraid that he is always like this."

In the drawing-room, it was evident that the Countess was on edge, possibly guessing at how the Earl had already behaved and fearful that he would continue his assault on everyone when he had finished the decanter of port and the other bottle that he had told Georgeson to bring him. Daphne was most sensitive to the Countess's unhappiness and almost at once apologized that she was exhausted from the trip and would retire. Giles promptly asserted that he would accompany her upstairs. Lady Marianne declared that she and her daughters were tired and urged the Countess that she needed rest. Captain Gregg had no desire to remain in order to discover how the Earl might choose to insult him or his regiment.

The Earl missed breakfast the next morning and even had to hurry after the others as they walked to the service. The mortician had already placed the caskets in the church. The party from the Abbey were the only mourners, aside from the servants who had been ordered by Georgeson to attend. The minister had arranged for the organist and choir to be present, and they did their best to fill the empty church with doleful music. The Reverend Mr. Medcraft preached a long, tedious sermon which no one listened to except Lord David, and he only did so to get ideas in case he was ever called upon to officiate at a funeral with no genuine mourners. Lord David concluded that, if he were ever faced with the problem, brevity would be the most welcome aspect of any sermon he delivered, a feature which Mr. Medcraft's effort sadly lacked.

Georgeson had arranged for two of the footmen to act as pallbearers with himself, and he was joined by Giles and Lord David. Captain Gregg was pressed into service when the Earl refused to take any role. With the appropriate words from Mr. Medcraft, the coffins were lowered into the ground, and all that remained was the ceremonial throwing of the first handfuls of dirt into the graves. The earth was damp, and the Earl, who led the way, first compressed the earth into hard balls and then flung them onto the coffins as if he were trying to break them apart. He had already spoken to a groom and had his horse ready as soon as they reached the churchyard gate. Off he went, leaving the poor Countess to act as host for the others who had come for her step-sons' internments.

The memorial gathering after the funeral was not a lengthy affair. It's most notable feature was how few reminiscences there were of the brothers. Daphne insisted that the Countess should visit Dipton Hall in the immediate future and would not take 'no' for an answer. Daphne had, for the first time, realized how lonely the Countess's existence at Ashbury Abbey must be, and she herself would be quite glad of more company when Giles was away. Besides which, she knew that her father rather liked the Countess.

Chapter VI

"Damnation!" Giles exclaimed as he put down a letter he had just received.

"What is it?" Daphne looked up from a letter she was reading.

"Ashton wants to take up even more of my precious time before I have to sail."

"What is it now?"

"Edwards has confirmed what that ass of a solicitor said about it being desirable if I stopped in town to see about some of Ashton's more private affairs. Add that to my need to visit Thomas's regiment, and the trip to Butler's Hard is going to take two full days more than it should. "

"So when do you have to leave?"

"I need to be in Butler's Hard by Thursday morning."

"So, you will have to leave on Monday. That is terribly soon. I knew, of course, that you would have to go, but I was just ignoring the fact. We have almost no more time together! Can I come with you? Monday, Tuesday, Wednesday. Three more days and maybe some of Thursday. Oh, it would be wonderful to have the extra time together, even though you will be busy."

"It would be fine by me, but I hope you won't get bored. Actually, Lady Ashton, it would be a good idea for you to know all about these problems so that you can give Mr. Edwards guidance when I am away."

"Am I now Lady Ashton? I am not even used to being Lady Giles. I don't feel like a Viscountess. I am still just me. However, I do think it would be a good idea to spend the rest of today riding around the estates so that you can give me any additional instructions you think of before you go to Russia."

"Glad to, but we both know who actually manages the estates. I just make suggestions. With Ashton Place coming on board, you really should think some more about getting professional managers for you to oversee."

"Ashton Place?"

"Yes, Ashton Place is the ancestral home of the Viscounts Ashton. There is a house, I think, and some tenant farms. That is probably partly what this lawyer is on about. And, yes, you are now Lady Ashton, or, if you prefer a bigger mouthful, I suppose that you could be called Lady Daphne Giles, Viscountess Ashton, but I think Lady Giles will do if you want. You can ask Steves. I am sure he knows the proper forms of address."

"It was simpler when I was just Miss Moorhouse."

"It was, but I am very glad that you are no longer Miss Moorhouse."

The trip to London was much less fascinating for Daphne than her previous journey, and she settled into Nerot's Hotel as if it were a second home. The morning found them taking a hackney cab to an address in Holborn near Chancery Lane. They found the address to be in a dirty brick building with windows that must have dated from more than a century ago. A brass plaque announced that the chambers of Snodgrass and Delancey lay within. Mounting to the second floor, they were ushered into a large room lit by dirty windows. There they were greeted by a red-faced, portly man with mutton-chop whiskers and a serious look belied by the smile lines about his mouth and crinkles about his eyes.

"Lord Ashton, Lady Ashton. I am Jeremy Snodgrass. My grandfather, my father, and now I have acted as solicitors for the Earls of Camshire, and I have also managed the legal affairs of your half-brothers. Thank you for coming so promptly. It will help immensely. I need to read your half-brother's will to you and then go over some rather tricky matters." The will was simple and left everything to Giles, referred to in the document as "my snot-nosed toady of a step-brother, Richard." Mr. Snodgrass rather stumbled over that part of the reading.

"Almost everything is entailed, so your brother only had a life-interest in Ashton Place and its income. I am afraid that he borrowed heavily against that annual income. In fact, his own revenues will not cover the debts, and they do fall to his heir. They are at a scandalous interest rate, fourteen percent. Ashton Place is leased, and the rent is paid until Michaelmas. The tenant has paid without fail, on time, so far, so I don't think you need worry about that. The late Lord Aston had borrowed against that income also for the next year. He did have an account at Coutts's bank, but it is overdrawn. There are also some gambling debts to various gentlemen. I believe that most of them have already shown me the notes he gave to cover his debts, but there still may be some that I don't know about. Of course, gambling debts are not collectible really, but they certainly would be regarded as debts of honor that his heir should repay. He also has a lease on a house in St. James's, which runs to Lady Day in two years' time. The rent on that property is past due. There is some furniture in it that belonged to your brother, I understand. Your Mr. Edwards looked into those premises and tells me that there are some difficulties with breaking the lease or making use of the house for your own purposes. Another debt of honor, I believe. So I am afraid, Lord Ashton, that there is no good news for the immediate future, though when it is all straightened out, you will have a handsome income from Ashton."

"I suppose. Is Ashton Place mine automatically, or does it formally revert to my father?"

"It is yours. It is a very complicated entail. I imagine that your grandfather, who strengthened and extended its terms, had a low opinion of his son's – your father's – ability to manage his affairs. The property automatically goes to Lord Camshire's oldest son over the age of twenty-one, as does the title. They are not really in your father's gift – and never were."

"I suppose that he will leave me in the same position when he dies."

"I would expect so. You can publish notices that you will not honor debts on notes extending more than two quarter-days* after his death or some such terms."

"Can you arrange to have the notices placed, Mr. Snodgrass?"

"I can, my lord, but it will alienate your father."

"That's of no concern to me. We could hardly be farther apart."

"Very good, my lord."

"Now, I will have Mr. Edwards pay all the debts for me. Just send the needed documents to him. I don't like paying the gambling debts, but I suppose I really have little choice. I imagine that the notes backed by the income from Ashton-Place estate can be paid as the income comes in."

"Might I make a suggestion, Lord Aston?" Daphne intervened.

"Yes, my dear?"

"It might be better if you paid the notes based on Ashton Place as well. Your spare funds are invested in consols*, yielding four percent, while Mr. Snodgrass said the notes are at fourteen. It will be much cheaper for us to pocket the extra ten percent."

"Of course, you are right. I shall so instruct Mr. Edwards. I think that we are finished, Mr. Snodgrass. I will look into the subject of the London lease or have Mr. Edwards do so. Are you also the executor for my brother Thomas?"

"Yes, I will read his will to you now if you wish. It is much simpler."

To Giles's surprise, Thomas's will left everything to him as well. "Originally, he was going to leave whatever he had to his sister, Marianne, but he came in a while back and told me that you were assuming her expenses. He then said he would leave it all to you since there was no point in Lady Marianne double-dipping, as he put it. There isn't much, I am afraid. Some debts, of course, and unpaid bills, mess bill too, probably, maybe some gambling debts and some that may be owed to him. There is, of course, his commission. I don't know what that might be worth."

"Mr. Edwards may know the ins and outs of disposing of an army commission. We do things differently in the Navy. I am surprised that neither of my brothers left anything at all to Lady Marianne Crocker. She was their sister, after all."

"That may be because they knew that there was nothing really to leave. Captain Thomas Giles, as I mentioned, knew that you were looking after her expenses."

Bidding Mr. Snodgrass farewell, Daphne and Giles made their way back to the Strand, and, from there, they took sedan chairs to Mr. Edwards's offices in the City. It was quite evident from his greeting that Giles was a very valued customer and that he regarded Daphne as someone who had to be taken very seriously in her own right. He was glad that she had come with Giles: if any financial decisions had to be made, he was sure that Daphne would understand.

"I am sorry about your brothers, Captain Giles. It is a sad time."

"And a nuisance. We have just been to see Mr. Snodgrass, and I seem to have inherited more debts and problems than assets."

"True enough. Did you get everything straightened out?"

"Yes, except this mysterious matter about the lease on the London house. And how to sell Thomas's commission. Do you handle such sales?"

"No, but I have a good friend who can manage it for you. Now, to the problem of that lease."

"Yes?"

"There is more than one lease, my lord. The one that Mr. Snodgrass knows about, and then another one, which has rather different terms for the tenancy and how the rent will be paid. "

"Yes?"

"It mentions services and some duties owed to a Mrs. O'Brien and a Mrs. Marsdon, and alternative ways of clearing the rent required by the lease. It came to light after the first one, and Mr. Snodgrass doesn't really know what it means nor does my solicitor, but he is really only familiar with legal matters having to do with prizes and ships, not real property and leases."

"It sounds very complicated. What do you think, my dear?"

"I don't know," stated Daphne. "I think you would have to learn more about the circumstances and the property and how the lease is involved in it. Mr. Edwards, could we go there now?"

"I don't believe that it is a place for a lady, my lady. It is not an entirely respectable area, and I am not sure how proper the activities that have been taking place there are," said Mr. Edwards.

"Oh! Well, I am not going to fall down in a faint if things are a bit ugly, you know. I suspect that you are referring to something to do with — ugh — with — ugh —

strumpets. I am aware that they exist and that they are not very savory, but nor is a cow birthing, and I have attended that in the past and will undoubtedly do so again. If it is something unpleasant about Ashton's whore that is involved, maybe a woman is needed to sort it out. It sounds like the sort of a problem that only a man would concoct and then be unable to see the way to rectify. Richard, what do you say? The house is close to our hotel, and we could go there on our way back to Nerot's."

"Daphne, are you sure you want to be exposed to the nastier side of London life?" Giles asked. He wasn't at all confident that Daphne could handle revelations about the seedier side of London life with aplomb. It was certainly completely outside her own experience.

"If your brother got involved in it, I think it is up to us to sort it out. If you didn't have to leave first thing tomorrow, you could go by yourself, of course, as would be much more proper, no doubt. However, we have to leave early tomorrow so let's do it now on the way back to the hotel. Can you come, too, Mr. Edwards?"

"I am afraid not, Lady Giles. I would be available tomorrow or some other time. I would very strongly advise against your going, my lady. It is not a fit place for a respectable lady."

"I don't see how it can harm me, Mr. Edwards. I will be quite safe with Captain Giles to protect me and my virtue. Let's go now, Richard," Daphne suggested. "If we can't sort it out, you will have a better idea of what is involved, and I may be able to deal with any problems after you have sailed."

Giles and Daphne took a wherry* back to Westminster Bridge, and, from there, a hackney cab to the address in Arlington Street. The house was even closer to their hotel than she had guessed from the address. Apparently, in London, quality establishments of an impeccable reputation rubbed shoulders with ones of much more dubious purposes. She idly wondered just how many houses of ill repute she might have passed on her shopping trips the previous time she had been in London. This was certainly one of them if Mr. Snodgrass's and Mr. Edwards's beating about the bush when talking about them was any indication. Until very recently, she had not even been aware that they existed! She was also aware that she still had only very vague ideas about what might go on in them. Her father's explanations about parts of Shakespeare that her governess did not seem able to discuss had left her with only a partial knowledge of what might be involved.

The house was a four-story gray-stone building, with possibly an additional attic floor above the parapet. It had a large, enameled, green front-door which was adorned with bright brass fixtures. Giles and Daphne ascended the steps, and Giles used the well-polished knocker to seek admission. The door was opened by a footman, dressed in a gold-colored coat and white knee britches and stockings with a white, powdered wig. He stared with some surprise at Daphne.

"Do you have an appointment with Mrs. Marsdon, sir?" he asked Giles.

"No. I have come about the lease on this property."

"I am afraid, sir, that you will have to make an appointment with Mrs. Marsdon. Just send a note to this address, and she will inform you when you may visit, sir."

With this brush-off, the supercilious footman started to close the door. His actions were halted by Daphne having placed her boot in the way.

"I believe that you have misunderstood the situation, my good man," Daphne declared in a loud, affected voice. "Captain Giles is the owner of the lease on this property, and if your Mrs. Marsdon does not see him immediately, he will have no choice but to get the bailiffs to remove her --- and you."

The servant backed down immediately, swung the door open, directed them to a large parlor on the ground floor, and announced that he would inform Mrs. Marsdon that they were here. What names should he use?

Giles answered before Daphne could respond, "Tell Mrs. Marsdon that Captain Sir Richard and Lady Giles are here to see her about the disposal of this property."

When the footman had left, Daphne asked, "Why didn't you introduce yourself as Ashton?"

"I was afraid it would be confusing since Ashton is the title by which my brother was known here. Also, it would give this Mrs. Marsdon less warning about who is actually here."

The room they were in was furnished with several settees and chairs with small tables scattered about. It featured a pianoforte, with music set on the rack that indicated that it was well used. On the walls were hung framed copies of cartoons that depicted aspects of London's seamier haunts. Over the fireplace hung a portrait of a striking woman. It was the highlight of the room.

After a short wait, a woman came bustling in. She was quite tall and slender, with dark blond hair, arranged loosely to fall down her back, and icy-blue eyes. She was dressed in a long gown made up of layers of diaphanous material that matched her eyes. It was tied just below her bosom and then allowed to flow freely. The gown was lightly draped over her shoulders, leaving her arms bare and featured a wide and revealing cleavage. The effect was somewhat spoiled by her face being heavily painted in a way that largely prevented her from exhibiting any expression. She was clearly the subject of the portrait over the mantle, but the artist had smoothed out the harsher features of her face, and, in the portrait, there was no evidence of the artificial make-up that rather spoiled her good looks.

The woman stared at Daphne pointedly, from head to toe, before turning to Giles, who received a similar examination.

"You wanted to see me," she began.

"Yes. I am here about the lease on this house."

"You have been misinformed. The house is already rented."

"You misunderstand me, madam. I have inherited the lease and am examining the terms and the use to which the property is being put."

"You have inherited the lease? I know that Ashton is dead, so I was expecting to be contacted by his heir, but you are not Captain Giles. I know him. A better 'swordsman' than Ashton, though not as daring. You are not Captain Giles."

"I think you have me confused with my other brother, who was a captain in the army. My other half-brother. I am afraid that I have to inform you that he also is dead, and as a result, I have inherited his estate, including anything he might have received from my oldest brother's will, which, in fact, was nothing. In reality, I only inherited debts from Lord Ashton and the lease on these premises."

"I see." Mrs. Marsdon stated thoughtfully. She turned to call through the door which she had left open on her entry. "Jacob, go and summon Mrs. O'Brien. Tell her that Ashton's heir is here." This was followed closely by the sound of the front door opening and closing.

"You are correct that Lord Ashton -- I suppose that you are Lord Ashton now, but it will prevent confusion if I address you as Captain Giles – that Lord Ashton had a lease on this property from the Earl of Knockingdon. I understand from the Earl that the rent is in arrears, so he will be glad to get your payment. You must be aware that the property is also covered by assignments and contracts that Lord Ashton made concerning the continued use of the property by myself and that details in these documents specify the interest that Mrs. O'Brien also has in the property."

"Mrs. O'Brien?" questioned Giles.

"Yes, Mrs. O'Brien. You must have heard of her. A prominent arranger of entertainments for gentlemen. She is very well known among the *ton*,* you know," Mrs. Marston added condescendingly, "the most elegant part of Society. I have asked my footman to summon her since she has as much of an interest in the use of these premises as I do. Of course, as Ashton's heir, you will have to honor these other agreements as well as the terms of the main lease."

Giles seemed to be at a loss for words as it dawned on him that Ashton seemed to have become enmeshed in a web woven to ensure that his half-brother's and now his own hands were tied tightly in dealing with the debts and other obligations associated with the lease.

"Mrs. Marsdon," Daphne broke in. "Do you have copies of these documents?"

The woman spun towards Daphne, her movement causing one of her breasts to pop out of its covering. She seemed to have little interest in quickly returning it to its proper place. Daphne noticed and was both intrigued and shocked to discover that the nipple was rouged, something she had never even thought would be done.

"Of course we do. I have just sent my footman to Mrs. O'Brien, who has the documents. She will bring copies – notarized copies, not that it is any of your business. If you think you can poke into our affairs or participate in them, you are quite mistaken. We won't allow it. Mrs. O'Brien is very particular about who she will employ and what activities will occur. She and I are in charge. We were in Lord Ashton's time, and these documents will guarantee that we are in future."

Before Daphne could reply to this statement, a rather disheveled man thrust his head into the door. "April, my dear, I must be going. Very good romp today. I've left the gratuity on the nightstand."

"I apologize for this interruption, Teddy. I hope to see you again soon, dear," Mrs. Marsdon replied.

When he had left, Daphne remarked in a shocked voice, "Why, you are nothing but a common whore."

"Not common, my dear, not common at all. I only take the most elevated gentlemen. Like that one, who I'll have you know, is Sir Edward Farthingale. Five guineas a time they pay, but they get the best ride in London."

Before Daphne could reply to this outrageous claim, the door opened to admit a rather buxom woman, expensively dressed with hennaed hair and a heavily painted face.

"Whoever you are, you are not Captain Giles, sir," the newcomer accused Giles. "And who is this country mouse?"

"Madam, I most certainly am Captain Giles, Captain Sir Richard Giles, Viscount Ashton. And this lady, who, in my opinion, is the height of proper elegance and true, unblemished beauty, is Lady Giles, Viscountess Ashton. I am the heir of my half-brother, the late Viscount Ashton. I require information about the lease on this property, which I am beginning to suspect, involves a most shameful contract. And who might you be."

"Why, I am Mrs. Hilda O'Brien, of course. Well-known, I would have you know, in all the most elegant circles."

"No doubt only among the gentlemen. I have heard of you, Mrs. O'Brien. The names of common bawds are well known among naval men. Mrs. Marsdon here tells me that you have documents adding to the lease on this property that prevents me from simply throwing her and her entourage out onto the street immediately."

"I do, indeed. Of course, the originals are kept in a safe place, but I have brought true copies of the papers as witnessed by a notary public. As Ashton's heir, you will find that they bind you to maintain Mrs. Marsdon in a proper style and establishment. You may, of course, use her services yourself or, to a specified extent, employ them to raise funds at specified amounts and reimbursement to Mrs. Marsdon and myself. You have no choice about that, though I am sure that you will find Mrs. Marsdon a very skilled partner and a most pleasant change from your lady here."

Giles was taken aback by this attack on Daphne, but, before he could respond, she intervened in an icy voice.

"Are these documents signed by you, Mrs. O'Brien?"

"Of course, they were signed and notarized by Lord Ashton, Lord Knockingdon, Mrs. Marsdon, and myself. Lord Knockingdon is the owner of this house. All the contracts are in order and quite unbreakable. Here are the copies."

"We'll see about that," Daphne spat out as she intervened to take the documents herself. A quick examination, more for show than for information, led to her continuing, "It looks to me that these documents will provide *prima facie* evidence that you are all involved in criminal activities and now a conspiracy to defame Viscount Ashton. Lord Ashton will give them to his man of business and his lawyer, and you will hear, in due course, what actions they recommend against you leeches. Come along, Lord Ashton. Our business here is finished."

Daphne turned to leave the room in a most imperious fashion and the startled footman only just had time to open the front door so that she could sweep through it, followed by a rather flummoxed Giles. He had never seen this side of her before. Daphne was down the stairs and had turned towards their hotel before he caught up to her.

"That was magnificent, Daphne!" he chortled. "I didn't know you had it in you."

"Neither did I. But that doxy made me so angry presuming that she had you firmly caught in her spider's web so that you for a few would have to partner in her … her … her brothel just made me very angry." She was silent moments before continuing in a joking tone, "At least, I hope that you were not wishing to explore her suggestions."

Giles laughed. "Of course not. I already told you that my father and Ashton cured me of all wishes to engage with ladies of pleasure. It is not as if I was unaware of what was available in London. The midshipmen's birth in old *Euryalis* had a very well-thumbed edition of *Harris's List**, so we all knew what was on offer in London, and I suppose in other ports as well."

"Harris's List?"

"Yes. There used to be a catalog of the available ladies of pleasure and what they would do. I don't think it is published anymore. I imagine Mrs. O'Brien would have been featured in it. I read it, of course, but was never inclined to pursue its wares."

"I seem to be learning more and more about this disgusting side of life. What a family you do come from,

Richard! I suppose that it is only thanks to your mother that you and David have turned out to be real gentlemen. Your older half-brother, just like your father, seems to have been totally despicable. I wonder what we will find out tomorrow about Thomas."

"So do I! I am not looking forward to discovering what problems he has left that require my attention."

With those somewhat gloomy thoughts, they walked off towards their hotel.

Chapter VII

Giles and Daphne arrived soon after midday at the headquarters of the East Hampshire Regiment. They were directed to the Adjutant, Major Brindsley, a small, dark, harried-seeming man.

"Captain Giles, I am very sorry about your step-brother. Such a senseless waste! I am afraid that Colonel Jenkins is away as is our Lieutenant Colonel, but they gave me full information about your business. Did you know that you were a great hero to him?"

"I did not. I am surprised."

"Oh, yes, he followed your career closely though, I am afraid, somewhat enviously. He subscribed to the Naval Gazette and made sure that the mess knew whenever you were mentioned. He did rather wish that he had gone into the Navy instead of having his father buy him a commission."

"How did he die, Major?" asked Giles. "I have received only the most minimal of news."

"It is a sad and rather stupid tale, I am afraid. The news of his brother's death was brought to Captain Giles by a couple of other captains who were returning from a visit to London, where I believe that they had encountered Lord Ashton at some establishment where he was well known as a reckless gambler and heavy drinker. He was in his cups that night and losing rather heavily. They observed him as they were gambling at another table. About dawn, they said, Viscount Ashton threw down his cards, announced that the game was rigged and that he needed some fresh air. He staggered out of the room without settling what he owed. The men with whom he had been playing seemed startled by his behavior, but soon they resolved as a group to pursue him to get what they were owed, at least in the form of notes that acknowledged the debts. They went to the house where he lived, only to be told that Lord Ashton had taken his horse, mentioning something about going riding in Rotten Row to clear his head. After some delay, his pursuers obtained horses and set off after him. They found him coming towards them, and when he saw them, he apparently tried to turn his horse to avoid them. Unfortunately, however, he must have pulled on the reins or spurred the creature in some strange manner. The beast reared suddenly, and Lord Ashton was thrown to the ground and apparently broke his neck. Having established that he was dead, the group returned to the same location to discuss the situation and toast the memory of the man who had just bilked them of their winnings.

"My colleagues were still at the club and heard all the details. They were highly interested since they realized that the victim was the brother of their messmate. When they returned to the mess, rather late the next night, they found Captain Giles somewhat advanced in his cups and quite unaware of his brother's demise. One of my colleagues, Captain Hershey, who is a belligerent and rather uncouth man, not at all popular in the mess, announced the death to Captain Giles and started to berate him on how typical the whole thing had been of the Giles family, or so I am told; I wasn't there.

"Captain Giles objected to this description of him and his relatives and several colleagues tried to get Captain Hershey to desist, but instead he became more vocal in abusing both Captain Giles and his family. Captain Giles, understandably, had had enough. He challenged Captain Hershey to a duel. Unfortunately, neither side was willing to back down. Captain Hershey is a very good shot, and the same could not be said of your brother. They met at dawn, and Captain Hershey mortally wounded your brother."

"What happened to Captain Hershey?"

"He fled. He has, of course, lost his commission. No great deprivation to the Regiment. I hope you are not thinking of taking revenge on him."

"No. It sounds as if Thomas got his due desserts. If there is a case, I trust that the authorities will deal with Captain Hershey. Now, I understand that there are some matters that are a concern to me.

"Yes. There are three things. First are his possessions. There is not much. Only his pistols and his sword are of value. Do you want them?"

"No, I am adequately equipped myself. Do you have a tradition of auctioning off a deceased officer's effects to cover his mess bills?"

"We haven't in the past, as far as I know. But we have not been on active service since the American War."

"Quite. I suggest that you auction my brother's effects and use the proceeds to pay his mess bill. Anything remaining should be used to raise a glass in the mess to his memory on as many occasions as it may take to exhaust the funds."

"That is very good of you, sir. Now the second matter is his commission. It is worth a bit of money, though not as much as you might expect since we are not a fashionable regiment, and there is the prospect that we may be called to active service. I might mention that the proceeds might be used to deal with one of the less attractive things that Captain Giles left behind."

"What is that?"

"Ah, well … ah … Captain Giles left behind him a bit of unfinished business."

"Yes?"

"Well, he got a country girl near here, a dairymaid, with child. It is not unusual near a regimental depot, as I suppose you know. Nevertheless, Captain Giles seemed to be quite attached to the woman, and, when a boy was born, he was concerned about the mother's and baby's future. I admit that I was somewhat surprised by his reaction. Most of our soldiers just walk away when something like that happens.

"Anyway, he did something to support the wench until her time came, and afterward, I believe. The problem is that she has been shunned by her own family and all of the village. She is living in a barn with her baby and hardly making ends meet since your brother died. There is a man in the village who is prepared to marry her, for a hefty sum of money, and raise the child as his own. He demands £500 to do so. Captain Giles was trying to raise the sum, but it was not likely to occur. Selling his commission might cover the sum, but I would recommend against that wedding even if it could be financed."

"Why?"

"The man is a brute. Both the woman and child would likely be ill-treated. In fact, he was suspected in the death of his previous wife from beating her, but it never came to the assizes."

"This is awful. Oh, the poor child," Daphne broke in. "Richard, we must do something. The child is your nephew."

"I suppose we must. Major, do you know how one sells a commission?"

"The best thing is for the Regiment to do it. We can get as good a price as anyone for you, and there is then no problem with whether the purchaser is acceptable."

"Will you do it for me, please? My wife and I will see the woman and decide what to do about the situation."

"Certainly, Captain Giles. I should be delighted to deal with the commission. If you can find a satisfactory solution to the problem of his child, it will help the Regiment too. Though these things do happen, unfortunately, our taking some responsibility for the deleterious outcome of dalliance between our officers and the local girls will ease our relations with the town."

Giles and Daphne set off to see the woman. Indeed, she was living in a barn with her child and seemed to be badly in need of everything to sustain them. The baby was dressed in rags and had a charming, grinning face, though it was covered with dirt, as were his hands and feet.

"Richard," Daphne whispered when she saw the situation, "we can't just leave her here."

"Let's find out more, my love, before we become too involved."

Questioning the woman, whose name was Nancy, revealed that her plight was indeed dire. Her family had rejected her totally, and the village had abandoned her when her son was born. Somehow, the parish had succeeded in shirking its duty. Captain Giles had promised to take care of her, but he hadn't done much, and then he got killed. It was only through the kindness of the farmer that she had use of his barn, but he provided no support and had made it clear that he wanted her to go soon. The proposed suitor was a brute, whom she feared greatly, but she could see no other alternative if the money should be raised. Otherwise, she would have to go to Portsmouth or, maybe, Southampton, where she might be able to sell her favors.

Daphne drew Giles aside. "Richard, this won't do. The child is your nephew, even though he is a bastard. I can't stand to see the poor woman abused in this way."

'Daphne, such a fate is the all too common lot of girls who do not guard their chastity better and get swept away by an attractive man and his false promises. We cannot rescue all of them."

"Of course not. But this child was the responsibility of your half-brother, and you are his heir, no matter what you may think of him, and so this is just one particular woman whom we must help. It is not a question of rescuing them all. I would feel badly about abandoning her here, especially when I know how well our child will be treated when he – or she, of course – arrives."

"What do you suggest?"

"Nancy would be better off well away from here. Not only is her reputation destroyed, but also the local people have disowned her. We need another milkmaid on the Dipton Hall farm. That position would give her a place to live. And there might well be someone in the area to marry her, if it was thought that she had had a husband who had died. Even if there isn't anyone to marry her, her situation would be better on our estate than what she faces here. And it would be cheaper for you than if you have to pay that brute what he demands in order to marry her."

"Trust you to think of my purse for me," Giles teased. "But you are right. We owe it to the family honor, tattered as that seems to have been rendered by the actions of my father and stepbrothers, to do something for Nancy and her child. I don't want it advertised that the child is Thomas's, though I don't doubt it. We could suggest that she say her husband had been taken by the press-gang and had died at sea. That would account for us taking an interest in her and make her having the child seem respectable. I don't even care what suspicions our neighbors might have about how the child came about if it would not bother you."

"It would not. And he is a lovely little baby boy under all that grime."

"Then let's do something about it."

Giles and Daphne turned to Nancy and outlined what they had in mind. She would get employment at Dipton Hall as a dairymaid, and with it would come a small cottage. They would also supply £20 for furnishings and clothes for the baby. Daphne would pick her up in the coach as she traveled from Butler's Hard to Dipton in a couple of days.

With this problem settled, Daphne and Giles were able to set off again for Butler's Hard. They arrived late at their destination, but again Mr. Stewart stopped them going to the inn, insisting that Mrs. Stewart would be heartbroken if they did not again stay with them. He reported that *Glaucus* was ready to sail; all that was needed was Giles's final inspection and approval.

Mr. Stewart did have a letter for Captain Giles from Sir Walcott Lainey. He, it seemed, had decided not to join the ship at Portsmouth, as had been arranged after he refused to brave the wilds of a trip to Butler's Hard, though why that was unacceptable had been totally unclear. He now claimed that he still had urgent business in London, which would prevent his joining the ship at Portsmouth. Instead, Sir Walcott now expected *Glaucus* to proceed to Chatham, where he would embark.

Giles was highly annoyed. Sir Walcott had claimed that he was in a hurry to get to St. Petersburg, though he had delayed departure so much that the Admiralty had decided that the trip could serve as an initial cruise for the new frigate. *Glaucus* would have to put into Portsmouth to pick up her cannon, powder, and shot in any case, and it was, therefore, the best place for the special ambassador to join her. Going to Chatham would delay them considerably, especially if the winds were not auspicious. However, there was nothing he could do about the changed situation. He would send Sir Walcott a message saying that it was important that he meet the ship as soon as it was likely to get to Chatham, specifying a precise date. The note stressed that further delay would jeopardize their hope to complete a worthwhile mission before it would be necessary to leave St. Petersburg for fear that the Baltic would become blocked by ice.

Daphne was amused at how annoyed Giles was at having his plans disrupted, though, in fact, it did not really matter. She pointed out the benefit of the new arrangement to Giles since he would have to put up with Sir Walcott for several fewer days. It would really be better for Giles than if the Baronet had appeared at Portsmouth when he was expected or, even worse, ahead of time. This argument did not improve her husband's mood until he thought of the implications of his cabin being entirely his own for a few more days.

"Daphne, my dear, how would you like to go on a cruise for a few days with me on *Glaucus*?"

"What do you have in mind?"

"Well, when we leave here, there will be a couple of very hectic days in Portsmouth loading our armament and supplies. We would have had to divide the main cabin in case Sir Walcott showed up on time, so it would be cramped if you were also present, so I did not think to ask you because you might find it uncomfortable, especially since you are with child. Now, the whole of the cabin is available, and there will be at least another three days, more likely four or five, quite apart from those in Portsmouth, until *Glaucus* reaches Chatham. I would love it if you came with me. We could send the carriage back to Dipton with orders to proceed then to Chatham, and it could pick up Nancy on the way to Dipton. It would certainly be there in time, given that we are not making a direct passage to the Medway."

"I thought that sailors were superstitious about women on board being bad luck."

"That's nonsense. Many ships have women, often wives of senior petty officers. And very useful they are too. Quite a few captains take their wives to sea, but most prefer not to. I think the story of the superstition is spread by captains who take a casual view of their marriage vows."

"All right. But what about Betsey?"

'She can come too, of course. Carstairs can find her a place, or we can set off part of the cabin. Or she can go back with the coach if she is afraid of the sea."

"You have an answer for everything. Yes! Oh, yes! I would love to come with you. If it weren't for the baby about to arrive, I would try to persuade you to take me all the way to St. Petersburg."

The next morning, after a pleasant evening spent with Mr. and Mrs. Stewart, Giles and Daphne were rowed out to *Glaucus*. Giles was piped aboard with full ceremony, even though he had yet to accept the vessel on behalf of the Navy. Daphne was whisked aboard soon after. Mr. Stewart was on hand to lead the way in showing the changes in the vessel.

The first surprise occurred when they entered the captain's cabin. Mr. Stewart explained that it was currently laid out as it would be for the voyage to St. Petersburg. Under this arrangement, the first room consisted of a dining room with a large, elegant walnut table, in simple lines and fine workmanship. It was surrounded by matching chairs.

"Good heavens, Mr. Stewart. This is surely not your usual furnishings," exclaimed Giles.

"No, sir, it is a gift from Mrs. Stewart and myself. We have very much appreciated the progress Daniel has made under your tutelage."

"He is a fine lad, Mr. Stewart. There is no need for you to make such a splendid gift."

"It is our pleasure, Captain."

"Then, thank you very much, very much indeed. Isn't it a magnificent set of table and chairs, Daphne?"

"It most certainly is!"

"Now,' said Mr. Stewart, "let's examine the captain's own cabin and the guest one."

Giles's compartment also was furnished in the same style as the dining room had been.

"Surely, this is not also from you, Mr. Stuart, is it?" Giles asked.

"No. You have Lady Giles to thank for these furnishings."

"Daphne? So that is what you were doing when you went shopping, and no packages showed up! This is magnificent! Thank you so much. It was so thoughtful of you. How did you even know what to order?"

"Mr. Stuart suggested what was needed when we were last here and where to purchase it. He showed me the usual furniture that he would supply, and it was not very nice. He said he knew that, on *Patroclus,* you never changed what the shipyard had supplied. I thought you might like to have better surroundings."

"I certainly do. And every time I am in my cabin, I will have an extra reason to remember you."

"Now," said Mr. Stuart, "let's look at the guest accommodation next door."

The space was a mirror image of the Captain's cabin, on the starboard rather than the larboard* side. It also had high-quality furniture quite unlike what the boatyard would have supplied. Unlike the pieces in Giles's own cabin, these ones featured a great deal of gold inlay work. To Daphne's eyes, it appeared rather garish.

"Surely you did not supply this ... this furniture, did you, Mr. Stuart?" Giles asked.

"Oh, no. It was delivered at the same time as Lady Giles's order. I understand that Sir Walcott ordered it himself."

"How in the world did he know what to buy?"

"I suspect that you will have to ask Lady Giles that question."

"Daphne?"

"Richard, Mr. Stewart mentioned when we were at Butler's Hard that many captains acquired their own cabin furnishings since those supplied otherwise are rather Spartan and crude. He also told me about the table but asked me to keep the news as a surprise for you."

"Yes?"

"I found out from him who could supply first-rate cabin furniture that would match the table he intended to give you. He also gave me a copy of the ship's plans, including the cabin, of course, in case I decided to order some furniture. So, yes, when I was in London, I did place an order."

"That is all very interesting, Daphne, but it doesn't tell me how Sir Walcott came to order his own furniture and why it fits the space just like mine does. Surely, you didn't buy a set for Sir Walcott too."

"Of course not. Do you remember how, at the reception where we met Sir Walcott, you went off with Sir David to huddle in a corner about something and left me with him?"

"Yes."

"Well, I had already sized up his character and was pretty sure that if you had nice furniture and he did not, he would make life so miserable for you that you would give him your own quarters."

"I suppose I might have done so, or even offered my cabin from the start."

"I didn't want that. So I took the opportunity to tell Sir Walcott how plain the standard fittings of a frigate would be. Not at all suitable for an important ambassador to Russia. He could not be sure that he might not have to entertain important Russian officials, even possibly the Tsar himself. Well, that got him into a most anxious state, especially as I knew that, in the past, you had always been content with the boatyard-supplied furnishings. I told him that I did know who supplied elegant furniture for captains' cabins and gave him their name and address. I was pretty sure that his self-esteem would make him decide to furnish his cabin. I even told him that I knew that the plans for *Glaucus* would have been provided to the shop. I just didn't say that I knew it because I was delivering them myself. I guess he must have taken my hints."

"Thank you very much. I am sure it would have been very awkward to have Sir Walcott housed with anything but the best furniture. But I am afraid that his taste is not such that I will buy it from him at the end of the voyage."

"You will be interested to hear," Mr. Stewart resumed, "that both your orders from Fortnum and Mason's have arrived."

"Both?" Giles questioned.

"Yes," replied Mr. Stewart with a smile. "There is one from you, Captain Giles, and one from Lady Giles."

Giles was not about to let on that he had already known about Daphne's visit to the shop. "I had no idea that your mysterious shopping expedition would include Fortnum and Mason's. What a delightful surprise! We will certainly be very well supplied for our short cruise. Thank you very much, Daphne!"

"On a more serious note, Captain Giles," resumed Mr. Stewart. "I should point out a couple of different features in this part of the ship. Mr. Hughes, from the Ordinance Board, suggested them. He thinks that stern guns should be more powerful than the usual pop-guns mounted at the taffrail*, partly as better weapons in themselves, and also as a discouragement and diversion against ships that are positioning themselves to rake your stern."

"Oh?"

"The first is the stern windows. I have made them removable so that they can be struck below* when you clear for action. If you have the misfortune of an enemy firing into your stern, that might limit the damage because there will be fewer pieces of glass and splinters flying about."

"That strikes me as a very good idea. And the other changes?"

"The windows can then serve as gun ports."

"What? Surely I am not supposed to share my space with another couple of enormous cannon. Having some of the broadside guns in my space is more than enough."

"There would be no more guns in the cabin, Captain Giles. If you look at the ceiling, you will see several deadbolts. You can't observe it, but their backing has been strengthened relative to what you might expect, so they can take the weight of a gun. Mr. Hughes has devised a very clever system of slings and tackles, so the existing guns can be repositioned as stern chasers if the need arises, and the stern has been reinforced to take the recoil. He tried it out with some of your crew and found it to be perfectly feasible, at least as far as moving them; he couldn't fire them through the windows, of course. Shifting the guns all took almost thirty minutes, but he is sure that time can be shortened with practice."

"This wasn't part of the original design, was it, Mr. Stuart?"

"No, sir. Mr. Hughes only suggested it when he heard that you have been given *Glaucus*. He said you were the only captain who would be willing to explore the capabilities of his design. I confess that Daniel was very enthusiastic about the idea also. He said that the heavy bow chasers in *Petroclus* had played a significant role in her success – and in the prize money he got."

"What did the Admiralty inspectors say about this change?"

"They did not notice them, I am afraid."

"Are they paying for them as an extra?"

"No. The expense will be borne by me. Daniel will be sailing with you, and anything that might make him a bit safer has my full backing."

"That is very generous of you, Mr. Stuart. I will be eager to try them out as soon as possible. Now, let's get on with my inspection so I can accept the ship."

Chapter VIII

Daphne stood at *Glaucus*'s taffrail as the day was fading. There was a light wind, and the sea was barely ruffled, so *Glaucus* glided along with hardly any pitching or rolling. The weather was sufficiently mild that she had left her boat cloak in the cabin, but she suspected that she would need it by morning. Giles had arranged for Daphne and Betsey to go ashore in Portsmouth while he was loading the guns and ammunition so that they could obtain some clothes more suitable for a sea voyage than the ones they had brought on the trip.

It had been a varied three days since they left Butler's Hard. They had slipped down the river peacefully, with slowly changing vistas opening up on either side, as *Glaucus* was towed and sailed down the river. Then there had been bustling times in Portsmouth as the ship's guns and supplies were loaded. Daphne was amazed at how smoothly the sailors worked and how they used pulleys and ropes to make it possible for groups of them to manage huge loads. Daphne was no stranger to seeing hard work done, but there were no horses or oxen on the ship to aid with the heavy tasks, just teams of men. They had funny terms for everything too. A pulley was a block, a rope was a line, and "Avast" was the order to stop. After two days of loading, they had sailed out of Portsmouth and through Spithead on the way to the English Channel. They were well out to sea as night fell.

The following day had been marked by constant drills with the sails and the guns as Richard and his lieutenants were learning the ways of the ship. Daphne had spent most of the time in a chair that Richard had installed for her on the quarterdeck since their cabin had been made unusable as the crew practiced shifting the guns in the stern cabin again and again until Richard was satisfied that the changes could be performed quickly in battle. She had had a book with her that she had bought in London, but most of her time had been spent admiring the incredible dance that was performed by the crew as they performed their tasks, some high above her in the rigging, others in well-coordinated movements of the heavy cannon taking all the steps necessary to use them efficiently. She had been thrilled as the final parts of the gun drills were accomplished with the cannon firing with real powder and shot, and the evident fun that the crews had when finally getting to use the results of their practice to produce loud noises.

Betsey sat on a coil of rope behind Daphne, looking very uncomfortable with the ship's motions. She seemed to be thinking that she would have been better to have taken the carriage back to Dipton and then met Daphne at Chatham. Her misery was only slightly relieved by the sailors who tried to flirt surreptitiously with her when they thought no one was looking. One crew member seemed to have raised her interest when he was helping her to stow their luggage and to make a corner of the deck near the petty officers' quarters private for her. He was a redheaded, confident, cheerful carpenter's mate called Russell. The carpenter's wife, when he introduced Betsey to her as someone to ask about the details of living on a ship, had indicated that he would make someone a good catch as she was showing her how to attend to the more delicate matters of everyday life. Nevertheless, Russell failed completely to raise a smile when he happened to pass where she was sitting to make some cheerful comments, even though he seemed to pass by her a large number of times.

Daphne's reading and her reveries had been frequently interrupted by the officers stopping by to chat.

She was quite amused to find that the midshipmen were awed by her presence, terribly awkward in talking to the captain's wife, sometimes almost tongue-tied and at other times spouting out miscellaneous information in bursts. It was evident that they all suffered from a bad case of hero-worship when it came to her husband. She had been charmed herself when she overheard two of them, who did not realize that she might hear them, express complete admiration that their hero had the most beautiful and lively of women as his wife. Richard regularly stopped by where she was sitting under some shade, which some sailors had ingeniously rigged to protect Betsey and her from the sun without obstructing her view, partly to apologize that he did not have more time for her and partly to explain the baffling steps involved in the work. He admitted that he had not really thought through the details of the first few days on a new ship and how busy and distracted he would be when he asked her to join him on the voyage to Chatham, but it was very evident that he himself was delighted to have her on board. Remembering that, for her, the greatest pleasures of the trip so far had come from sleeping in his hanging bed, she could only say that she was delighted that he had asked her on the voyage without going into what its highlight had been so far. The first night had started with him hanging a separate hammock in the cabin, saying that the hanging bed was too narrow to be comfortable for two, but somehow she had got him to relent. It had been crowded but not unpleasant! She wasn't even embarrassed when Betsey entered in the morning and saw the nature of her sleeping arrangements.

Her reflections were interrupted by Mr. Brooks, the master. He came to the taffrail and stared towards the sunset.

"I am afraid we will have a bit more wind by morning, my lady," he announced as he turned around to face forward.

"Will it become rough?" Daphne asked.

"Not very, only a little more heel than we have now and more motion. Are you a good sailor?"

"I don't know. This is my first time on a ship."

"Is it? You have adjusted very well, if I may say so. Hopefully, there will not be enough motion to bother you." Mr. Brooks seemed to be oblivious to poor Betsey, who was clearly not a good sailor.

They were joined by Giles.

"Daphne, I hope that Mr. Brooks has not been alarming you."

"Quite the contrary, Richard. He has been trying to alleviate any fears I might have about the *Glaucus* rolling or pitching more. See, I have already learned some nautical terms."

"So you have! Soon you will be speaking naval English as well as French. Well, I don't think the wind will become serious, but Mr. Brooks is a better judge of weather than I am. I think we should have supper now if you are ready. We will have to be up before dawn, you know, so that the crew can clear for action. It is our usual custom, and it will be especially necessary with the crew still becoming used to *Glaucus*. Let's go below where the table is laid."

The next morning, Daphne was on the quarterdeck* with Giles well before dawn. The wind was from the east, kicking up whitecaps that could be seen even in the dark. It was coming over the right side of the ship, but she supposed that she should get used to thinking of it as the starboard side. Noises and rumblings below her feet indicated that the cabin was being dismantled, and the guns moved to their unusual positions as stern chasers. Her boat cloak kept her warm, and she clutched a steaming mug of tea, which Giles's servant had prepared for her. The stars were fading, and there was a definite glow in the east when a lookout called. "Land ho. Ahead and to larboard. Five miles."

"This should be Pevensey Bay, with Hastings ahead and a bit to starboard," Mr. Brooks announced. "We should come about soon, sir."

Before Giles could issue the command, another hail interrupted him.

"Ship ho! Three points off the larboard bow! Half a mile." Giles peered off to larboard. There was, indeed, a ship to larboard of *Glaucus*, closing with them on the larboard tack. In the rapidly increasing light, she appeared to be a frigate, with her gun ports closed, and not picked out with special decoration. Probably also a thirty-six, like *Glaucus*. She seemed to be flying no flag, at least not one that could be seen in this light.

"Mr. Dunsmuir, raise the private signal and our number."

The signals rose promptly on their halyards, while the officers on the quarterdeck stared at the unknown vessel waiting for the response from the stranger.

"No reply, sir." Mr. Dunsmuir announced unnecessarily. "But look, sir, she has just broken out the French flag."

"Furl the top-gallant sails," called Giles as a first step to engaging the enemy.

"I see no signs that she is about to reduce sails to go into battle, sir; I think she is hoping to slip past us and get away," remarked the master.

"Belay* that order. Quite right, we'll pass ahead of her, Mr. Brooks, and then come about to engage her on our starboard side," Giles informed the Master. "I wonder why she doesn't want to engage." Then he twisted towards the bow and bellowed, "Stand by the larboard guns. Fire as you bear. Then reload and secure the guns. Carstairs, escort Lady Giles to the orlop* immediately!"

The other ship had its own ideas about how the encounter should proceed. Just before *Glaucus* was to cross her bows, she turned off the wind, obviously intending to avoid presenting her bow at close range to *Glaucus*'s guns and hoping that, as she turned, her own broadside would get in a strong blow against her opponent. Giles thought that he had a surprise in store for the enemy. "Standby to come about," he roared. Then, with hardly a moment's pause, counting on his well-trained crew's being already for the order, "Helm alee*." Immediately the reply came from the quartermaster, "Helm's alee, sir."

Even as *Glaucus* started to turn, her opponent's bow chasers opened fire, with her starboard gun being the first to get off her shot. The ball, probably only a nine-pounder, did not reach *Glaucus*. The next couple of shots from her larboard bow-chaser had the same fate as the balls sank without reaching Giles's ship. *Glaucus*'s broadside began to bear and fired at the enemy. Then it was her own turn to receive unanswered shots as the turning enemy's guns bore on the frigate.

"Stand by to come about. Stand by the stern guns" was Giles's next order. "Single shot and double charge the guns. Fire as you bear. Mr. Brooks, bring us about."

Almost immediately, the four aft-most guns, now positioned to fire through the window openings that were serving as makeshift gun-ports, roared out. All of them struck the enemy, three of them whistling in to wreak havoc on her deck with one gun upended and wood splinters from other hits sweeping across to wound many of her crewmembers. The fourth ball thumped into the mizzenmast, spraying deadly splinters all over. Possibly, because of the dangerous excess of powder that Giles had ordered, the shot had enough strength to damage the enemy's mast so that it cracked and then started to fall to starboard. With *Glaucus* now turning rapidly to starboard and with the opposing ship's losing her sails, the remainder of her broadside missed *Glaucus*. The English frigate continued to turn, and now her starboard guns bore on the enemy. Her broadside rippled out, and so did the next one until the continuing turn left the guns no target, while she was once more in range of the enemy's cannon. Their next broadside again swept *Glaucus* with splinters, but it did no other damage to the guns and the rigging. *Glaucus's* bow chasers next fired, wreaking more havoc, and then her turn brought the larboard guns into play. Some of the opposing frigate's guns were still in range, but that soon ceased to be the case as *Glaucus* continued to advance so that she could take up station on her opponent's quarter. Now she could fire into the French ship with impunity. Some of the additional damage she had caused to the French ship's rigging meant that the enemy still could not maneuver effectively even though she had cleared away the wreckage of the mizzenmast. In this position, Giles could reduce his rival to matchwood if the fight continued.

"She's struck," Midshipman Stewart roared. His job had been to watch for the first signs of the French surrendering.

"Cease fire," ordered Giles. "Mr. Hendricks, Mr. Macauley, take possession of the frigate. Take Mr. Miller and Mr. Dunsmuir with you. Send their officers here when you have accepted their surrender. Then evaluate the damage and report to me, Mr. Hendricks. Mr. Macauley, secure the French crew using your marines. Carstairs, take my barge and search for anyone knocked overboard, especially from the Frenchman. Check all the wreckage in the water. Mr. Fisher, go to the orlop and tell Lady Giles that it is safe to return on deck. Mr. Correll, you can start restoring the ship to its normal state after the bosun, the carpenter, and the gunner have assessed the damage."

Giles turned to survey the damage to *Glaucus*. It seemed to be mainly cosmetic in the sense of only splinters begin knocked from the wood that was. The carpenter would be busy, but none of the damage was a threat to the ship. He couldn't help wonder how much injury the splinters had caused. Probably a great deal since Dr. Maclean had yet to report. Aloft, they had been lucky. There were numerous holes in the sails that he had not been able to furl until the battle was over, and many lines had been severed, but nothing that could not be quickly and easily repaired. *Glaucus* could proceed as soon as she had determined that the captured ship was seaworthy and could navigate under her own sails. He probably should send her into Chatham rather than Portsmouth since it would take about as long either way, and he was going to Chatham where he would be able to pick up his prize crew immediately. That destination might also help in making sure that *Glaucus* got the proper credit and prize money. He might even accompany her there, if she was not too much slowed by the damage she had sustained.

He felt a surge of relief followed by anxiety as Daphne appeared on deck. He had been worried about her, even though she should have been perfectly safe in the orlop. Here she was, but looking very disheveled. Her dress was bloodstained, and there was blood on her face. The hem of her petticoat was showing, looking like it had been ripped somehow.

"Daphne, are you all right? Are you hurt?"

"Of course, I'm alright. The orlop is perfectly safe if a bit dark and scary."

"But you are covered in blood, your clothes are disheveled, your hair is out of place, and you are reeking of rum."

"I am. You know that the orlop is where the surgeon treats all the men with wounds. There was a terribly large number of them."

"I know, but weren't you safely out of the way?"

"I suppose I was, at first, but Dr. Maclean and his assistants had more than they could handle, so I tried to help out."

"You did what?"

"I helped out. Swabbing wounds and helping to remove splinters and cleaning out areas of the victims where Dr. Maclean was trying to operate or sew up wounds. He said that pouring rum on the wounds made them less likely to fester — and pouring it into the victims made their wounds hurt less. Some of it splashed onto me."

"Hamish," Giles spoke to one of the ship's boys. "Get a basin and some water and a cloth for Lady Giles. And pass the word that Betsey, her maid, is wanted on the quarterdeck. Where is Betsey, anyway?"

"She fainted when the first of the injured were brought into our space, and she continued to feel very wobbly even after she had recovered consciousness. She may still be in the orlop. It would be a good idea, Richard, to bring her on deck."

"Hamish, just bring the water. Tell one of the seamen that Lady Giles's maid needs to be brought on deck from the orlop."

At that point, Midshipman Stewart appeared. "Sir, the captain's cabin has been restored. It suffered no damage from the enemy."

"Very good. Please accompany Lady Giles to the cabin and get Ferguson to arrange for water to clean herself. Tell him to make tea as soon as the stove is lit, and water can be heated."

A large number of seamen was working on the main deck as Daphne and Mister Stewart approached the companionway. Word had already spread about Daphne's role in the orlop. One of the men cried out, "Three cheers for Lady Giles." From the enthusiastic response by everyone present, one would never have guessed that they were suffering from the exhaustion that followed hard work and being in action. Daphne, who had seemed quite unperturbable when describing her role in the sickbay, blushed a deep crimson and did not seem to know where to look before she rallied to wave and smile at the cheering men.

Giles turned to examine the deck to discover what his next task should be. Carstairs was approaching, holding a stout-looking canvas bag.

"Did you find anyone, Carstairs?"

"Aye, sir. Three frogs, sir. They are being looked at by Dr. Maclean. And we found this bag. It was in the sails that had been alongside the Frenchie."

"Give it to me."

The bag had been loaded with papers and an iron cannonball – a nine-pounder – to make it sink. It must have been thrown overboard from the French ship when capture became inevitable, but it became entangled in the rigging that was dragging over the side due to the damage that had already been inflicted. Before opening the bag, Giles looked toward the captured frigate. A boat was approaching *Glaucus* with what must be the French officers on board.

"Get this out of sight before the Frenchmen appear on the quarterdeck," Giles instructed Carstairs, giving him back the bag. "I don't want them to know that we found it."

"Aye, aye, sir."

118

Three captured French officers were coming through the entry port.

"What have we here, Mr. Hendricks?"

"The French ship's officers, sir. Three lieutenants. They have all given their parole. Incidentally, the ship is called *Le Jour de Triomphe*."

"Where is the captain?"

"He is dead, sir. That may be why they were so slow to strike*."

"Maybe. And what is the state of the … what did you call her?"

"*Le Jour de Triomphe*, sir. It means the day of triumph. She carried no spars that could be used for the mizzenmast, sir. The carpenter and the bosun are hopeful that they can fish the mizzen topmast to the stump of the mizzen and raise a driver* on it. There will be no mizzen square sails if she is rigged that way. It will take a couple of hours. There is a lot of damage to the woodwork and the standing rigging*, but nothing stops her from getting underway soon. None of our balls hit her near the waterline. The carpenter says he can patch the holes quickly, though she may leak a bit. I guess that the ship will be ready to get underway in about two hours."

"And the crew?"

"We counted twenty-seven corpses, sir, but there may be more who were thrown overboard. Forty more wounded. I wonder if Dr. Maclean might be able to go across to help their surgeon who, by the way, is drunk. The rest of the French crew and the petty officers are confined to the hold."

"Very good, Mr. Hendricks. Return to *Le Jour* with Dr. Maclean when he is through here and return when he is finished. Ask Mr. Miller to select a crew to take her into Chatham with us. Oh, and Mr. Miller should have a master's mate to help him and act as an officer. Ask Mr. Brooks to arrange that. Also, take Mr. Fisher to go with Mr. Miller. The experience of having more responsibility will be good for him."

"Aye, aye, sir."

"Now, let's see to these officers. Introduce them to me, please, before you go. Do any of them speak English?"

"No, sir."

"Then, let's see to them. Come along and tell them who I am and that they are welcome on board. Oh, you should send their sea chests over when you can."

"Aye, aye, sir."

The introductions were completed quickly, and the three French lieutenants, whose strange names Giles forgot as soon as he heard them, were sent to the wardroom with Mr. Fisher to get cleaned up and given some refreshment.

"Now, Carstairs, what have you done with that bag?"

"It's in your cabin, sir. I handed it to Lady Giles directly, since Betsey is not really recovered from seeing the wounded in the orlop."

Giles felt able to leave the deck at that point since everything requiring his immediate attention had been dealt with. *Glaucus* had only minor repairs to complete and could get underway at any moment. The prize was in good hands. He had decided to have *Glaucus* accompany her into port so that there would be no danger of having to leave his prize crew behind.

As he started down the companionway, Giles felt a sharp tinge of guilt. He should not have put Daphne in harm's way by inviting her to cruise in the English Channel. There had indeed been a risk of combat, even though not a great one, and the outcome of a serious fight was never foreordained. He had put her and their unborn child at unacceptable hazard. However, the guilt was partly allayed by recalling Daphne, appearing like an evil ghost from the orlop, cheerful and steady as always, and then responding with embarrassment to the salute of his crew. He would wager, if anyone on board had tried to predict what would happen if they came to battle, that it would be the lady who would faint away and the servant who would be a pillar of strength, but that would just show that they did not know Daphne.

Chapter IX

Giles was still worried about the effect the battle might have had on Daphne. He knew from his own experience that the horrors that one observed in battle were harder to deal with mentally in the aftermath of the fight when there was no longer anything of urgent importance to prevent one from reflecting on them than while the action was happening. He feared Daphne's reaction, especially as she had certainly not been expecting to go in harm's way on this trip with her husband, particularly not when she was with child. He need not have worried.

"Oh, Richard. I am so glad you are all right. I was so frightened for you while the fight was going on," Daphne greeted him.

"I'm sorry, Daphne. I should never have asked you to accompany me on this little voyage. I didn't think there would be any danger to you."

"I wasn't really in any danger. And I am glad to see what being in a ship in battle is really like, at least in terms of what happens to the unlucky members of the crew. I knew that it must happen, of course, but somehow I never really thought of what it must be like to be amongst men who had suddenly been wounded or had their shipmates killed. I know you have to fight, but, oh, how I long for peace now!"

Daphne started to cry, and Giles took her into his arms. After several moments, where her thoughts were elsewhere, Daphne pulled back enough to say, "Did you know that Carstairs delivered a bag to the cabin which he said was important?

"Yes, I told him to bring it here."

Giles opened the bag. It contained a nine-pounder ball, several bound books, and another small book that looked like a notebook or sketchbook. Giles opened the first book. It was, of course, in French. Even with his very limited knowledge of French, however, he could make out that it was the ship's log*. He showed it to Daphne, who confirmed that it was indeed the ship's log. The other books turned out to be the captain's log, and what, with Daphne's aid in translation, seemed to be the master's log. The booklet contained rather clumsy sketches that might represent military installations and a lot of writing in a rather poor hand. Daphne struggled more in making out the handwriting than in translating the words.

"They seem to be reports written after night explorations of the English shore. It mentions several towers with sketches and other places where the writer suspects there are fortifications," she said before putting the booklet aside.

"These may be more informative," Giles said, holding up a folded set of papers. "They seem to be the ship captain's commission and orders. "See if you can make anything of them."

Again, the two heads bobbed over the papers. Daphne could make out the content of the first paper even though it seemed to have a rather formal, elaborate, and old fashioned composition. Giles remarked that it was very similar to the language employed in his own commissions. On translation, the document simply ordered the captain to take command of *Le Jour de Triomphe* and to carry out the orders he had been given previously.

The second document was more interesting and caused Giles some concern. It consisted of the orders given to the captain about what to do with his ship. It contained several distinct parts.

First, the ship was to approach Pevensey Bay well after dark. It was to approach, as close as the captain dared, to the western part of the beach and wait for a specified signal to be flashed from the shore. He was then ordered to land an agent, a *Monsieur l'Eveque*, who would meet with French sympathizers who would conduct him inland.

Second, following the successful landing of the agent, or else after waiting for one hour with no signal, the captain was to land a party to explore as much of the beach as they could during the night, recording as much as they could make out of the location and nature of the shore defenses. They were to avoid, at all costs, being observed by soldiers ashore. If they were challenged, they should pretend to be smugglers, but under their smuggler disguises, they were to wear uniforms so that they might escape execution as spies.

Third, *Le Jour de Triomphe* was ordered to be well offshore by dawn, and on a tack that would make it appear that she was beating up or down the English Channel, whichever direction was appropriate for the wind at the time. When she was out of sight of the British, she was to go to Cherbourg.

Fourth, three weeks after the landing the agent, *Le Jour de Triomphe* was to return to Pevensey

Bay to pick up *Monsieur l'Eveque*. Rather surprisingly, the orders contained both the location where the rendezvous would occur and the signal codes to be exchanged to verify that it was not a trap.

Giles was surprised that the information about how to reconnect with the agent was part of the orders until he realized that the orders also said that he should rehearse the codes with *M. l'Eveque* before he was taken ashore.

Giles could not hide his excitement. "This is a real windfall, Daphne! We now know that the French have landed an agent and when and where he is to be picked up. Our side should be able to trap him. And maybe capture another frigate if they send one to replace *Le Jour*. We'll have to make sure that our finding this information does not become common knowledge. I had better see Carstairs at once.

"Sentry, pass the word for Carstairs," he called in a much louder voice.

Carstairs appeared almost immediately.

"Carstairs, who knows about the bag you found?" Giles asked his Coxswain.

"The boat's crew, sir."

"Any of the French prisoners?"

"No, sir."

"Tell everyone who knows about your finding not to spread the word, especially make sure that the crew of the barge do not gossip."

"Is that wise, sir? I don't know how many other people may have been told by the crew of your barge or how much farther that information may have spread. If you emphasize its importance by ordering that it not be discussed, it is much more likely that the news will spread since it will be thought to be important. Otherwise, it is not likely to go beyond this ship."

"What about asking the ship's crew not to talk to others about how we happened to take the frigate. If we tell them it is about trying to keep the French from finding out what happened, would that make sure that people hold their tongue when we are in Chatham?"

"Probably, sir."

"Very well, Carstairs. Pass the word and include any other ships we happen to visit. Say that I don't want to announce it because the French prisoners might hear about it."

"Aye, aye, sir. The idea that they are part of a plot to fool the French is likely to keep everyone mum."

"This complicates matters, Daphne," Giles said when Carstairs had left.

"Why, dear?"

"I have to report this immediately, and I also have to pick up Sir Walcott as soon as he gets to Chatham. But I don't want to report what we have found to the port admiral at Chatham."

"Why not?"

"Because I don't really trust the port admiral's wisdom in these things. Port admirals are better than yellow admirals* usually, but they have been awarded an office that is purely administrative and has nothing to do with actual fighting or strategy. They are just one step up from yellow admirals."

"What are yellow admirals?"

"They are former captains who have risen to the top of the captains' list, so they are next in line to be admirals, but the Admiralty doesn't believe that they should have a command. In theory, it is one way to prevent totally unsuitable men from becoming admirals. Often, though, it does mean that good men are promoted only to let someone with influence, rather than exceptional merit, get promoted ahead of time."

"So, what are you going to do?"

"I am tempted to see Admiral Gardiner of the North Sea Fleet. He is usually on station east of the Godwin Sands, and he has experience and understanding in this sort of situation."

"Then do it. Sir Walcott can wait. One more day isn't going to affect his mission. After all, he has imposed both inconvenience and delay on you by not showing up at Portsmouth. Furthermore, I have heard so much about the Admiral from your letters that I would like to meet him. I promise not to tell him the derogatory remarks you have made about him in your letters."

"You better not! My career would be cut short, I am sure. But you are right. It is what I should do."

"Well, with that settled, we can probably have dinner. I imagine you will be hosting the French officers."

"I hadn't really thought about it. I just presumed that they would eat in the wardroom."

"I think it would be a good idea for you to have them dine with your own officers and with us. After all, with one lieutenant on *Le Jour* and another one on watch*, there might not be many people to entertain them in the wardroom, especially as your best French speaker is on *Le Jour*. It would also be very good for you."

"How did you reach that conclusion?"

"You need experience in hearing French. Even with a little of my help, you may understand conversations better when you reach Russia if you hear it spoken now, especially as I can do some translating. I will engage the lieutenants in French if they do not speak English. They have shown no knowledge of the language so far, I believe. They communicated with young Mr. Fisher, your midshipman, who is the only one of you who talks anything like decent French."

"I'll try. But don't expect me to participate."

"Say a few words, if you can. But remember what I said about the advantage of understanding what other people say when they believe that you don't speak their language."

Glaucus's officers who were free, namely Mr. Correll and Midshipman Dunsmuir, together with Mr. Brooks, Mr. Macauley, and Dr. Maclean, arrived before the French captives were shown in by Mr. Fisher, who had been told to look after them. He introduced them around the room and then explained to the French officers that he would have to be on deck. Before he left, Daphne took him aside to verify what he had learned about their guests. While she was so occupied, Giles overheard one of the French officers ask another one – he still couldn't remember their names – something about a sack. The other one replied with something that included 'jeter' and 'sac.' The first one said 'bon' and seemed to be relieved at the answer. Giles suspected that he had just heard one officer reassure the other that the captain's critical documents had been thrown overboard before their ship was captured. He couldn't be sure, of course, but he thought it possible that, when the French officers were landed as prisoners who had given their paroles, they might well be approached by French agents. If there were confirmation that the reason for the French ship's being in Pevensey Bay should remain unknown to their captors as well as the subsequent rendezvous, the French might well not alter their plans, and the chances of capturing the spies as well any ship sent to replace Le Jour de Triumph at the pick-up would be enhanced. It confirmed to him the wisdom of trying to turn the documents over to Admiral Gardner.

Daphne made sure that the dinner went smoothly despite the difficulty that in neither group did anyone talk the other's language except for herself. She spent some time translating and, in some cases, summarizing. From Giles's expression, she could see that he understood more and more of what was being said in French, though he was not attempting to express himself in that language. The diners did not linger at the table after the meal was finished, but, nevertheless, Daphne felt that she could count the social gathering as a success.

That was confirmed later by Giles, who was delighted both with Daphne's ability to handle what could have been an awkward situation and with the fact that he had gleaned some important understanding of the conversations largely because of her efforts. He regretted even more deeply than before that he could not take her to St. Petersburg, not only as a companion but also as an invaluable aid.

Admiral Gardner's fleet came over the horizon later in the day, just where Giles had expected them to be. Giles and Daphne went aboard the flagship immediately. Daphne was getting quite accustomed to the ceremony involved in a post captain's coming aboard a ship and was becoming adept at retaining her dignity while being hauled by a crude contraption onto the deck of a ship.

Much to Giles's surprise, Admiral Gardner came on deck to greet them. "Welcome aboard, Lady Ashton, I have heard a good deal about you, but the reports do not do you justice."

Daphne was surprised by this greeting, for she was not at all used to her new title. She always thought of herself as Lady Giles if she thought of her formal name at all. However, with no show of surprise, she curtseyed to the Admiral while extending her hand so that he could kiss it. "I am surprised that you have heard much about me. It is unlike Captain Giles to talk about his personal affairs or activities."

"Oh, I have other sources of information. You are quite right about Captain Giles. I believe that he contented himself with saying he had found the perfect wife for himself, though he did make occasional references that indicated that you were managing his estate. No, I heard about you from Captain Bush, whose ship is under my command, and from Mr. Edwards, who is my prize agent as well as your husband's. They are both convinced that you are a wonder in your endeavors as well as in pulchritude. My condolences on the loss of your brothers, Ashton."

"Thank you, sir, though we were not close. Incidentally, I intend to use my naval rank in the service, not my title."

"Very wise, I believe. I must confess that I am very happy to know that you will inherit the earldom, rather than your brother. We can use all the men of ability and integrity that we can get in the Lords, and your brother promised to make your father look like he had been an asset when the time to transfer the title came.

"Now come below and tell me why you are here and what that prize you brought with you is all about. I did not expect you but had heard you were on some sort of undertaking for the Admiralty. I have to tell you, Lady Giles, that one of the joys of commanding your husband is that he tends to have good tales to tell when we meet."

The Admiral had rearranged his furniture so that this time his guests were not lined up on one side of his desk while he sat on the other with the light behind him. Instead, he had had his servant make a circle of chairs. He fussed about making sure that coffee and biscuits were served to his guests before signaling that he was ready to listen. Giles told the tale of his battle in Pevensey Bay and gave his superior the documents that had been found in the bag. He also mentioned his certainty that the captured French officers were convinced that the documents were all at the bottom of the sea. Admiral Gardner examined the recovered papers carefully and then looked up.

"You were quite right to bring this discovery to me, Captain Giles, though you have now posed a pretty problem for me. We don't want it known generally what you have discovered, or even where and when you captured the French frigate. I can help with that by keeping your prize and the prisoners with me for a while. In fact, I'll arrange it now."

The Admiral broke off to summon his flag lieutenant and issued a string of orders to send a prize crew to *Le Jour de Triomphe* and then take Giles's prize crew to *Glaucus*. That task completed, he resumed his comments on the situation.

"As I was saying, we want to keep the capture unknown ashore for a while. On the other hand, the news has to be given to the proper authorities as soon as possible so that they can deal with the espionage danger and arrange to make sure to capture any vessel the French send to replace *Le Jour de Triomphe*. Admiral Smithers, the port admiral at Chatham and the Nore*, is the obvious man, but he is a time-server who was very annoyed not to get a lucrative posting at sea and does everything he can to try to magnify the importance of his role. He is certain to spread the word incautiously that he is involved in catching spies. The Admiralty has to be informed at once as well.

"The easiest thing would be for you to go to London immediately, but you are not under my orders, and you have to go into Chatham to pick up Sir Walcott Lainey. If you left him in Chatham while you went up to London, he would raucously broadcast your irresponsible insult to him far and wide. Almost anything else that I could do to get the news to the proper authorities might let the cat* out of the bag* since we do not know where idle conversations might be overheard by agents of our enemy."

"The answer to this part of your problem is simple, Admiral Gardiner," Daphne broke in. "I have to return to Dipton. Indeed, I expect that my coach will be waiting for me in Chatham when we get there. I can easily go through London on my way and deliver the material and your comments to the Admiralty. If it causes any gossip in the Admiralty, it will be about Sir David's wandering eye and his charming the ladies and not about any special messages."

"I am not sure that I like that. How do you know about his roving eye?" huffed Giles.

"A woman has to be in his presence for only a couple of minutes to recognize it. I'll make sure on leaving that it is quite clear to all that I am on my way to Dipton if you are worried about that. No, the gossip, if any, in the Admiralty will be how I was trying to play to his weaknesses to advance your career."

"You are quite right, Lady Ashton," said Admiral Gardner. "You have married a really amazing woman, Captain Giles. She is correct about how her visit would be interpreted. In fact, ladies' attempts to use their wiles on Sir David to advance the careers of their husbands is almost a standing joke in the Admiralty. Their endeavors are not always unsuccessful, either, I might add."

Giles still did not seem to be happy with the arrangement, but he could see that it really was a good solution to the Admiral's dilemma. It was also clear that Daphne was eager to undertake the task. If he objected, she might believe him to be a meddling, huffy husband, such as one might find on the stage, rather than the sagacious and open-minded man who he was sure he was.

"I don't want to seem rude," Admiral Gardiner continued, somewhat to Giles's amusement for it was a phrase he had never heard his superior use before, "but time and tide wait for no man – or woman. More precisely, a few minutes wasted at the start of a voyage can turn into hours by the end when one relies on winds and currents. If you leave now, you can be in Chatham in time to leave for London first thing in the morning, Lady Ashton."

The Admiral escorted Daphne and Giles to the entry port with no further waste of time, and after the usual ceremony and the swaying of Daphne into the barge, they were off again to *Glaucus*. On boarding, Giles issued a string of orders that would see them underway just as soon as the men from *Le Jour de Triomphe* were aboard, and the flagship's boat had taken charge of the three prisoners.

Well before eight bells of the forenoon watch*, they were underway for an unremarkable trip on a decreasing wind that had just enough strength to get them into the Nore as the sun was setting. Admiral Gardner had probably been right; they might have had trouble getting into the Nore and finding an anchorage if they had delayed their departure by much.

Chapter X

Daphne and Giles boarded his barge early in the morning for the trip to Chatham from the Nore. The wind and tide were such that it made no sense for *Glaucus* to work her way up the Medway to Chatham just to turn around and come back down. As their boat moved through the other ships at anchor, Giles noted a large number of telescopes pointed at them from the various quarterdecks. It did not surprise him. He knew that he was the subject of gossip and speculation throughout the fleet. Talk of his marriage to someone about whom none of them had ever heard had spread widely, both by members of his own crew and also by those who did know her, such as Mr. Edwards and Captain Bush, his longtime friend and fellow resident of Dipton. Typical of Daphne, the hood of her boat cloak was thrown back as she sat in the sternsheets* so that she could get a good look at all the vessels, thus providing the gawkers a fine view of her lovely, intelligent face. Giles himself was almost overcome, reveling yet again in his good luck in winning her hand.

There was, in fact, very little wind, and the glowering skies did little to enhance the drab view of mudflats and salt marshes as they proceeded up the Medway River from its mouth. The barge skimmed swiftly through the water, and Daphne could study the Chatham Dockyard when it came into view with the town of Gillingham spread over the hill behind it. It took no time at all before they tied up at a dock near the coaching inn where Daphne's carriage should be waiting.

The vehicle was, indeed, at the inn. While the horses were being harnessed and the luggage loaded aboard, Daphne and Giles had a farewell cup of coffee in the inn's private parlor. Much as Daphne would have liked to stay until Sir Walcott Lainey appeared, the need to get to London took precedence. Carstairs helped Betsey into the coach while teasing her that she had certainly turned Carpenter's Mate Richards's head. With a last embrace from Giles, Daphne followed her maid into the carriage, and they were on their way.

As the coach set off, Giles saw that Viscount Ashton's coat of arms had been painted on the door. He hadn't ordered it, so he wondered if it was there at Daphne's order or at Steves's. Both were likely suspects. Steves was always ready to glorify his employer, especially as, in terms of prestige, service to Captain the Honorable Sir Richard Giles was a comedown from serving the Earl of Camshire, even though his present position was a much more agreeable one. On the other hand, Daphne had been conscious of snubs delivered by the most elevated of the ladies in the Ameschester area and of attempts to put her in her proper place. She would not be above rubbing their noses in the fact that she now took precedence over all of them since the highest title among them was Baroness and others were at most the wives of Baronets.

Had Giles been able to ask Daphne about the crest on the carriage door, he would have discovered that she hadn't even thought about the coat of arms that came with Giles's courtesy title. She also would not have confessed that, if she had thought about it, she certainly would have had it emblazoned on her coach's door to annoy a few particular ladies, though that is certainly what she would have done. Her thoughts as the coach pulled onto the turnpike going to London were on how to spend her time in the city once she had completed her mission to the Admiralty. She had unfinished business there concerning that wretched lease on the house in Arlington Street.

It was well past noon before Daphne's carriage came through the arch in the Adams Screen to enter the Admiralty courtyard from Whitehall. The crest on the carriage door possibly served its purpose, for she was ushered without delay into the First Lord's presence.

"Lady Ashton," Sir David greeted her once she was properly seated, "to what do I owe this unexpected pleasure?"

Daphne summarized concisely the fight with the French frigate and the discovery of the contents of the bag that had been thrown overboard. Sir David was struck with what an orderly and complete presentation she made. He expected that, on naval matters, ladies would be scatter-brained and incoherent.

"My lady, I am very grateful for your bringing me this material. I must say that it is a pity that you are not accompanying Captain Giles to St. Petersburg. I am sure that you would be much better able to discover the real attitudes to joining us or about Bonaparte in St. Petersburg than will Sir Walcott. Now, let me see these documents, please."

Sir David rapidly skimmed the materials that Daphne had brought. "You and Captain Giles are quite right. These are matters requiring immediate attention and discretion. I am not sure the officials in Chatham would have provided either. However, you have certainly disrupted my day. I must deal with this at once, even though I had a very busy afternoon already scheduled. I hate to rush you away, Lady Ashton, but these problems are very pressing."

"I quite understand, Sir David," said Daphne, who had no desire for chitchat with the First Lord now that her task was completed. She quickly found herself in the Admiralty courtyard, where her carriage was waiting to take her to Mr. Edwards's offices. The coat of arms was certainly proving its worth since, otherwise, her carriage would not have been allowed to stay in the small courtyard. They proceeded up Whitehall and down the Strand, but their way was completely blocked at Fetter Street. Daphne resolved to take a sedan chair the rest of the way when she noticed one depositing its occupant near where her carriage was halted.

Two burly chairmen picked the conveyance up and took off at a good pace. They maneuvered around the blockages in Fleet Street and over the ditch into the City. Daphne had trouble deciding which side to look out on as they passed worthy sight after worthy sight. They surged through the pedestrian and horse-drawn traffic in a way that would have been impossible with a carriage. She suspected from the looks of some people whom they passed that the leading chairman was not above using one of the long poles at the front of the chair to forcefully clear the way ahead. She was deposited in front of Mr. Edwards's offices after an amazingly quick trip.

Daphne was shown immediately into Mr. Edwards's own room, even though she had no appointment, and he was busy with another man. "Lady Ashton," he greeted her. "Mr. Longshank and I were just discussing the documents Captain Giles sent us about the lease in Arlington Street. Mr. Longshank is a solicitor specializing in leases and contracts on real-estate properties. He is also a neighbor of yours, at least his parents are, or so he tells me."

"Oh, of course, you must be Andrew, the son of Mr. and Mrs. Longshank of Cobbdale House. Your mother talks about you when we visit each other. Weren't you at the Hunt Ball last spring?"

"Yes, I was. I was introduced to you then, but I don't expect that you remember me. You were very busy that evening."

"I was, but now that you mention it, I do remember meeting you. Weren't you talking with my niece Catherine when we were introduced?"

"Yes, I was." To Daphne's surprise, Mr. Longshank blushed at the mention of Catherine.

"Enough of this," broke in Mr. Edwards. "I am sure that Lady Ashton did not come here today to renew connections with people from Ameschester. I imagine that she is here about that wretched lease, and that is why you are here too, Mr. Longshank. What have you found out about it?"

"Quite a lot. At first sight, just looking at the lease itself, it seems very straightforward. It is a lease on a house owned by Lord Knockingdon. The lease is for a period of several years, terminating in about 30 months. The rent on the property is in arrears, which doesn't help matters, especially as Viscount Ashton is probably less experienced in avoiding debtor's prison than was the late Viscount Ashton. It is confusing that they both have the same name."

"You are right. My husband hates being in debt. Incidentally, you might as well refer to him as Captain Giles," said Daphne. "That is how he is known in the Navy, and I expect that Mr. Edwards thinks of him by that name. It will make this discussion simpler."

"Very good, my lady. This would, at first sight, appear to be straightforward. You could get rid of the lease by paying two extra quarters' rent in advance or by selling the lease with Lord Knockington's approval. Since the rent is so high, the first option would be better. However, the other documents pretty well render moot the provisions for ending the lease."

"Why is that, Mr. Longshank?" asked Daphne in a very puzzled voice.

"They are an interlocking web of provisions. For instance, this contract between Viscount Ashton and Lord Knockingdon and Mrs. Marsdon guarantees Lord Knockingdon two free lessons with Mrs. Marsdon a month. The guarantee runs up to the time the lease runs its full course, not to any earlier date at which it might be terminated."

"Lessons? What sort of lessons could she give?"

"It says that the lessons are in deportment, dancing, and theatrical presentation."

"Oh. It seems strange to me that Lord Knockingdon would desire such lessons. Or that Mrs. Marsdon could supply them."

"It does. I am afraid that these are euphemisms for more dubious — more dubious — carnal endeavors. Not the usual sort of lessons. The terms are used, possibly, in order to allow misinterpretation by third parties such as ourselves, or by some magistrate whose attention was called to them."

"I see."

"Special 'lessons' are mentioned in other documents. For instance, in one of them, Mrs. O'Brien is allowed to book some particular rooms for her employees to give lessons. In another, there is a schedule of how the fees are to be split if the lessons are arranged by Lord Ashton."

"What? Why would he do that? Is this also referring to carnal activities? Doesn't that make him a …a…what is the word?"

"Pimp, my lady? Yes, I suppose that it does."

"Is that what all these documents are about — running a — a —?"

"No. There are arrangements for Viscount Ashton to pay the interest on Mrs. Marsdon's debts to Mrs. O'Brien, and provisions for Mrs. Marsdon to accompany him as desired to routs* or banquets or similar functions, though only to a limited extent. Then there is one arranging for Mrs. O'Brien to provide cleaning services by maids at specified rates."

"She provides maids?" Daphne asked in surprise.

"Oh, yes. The women are probably low-grade prostitutes, ones whom Mrs. O'Brien is training to become better companions. She pays them for the menial work with better opportunities and fees and possibly with lessons on how to attract and please men of quality."

"But if they are working as maids, why don't they just get employment as maids?" Daphne asked.

"They probably cannot get a good reference, or they have been with child, or they just prefer the better pay and lighter work than most regular maids have. I don't know for sure. Just what the documents say." Mr. Longshank was blushing again, clearly unhappy about being questioned about the activities referred to in the documents.

"So you are saying that there is no way out of the dilemma of owning the lease on — on —" Daphne again could not think of a word to describe what she was discovering.

"A disorderly house?" supplied Mr. Longshanks.

"Yes."

"Not that I can see. I imagine that the only way to do so would be to pay everyone very, very heavily – Lord Knockingdon, Mrs. O'Brien, and Mrs. Marsdon, at the least."

"I wonder how Lord Ashton got trapped in this spider's web," Daphne mused.

"He was not really trapped, I suspect. The late Viscount Ashton was not a man of high moral character, my lady. He possibly became infatuated with Mrs. Marsdon and arranged with Mrs. O'Brien to keep her as his mistress. It is quite common, though the man still has to pay the bawd – the abbess --," Mr. Longshank sought for the appropriate word seeing a look of bafflement on Daphne's face, "the keeper of the … the brothel, in which Mrs. Marsdon worked as a courtesan before she took up with

Viscount Ashton. Then when Viscount Ashton became short of funds, he probably thought he could get himself out of difficulties by becoming a whore-master himself only to find himself in even more of a financial pickle."

"How do you come to know so much about these matters, Mr. Longshank?" Daphne asked.

"Ugh — ugh — well the firm I articled with — basically was apprenticed to — specialized in land-problems, and quite a few of those problems involved matters of this sort. I got to know far more than I wanted to about the sporting life in London while working on such problems. When I completed my time, the partners asked me to join the firm. This sort of work – on the more dubious uses of property -is usually very lucrative – disputes arise all the time – and it has been growing steadily, especially as more of these high-class establishments have been moving into Mayfair and other areas. Not much of the quality trade still remains around Covent Garden or even St James's now. I am, of course, referring only to the better class of establishments with only the best patrons."

"Thank you, Mr. Longshank. You have been very informative. I do not like getting landed in this situation. I don't like it at all! And I thoroughly dislike the idea of enriching these creatures or Lord Knockingdon. The man seems to be a disgrace to the aristocracy and the country – as was, it seems, my brother-in-law. I am distressed, I can tell you, very, very distressed. I must think about the situation. Can you give me the documents so that I can see if I may be able to see a way out?"

"You are welcome to them, my lady. However, I am sure that you will find nothing. These papers were obviously drawn up by experts in this aspect of the law. I know that they are impervious to alteration or misinterpretation. They have woven a very tight net about not only Lord Ashton but also about anyone who might inherit the lease from him. They certainly ensure that the arrangement will continue to the benefit of the other parties."

"I cannot believe that my husband is required to pay for and assist this…this…bawdy house. Surely there are laws against it. Aren't there, Mr. Edwards?"

"There are some, yes, some weak ones, but they are used only against establishments that are causing regular disturbances or are stepping on the toes of ones with influence. Houses like the one involved in this lease are protected by the illustrious nature of some of their clients who seem to regard the services they provide as being completely necessary."

"Mr. Edwards is quite right," broke in Mr. Longshank. "I am sure that the perpetrators are exempt from the law. Trying to bring them before the law would change nothing, but Lord Ashton would probably receive a fine for allowing dubious activities to proceed while the real villains get away scot-free."

Daphne thought that she saw a fleeting smirk on Mr. Longshank's face as he pronounced his opinion. She bid Mr. Edwards farewell as well as Mr. Longshank, rather warmer in the first instance than the second. Mr. Edwards arranged for her to take a sedan chair to the pier where she could take a wherry to Westminster Bridge. From there, he pointed out, she could get a hackney cab to her hotel.

She was fuming all the way back to the St. James's neighborhood about the insidious position in which his half-brother had placed her husband. She suspected that there must be some way out amongst the convoluted language employed in the myriad of contracts. She was also dubious that Mr. Longshank would necessarily show it to her, even if he knew what it was, since he seemed to be heavily involved in such contracts and in the habit of adding much incomprehensible verbiage to legal documents. Furthermore, he seemed to be all too pleased with the trap in which she and Giles were caught.

When Daphne returned to Nerot's Hotel, she was in the process of arranging for dinner when Captain Bolton came into the hotel lobby. "Lady Ashton, what a pleasant surprise. Is Captain Giles here as well?"

"No. I just saw him depart in his new ship to go to St. Petersburg. I stopped in London to complete some business."

"Then, can I persuade you to dine with me? I was just going to make arrangements here."

Daphne accepted the invitation at once. Captain Bolton had proved good company on her previous visit to London, and she might get a chance to find out about her husband from his naval friend. One somewhat annoying aspect of Giles's character was that he spoke very little about his past doings and hastily turned the conversation when Daphne tried to pry from him more information about his naval life.

Captain Bolton was a pleasant and talkative man. It was evident that he was in awe of Giles's accomplishments. He had known him well in the West Indies when they had both been lieutenants and had crossed paths regularly in Port Royal and English Harbor.

"He was always a very pleasant fellow," Captain Bolton remarked at one point. "Not given to airs for being an earl's son. Not that his family did anything for his career. We were all struck with how little influence he seemed to have. You know it is usually critical for advancement in the navy, so we thought he would have a leg up on us, but he didn't. He got his step entirely because of his bravery and initiative in battle. He was made post-captain for the same reason. We had many a good time ashore, though he was always a bit of a prude when it came to sailors' pleasures. Indeed, very much a prude though he never actually condemned others for partaking. It was just that such activities did not appeal to him."

After their service in the West Indies, Captain Bolton and Giles had seen very little of each other, though it was evident that he had followed Giles's subsequent career with admiration and apparently little jealousy. His own career had been much more pedestrian, and he had only been made post-captain recently and was still waiting for his first command in that rank. He remarked that he had received the promotion only after a furious and very bloody fight with a French privateer.

Daphne expressed her horror at the carnage involved in naval warfare and recounted her own recent experiences when *Glaucus* had encountered *Le Jour de Triomphe*. Captain Bolton listened eagerly, like all naval captains relishing any tale of combat at sea. Daphne could not help the details since she had spent the time in the orlop helping with the wounded.

"Were there many wounded or killed on *Glaucus*, my lady?" asked Captain Bolton.

"Oh, yes. It was awful, though the French ship suffered far higher numbers." Daphne recited the numbers whereupon she was startled when Captain Bolton burst out laughing.

"I am sorry to laugh, Lady Giles. I know it is not funny, but *Glaucus*'s losses were amazingly small for an engagement between two evenly matched frigates. It just goes to show Captain Giles's amazing ability to win naval battles. My own losses were very much larger, even though I commanded only a brig*, and the French privateer was weaker than me.

Daphne was becoming tired of naval conversation. She remembered how Captain Bolton and her niece, Catherine, had been drawn to each other and decided to explore more details about him. Captain Bolton was the third son of a country parson in Norfolk. He had become enamored of a local woman and had thought that he could marry her when he was made a commander, but he had been immediately sent to sea and had not returned to England for several years, by which time she had married someone else. Now, as a post-captain, who was being given a frigate that was undergoing a renewal of its copper at the Portsmouth Dockyard, he was very much in a position to marry. Especially as he had been fortunate in the matter of prize money. Not nearly as much as Captain Giles, of course, but enough to allow him to set up a very comfortable establishment, even to buy a modest property suitable for a gentleman. Listening to all this, Daphne began to suspect that Catherine might have told him who, in reality, would grant permission for her to marry. When Giles was away, Daphne had all the power to make decisions in his absence. That applied to permitting Catherine to marry and providing a dowry.

This reflection caused Daphne to recall her duties as someone with responsibilities for an unmarried relative. "Captain Bolton, to change the subject, Catherine was delighted that you showed her the paintings when she was here. You must know a great deal."

"Well, it is a bit of a hobby with me, rather like your husband's interest in agriculture, I suppose."

"Dipton Hall — my home, you know — has hardly any paintings that I like, and we need to start collecting better ones. There are, of course, few experts in our area of the country. I wonder if I can persuade you to visit to give me advice on what might be suitable, and whether any of the existing ones have merit."

"I would be delighted to. It would have to be soon, however, before my ship is ready."

"Of course. I wonder if you are free for the next few days."

"Oh, yes, though I have some business I have to attend to in the morning. I am free after that. I could go to Dipton on the following day."

"Better yet, I also have engagements in the morning. You could come with me, in my coach, in the afternoon, if it is convenient. Of course, with Captain Giles away, I couldn't put you up at Dipton Hall, but my father lives nearby and would be delighted to accommodate a friend of my husband." Daphne had realized only at the last moment that it would not do to have Captain Bolton stay at Dipton Hall.

One young gentleman in a house with several highly desirable young ladies would have tongues wagging without stop, and all their reputations would be ruined. It might be disastrous for Lydia and Catherine, and it certainly would not help her endeavors to make sure that Captain Giles's house was the leader of society in their area.

"That would indeed be very convenient, Lady Ashton."

As Daphne was getting ready for bed, it struck her that she really might have business to attend to before leaving London. Her original claim was based on nothing more than the desire not to let her trout off the hook. Now she realized how she could profitably spend the extra time in London. Her mind must have been playing with her problem of the lease all through the dinner with Captain Bolton. Now it was clear to her that she would have to examine the house in Arlington Street again to see if doing so would stir up some ideas on how to escape from the trap into which she and Giles had stumbled.

She particularly recalled that Mr. Longshank mentioned that, in some of the documents, reference was made to special rooms that were to be used by Mrs. O'Brien's minions. What was special about the services being rendered that they needed special rooms? Surely, for the purposes that Daphne was now convinced was the prime function of the house in Arlington Street, all that was needed was a bed and some furniture for hanging clothes and possibly a stand for washing. Maybe even some chairs and tables if the participants desired to indulge in drink and talk before engaging in the more carnal activities. Surely, that wasn't enough to require special facilities that courtesans from other brothels could use. Come to think of it, Mr. Longshank had appeared to be very knowledgeable about the documents and treated their terms in a very off-hand manner. Furthermore, there had been that smirk of his that she couldn't forget. Could he have been involved in drawing the documents up? How she would have preferred Ashton not to have died or, rather, if he was going to do so, that he had made someone else his heir.

"Betsey," she said, "what do you know about prostitutes and the places they practice their trade?"

"Oh, Lady Ashton, I'm a good girl."

"I know you are, Betsey. But I think all girls must whisper to each other about ones who are not good."

"Yes, I suppose we do, but we don't know much about it."

"I don't either though I am finding out more than I want to know. I don't think there are any prostitutes at Dipton."

"Not anymore, my Lady."

"What do you mean?"

"Do you remember Sally Walker? She worked as a barmaid at the Dipton Arms. Elsie found out that, for two shillings, she would accommodate men in one of the rooms, and often she would spend the whole night with travelers for a fee. Elsie dismissed her without a reference when she found out about it, but it had been going on for some time when Tom Arbuckle was the landlord, Elsie told me. I heard that Sally was seen in Ameschester, looking for — for clients."

"I don't really see why men would want to use women like them."

"My mum says that men are like dogs and are eager to mate with any woman who will let them. I just don't know why the women would let them if they were not married. Even if they were paid. I wouldn't!"

Their discussion didn't reduce Daphne's puzzlement about why such improper activities occurred, but it did make her more aware of doings in her part of the world. She was not overly surprised to learn that prostitutes were to be found in London. Could it really be true that they were to be found in Ameschester or even in Dipton? She still found it hard to believe Betsey's words. Maybe these loose women were only meeting the needs of men of the lower ranks. But the London courtesans certainly catered to men of the most elevated level of society. If such ladies of ill repute existed in the Dipton area, would Giles be tempted to use them? She couldn't believe that he would be tempted, but then, surely not all the wives of customers of Mrs. O'Brien's customers knew about what their husbands were doing. Should she worry when Giles went off by himself for a ride? She couldn't possibly insist on accompanying him everywhere. It was all very puzzling, especially as she had no idea of who among gentile ladies she was acquainted with could she raise such a topic.

Chapter XI

Daphne had trouble falling asleep, partly because of some discomfort caused by the baby she was carrying, but more because she had been mulling over the questions about the leased property. She awoke, ready to take the bull by the horns and deal with the lease problem. Unfortunately, a moment's reflection suggested that the morning's early hours might not be the best time to examine the house. She knew that debauched activities could go on to all hours of the night. After all, her brother-in-law had met his death while riding immediately after a night spent drinking and gambling. It was even unlikely that the maids who had been mentioned in one of the documents would start work at the crack of dawn, even though in Daphne's experience, that was the usual pattern for maids in the better houses in Dipton. Ten o'clock would probably be a suitable time to call. She would just have to find some other way to spend her time before that. It was infuriating that coffee shops would not serve women!

Ten o'clock found Daphne, with Betsey in tow, knocking on the door of the house in Arlington Street. It was opened by the same flunky as before, though now he was not dressed in his showy livery and seemed rather uncomfortable in his movements. Her demand to see Mrs. Marsdon was met with a rather surly acquiescence and a warning that it might take some time for Mrs. Marsdon to appear.

That was only partly true. After about ten minutes, the doxy came into the parlor. She was dressed in a loose, semi-diaphanous wrap that left no doubt that time had not been kind to her figure. She still wore last night's make up, but it could no longer hide the wrinkles in her complexion. Her rather elaborate hair dress had become somewhat undone, with random, scrawny locks cascading in odd directions.

"What are you doing here?" this apparition began obnoxiously. "Don't you know that it is far too early to rouse a lady of pleasure? Come back later."

Daphne chose to ignore this. "I am here to inspect the premises. I have the authority of Viscount Ashton to make whatever arrangements are needed for this house because it is his leased property. I have every right to see all parts of the property whenever I want: the lease so states. I am doing you the courtesy of informing you of my intentions and to invite you to accompany me to explain anything that I may question. If you try to interfere, I will call the watch* and have you hauled up before the magistrates for running a disorderly house. I have no doubt that they will happily condemn you to Brideswell* Prison."

"You have no right to do any such thing. The documents guarantee that I am entitled to live here as long as I like."

"That is not quite what they say, just until a specified date in the future. I am not disputing that. I am simply noting that, of course, the leaseholder or his agent has not given up his rights to use and to determine the use of the house as long as the exact terms of those documents are fulfilled."

Daphne had no idea if any of this was correct, but she doubted that the strumpet in front of her had any better knowledge. She had no intention of letting her adversary take over the confrontation. "I have already seen this rather seedy room, now we will explore the rest of the house. You can have your lackey inform anyone else who is still in the house that I am coming. Any other doxies here can be warned to make themselves presentable, or I shall seriously consider having them treated as common whores."

Daphne marched across the hallway and opened the door to the room facing the parlor. It was set up for the entertainment of many people. At one end was a small stage with curtains that could be drawn across it. Around the room were scattered various settees, with cushions to encourage reclining and each with a good view of the stage.

"What goes on here?" Daphne demanded.

"This is where I and some of my helpers present our attitudes. Tableaux vivants, you know. Very popular with the sporting gentlemen. Gets them nicely warmed up."

"I see. Interesting," Daphne proclaimed even though she had no idea what the bawd was talking about.

The rear of the ground floor was given up to a kitchen and a large butler's pantry that seemed to be used for preparing drinks, judging by the dirty glasses awaiting washing. On the first floor, the two rooms, which would probably have formed the drawing-room and the dining room when the house was first planned, had each been divided. All four contained beds, in one of which a very young girl huddled under the covers with just her face appearing. She seemed to be terrified at the intrusion. Daphne hardly glanced at the girl but noticed that scattered about were various items of women's clothing of a sort she had never encountered before, as well as some men's clothing. There did seem to be more lumps in the bed than the young girl could be responsible for, but Daphne decided that she would rather not find out what else was under the covers.

On the second floor, Daphne discovered what must be the special rooms she had heard about. The first one she looked into contained a collection of large items made of wood. Daphne could not even guess what their purpose was. On the walls were hung several whips. There was also a large container filled with water in which was sitting a variety of wool balls. "What in the world is this?" Daphne asked.

"This is our flogging room. We bind our customers to the equipment and give them a thorough whipping or caning. Particularly popular with men who have been to the best public schools."

"Of course," Daphne said, though she had never even imagined that men could get pleasure from being placed in such a position. She had thought that men were always in charge, or so they thought. "But what are these wet balls?"

"You must know that many men dream of being exposed in the public pillories and of having rotten vegetables thrown at them. This room simulates that situation. The fee is doubled if the client wants real rotten fruit used because of the extra work to clean up the mess afterwards. Among those who enjoy this activity, it produces a most impressive phallus," Mrs. Marsdon drawled in a matter-of-fact voice that Daphne suspected was designed to make her feel embarrassed and unsophisticated.

Daphne was revolted by the whole idea of the perversions being indicated, but she wasn't going to let this harridan know how nonplussed she was at this unbelievable account. "I suppose that the other special rooms here appeal to similar tastes?" she demanded, still trying to hide her revulsion.

"Yes, indeed.' Mrs. Marsdon was almost gloating. "One is specially equipped to cane and whip gentlemen. The next one is for disciplining some of our young women, who are willing to submit for a very large fee. That is very popular among our clients. Marquis Sombutler, especially. Very distinguished and well-respected men use it regularly. Of course, the fee has to be very high for, often, the ladies cannot resume their work for quite a time, and it may leave scars. The fourth room is for our clients who enjoy being dressed as women. Also very popular, I must say. You would not believe how many men have to be entertained by our attitudes downstairs while waiting for access to our special rooms. I am sure you want to inspect them also. Maybe you would even like to take a turn in the ladies' discipline room, Lady Ashton. I would be happy to whip you properly though I would, of course, count it against the services I am supposed to give to Lord Ashton, even though the former holder of the title felt that it was more blessed to give than to receive, so I had to take some of his whippings."

"No, thank you, Mrs. Marsdon." Daphne momentarily turned on the charm to hide her astonishment. She refused to be intimidated by this woman. "I am not inclined to repeat my half-brother's endeavors, even though I am sure you deserve to be flogged. I don't need to see these special rooms. I expect they are in the same shoddy condition as the first one. I expect that if Viscount Ashton should continue to use the premises for these purposes, he will have them completely redecorated and refurnished with higher-class equipment. And while I might like to give you a thorough thrashing, just as you deserve, in the ladies' room, my time is too pressing now to indulge my pleasures. Let us see what is on the third floor."

Mrs. Marsdon led the way up the stairs. Daphne noticed that Betsey's mouth was open in consternation, and there was a slightly glazed look in her eyes.

"Are you all right, Betsey?" she whispered.

"Yes, my lady. I just cannot believe any of this. Why would anyone want any part of this, or why would women want to work here?"

"I don't know. I can't even imagine it. I have never heard of such things before now."

"But you seemed quite knowledgeable, my lady."

"Play-acting, Betsey. Just play-acting. I know no more than you."

The third floor had been divided into several small bedrooms, more clearly equipped for what one might expect in a brothel, rather than with any extensive furnishings to accommodate a longer tryst. "These are where our less talented ladies entertain gentlemen who are in more of a rush or who can afford to spend less time with them than the ones who use the first floor rooms."

"I see," said Daphne, though, in fact, she was having a hard time not revealing how shocked she was to hear prostitution discussed in such matter-of-fact terms. "And what will I find on the next floor?"

"Oh, just my own rooms. Never opened to others except, of course, the late Lord Ashton."

"Of course," Daphne agreed, not believing a word of it. "Nevertheless, I am afraid that my inspection cannot be considered complete without viewing those premises."

Daphne, without waiting for any comment from the other woman, proceeded up the stairs, followed by Mrs. Marsdon and trailed by Betsey, who still seemed to be totally disoriented by the sudden exposure to a whole side of life which she had never even imagined could exist. Daphne, too, was having a hard time visualizing the seamy side of human nature that the visit was revealing even as she strove to give the impression that she considered it all normal.

The upper floor, which from the street had been largely hidden by the pediment, turned out to have unexpectedly high ceilings and large windows facing the back of the house. The two rooms facing the street had low ceilings and were poorly lit by the dormers. They were given over to a dressing room and a place to hang innumerable dresses of all types.

One of the main rooms facing the rear of the house had been fitted out as a sitting room, and it would have been very pleasant were it not for the garish clash of colors in the furnishings and the wallpaper. Its most notable feature was a large portrait of a much younger and very voluptuous Mrs. Marsdon lounging provocatively in the nude in the style of many classical, salacious pictures. Daphne recognized the style of a renowned artist whose portraits were often shown in magazines after being converted into etchings. Either the artist had been flattering his subject outrageously, or else the younger Mrs. Marsdon had had a much more attractive figure, face, and complexion than she now possessed. The other room facing the rear of the house was a large bedroom, very comfortable looking if one could ignore the poor taste revealed by the choices of colors, curtains, and furniture.

"How very nice!" exclaimed Daphne hypocritically. "You must be very happy here. I am glad to see that these quarters are eminently suitable for your lessons in deportment and acting. Very suitable! And I am sure you can use the bedroom to instruct kept women or the daring wives of wandering husbands how best to keep their men's interests. No doubt, you instruct them in how best to hold elevated conversations. However, I am sure that we can find much better uses for the rest of the house when we have refurbished it to the very best standards and got rid of much of the special equipment."

"Don't you dare try to make changes to my establishment!" was the response. "I'll have you know that many very prominent men are most partial to my special services and would come down hard on anyone who tried to interfere with them. Why I'll have you know that the Bishop of Stanbury is very partial to the women's dressing room while Sir David McDougall very much enjoys reddening and striping a wide variety of backs and backsides in the discipline room. Hector, the footman who let you in, had his back well flogged by Sir David before providing his more common molly-boy use. If you think that the law would help, Sir Toby Constips, the local magistrate, is an enthusiastic patron and Justice Brownwater is very, very needy when it comes to receiving a good flogging."

"Thank you very much for the tour, Mrs. Marsdon. I shall be letting you and, of course, Lord Knockingdon and Mrs. O'Brien know that we shall expect all of you to uphold the terms of the lease." -With head held high, Daphne led the way down the several flights of stairs and through the front door, even eliciting a bow from the lackey who must have been the well-flogged Hector.

"Thank God that is over!" she exclaimed to Betsey. "I am sorry to have exposed you to that — that — abominable place and what goes on there. I had no idea of how the house was used. In fact, I never knew that such things happened at all. I didn't really know what occurred in the brothels that are whispered about and never even imagined any of this."

Captain Bolton was waiting for Daphne when they returned to Nerot's Hotel. The carriage was soon rolling along on the way out of London. Captain Bolton took a keen interest in everything they were passing, and his delight in the changing sights kept Daphne from brooding too much on the shocking tour she had taken with Mrs. Marsdon. Captain Bolton confessed to knowing very little of England apart from East Anglia, London, and the routes to the major naval bases. The different types of landscape as they traveled to Dipton kept him enthusiastically commenting on all he found charming, and Daphne found that she was starting to see the countryside with newly awakened pleasure.

This led to a discussion of depicting landscape in paintings and Captain Bolton's fascination with art. He waxed lyrical in describing the developments that an artist called Turner was making, quite catching Daphne's attention. She really should find out more about current artists and what paintings would be suitable for Dipton Hall. She and Richard had never talked of art, and she wondered what his tastes were. She knew that his profession meant that he would be away from home for long periods. She had never imagined how much she would miss being able to ask him small things and get an immediate answer.

The trip passed easily, though darker thoughts concerned with this mornings' inspection kept intruding into Daphne's thoughts. She even wondered idly if Captain Bolton was one who indulged in the types of services that were offered in the sort of establishment with which she was now so unwillingly associated. Surely, no gentleman would. But then the names that Mrs. Marsdon had dropped kept intruding into her thoughts. Who could she talk to about the house, and what was happening there? Ladies were not supposed to know anything about such things, and she could think of none who would be helpful. That supposed innocence included herself, so how could she ask assistance of any male acquaintances – and if she did, would they be all too knowledgeable, not about how to extract Richard from the tangled web, but about the forbidden joys that her unwanted establishment provided? She had never wanted to be a viscountess, and being one certainly had brought many problems.

They arrived in Dipton just in time to stop first at Dipton Manor to introduce Captain Bolton to her father and to invite them to dinner. She discovered that Mr. Moorhouse was already supposed to dine at the Hall, and received the news that the Countess had arrived and was staying there. Daphne had invited her to visit while she was at the funeral. It was just a pity that the unexpected length of her own time away from Dipton meant that she had missed her mother-in-law's arrival. Would there be ruffled feathers to smooth out at Dipton Hall because she had not been there to greet the Countess?

There was, in fact, none. Lady Clara was very understanding about why Daphne's return had been delayed; indeed, she sounded a bit envious that her son had wanted his wife along on even a short voyage. She instead confirmed how grateful she was for the invitation to visit Dipton Hall. She seemed to be much less imperious than she had been when Daphne first met her.

After the ladies had withdrawn after dinner, Captain Bolton's irrepressible curiosity got the better of him. The Countess had invited Lord David to dine, and he had been introduced by that name to the naval visitor.

"I am puzzled, Lord David," Captain Bolton began, "that you are addressed as 'Lord David.' I always had heard that the proper address for the younger sons of earls is 'The Honorable' or, I suppose, in your case, it would be 'Reverend the Honorable.'"

"You are quite right about the proper form of address," Lord David responded happily. "The 'title' is our own family quirk or joke that has no official warrant. It came as a result of my father's bad temper, I am told. It was soon after Lady Marianne left her home, much to my father's annoyance. We had a butler at the time who was a bit of a stickler for protocol and insisted on announcing even members of the family when they had been away. As a result, when my half-brother, Thomas, returned from a trip, the butler announced him as 'The Honorable Mr. Thomas Giles.' My father is said to have bellowed something like 'The Honorable Mister! The Honorable Mister! Peter was 'Lord Peter' before he became Ashton. 'Marianne' is 'Lady Marianne.' If 'Lady' is good enough for that traitor Marianne, 'Lord' is the right title for my other sons. Thomas is 'Lord Thomas' around here!' The idea caught on, and Richard and then I became 'Lord Richard' and 'Lord David.' Family acquaintances picked it up, and it has become habit for us to introduce each other with the incorrect title. I am afraid that my sister-in-law has little use for the finer points of protocol, so she introduces me as Lord David without thinking."

"Makes wonderful sense to me, *Lord* David. I have never actually been in a position where the difference would be relevant until this visit."

"With that resolved, I imagine that we are ready to rejoin the ladies," responded Lord David.

When Daphne had led the ladies into the small drawing-room, her niece, Lydia, immediately approached her. "Aunt Daphne, do we have to still be in mourning?"

Daphne had actually been surprised that her relatives had all been in mourning with the exception of Lord David. She herself had abandoned it for the trip to London. "What does your mother say?" she prevaricated.

"Oh, she would abandon it right now, but she was afraid that it might insult you or Mr. Dimster's parents."

"And your grandmother? She knows far more about these things than I do."

"I haven't asked her. She isn't my real grandmother."

"Let's get her opinion anyway."

"Of course, you can come out of mourning, Lydia. Your uncles meant nothing to you or to your mother. It is quite meaningless to pretend to mourn them. Nevertheless, you should first ask Mr. Dimster what his parents would think. You don't want to start marriage on the wrong foot, especially with his father supplying the allowance."

"That is something we need to talk to you about, Aunt Daphne. Tomorrow morning?"

"Of course. Around noon? Ask Mr. Dimster to come for luncheon if he is free."

Lady Marianne and Lydia soon excused themselves. Captain Bolton's attention was directed entirely at Catherine, while Lady Camshire and Daphne's father held a quite animated conversation. That left Daphne with Lord David, and even before she could think of how to begin a conversation, he took the lead.

"At the funeral, Captain Gregg said that Richard should go to the regimental headquarters to straighten something out. I hope it all went well."

Daphne had completely forgotten about Thomas's love-child and his mother and the steps she was supposed to take on their behalf. That was something else she would have to see to immediately. But she didn't think that she should enlighten Lord David about the matter. He probably could be discreet, but he was likely to treat the newcomers in a special way if he knew why they had come to Dipton.

"Yes," she answered after a moment to think about her reply. "It was really quite straightforward. I am afraid that it was your other brother that caused the real problems. Part of his financial affairs are in a terrible tangle, and it is not clear how to straighten them out. They arise, I am afraid, from his rather dissipated way of life. They, in fact, are the major, delicate problem he left Richard. Mr. Edwards was not much help in straightening it out, and

Richard had to leave before he could tackle it. I really am not quite sure what to do."

"Why don't we talk about it soon?" Lord David replied. "I don't know much about debauchery, but probably more than you do. I might be able to help."

Daphne again had trouble falling asleep that night. There was again some discomfort from being with child. How convenient it would be if she could somehow speed the process up and still have a healthy child. She also had much on her mind. She had to find out how the various projects at Dipton were progressing. She should also inspect the farms and talk to her tenants to see what were the prospects for a good harvest. Then there were the problems that had arisen in her trip with Giles: Thomas's love-child and Ashton's whorehouse. In addition, what could Lydia and her fiancé want? Furthermore, she really should find time to see to the needs for better art at Dipton. It was all very well to tell herself that there was nothing to be done until the next day, so she might as well sleep; her mind didn't work that way.

Chapter XII

Giles turned away as the coach carrying Daphne disappeared at the first bend in the road. He entered the inn where he presumed that Sir Walcott must be staying. However, the innkeeper had no news of the man. Giles sent Carstairs to find out if any of the other inns in Chatham knew where his passenger might be staying and settled into the lounge with a cup of bad coffee, for which he soon substituted a pint of ale. He was growing steadily more annoyed. Carstairs returned to report that he could find no trace of Sir Walcott in any of the likely places in Chatham.

After remaining at the inn for another hour, Giles gave up on Sir Walcott's imminent appearance. He returned to *Glaucus* in his barge, where he detailed Midshipman Stewart to take the cutter and return to Chatham to await the special ambassador. He had better ways to spend the time than cooling his heels in Chatham until his wayward passenger should appear. He did occupy his time by reading and visiting other ships whose captains he knew to renew friendships and exchange gossip. He was pleased to discover that his capture of *Le Jour de Triomphe* was still unknown in other ships, so there was some hope that Sir David could put things in motion to deal effectively with the spies and traitors.

Midshipman Stewart returned with no news about Sir Walcott. The next day, Giles dispatched Mr. Fisher to wait for the tardy envoy and Mr. Dunsmuir on the following one. He was about to send Mr. Stewart again on the fourth day when a dangerously overloaded boat appeared through the early morning mist. In it was a clearly angry and disheveled Sir Walcott along with innumerable pieces of baggage and six liveried servants.

"Captain Giles, you have been derelict in your duty. I arrived in Chatham to find no welcoming party. I had to hire a boat to take me out here. This will not do, sir, this will not do! I demand an apology."

"Apology! Apology!" roared Giles, rather to the poorly suppressed delight of the onlookers. Captain Giles rarely lost his temper, but when he did, it was the stuff of legends. "You dare to come onto my quarterdeck and accuse me of a court-martial offense? You, who are six days late in coming to Chatham without sending any note of explanation! You, who caused delay by not keeping to the Admiralty's schedule about when we should meet in Portsmouth! Apology? It is you who should apologize to me and to all my crew!"

Only when this outburst was out of his mouth did Giles remember that it might not be the best idea to issue such fighting words to a man whose courage and skill with pistol or sword were unknown to him. A duel would certainly not be conducive to getting underway soon. Moreover, Daphne would be furious if she found out that he had fought a duel.

Giles need not have worried. "Captain Giles," replied Sir Walcott, clearly cowed by Giles's greeting. "I could not be in Portsmouth on the appointed date. The Prince of Wales was having a rout the next day that I simply had to attend. Such an event! All the *ton** were there. And it was clear that the Prince was leading the way for the most elegant fashions. It was Mrs. Fitzherbert* herself who pointed out how elegantly Georgie* was dressed. I couldn't possibly go to St. Petersburg, representing his Majesty, in my out-of-date wardrobe. It took my fool of a tailor all this time to make the new clothes. Why, I only received them yesterday afternoon,

and then I had to, simply had to, comfort my friend Allen –
Lord Allen Hatch, you know, who had had such a bad time
with his friend – that I could only leave London late in the
evening. Do you realize that I have been up all night to get
here!"

Giles recognized that there was no point
remonstrating more on his passenger's lateness. Instead, he
turned to the next matter. Sir Walcott's servants were lined
up behind him, waiting for instructions. They were in for a
surprise.

"Didn't Sir David tell you that there was room for
only two servants, and wasn't that included in your written
instructions, Sir Walcott?"

"Yes, but I took them to be standard orders; they
don't apply to *me*."

"I am afraid that I have had the same orders, and,
yes, they do apply to your men. Choose two to be your
servants; the others will have to join my crew. Those are
my orders." Giles deliberately made it unclear whether he
meant that he had been ordered to take this action or it was
being taken on his own initiative.

"Oh, good. So the others will still be serving me,"
Sir Walcott seemed much relieved by Giles's statement.

"No, they will be enrolled as landsmen, hopefully as
volunteers but, if necessary, as pressed men. They will be
assigned duties that will keep them busy. Now, please
indicate which two you want. The others are becoming
seamen,"

Sir Walcott's men were all very handsome individuals with faces unmarred by scars, warts, or pox marks. They were all quite tall and varied between being slim and of graceful stance to being stocky and standing solidly. Giles was relieved that Sir Walcott, after much humming and hawing, chose the two most graceful individuals. The others might be made into useful seamen.

"Very good," Giles commented. "Mr. Hendricks, enroll these four men as landsmen. Offer them the King's shilling*; otherwise, list them as pressed. It doesn't really make much difference. They are in for the duration of the war. They have lost their protections from being pressed by Sir Walcott having them accompany him here, knowing that they would then be vulnerable. He had been warned explicitly about what would happen. Oh, and have the purser give them some more suitable clothes."

"Aye, aye, sir."

"Now, Sir Walcott, most of your belongings will have to be stowed in the hold. They won't be available to you on the voyage, and you may have only limited access to them when we reach St. Petersburg, where, presumably, you will be housed with the Ambassador, and I have no idea of how much space he will be able to afford you."

"What? But they are packed in such a way that *each* day I have to get at different trunks. Breeches in one, shirts in another, and so on. I cannot do without *any* of them in my cabin."

"I am afraid that that is impossible. Maybe one of your men can repack your things before we have them stowed. I'll be getting us underway immediately, so you must have it done before we get into rougher water. I do hope that you will dine with my officers and me later. We usually dine at sea at noon, except for special occasions, so tonight we will make it later. I should warn you that we also rise early in the morning. The ship has to be cleared for action before dawn, and that involves dismantling our cabins, I am afraid. You will have to be up and dressed an hour before dawn."

"What! I can't. I simply *can't* get up at that hour! I always sleep until noon."

"Not on this ship, I am afraid, Sir Walcott. There is no choice. We will be in possibly hostile waters, and we must be ready for any surprise encounter at dawn. You will, of course, be at liberty to resume your cot when the cabins are restored."

Giles was delighted, even though he knew that he should be ashamed, at the pleasure he felt in his guest's being put upon to follow the ship's routine. "Bear a hand there," he ordered two passing seamen. "Help Sir Walcott get his belongings to his cabin. Though I imagine most of those crates can be stowed in the hold immediately." The crates in question were clearly filled with wine. There were a couple of dozen full crates, even though their total trip would not last more than nine weeks, and much of the time would be spent in St. Petersburg, which could be presumed to have adequate supplies of wine. In addition to being saddled with a pretentious fop, did he have to cope with a serious drunkard as well?

Giles turned away from dealing with Sir Walcott's arrival to give the orders to get *Glaucus* underway. Although his crew had only done the maneuver twice before in this ship, it went very smoothly. Soon they were out of the Nore and traversing the Thames Estuary. They sailed on a light northerly breeze that was just strong enough to hold the ship steady in the small waves hitting her side. Sir Walcott, however, did not appear for luncheon, his servant mentioning that he was fast asleep in his hanging bed.

The wind freshened and veered somewhat as they sailed into the North Sea, and soon they were pounding along close-hauled in a fresh breeze. The shallow water guaranteed rough seas, and *Glaucus* had to corkscrew her way through them. It was soon evident that seasickness had struck Sir Walcott, as well as the men whom he had brought with him. Nothing was seen of the baronet for the rest of the day or the next one, except when he was turned out of his hanging cot so that the cabin could be struck below* as the ship cleared for action. The following morning, Giles had mercy on him by ordering only a partial clearing for action before dawn that left the stern cabins untouched. Sir Walcott remained all day in his cabin, and it was evident that he had yet to find his sea legs.

By noon on the fifth day of their voyage, the Skagen* marking the north tip of Denmark was to starboard. That was the name given to the place on Mr. Brooks' chart, which had been copied from a Danish one. The English usually called it 'The Scaw.' Giles had decided that it would lessen confusion if they used the chart names rather than the English ones when they differed. Soon they started easing their sheets* as they turned southward down the Skagerrak*. The wind had moderated a bit, and, before long, they were running before it with the *Glaucus* gently making her way up and down the much smaller waves. Giles cracked on all sails, including the studding-sails*, and they surged along very smoothly. Sir Walcott appeared, still looking rather green around the gills. He complained vociferously about the awful conditions he had to endure to carry out his duties and how badly he had been served. It apparently never occurred to him that the conditions had been equally bad for everyone else on board and that the servants he had brought with him would have had a much more disagreeable experience.

The eased conditions did, at last, enable Giles to have the dinner to welcome Sir Walcott aboard. It was not a particularly happy occasion. Sir Walcott showed no interest in the officers with whom he was dining. Instead, his conversation consisted of long harangues about his own importance, how many fashionable events he attended, and people he knew, demonstrating how important he was. These were matched by complaints about how badly he was being used by the Admiralty in not supplying a proper warship for his transportation. He seemed to think that nothing less than *Victory* would be suitable for his importance. This complaint was interrupted by grumbles about everything to do with *Glaucus,* including this dinner where the joint of fresh beef, which was its centerpiece, was, he claimed, greatly inferior to what he was used to.

After a few attempts to enter the conversation, spurred on by Giles's remarks about their trip and about their various experiences, the lieutenants and doctor lapsed into silence, and Giles soon stopped making any effort to have a conversation. The lieutenants found excuses for their being required urgently on deck so that they might escape to the wardroom. Even the midshipmen, who usually were so hungry that they never left the table until long after the cloth* was drawn in the hope that nuts or fruit might accompany the port, found that they desperately needed to study so that they could pass their lieutenant's examinations.

Sir Walcott was quite happy for Giles's participation in the conversation to consist of various grunts. The baronet's monologues became more and more rambling and incoherent as he downed glass after glass of port, and Giles was starting to worry that he was on the verge of becoming privy to liaisons of a disgraceful nature when the baronet's head started nodding, and he planted his nose on the table. Giles promptly summoned Sir Walcott's servants to put their master to bed.

Giles could not believe how much wine his guest had consumed. Sir Walcott would quite exhaust Giles's supply if he entertained the special envoy often while they were at sea. Giles was glad that he had intercepted his original orders to serve delicacies from his collection of cabin supplies at the end of the dinner. He now ordered his servant to bring them and the port wine to the wardroom, where he could expect to find much more congenial and appreciative company.

Glaucus continued to make good progress during the night. The sky was clear, and the moon was almost full. Giles took silent glee in ordering a full clearing for action before dawn and seeing an obviously hung-over Sir Walcott shivering on deck as he waited for his cabin to be restored. After it was clear that all was well, Mr. Brooks approached his captain with a navigational problem that they had discussed without a firm resolution, partly because the most advantageous way to proceed through the passages that led to the Baltic would depend to some extent on the wind. With the wind that was presently blowing, it was clear that the best way would be through the Øresund, the straight that passed between the entrance to Copenhagen and Sweden. It was the most direct of the three ways, though it was also the one that would call the greatest attention of the Danish authorities to *Glaucus*'s presence. Giles felt that this was preferable to having vague rumors about their possible purpose and destination being circulated. As he passed Copenhagen, he was sure that some sort of vessel would intercept him to question him about his destination. He could only hope that it would not try to detain him.

Mr. Brooks was completely confident that he would have no trouble navigating the channel, especially with a northerly wind. The passage ran in an almost straight line for about sixty nautical miles, he said, though, at its narrowest, it was hardly two miles wide. It would be no joke to have to beat up it, but it would be easy to traverse with a following wind – far easier than either of the other two passages. Giles agreed with his master and ordered him to steer the course that would take them to the mouth of this passage.

Glaucus arrived at the entrance to the strait at two bells of the forenoon watch to find two Danish frigates on patrol. After being hailed by one of them on friendly, even welcoming, terms, and after Giles explained that they were on their way to St. Petersburg on a peaceful errand, the British frigate sailed down the Øresund without reducing sail. Soon they were approaching the narrowest section, with the towns of Helsingør to starboard and Helsinborg to larboard. Giles started to worry about the possibility that the Danes or Swedes had joined Napoleon. Batteries on either side of the strait could easily hit *Glaucus* as she moved along. He need not have worried; his ship sailed uneventfully past the towns, dipping her flag to the fortresses and receiving reciprocal salutations from each.

The Øresund then widened considerably. Giles debated whether he should keep to the eastern side, which was the more direct route, or to go along the side on which

Copenhagen was located so that it would not appear that he was trying to avoid the Danish capital. He decided on the latter course. He was somewhat surprised to see a powerful Danish armada anchored at the entrance to Copenhagen harbor with what he thought must be an admiral's flag on one of the largest ships of the line. Like many others hearing news of the battle three years earlier, he had thought that Admiral Nelson had destroyed the Danish fleet completely, but this was a strong fleet, and clearly not newly built. As he examined the flagship, he saw a small boat with sails raised peel away from the mammoth warship and head towards *Glaucus*.

The boat sailed up to *Glaucus* and, after receiving permission, hooked on to her side. Giles went to the entry port to greet the smartly dressed captain who, Giles presumed, was the flag captain to the Danish Fleet's admiral. Giles's order that the standard honors for a captain coming aboard be made to welcome the Danish officer had been appropriate.

"Captain Madsen," the arrival declared himself, in clear though heavily accented English, after saluting the quarterdeck. "Greetings and welcome from Admiral Holm. He would like to know your purpose."

"Captain Sir Richard Giles," responded Giles, quite forgetting that he was, in fact, a Viscount, even if it was only a courtesy title. "We are in transit to St. Petersburg with a special envoy on board, Sir Walcott Lainey. Are we still at peace?"

"Yes, we have no news of any change in that. Might I suggest, Captain, that you salute the Admiral? A fifteen-gun is what is customary among us. The Royal Family is not in residence, and, in any case, you would not be able to see the Royal Standard over the Palace, so a full salute would not be appropriate."

"I intended to begin the salute when we were closer, Captain Madsen," Giles replied. "After it is completed, perhaps you will join me for some refreshments."

Having ordered the fifteen-gun salute and staying on deck for the flagship's response, Giles led the way to his cabin. There was still no sign of Sir Walcott, who had retired to his bed again after being forced to rise for the pre-dawn ritual. Giles ordered his servant to pour two glasses of the excellent Madeira, which Daphne had included in the cabin supplies that she had chosen for him, and the two Captains settled down to a friendly chat.

They got on well, as professional sailors often did on first meeting. After the standard exchange of complaints about the ignorance concerning naval matters of the governments they served, they ventured into the political situation. The Danish captain was quite frank about their worries about Bonaparte. The Danes were puzzled by his inaction. It was not like him to sit idly by, though they did realize it was partly on account of most of his attention being directed at preparations to invade England. However, while he was waiting to accomplish that endeavor, they were surprised that he had not seized their country or forced them to ally themselves with France in the way that the Dutch puppet-government now was subservient to the Emperor, the title with which Bonaparte had recently awarded to himself. Possibly, he was waiting for his coronation, which was rumored to be planned on the most elaborate scale, before taking hostile actions against his neighbors, but somehow there were still anxieties about what he would do even before that.

Giles happily concurred in the reality of the worries, but he then very much exaggerated the extent to which England would be defended against a French landing even if the French were able to seize command of the Channel. He also stressed the Royal Navy's strength and how all their captains were itching to get at the French fleets. Giles suspected that his remarks about the importance of Danish neutrality, though delivered in no official capacity, would reverberate with the Danes. He even mentioned how surprised he was to be unable to see any of the effects of Hyde Parker's and Nelson's most regrettable attack on the fleet at Copenhagen. The last was most certainly a delicate subject, he realized, and his raising it was inviting an official reprimand if it ever became known to his superiors. He had been given no explicit instructions on what to say Britain's position on Denmark might be, but his thoughts were out of his mouth before he realized how inappropriate they might turn out to be.

Glaucus had sailed well beyond the Danish fleet before Captain Madsen declared that he must leave. Giles saw him over the side, again with the appropriate ceremony. It was only when they were nearing the end of the strait that he realized that Captain Madsen might be playing him in the way that he had been attempting to fool the Danish captain. Giles would have to include that possibility in his report, not that it would matter much. He would need to reach Russia before the report could be included in the Ambassador's dispatches, and then it would still have a long journey to England and the Admiralty. Giles was unhappy that he should have to learn to curb his tongue when dealing with the seamen. His own inclination was to be straightforward and not guard his thoughts to conform to some complicated diplomatic chess game that he found very hard to figure out.

Chapter XIII

Daphne's first task on returning to Dipton was to make sure that everything was well with the girl by whom her half-brother-in-law, Thomas, had had a baby. Of course, she knew that the child could never be acknowledged as part of her husband's family, but, even so, she felt a responsibility towards the girl. She found her in the dairy barn with the new-born baby close at hand in a basket.

"Nancy, you have arrived safely, I see. Are you being looked after adequately?"

"Oh, yes, my lady. Mr. Scramps, the head cowman, has made sure I know my duties and that my cottage has everything I need. And Mrs. Wilson has been very helpful. I never knew that a housekeeper could show such concern for someone like me. She even insisted that Thomas here needed better clothes."

"Thomas is your baby's name?" Daphne asked. Her own baby took this moment to start kicking again. She thought wryly that he must be trying to greet his half-cousin. The thought sobered her. She should indeed feel an obligation to this girl.

"Yes, my lady. I named him after his father, much good that that did us." A tear glistened in Nancy's eye.

"Well, Nancy, I hope you will be happy here. If you need anything, tell Mr. Scramps."

Daphne's next task was to find out how work on the new vista was proceeding. The men in charge had their usual list of difficulties that they had encountered and overcome, and they were still on schedule. From what Daphne could see, things were progressing well. It was likely that the main work could be done before winter weather turned some of the low-lying ground to mush. She did realize that while they asked her approval of some steps they were about to take, they had mastered many similar problems in her absence. She had been very careful whom she had chosen to do the various jobs, and she was very pleased to see how capable they were, even if it made her realize that she was not quite as indispensable as she had presumed.

The new stables were also progressing nicely. Mr. Griffiths was full of information about how the training of the few horses they had was advancing and how the new acquisitions they had obtained at auction were shaping up. Their equine venture had started too late in the year to have their own colts by spring, but the two pregnant mares he had bought were doing well.

As Daphne was returning to Dipton Hall to change before meeting with Lydia and her fiancée, Daphne reflected that her absence had not led to serious crises and that everything had been going smoothly without her every-day supervision. Maybe she should take more seriously the possibility of hiring stewards for the estates in her care. With the new baby, she really couldn't provide the detailed oversight that she had believed to be necessary for the success of the various ventures.

These musings turned out to be prescient. When Daphne was alone with Lydia and Mr. Dimster, the conversation was started by Lydia.

"Aunt Daphne, you said that I could come out of mourning. I did. I think we all will. I asked Lady Clara, and she saw no reason not to. So when can we get married?"

"Whenever you wish. The house your uncle is providing for you and Mr. Dimster will be available on Michaelmas. But you can, of course, live here until then. The dowry is ready to be transferred when you have married, so with your father's allowance or wage or whatever it is called, Mr. Dimster, you should be able to live comfortably."

"That is the one item that is in question, Lady Ashton," intervened Mr. Dimster at this point.

"Yes?"

"It's about my allowance. My father has changed his mind and will only give it to me if I become the Member of Parliament for Dipton."

"I thought you didn't want to do that."

"I don't, but what choice do I have?"

"Well, I can tell you that you won't become the Member for Dipton. Both Captain Giles and my father are agreed that it would not be suitable for you to take the seat because of the demands your father would make of you. In any case, I don't think that it would be a good idea for you to be dependent on your father's wishes, whether in connection with the Dipton seat or another. If he will cut off your allowance for not doing what he wants in this matter, he will also cancel it for disobeying him on something else. Giving in to him now means that you will have to do whatever he asks in order to make ends meet."

"I know, Lady Ashton, but what can I do? If I refuse, I won't be able to afford to marry Miss Lydia. I should tell you that my father has already made arrangements to have the election writ* moved by one of his cronies tomorrow."

"Has he? How very inconvenient. I will have to consult with my father as to who the member should be. However, that doesn't solve your problem, does it?"

"No, it doesn't. I still have to choose between marrying Miss Lydia and keeping my allowance."

"There is another way out, you know."

"What is that, Lady Ashton?"

"Why, to find work elsewhere, of course. You have been helping to manage your father's estate, have you not?"

"Yes, but he has hired a new steward who will start at Michaelmas, and he has told me that I won't have a position with him, or an allowance, if I won't stand for Parliament. He really has me blocked off."

"I think there is at least one way to solve your problem. I need a steward. Acting as my own manager for both Dipton Hall and Dipton Manor is becoming too much for me." Daphne unconsciously patted her tummy at that point. "You could become my steward. The salary would be more than adequate to allow you to marry even without the dowry. Which, of course, you will also get."

"Oh, thank you, Lady Ashton! Of course, I'll take the position."

"Aunt Daphne, this is so kind of you," said Lydia, coming around the table to throw her arms around her rather startled aunt.

"Nonsense. I am not being generous. It is a genuine position, not something cooked up for Mr. Dimster. And I warn you, Mr. Dimster, I am a hard task-mistress and will be keeping an eagle eye on what you do."

"I am glad to hear it. I have heard of too many instances where the landowners give their stewards no directions or oversight and then blackguard them for not getting the best return or, worse still, for lining their own pockets. I don't want anyone to think that I am in that category."

"It does happen, unfortunately, but not at Dipton Hall, I can assure you," Daphne replied. "Now I imagine that you two want to set a date for the wedding and to arrange to have the service conducted by Lord David. I can spare you for one week after the event to have a honeymoon, Mr. Dimster. No, let's make it ten days. Lydia, and as a gift from your uncle, who will not be able to attend, I will give you fifty guineas to finance your going away and to help you get started in married life."

"Oh, Aunt Daphne. You are the very best aunt in the world!"

Daphne laughed and waved the two lovers away. What a difference four years in age could make. Had she ever been that spontaneously enthusiastic? Up till now, the family she had acquired by marrying Richard had largely been a nuisance and an irritation, but today she had got quite a bit of satisfaction from being able to help one of them.

Helping Lydia made Daphne think that she should look for Captain Bolton and at least pretend to be interested in his alleged purpose for being at Dipton. However, glancing out the window, she saw that Catherine was apparently explaining to him how the vista was being improved. She had the sketch that she had prepared to show how it would look when finished. Daphne thought it an excellent way of conveying not merely the rigid plans but for endowing the scene with a sense of what it would look like and what one might feel looking at it. Her interrupting them to talk about paintings, she was sure, would not be appreciated. Instead, she went to see Lord David in his vicarage.

As always, he was welcoming. Somewhat to her surprise, she found herself telling him not only about her adventures on *Glaucus* but also about the problems associated with the house on Arlington Street.

"I always knew that Ashton was a rotter," he declared when Daphne had outlined her problems, "but nothing like this. We will just have to find a way out of it."

"I don't see how. It's not the money, though that is not inconsiderable. It is just that I hate being bilked by these horrible people."

"I agree. I really wasn't fully aware of what sorts of things happened in London. They are awful, and you and Richard shouldn't be caught up in them. Now let me study the documents. I am not a lawyer, but quite a few of my acquaintances have followed that vocation, and they have always told me that the details are what matter and that a lot of solicitors are far from being careful enough in drawing up papers, especially when they think that no one will examine them carefully. I am thinking about this solicitor that Mr. Edwards consulted and, you are sure, drew up the documents. That strikes me as being sufficiently unethical that it should land him in a great deal of trouble if it were to be exposed. I also think that a man who behaves in that way is likely to be lazy as well as unscrupulous. It is possible, indeed likely, that, being lazy, he has allowed some weaknesses that we can take advantage of."

"We?"

"Of course, 'we.' Ashton may have stuck Richard with the problem, but it is a family disgrace, and I am bound to try to help overcome it with you."

"Oh, David! That is very good of you, and it helps so much being able to tell someone about our problems. It is so shameful! I haven't even told Mr. Edwards what it is really."

"Just leave the documents with me, and I will see if I can think of anything."

Daphne's next stop was her father's home. She wanted to see him in order to tell him all about her adventures, though she did not expect him to be of much help with her dilemma. Thinking it over, she thought she would avoid altogether telling him about it. She rather thought that he had no idea about the debauched life of some quite respectable-seeming men. He would certainly be horrified to learn that she was now all too well aware of the nefarious dealings that accompanied such activities. He rather liked the Countess and might see her as being tarred with the same brush, and that could spoil their friendship. However, Daphne did need to discuss with her father Mr. Dimster's mention that Sir Thomas Dimster had arranged for the by-election for the Dipton seat in Parliament since the election could be controlled by her father and herself.

Father and daughter settled down comfortably in front of a blazing fire in the parlor of Dipton Manor, with tea and toasted crumpets. Mr. Moorhouse listened with fascination to Daphne's account of her adventures. He was greatly concerned to learn that she had been in a battle, though he resisted remonstrating with her about the dangers of sailing in a warship in time of war. He knew that she would take it without concern for or even remembering her pregnancy if the opportunity arose again. She did avoid telling him about the house in Arlington Street or about how she had come to bring a dairymaid to Dipton. In the latter case, she suspected that her father guessed the essence of the situation and had no wish to know the details.

They then turned to the matter of the by-election. The MP should be someone with direct involvement in the riding. A variety of names was considered, but they all were unsuitable for political or personal reasons, or else they had already firmly indicated that they were not interested.

"The best person would be Richard," Mr. Moorhouse remarked, "except he can't run."

"Why do you say that, father? We talked about it earlier, and he was very reluctant to stand for the riding, but maybe when it is pointed out that we have no candidate, he might change his mind. However, I most certainly would prefer him not to be elected. I suppose that we could get Sir David McDougall to suggest someone. I suspect that he has the names of many people who are looking for a seat."

"Probably, Daphne, but I would not be happy about it. I think members of Parliament should know their ridings, and I am not convinced that a party-man is what we need."

"Well, we have to find someone or stay out of it and allow whoever Mr. Dimster puts up to take the seat."

"You know, Daphne, I really think that we have overlooked the best candidate."

"Who is that?"

"Your brother-in-law, Lord David."

"Lord David? But doesn't he have duties here that would prevent him serving?"

"He could get a curate. I agree that he is a very good vicar, young though he is. Parliament doesn't meet all that often, and the lack of a member has not troubled us so far. If he attended some sessions, especially where important matters are being considered, it would be a contribution. You know that his mother wants him to become a bishop, and I am sure that he would be a very good one. Being an MP would be a good introduction to the fiercely political nature of being a bishop."

"If he is willing to do it, I think he should, though he does add a great deal to the parish – and our society."

"He won't be gone that much, I imagine. Unless he becomes a member of the government, of course. I'll ask him if you would like."

"Yes, that would be good. I confess that I don't really understand why the two of us can determine who the MP will be."

"Technically, we do not. In this borough – it is ridiculous for Dipton to be a borough while Ameschester is not, but that is how it goes – in this 'borough,' there is a very limited number of electors. I don't really know how they are selected, but I think the list consists of the gentlemen who reside here and the wealthier of the tenant farmers. I think it depends on who pays taxes or how much they pay. Since the tenants are the largest group, apart from laborers, and most of those who qualify to vote hold their leases from Richard or from me, they will vote as we suggest. In the past, old Gramley and his friends had an automatic majority, so he was nominated, and no one else stood. Now we can control the election in the same way."

"It all seems very odd to me. Will Richard become a member of Parliament automatically when his father dies?"

"Well, in a way. He will be a member of the House of Lords automatically."

Daphne left still feeling that she didn't really understand all the various ways men could enter Parliament. She realized that, in one respect, it did not matter. She could never become a Member or have to worry about for whom to vote. She already had enough choices to make without bothering about that. She did realize that she and Giles would have to make some decisions about his attendance in the House of Lords when the time came. Would they need a London house? But this was taking her jumps before they even came in sight.

She arrived at Dipton Hall to find Lydia and Mr. Dimster very perturbed.

"Aunt Daphne, something terrible has happened," her niece broke out as soon as she entered the small drawing-room.

"What is it, Lydia?"

"Thomas couldn't wait to go home and tell his family that everything was ready and all we had to do was decide on the date of the wedding. He thought they might have some opinions on who should be invited and so on and when it might be held."

"Yes, that sounds sensible. So, what is so terrible?"

"He told his father that he would not be standing to become MP for Dipton and that he was not going into Parliament at all. Before he had a chance to give his reasons and how he would support himself, Sir Thomas flew into a rage. Called Thomas an unprincipled weakling who had taken money from his father and was not ready to repay it properly. It wasn't just about the job; Sir Thomas could find someone else for the seat. Furthermore, he was cutting off Thomas's allowance immediately. He also forbad Lady Dimster and his daughters to attend our wedding. He announced that he was disinheriting Thomas and told him to leave the house and never return unless he gave up his position with you and did what he was told."

"Well, first things first," announced Daphne. "Mr. Dimster, you are welcome to stay with my father at Dipton Manor until the marriage. It would not be seemly for you to stay here. Captain Bolton is also staying with my father.

You can start your position as my steward as soon as you like."

"Tomorrow?"

"Certainly. Now, have you decided on a date for your wedding?"

"Can we have it the day after tomorrow?" asked Lydia. "Mr. Dimster's family are not going to attend, and all of mine are already here."

"Is that wise? Do you think that your brother won't attend, Mr. Dimster?"

"No, I think he will want to come. He is in London, of course, but he has crossed swords with my father already and is independent. I would like him to stand up with me."

"I think, Lydia, that you should wait a couple of weeks. You are going to continue to live in Dipton, and you know many people here, even if you do not know them very well. One way to get them to accept you into the community more quickly is to invite them to your wedding. And it will take a few days to get the invitations out and for people to respond."

"But, Aunt Daphne, we don't have any money for invitations or for a wedding breakfast."

"Don't worry, Lydia. Captain Giles has already decided that he will pay for all that. You should talk with your mother, of course, first. I don't know much about the proper form for an invitation, but I am sure that Lady Camshire knows how everything should be done and can help you draw up a list. I think you will want to invite all the gentry in the immediate area, and Mr. Dimster, there is no reason not to ask people near your father's estate. You could get the invitations out quickly if you take the wording for the invitations to the printer in Ameschester tomorrow. If you think about it, you will realize that you don't want to rush your wedding too much. You will have only one wedding in your life, and you want to make the most of it. Furthermore, you don't want people thinking that you have reason to rush into marriage.

"Mr. Dimster, you will be busy with the wedding arrangements for the next couple of days, I imagine. We can wait a while before I start showing you all the details of the estate."

Dinner was a lively affair, with most of the discussion centering on the upcoming wedding. The date was easily settled: Saturday morning two weeks next. Lydia would have her sister as her attendant, while Mr. Dimster would ask his brother and, failing that, a friend from Cambridge. The Countess, of course, knew exactly what the proper wording of the invitation should be. Where controversy arose was about the name in which the invitation should be made. Lady Marianne favored herself, and Daphne agreed with her. The Countess and Catherine thought that it was only right that Daphne should be the one while Lydia could not make up her mind and just wanted the invitations to be issued as soon as possible. The gentlemen, wisely, had expressed no opinions, but, in the end, their views were sought. Mr. Moorhouse agreed with Lady Clara, while Captain Bolton was sure that Lady Marianne would be the proper name on the invitations. Finally, Lord David had to settle the matter, and he suggested that both could be named. That met with agreement all around, and Daphne sealed it by stating that

Lady Marianne's name should come first, a position that Lady Marianne endorsed happily.

When the ladies withdrew to the drawing-room, the wedding planning dominated their conversation. While they had all known it was imminent, somehow setting the date had brought forward a large number of matters to discuss. The gentlemen, by contrast, were very glad to leave that subject behind. Mr. Moorhouse and Lord David directed the conversation to two other topics: what a nice place Dipton was in which to reside and what Captain Bolton's experiences had been in the navy and elsewhere. He submitted to their questioning willingly and, in turn, sought to know about the social life and congeniality of the area. He was quite aware that his hosts were treating him as a possible suitor for Catherine's hand, and he had no intention of putting that option aside.

As he was leaving Dipton Hall, Lord David murmured to Daphne that he thought he might see a way out of her dilemma. She retired to her bedroom wondering what it could be and realizing all too well how exhausting had been her first day back in Dipton. Her back hurt, and the baby, which had been quiet for most of the evening, resumed active kicking. Surely things would get easier soon. She certainly couldn't keep up this pace when the child arrived. How long would it be before Richard would return? So much was happening while he was away. It will take days to bring him up to speed about the various decisions and activities, even if he does receive her letters.

"No, I think he will want to come. He is in London, of course, but he has crossed swords with my father already and is independent. I would like him to stand up with me."

"I think, Lydia, that you should wait a couple of weeks. You are going to continue to live in Dipton, and you know many people here, even if you do not know them very well. One way to get them to accept you into the community more quickly is to invite them to your wedding. And it will take a few days to get the invitations out and for people to respond."

"But, Aunt Daphne, we don't have any money for invitations or for a wedding breakfast."

"Don't worry, Lydia. Captain Giles has already decided that he will pay for all that. You should talk with your mother, of course, first. I don't know much about the proper form for an invitation, but I am sure that Lady Camshire knows how everything should be done and can help you draw up a list. I think you will want to invite all the gentry in the immediate area, and Mr. Dimster, there is no reason not to ask people near your father's estate. You could get the invitations out quickly if you take the wording for the invitations to the printer in Ameschester tomorrow. If you think about it, you will realize that you don't want to rush your wedding too much. You will have only one wedding in your life, and you want to make the most of it. Furthermore, you don't want people thinking that you have reason to rush into marriage.

"Mr. Dimster, you will be busy with the wedding arrangements for the next couple of days, I imagine. We can wait a while before I start showing you all the details of the estate."

Dinner was a lively affair, with most of the discussion centering on the upcoming wedding. The date was easily settled: Saturday morning two weeks next. Lydia would have her sister as her attendant, while Mr. Dimster would ask his brother and, failing that, a friend from Cambridge. The Countess, of course, knew exactly what the proper wording of the invitation should be. Where controversy arose was about the name in which the invitation should be made. Lady Marianne favored herself, and Daphne agreed with her. The Countess and Catherine thought that it was only right that Daphne should be the one while Lydia could not make up her mind and just wanted the invitations to be issued as soon as possible. The gentlemen, wisely, had expressed no opinions, but, in the end, their views were sought. Mr. Moorhouse agreed with Lady Clara, while Captain Bolton was sure that Lady Marianne would be the proper name on the invitations. Finally, Lord David had to settle the matter, and he suggested that both could be named. That met with agreement all around, and Daphne sealed it by stating that Lady Marianne's name should come first, a position that Lady Marianne endorsed happily.

When the ladies withdrew to the drawing-room, the wedding planning dominated their conversation. While they had all known it was imminent, somehow setting the date had brought forward a large number of matters to discuss. The gentlemen, by contrast, were very glad to leave that subject behind. Mr. Moorhouse and Lord David directed the conversation to two other topics: what a nice place Dipton was in which to reside and what Captain Bolton's experiences had been in the navy and elsewhere. He submitted to their questioning willingly and, in turn, sought to know about the social life and congeniality of the area. He was quite aware that his hosts were treating him as a possible suitor for Catherine's hand, and he had no intention of putting that option aside.

As he was leaving Dipton Hall, Lord David murmured to Daphne that he thought he might see a way out of her dilemma. She retired to her bedroom wondering what it could be and realizing all too well how exhausting had been her first day back in Dipton. Her back hurt, and the baby, which had been quiet for most of the evening, resumed active kicking. Surely things would get easier soon. She certainly couldn't keep up this pace when the child arrived. How long would it be before Richard would return? So much was happening while he was away. It will take days to bring him up to speed about the various decisions and activities, even if he does receive her letters.

Chapter XIV

Daphne's morning on the following day promised to be less hectic than her first day back at Dipton had been. With the help of Catherine, Mr. Dimster, and Lady Camshire, Lydia was busy designing the wedding invitations so that Lydia and Mr. Dimster could take the finished draft to Ameschester to be printed immediately. Daphne would hardly be surprised if the team should be fully occupied on the next day or so with filling in the names and getting the invitations delivered. Hopefully, that would be the end of that part of the arrangements, though Daphne feared that the dislike that Lady Marianne had taken to some of their neighbors might lead to disagreements about who should be invited. Luckily, Saint Michael's and All Angels, Dipton's parish church, was large, so there would be no lack of space to accommodate as many people as they could possibly want to invite.

She would spend the morning with Captain Bolton on the subject of paintings for Dipton Hall. In the afternoon, she would attend to her own interests except for following up on Lord David's intriguing remark about how the problem with her London house might be solved. She simply refused to feel guilty about not attending to the affairs of Dipton Manor. That could wait another day, at least. She briefly thought about approaching her father as to how he felt about appointing a steward for Dipton Manor, pledging, of course, that she would oversee any such appointment herself.

Captain Bolton was not much impressed with the paintings he saw, with one exception. That one was a picture of a horse that he said was by a very well-known artist, a man called George Stubbs. Mr. Gramley or his father must have been very proud of the horse, which indeed looked like a splendid steed. Captain Bolton suggested several artists whose paintings Daphne might like. He even went so far as to say that he thought good portraits of Captain Giles and herself would enhance the house. If they wanted to have them painted, they should get a first-rate artist. He could introduce them to several exciting, up-and-coming painters, some of whom might also provide landscapes for Dipton Hall. He would be happy to show Daphne around the better galleries and studios if they both happened to be in London at the same time.

During the conversation, Captain Bolton let slip how much he admired the drawing that Catherine had made of the intended vista that was now being realized. It was much more than a formal translation of the construction plans into a literal representation. Instead, it revealed both the look and the feel that the vista would have in the middle of summer when it was finished. Catherine, he thought, should be encouraged to paint the same scene in the more robust medium of oils on canvas. Indeed, he could see her as a very fine landscape artist.

Daphne made a mental note to herself to talk soon to Catherine about suitors. She thought that Captain Bolton would be an eminently suitable spouse, but she didn't want him to be too encouraged if his obvious interest was not matched by her niece's. She reflected wryly on how her attitude towards her niece had changed from the time when she had first joined her in Dipton Hall. Then, she would have been happy to use any pretext to get rid of her in-laws.

Later, in the afternoon, she went to see what her brother-in-law, Lord David, had had in mind. Before getting into the problems concerning Arlington Street, she thought she should ask about his own interests.

"Has my father talked to you, David?"

"About standing for Parliament? Yes, he has."

"What do you think about it?"

"I am tempted, I must confess. I enjoy what I am doing here, but I am not sure that I am not called to a higher office. My mother makes no secret that she would like to see me a bishop. At first, I thought that that would be the last thing I would want, but now I am not so sure. I am afraid that there is getting to be a real need for men to step forward to counter the tendencies of the high-church people. Experience in Parliament would stand me in good stead as preparation for the Church's politics and for the House of Lords where bishops also sit. Being in Parliament would, I regret to say, produce more influence that might help me to being made a bishop. However, I have a responsibility to see that this parish is properly served. I think we have come a long way since I started here. I would have to get a very good curate. Luckily, I think I know one."

"Who is that?"

"My friend, Geoffrey Foster. We were in college together. He is the son – second son -- of a landed gentleman in Derbyshire. Very pleasant fellow. He took orders a bit after me and has yet to find a living. His father doesn't have much influence. He would be a very good curate for this parish. And he could share the vicarage with me."

"Is he married?"

"No. He couldn't afford to be without a living of some sort. I am thinking of going to London in a day or two to sound him out. I have to decide soon. Mr. Dimster has made sure that there is a minimum amount of time for the candidates to be nominated. Now, about the lease on that London house."

"Yes? You said that you had found something useful."

"I think so. The same lawyer drew up all these interconnected contracts, and he filled them up with the same verbiage towards the end of the various documents. Word for word in each case. They probably come from standard leases or contracts like that. Each one contains a badly worded provision for when the contracts can be suspended, and you might be able to take advantage of it to get out of the mess."

"How could that be?" Daphne asked eagerly.

Lord David explained his rather nefarious scheme. It involved using the clause so that all the other principals to the contracts would be harmed while Giles's expenses would be reduced. It would take a lot of bluffing to make sure that the provision could be exploited. Did Daphne think she would be up to it? She would have to act as a most unsavory character.

"I don't see how I could carry it off, David. It isn't like me at all."

"I know it isn't. Think of yourself as an actress. They don't have to be anything like the characters they are playing. It's not as if you would be going ahead with the scheme. As long as they think you might, and you have the confidence to carry it off, they will take our bait."

"All right. But don't be surprised if I get all tongue-tied when I am supposed to suggest outrageous things or that they just see right through me. I think I might be able to do it, though I do regard myself as a very straightforward sort of person, not given to trickery. But these people have made me so angry that I think I can pretend to be as corrupt as they are. However, there is one part of your scheme that I do not like. To carry this off, I will need to bring a lawyer, and I am not sure that I want anyone I can count on to know about the problems we face over the house or about the scheme to get us out of it. It doesn't smack of being entirely above board."

"I guess it isn't quite. I was thinking of acting as if I were a lawyer."

"Is that safe? Isn't it illegal?"

"Possibly, but I will be careful. I will only say things that are true though I expect them to be misinterpreted. It will be good practice for being a politician. Anyway, I don't think that these people will want to have anything to do with the magistrates. Now, I should go up to London in the next couple of days to see my friend Foster. Could you come, too?"

"I suppose so, and the sooner we can deal with the problem, the better. It is getting a bit close to the time when the baby is due."

"All right. Let's draft a note to Mrs. Marsdon to make sure that these wretches are all present at the house three days from now."

The two conspirators put their heads together to draft a missive that would be intriguing and slightly threatening. After several tries, they came up with

Mrs. Hannah Marsdon

11 Arlington Street

London

Viscountess Ashton requires your presence and those of Mrs. O'Brien and Lord Knockingdon at the house at 11 Arlington Street, of which Viscount Ashton holds the lease, at ten o'clock ante meridian on Friday inst.

The meeting is to inform you of the future uses to which the house will be put and to arrange for your departure while changes are being made.

The presence of the solicitor, who drew up the relevant documents, is also required.

The Honorable David Giles, counselor

"I think that will do the job, Daphne, don't you?" asked Lord David.

"Aren't you afraid of pretending to be a lawyer?"

"I'm not doing that. It just sounds as if I am. Calling myself 'counselor' is meaningless, but I hope that they will take it to indicate that I am a solicitor who likes to pretend that he is above the common herd. If you approve, I will just copy this out in a nice copper-plate hand such as a snotty solicitor's clerk might use."

"I didn't know that you could write that way."

"Oh, yes, I can. When I was a boy, I became interested in calligraphy for a while."

Daphne and Lord David traveled up to London, together with Betsey, in Daphne's carriage. Nerot's Hotel was becoming very familiar territory to Daphne. Lord David left her at the hotel while he went to have dinner with his friend. With no acquaintance appearing to relieve possible boredom, Daphne dined alone in a private room at the hotel.

Ten o'clock the next day found the conspirators knocking at the door of 11 Arlington Street. It was opened by Hector, now in his livery, though moving rather stiffly. He showed them into the parlor where Mrs. Marsdon and Mrs. O'Brien were seated with two men. One of them, an old man with a hawk nose, little hair, and a rather drab frock coat, was Lord Knockingdon; the other was Mr. Longshank. When introduced to the latter, Lord David opened the conversation by announcing, "You know, old boy, you really shouldn't try to have clients on both sides of a contract, especially when you draw them up so carelessly. I really should report you to the governors."

"What are you talking about, Mr. Giles," demanded Mrs. O'Brien.

"Didn't you know that Mr. Longshank was advising Lady Ashton about the lease and the other documents? Surely he must have told you since everything he said was to encourage her to believe that the main terms could not be broken or changed."

"But that surely is the case. He assured us that it was," interjected Mrs. Marsdon. "Originally, he was very proud of the way he had boxed in Viscount Ashton when he was first besotted with me."

"Oh, dear, did he really tell you that? Maybe he thought it, but then he really was not at all careful in drawing up the papers. The only one that is really foolproof is the lease, but even it is nicely flawed since it means that even though the period is stated, it provides that the lease must be renewed if the tenant wants it, whatever the landlord might wish, and at the same rent."

"How is that flawed?" asked Lord Knockingdon.

"Why, sir, properly equipped and managed, this property can turn a much bigger profit than seems to be contemplated in this document, while all the side benefits in the other contracts end at the time the lease ends."

"What, that cannot be."

"Oh, yes, it is. You see, the other documents all have no requirement of renewal, though the lease does."

"But … but…I presumed that it was in all that legal nonsense that filled out the documents. I didn't read them, of course, it just looked like the usual verbiage that lawyers use to make contracts look more impressive and pad their own accounts."

"Well, be that as it may, they are indeed part of the agreements."

"Well, even so, you and your client are bound to honor all the agreements until that time. And I want my rent now, or I'll have Lord Ashton thrown in debtor's prison. And of course, the payments to Mrs. Marsdon that are required must be made."

"Certainly. It is my client's objective to adhere most strictly to all the terms of the agreements. Most strictly. Indeed, Lady Giles has assured me that she intends to keep to the letter of the contracts in every detail."

"So she should," stated Mrs. O'Brien in a rather nasty tone. "And she had better realize that the special services of Mrs. Marsdon only apply to Lord Ashton and not to Lady Ashton. If she wants them – and I can assure you that Mrs. Marsdon is very skilled – that will be a separate charge."

"I am sure that Lady Ashton had no intention of exercising the rights of Lord Ashton," Lord David replied smoothly. "Now I would like to get to the heart of the matter, which is the reason that we required this meeting. I call your attention to the clause at the bottom of the page of the contract detailing how Mrs. O'Brien will be entitled to use the facilities of this house. It is drawn up in rather strange language, but its meaning is perfectly clear. I imagine it was taken from some other documents about rental property, probably one of a rather different nature, and incorporated into these documents willy-nilly by Mr.

Longshank. Such a common practice, isn't it, Mr. Longshank? So profitable, making the clients believe they have special, long documents tailored to their very own needs."

"I see that you are taking your own sweet time getting to the point, Mr. Giles," huffily remarked Mr. Longshank.

"Yes, of course. You do recognize all the tricks of the trade, don't you? But we digress. You will see that the clause stipulates that the terms of the contract will be suspended if the facilities of the property – if you check back through the convoluted provisions of this contract, you will find that what is referred to is this house. Yes, indeed. You will see that the contract stipulates that, if the facilities are not available on account of necessary work to be done to the house in connection with repairs or refurbishment needed for any reason, even if they would not then allow its current use to be maintained, the lease is suspended at the time that the work begins. However, the rent must continue to be paid, though it will be recalculated when the work is finished at whatever figure is agreed on by the principals. Only then can it be returned to its previous use. So, you see, Mrs. O'Brien, you would not be able to get to use the special rooms while the refurbishment is being done in such a case. Indeed, the refurbishment might alter the house so that they would no longer exist. And you, Lord Knockingdon, would have to forego your special lessons with Mrs. Marsdon. And I am afraid, Mrs. Marsdon, that you will not be able to use the facilities to entertain your … ah … students, neither by yourself nor by your assistants. Most regrettable, it would be for you if the interruption turned out to be lengthy. Most regrettable, since then you would undoubtedly lose your pupils."

Daphne noticed that Lord David was having a very good time playing his assigned role. She just had to hope that he wouldn't overdo it.

"Get on with it, man, get on with it. None of that has anything to do with us," growled Mrs. O'Brien.

"Quite the contrary, madam, quite the contrary. You see, Lord and Lady Ashton have decided to refurbish the house completely to make it more suitable for the entertainment of gentlemen of the highest standing and reputation for flawless moral character. Such men have an absolute need for privacy while enjoying their pleasures in the most elegant and attractive facilities possible. The current layout of the house would be quite unsuitable for that purpose. You may disagree, but the lease is quite clear that that decision is not up to you, and it is also clear that you would not be able to undo the changes."

"That is ridiculous. You won't know what you are doing. Word it how you like, you are still going to be running a bawdy house. It is the only thing that pays, but you have to know the trade from the bottom up to be able to make it work. You cannot just step in and expect the ladies of pleasure to pay any attention to you."

"We'll see about that," broke in Daphne. "You see, we intend to provide very special services for these most genteel of gentlemen. Landed lords and very well-to-do country gentlemen, not your usual fashionable riff-raff who demand only crude service and do not need complete discretion. Not the sort of men you attract. I can assure you that we can turn this house into a rousing success. We will give our clients entertainment using much higher-class surroundings than these rather tawdry ones. The ladies will be drawn from the elevated ranks of society so they will know how to talk in the right accents that will make the guests feel comfortable and have the correct vocabulary. They will also be skilled in all the arts of seduction, not your common whores. With these changes, we shall have no problem doing a most rewarding business, since our clients will be eager to pay far higher fees for our services than yours can command."

"But where will you get your whores? You certainly won't get them from me," Mrs. O'Brien sneered. "You can't make silk purses out of the sow's ears that you'll find available in London. The very best are already taken and trained by me and one or two other experts in the needs of gentlemen. We keep our whores sufficiently in debt that they can't abandon us."

"So you say. I don't think that you realize that for every one of your well-to-do clients, there is a wife at home. She also wants carnal satisfaction but will seek it in only the most discreet of circumstances. Many of them already have a stream of lovers, but they cannot really capitalize on their dalliance. Of course, they would never work in a tawdry house of pleasure, such as this one. But with the proper guarantee of confidentiality and reward, I don't expect that finding willing companions will be a problem among my connections. It is a source of talent that you have no way of tapping."

"And our special services?"

"Why there will be no problem. The ladies will most certainly delight in giving men a good thrashing, and some are quite accustomed to being beaten by their husbands with no return. They are used to dressing in elegant and proper fashions and will undoubtedly make people like the Bishop of Stansbury into the most ravishing of 'ladies' since they and their maids are accustomed to doing so themselves."

"That will be the day!" Mrs. Marsdon scoffed.

"It will. And of course, we have the entry to find any number of well-bred men all ready to take on Hector's other duties, and no doubt with far more skill, isn't that right, Mr. Giles?"

"Oh, quite. So many second or lower sons have endured and come to like the perversions endemic to the public schools that they are eager to pursue the pleasures in a safe environment. Oh, that will be no trouble at all. The gentlemen we have in mind are most willing both to give and to receive. It is definitely a quite feasible and rewarding part of the enterprise, since, Lady Ashton, you will be able to collect from both parties to such encounters."

"So," continued Daphne, "you are hereby warned that as of tomorrow morning, work on renovating this place will commence. I expect all customers, servants, and ladies of pleasure to be out of here before seven in the morning. I will be hiring some guards who will be here in a few moments to ensure that nothing of ours is taken away. Mr. Giles assures me that everything here, even the clothes that you are wearing, Mrs. Marsdon, belongs to us. They will, of course, allow you one dress which is more suitable for going abroad. Your clothes are ours by the terms of the documents. It was so good of Mr. Longshank to so vigorously protect our interests."

"But you cannot just take everything that is in this house," protested Mrs. Marsdon.

"Why not? It was all provided at the late Viscount's expense, and the current Viscount is the heir. That, incidentally, includes the one very fine picture in this house, Mrs. Marsdon. The one on the fifth floor. It is by a very fashionable artist, and I expect that the proceeds of having prints made of it to sell in the shops will bring in a pretty penny.

"Now, are we clear about everything? Come along, then, Mr. Giles. We still have other business to attend to."

Daphne and her brother-in-law rose from their seats as if to depart. This was the critical moment. If they left, their threats would turn out to be empty, and they would be back where they started.

"Don't be in such a hurry," said Mrs. O'Brien. "Maybe we can work something out to our mutual satisfaction."

"What do you have in mind?"

"I will have to talk with my associates."

"I can give you ten minutes, no more," Daphne responded.

The three trooped out to go into the opposite room and shut the door.

Lord David winked at Daphne and murmured in her ear, "The walls may have ears. We should keep up our façade."

"They had better be quick, Mr. Giles," Daphne said in a normal voice, taking up Lord David's hint. "The man who will be directing the work, Mr. Fitzsimmons, is supposed to be here by one o'clock, and he will start some of the preliminary tasks right away."

"Quite right, Lady Ashton," replied Lord David. "I doubt that those three can come up with any sensible alternative before then. After all, you should make a very hefty profit from this venture, not to mention the extensive favors you can expect from satisfying your clients' cravings so discreetly yet elegantly. Your influence will rise immensely as a reputable owner of a disreputable house. Any number of prominent men will be happy to pursue your interests to ensure that you do not happen to mention their little foibles. It is certainly important to get started on the changes right away."

Daphne was horrified by what Lord David was envisaging and was only saved from protesting by a large wink that he gave her. "I am just as horrified as you are by what I am suggesting," he suggested in a whisper. "Let's hope that they don't see through our play-acting. Especially as I don't see any other way to close down what is going on here. They will continue their business at our expense if they catch on to what we are really doing, so let's keep up the charade."

"All right, though it would quite sicken me if what we have described were really what we intend to do," Daphne whispered in reply.

They were rewarded for their bit of spontaneous play-acting by hearing the opposite door being opened and closed quietly. Hector, it seemed, had been eavesdropping and was now reporting the urgency to be deduced from Daphne's remark to the people in the room across the hallway.

"I hope that our ruse works on them as we hope," whispered Lord David with a grin.

Apparently, it did, for a few minutes later, the trio returned.

Mrs. O'Brien opened the conversation. "Lady Ashton, we all have the view that you are most unlikely to be a successful mistress of an establishment such as you propose. You are too naïve, too inexperienced. You are certain to fail."

Daphne was afraid that they had seen through her act all too easily and were not intimidated by it. However, before she could assure the disgraceful trio that she was quite capable of running a fine establishment for gentlemen, the bawd continued, "We do realize that in you attempting to create a different establishment, and thereby closing down this very successful one, we stand to lose a great deal of money. Possibly we can reach some compromise."

"What do you have in mind?" Lord David asked as Daphne tried to hide her astonishment at this development while retaining her haughty demeanor.

"We thought perhaps we could share some of the proceeds of the house with you while keeping to the same arrangements otherwise."

Daphne pretended to think for a moment, pushing herself back into her assumed character. "Madam, you won't be having any proceeds to share while the renovations are being conducted, while the contracts between us will all expire before the new establishment is ready to open. I see no advantage to me in your silly offer."

"Oh, you misunderstand; I meant that the construction should be abandoned."

"Ah … no, I can see no benefit to me in such an arrangement either. I will not have my good name associated with this tawdry enterprise. No, a partnership is quite out of the question."

"Then, can we come to some other arrangement?"

"Well, I would need some compensation —," Daphne had to think quickly, for this was going much better than she had expected, "— for the inconvenience you have put me to about this. What do you think would be fair, Mr. Giles?"

"Let me think —," Lord David was as unprepared for this turn of events as Daphne had been. It was far more promising than anything they had contemplated. "— I would think £5,000 might be a just recompense, and, of course, the rent arrears would have to be forgiven. Yes, at a very minimum."

"That is far too high," responded Mrs. O'Brien. "We would never get that vast sum back."

"Of course *you* wouldn't," said Daphne, now hugely enjoying the game. "You do not know how to run a really first-class establishment. The sum sounds a little low to me. I think Mr. Giles is being very generous. Of course, with that being the figure, we would have to retain the special equipment and see what sort of a price it would command. I imagine that there are other such houses that could use the trash."

"I will have to consult with my colleagues again, but I know that any transaction will have to include us keeping the furnishings," said Mrs. O'Brien. The three of them trooped out of the room again.

"David," began Daphne in a low voice, but she was halted by Lord David putting a finger to his lips, signaling silence. He tiptoed to the door and suddenly showed his head into the passageway.

"Ah, there you are, my good man. Hector, isn't it? Lady Giles requires some coffee to pass the time while the others confer. Fetch it now."

"Yes, sir. And sir, do you think it would be possible for me to retain my position if you are taking over the premises?"

"I suppose it is possible, but Lady Ashton expects the operation to be closed for a lengthy period, and I am sure she would not need your services in that period."

Lord David returned to his place beside Daphne. "I had no idea you could act so well."

"I find it very hard to believe that I succeeded. I had a very hard time not showing how revolted I am with the whole idea. It is so completely different from everything I was taught about society and those in elevated positions. Anyway, talking of acting, you are no slouch yourself. I thought I would explode when you named that figure."

"I don't know where I got it from. I also don't like what these people are doing at all."

"Aren't there laws or ordinances or something against such goings-on?"

"I believe there are. But I think the magistrates and judges turn a blind eye to such activities unless the trade becomes a public nuisance that inconveniences them. Many powerful men seem to enjoy this sort of thing. You may have given me the material for my maiden speech to the House."

"So, you are going to stand?"

"Yes. Foster is quite eager to be my curate. You will all find him to be an excellent man. Might even be a fall back for you, Daphne, if Captain Bolton escapes the web you are weaving for Catherine."

Further conversation was stopped by the return of the trio of procurers.

"We have talked over what you are proposing. It is far too much," announced Mrs. O'Brien.

Daphne rose to her feet. "In that case, there is nothing more to discuss. Expect my workmen tomorrow at seven o'clock."

"Let's not be hasty," intervened Lord Knockingdon. "I think we can work things out."

"What are you suggesting?" responded Daphne.

"We can offer £1,000, but the rent owing would be included in the figure. Also, we would want Lady Giles to give us the names of the women she will be using."

"Absolutely no to that last suggestion. I cannot possibly have their names bandied about. Only I could approach the ladies in question with any hope of their agreeing. I shall just tell those I have sounded out that it will not be feasible after all. Of course, you are free to ask your clients to enquire whether their wives would be interested in the positions.

"Now, about the figure you suggest. It is far too low, but this whole business is somewhat of a bother to me. Let's say £4,000 in addition to canceling all rents owing."

Lord David shook his head vigorously as if suggesting that Lady Aston was being far too generous. The two sides haggled for a while, settling on £3,000 and the rents owing and for the lease to cease immediately. Lord David quickly wrote out a memorandum of agreement for all to sign to confirm the agreement.

"That settles it, then," said Daphne. "Mr. Giles will arrange to have the more formal documents drawn up. Please be at Mr. Edwards's office in the city at 11:00 a.m. tomorrow to sign them. He has been appointed to handle all Viscount Ashton's affairs while my husband is away, with my approval, of course."

The two conspirators left. They were hardly around the corner from the house before they broke down in hoots of laughter. They had succeeded beyond their wildest dreams. Daphne was rid of the Arlington Street problem. All that remained to do was to go to Mr. Edwards's office so that he would know exactly what was required.

"What are you going to do with the money, Daphne?"

"I've only just started to think about it. I don't want to keep a penny of any money derived from that appalling enterprise."

"May I make a suggestion?"

"Of course."

"Use it to pay off some of my late half-brother's debts. If there is any money left over after that, give it to support the Magdalenes."

"The what?"

"It is a charity that tries to rehabilitate fallen women."

Still chuckling over some of the more outstanding moments of their confrontation with the proprietors of the house of very disreputable pleasures, Daphne and Lord David went to Mr. Edwards's office to arrange for the proper welcome when the whore masters visited him. Then they thankfully returned to Dipton and a way of life that was far more congenial to each of them.

Chapter XV

Glaucus left the Øresund and turned east before the sunset. It should be clear sailing to the Gulf of Finland from here. However, Giles felt apprehensive knowing that, if Denmark chose to block the passages out of the Baltic, he would be trapped, unable to return to England without overcoming impossible odds.

The winds were light and from the west. Mr. Brooks set a course to take them directly to Russia. Giles would prefer that the Swedish navy not have *Glaucus*'s presence flaunted in their face while nothing would be gained by sailing closer to the Germanic and Polish sides of the Baltic.

The autumn sun still had a good deal of heat. Sir Walcott emerged on deck on the morning following their leaving Danish waters and took up the shipboard habit of taking his exercise by pacing back and forth along the quarterdeck. Giles often joined him, but their conversation was limited. Sir Walcott discovered that he did not seem to impress the captain by the illustrious names he dropped. In fact, he and Giles had no common interests. The baronet refused invitations to the wardroom and the captain's table, preferring to eat alone, largely consuming the supplies he himself had brought aboard. Giles noted, on the basis of the many empty bottles that Sir Walcott's servants carried from his cabin, that he was making a large dent in the crates of wine he had brought aboard. Giles was happy to ignore his passenger, and his only regular annoyance due to Sir Walcott's presence came from muffled sounds from the other cabin, which suggested that most improper and, indeed, illegal activities might be taking place in the baronet's quarters. Giles felt he could do nothing about it. Putting Sir Walcott in irons would hardly advance the purpose of the voyage.

Michaelmas came and went, and Giles felt increasing uneasiness about the child that Daphne was carrying. It was due soon. Though Giles was convinced that Daphne would have the best of medical attention and knew that she was strong and healthy, he was also aware that the risks of childbirth, both to the mother and child, were not negligible without even contemplating the possibility of a stillbirth. He found himself in the unusual position of being helpless to do anything about the risks he faced. He knew that, even if he were at Dipton, there would be nothing he could do other than worry and that he would be excluded from both the labor and the delivery. Nevertheless, he regretted that he would not be present to give Daphne his support before and after the ordeal.

Glaucus's officers saw quite a lot of shipping as they sailed along, merchant ships sailing from St. Petersburg and other ports. *Glaucus* did not stop any of them in order to examine their destination. They were all neutral ships, and there would be no justification for trying to enforce a blockade this far from the French coast. Giles kept his crew active in polishing their skills, despite Sir Walcott's protests about the racket that they made. They were thumping on the decks loudly as they carried out practices on sail-handling or taking down and raising various spars or fixing rigging. These were all unnecessary preparations for their current voyage if it could be presumed that there would be no warlike encounters or desperate weather, but they were of crucial importance if *Glaucus* were to be in action or found herself in foul weather. Giles took particular pleasure in the gun drills using actual powder and shot. He moved the time of firing forward so that it would be most painful to a man with a wine-induced headache. Using real ammunition always delighted the crew members and particularly infuriated Sir Walcott with the noise.

The nights were becoming distinctly chilly as they became shorter, a reminder that they could not stay too long at their destination. Finally, Mr. Brooks announced that, by his reckoning, Kotlin Island, on which the Russian naval base of Kronstadt was located, should come over the horizon on the next day.

That was not quite what happened. Partway through the forenoon watch, the lookout at the masthead yelled, "Sail ho, two points to larboard." Mr. Dunsmuir was ordered to take a telescope aloft and report what he saw. When he had neared the main topgallant truck, he took a firm grip around the shrouds* before leveling the telescope. In a moment, his voice floated down. "The ship appears to be a three-master. She is on a course to cross our bow." Soon after, he shouted, "Deck there, the ship appears to be a frigate under all plain sail to the topsails. She is coming into the wind as if to beat up to us."

"Should we clear for action, sir," asked the First Lieutenant, Mr. Hendricks, whose watch it was.

"No," replied Giles. "She is likely a Russian picket ship, and we don't want to appear to be hostile. With this wind, we can tell if she appears to be aggressive long before we are in range, and we can clear then if necessary. However, do ready the guns for firing, but don't open the ports and run out just yet."

"Deck there," came the next hail from Mr. Dunsmuir. "There is a sail behind the first one ... in fact, several sails."

As time passed, it became evident that in front of them was a mass of ships, sailing in close formation, unquestionably a naval fleet. Giles surmised that it must be the part of the Russian navy, no doubt performing exercises. By the time all the ships were visible from *Glaucus*'s deck, they could see that the fleet was comprised of eight ships of the line sailing in two columns accompanied by three frigates and four smaller vessels, sloops-of-war and brigs. Almost at the same time, the lookout reported that low land had come into sight ahead.

"Mr. Hendricks, prepare to back our main topsail and restore the guns to their usual position so that it will not be evident that we were prepared for hostile action."

When the Russian frigate was almost up to them, she backed her main topsail to come to a halt. *Glaucus* did the same. The Russian ship lowered a boat that set off across the short span of water between the two ships. In the sternsheets was an officer. Giles guessed that he was probably a lieutenant, so there would need to be no special ceremony when he came aboard. Giles did wish that he had made more detailed inquiries about the ranks and uniforms of the Russian Navy when he was in London. He would just have to improvise.

The first man out of the boat when it pulled up alongside *Glaucus* was indeed a lieutenant. After smartly saluting the quarterdeck, he introduced himself as Lieutenant Boris Petrovitch Pirov. He stated, in flawless English, though with a thick Russian accent, that he was there to inquire about *Glaucus*'s presence in Russian waters.

Giles explained that they carried a special ambassador to the Court of St. Petersburg and introduced the Lieutenant to Sir Walcott, who elaborated at length just how important his mission was. Giles didn't mention that he himself had another mission involving the Russian Admiralty.

"Admiral Smolensky, the vice admiral who is exercising his division over there, guessed that there was some such explanation for your coming here. He told me to welcome you and to guide you to the naval anchorage at Kronstadt. It is a bit tricky if you don't know the waters, and there may be some signaling about where you are to anchor, which I can interpret for you."

Lieutenant Pirov went to the side and issued a string of orders to the midshipman who was in the sternsheets of the boat in which he had come. Then he turned back to Giles and his circle of officers.

"I must introduce you to my officers, Lieutenant Pirov, since we will be shipmates if only for a short period," Giles said, forestalling whatever the Russian might have intended to say. After he had named all the officers, he noticed that Sir Walcott had come on deck, dressed in the most impressive fashion, and was studiously ignoring what was going on. "Finally, Lieutenant, let me introduce you to the special ambassador whom we are taking to St. Petersburg. Sir Walcott Lainey, allow me to introduce Lieutenant Boris Petrovitch Pirov. Lieutenant Pirov will guide us into a safe anchorage."

Sir Walcott responded to Lieutenant Pirov's bow with a slight and condescending nod. He then launched into a discourse in French. From what Giles could gather, he was emphasizing how very important his mission was and how he must not be hindered in any way from reaching the Court. The lieutenant did not seem to be overly impressed, for after Sir Walcott had finished his lecture, the Russian officer turned to Giles and said, in English, "Captain Giles, you will, of course, have to visit Admiral Stroganoff in Kronstadt before proceeding, despite Sir 'Valgoff's' appeal. My orders are to direct you to where the main fleet is at anchor and to introduce you to the Admiral when you have anchored near the flagship." It was quite evident that Sir Walcott's harangue had not impressed the lieutenant, as clearly indicated by the deliberate mangling of the envoy's name.

Giles ordered them to get underway.

"That is Kotlin Island straight ahead. Kronstadt is on the southeastern corner. We should head to the channel to the south of the island," Lieutenant Pirov stated.

"Mr. Brooks, make it so. And you might as well take your instructions directly from Lieutenant Pirov rather than waiting for me to confirm them."

"Aye, aye, sir," replied the Master. "Lieutenant Pirov, I am surprised that the passage is to the south. The chart suggested that the north passage is wider and easier."

"You may have a copy of an old chart, Mr. Brooks. The North passage is wider, but it is very shallow with shifting mud banks. The charts can be misleading, especially if you have a copy of some of the earlier ones designed to fool the Swedes."

Glaucus slid into the channel separating Kotlin Island from the mainland, and all eyes of those not immediately involved in sailing the frigate were glued on the evolving scene. They passed outside a wall that enclosed a merchant-ship harbor, which was guarded with several forts. Lieutenant Pirov proudly pointed them out to Giles, "They are sited on artificial islands, created by Peter the Great by having cribs of logs filled with stones placed on the ice in the winter so that they then sank into place when the ice melted in the spring."

"Interesting," murmured Giles, his attention diverted by the appearance of dozens of masts and spars of warships beyond the merchant harbors. Much of the Russian Baltic Fleet must be at anchor, and the fleet that they had already seen was only a small part of the ships that the Russian Navy had in the Baltic. Lieutenant Pirov helpfully told Giles what the Russian custom for saluting the Admiral was and when to commence firing the guns. As they passed the end of the merchant harbor, the first of *Glaucus*'s guns boomed out. It was followed steadily by the rest of the salute, as Mr. Abbott, the gunner, could be heard muttering the time-honored patter that allowed him to space the firings properly. The wind was dying, but there was just enough for *Glaucus* to slide into the position Lieutenant Pirov indicated and to anchor off the flagship's quarter. The various adjustments to the sails to allow the frigate to sail through the fleet smoothly and then to stop at the correct place to drop the anchor, followed by the prompt and apparently well-coordinated furling of the sails, were all carried out with the precision that spoke of long training.

Both Giles and Mr. Hendricks heaved a sigh of relief when it was clear that *Glaucus* had fallen back to be brought up tight to the anchor-rode with the anchor holding. As always when under intense scrutiny, he had been afraid that some mistakes, possibly minor, would make a shambles of the apparently effortless anchoring and give the fleet's officers, who undoubtedly would be watching through their telescopes to see how the stranger would perform, and hoping for a chance to laugh at another's misfortune. He had feared particularly that the anchor might not hold so that he would be faced with trying to recover his anchor hastily while *Glaucus* drifted helplessly into danger. The smooth anchoring was important not only for Giles's own pride but also to demonstrate that the Royal Navy was a skilled and efficient force with which it would be sensible to become allies. Word of *Glaucus*'s smooth arrival would undoubtedly spread to a wider audience.

When it was clear that the anchor was holding, it was a task of only a few minutes to lower the captain's barge. Giles, who had already changed into his best uniform and shoes, descended into it following Lieutenant Pirov and Sir Walcott.

The Russian flagship was a gigantic three-decker. Its name, carved amid the elaborate woodwork adorning the stern, was written in the Cyrillic alphabet.

"What does that say?" Giles asked Lieutenant Pirov

"*Alexander Yaroslavich Nevsky*," was the reply. "He was an early Russian ruler and a saint."

As Giles rose from his seat in the boat to climb onto the mammoth vessel, Sir Walcott also stood up with the clear intention of leading the way. However, somehow, he tripped over Carstairs' leg and went sprawling onto the floorboards of the barge. Amid the coxswain's effusive apologies, Giles was able to take his proper place to lead the way onto the flagship. Carstairs's attempts to help Sir Walcott to his feet resulted, instead, in the baronet sprawling onto one of the rowers. Lieutenant Pirov, realizing that he would be needed to act as a translator as soon as Giles was aboard, followed him immediately out of the boat. Sir Walcott, with his finery in some disarray as a result of his mishaps, was finally able to board, though only after significant time had passed.

Giles was welcomed on board by the flag captain, who introduced himself as Captain Sergei Borisovich Panin. Captain Panin complimented Giles on *Glaucus*'s smooth anchoring and then asked if he was the same Captain Giles who had captured the French 74, *Le Jour de Gloire*. Giles acknowledged that he was the man who had captained *Patroclus* and had lost her. He reflected that the Naval Gazette must provide amusement to officers in navies that had seen little warfare. His past feats of war might well smooth his dealings with his Russian counterparts. He was also surprised to realize that Captain Panin had been speaking French, which Lieutenant Pirov had translated into English. He had been able to get the gist of what was being said even before it was translated. At that point, Sir Walcott arrived on deck. Lieutenant Pirov introduced him in Russian, again mispronouncing his name. Captain Panin responded in French, but he mangled Sir Walcott's name still more.

"Admiral Stroganoff will see you now," Captain Panin continued in French. "Come this way."

Somehow, while he was translating this, Lieutenant Pirov succeeded in blocking Sir Walcott's attempt to take the lead. As a result, it was Giles who first followed the flag captain into the Admiral's cabin and was the first to be introduced to him. Sir Walcott was presented next, with the flag captain following Lieutenant Pirov in mispronouncing his name again. The Admiral made some welcoming noises, following which Sir Walcott launched into a long diatribe in French. As far as Giles could make out, the lecture concerned the importance of Sir Walcott's mission and his own high status and how urgent it was that he get to Saint Petersburg as quickly as possible. Several times Giles heard him say 'Prince de Galles,' which he knew was 'Prince of Wales.' At one point, the baronet also seemed to be emphasizing how badly his name had been mispronounced. That got a raised eyebrow from the Admiral directed at Lieutenant Pirov, who responded with a slight nod. Giles wasn't certain, but he thought he saw the Admiral wink.

When Sir Walcott finished, the Admiral replied in words that the lieutenant translated, "Welcome to Russia, Sir Falsecost. I am afraid that some Russians have trouble with exactly how to pronounce English names. I am very pleased that you have set that straight. Unfortunately, Sir Falsecost, it is not possible for Captain Giles's ship to proceed to St. Petersburg until tomorrow.

"Captain Giles, I do hope that you and your officers can dine with me this evening. Many of my captains would like to meet you. News of your exploits has definitely preceded you. Sir Falsecost, you, of course, are also invited."

Sir Walcott was fuming all the way back to *Glaucus*. "That stuck-up sailor! Doesn't he realize that I am His Majesty's special ambassador? Suggesting that there is no urgency about my mission. Why the bumpkin couldn't even get my name right. Hopelessly limited interests. More about your silly old battles, Captain Giles, than about my important connections with the Prince of Wales, even though I specifically mentioned them to him. I have a good mind not to dine with him. That will show him!"

"Suit yourself, Sir Walcott. You may find it a rather boring occasion. Just a lot of naval officers, who are sure to want to talk about naval matters."

Giles couldn't know how much of a role his remark might have played, but Sir Walcott did announce that he was not going to dine with the Admiral. Giles found on reboarding the flagship with Lieutenants Hendricks, Miller, and Macauley that a sizeable number of Russian captains were on hand. Some were grizzled old-timers, others, young men only a bit older than himself. He guessed that the older men would be captains of the line-of-battle ships while the younger men would turn out to be frigate captains. That proved to be the case as introductions were made with each captain's vessel's name and size.

Before they all sat down at the table, the Admiral took Giles aside. "I hope that I did not cause too much offense by deliberately mispronouncing Sir Walcott's name."

"You did, sir, but I would not worry about it. He is a man who seems to take offense overly readily and is quite obnoxious. I cannot speak about why the British government chose him to be a special ambassador, for I am hard put to explain the choice. The only reason that I can think of was that the Prince of Wales used his influence so that he could more readily avoid him for a while."

The Admiral laughed. "I am afraid, Captain Giles, that the workings of governments and diplomacy are beyond us simple sailors."

Lieutenant Pirov, who was acting as interpreter during this exchange, looked decidedly relieved that the offense he might have caused Sir Walcott was not likely to cause any difficulties for himself.

The Admiral served up several dishes with which Giles was not familiar. He found some of them strange, but his liking of the wild boar and of a soup made from beets knew no bounds. Wine flowed freely. Besides the Admiral, those seated close to him were senior naval captains. They were obviously envious of his having experienced several years of war while they had been at peace. The older ones recalled their wars with Sweden, and Captain Obolensky, the captain of a seventy-four third-rate ship of the line, whose name Giles missed, waxed eloquent on how he thought that Sir Sydney Smith's service to the King of Sweden had been grossly exaggerated. They restrained their detailed questioning of Giles's exploits until the cloth had been drawn. Then nothing would do but that Giles told the whole table about how *Patroclus* had freed the British frigates and took the French line-of-battle ship. In setting the scene, he had alluded to *Patroclus*'s earlier capture of frigates and the story of the powerful bow-chasers involved both in those captures and also in his battle with *Le Jour de Gloire*.

Small glasses of a rather tasteless but fiery liquor called vodka were brought out to drink the Tsar's health as well as King George's. This vodka seemed to take the place of port or brandy. It appeared that there was no question of only sipping the very strong drink; instead, his Russian companions insisted that he must drain his glass on each toast. His account held them sufficiently spellbound that no one seemed to be drinking as he talked, but when he stopped, and questions started to flow, one captain after another suggested a toast, and everyone threw back another shot of the liquor. Lieutenant Pirov, who was acting as interpreter when necessary, told Giles that vodka was flavored in many different ways and that he should try various ones that were available with the feast, but Giles realized that after the third round, he could not distinguish one flavor from another. Glancing down the table, he saw that his officers were also being plied with the strong drink in the same way, with most attention being focused on Lieutenants Miller and Macauley, both of whom had participated in the adventures that he had been recounting. He would have to see about the possibilities of leaving soon. Otherwise, the whole contingent from *Glaucus* would have to be carried from the flagship.

Chief interest seemed to center around the use of heavy bow-chasers. All were intrigued by Giles's use of the innovation, but the discussion quickly became controversial. The standard argument against fore-and-aft guns was trotted out, namely that a ship could only carry so many heavy guns, and diverting some of them to shoot forward would inevitably weaken the broadside while engaging one's enemy broadside to broadside had long been the epitome of naval battles. Some of the frigate captains, who had experience in stern chases against pirates and smugglers, did feel that stronger bow-chasers would enhance their ability to catch their opponents. Giles realized that he should not mention how his aft-most guns on *Glaucus* could be used either as broadside guns or stern chasers. Neither of the innovations he had adopted was accepted by the Royal Navy, and the stern-chaser adaptation did not run the same risk of weakening the broadside. Giles would have to warn his officers not to mention what Mr. Hughes had done to make it possible to use the guns either as stern chasers or as broadside guns. He hoped that his lieutenants had not already mentioned the modification or that their Russian listeners at the other end of the table were now so drunk that they would not appreciate the significance of what they were hearing.

Admiral Stroganoff must have noticed Giles' discomfort in having to drink toast for toast with his enthusiastic captains and called the evening to a halt. Even so, Giles had to be assisted by Carstairs into the boat, for he was feeling a bit unstable and thought the deck was pitching in a way that seemed strange since surely the *Alexander Yaroslavich Nevsky* was in a well-protected anchorage. Lieutenants Macauley and Hendricks also seemed to be thinking the deck was very unstable as they walked a most peculiar path to get to the entry port. Lieutenant Miller did not have the same problem: he had to be carried on deck and secured in a bosun's chair for his return to *Glaucus*. The Royal Navy officers would have to either learn how to drink vodka in moderation or else risk disgracing themselves completely.

Chapter XVI

Giles came on deck only when the forenoon watch was well advanced. He had a splitting headache that pounded on the left side of his temple like a loose shutter in a gale. He had an overwhelming desire for water and strong coffee but not for food. Mr. Correll had the watch and greeted him cheerfully and, in Giles's opinion, too loudly.

"Surely you have not been on deck all this time, Mr. Correll?" The lieutenant had been on watch when they had gone over to the flagship and was still on deck when they returned.

"No, sir. I had the midshipmen stand the harbor watches. This is my regular watch today."

"Very good. Carry on." Giles turned away and thought that he might just have a few more hours' sleep before becoming active. That vodka was potent stuff! Unfortunately, there was to be no rest for him that day.

Sir Walcott appeared on deck as Giles turned to go below. The baronet had not attended the Admiral's dinner, and so he was no worse for wear than he was every morning, though this was unusually early for him to come on deck.

"Captain Giles, why are we still at anchor? I must get to St. Petersburg."

"Sir Walcott, as I explained to you yesterday, we have to arrange permission to go further up the Neva to St. Petersburg. Yesterday, Admiral Stroganoff sent a message about our arrival to the Admiralty in St. Petersburg, and he will let us know when we may proceed."

"What can be taking them so long? I must not delay."

"I see a boat leaving the flagship now, Sir Walcott. If I am not mistaken, that is Lieutenant Pirov in the sternsheets."

It was indeed Lieutenant Pirov in the boat. With him was a tall, rotund civilian who had a rather jolly countenance framed by mutton-chop whiskers. Lieutenant Pirov deferred to him in aiding the distinguished person to leave the boat first. As the new visitor appeared at the entry port, Giles had to step forward to prevent Sir Walcott jostling him aside to be first to greet the new arrival.

"George Malthampton, Captain. I am the British Ambassador to the Tsar's court. Welcome to St. Petersburg."

Giles was amused that the Ambassador had not named his title in introducing himself. He would do the same. "Richard Giles, captain of this frigate, my Lord," he responded. "And this is Sir Walcott Lainey."

"Ah, yes, the special envoy. Welcome, Sir Walcott. I hope you enjoy your time in St. Petersburg. You are welcome to stay with me while you are here. I have quite a spacious residence."

"I hope that the accommodations will be adequate," Sir Walcott replied. "I am tired of being cramped in this ship. I must get on with my mission as soon as possible. I trust that you have arranged a meeting with the Tsar at the earliest possible moment."

"That is not the protocol, Sir Walcott. You will have to meet first with Count Oblensky, the principal minister of the Tsar. Then you may have an audience with the Tsar. The Count will present you, and I will accompany you."

Turning back to Giles, he continued without waiting for Sir Walcott to respond, "Captain Giles, the Russian Admiralty sends their greetings. They request that you bring your frigate up to St. Petersburg to moor near the dockyard and the Admiralty. They believe that it would be a greater honor to ask for your ship to go to the capital rather than for you to leave it here, in Kronstadt, and proceed to the capital by smaller boat."

"Lieutenant Pirov, we have to proceed to St. Petersburg. Can you get us a pilot?" Giles asked.

"I can serve, sir. I am fully familiar with the hazards on the route, having guided ships up to the capital several times. Admiral Stroganoff anticipated your need for a pilot."

"Mr. Hendricks, prepare to get underway. Mr. Brooks, we are to go to the dockyard in St. Petersburg. Lieutenant Pirov will act as pilot."

The first lieutenant started to bellow orders that had crew members scurrying in various directions, seeming like ants whose nest had been kicked. The top men started up the shrouds; the line-handlers spread out across the deck to ready the myriad of sheets, braces, and halyards that would be involved. The ship's boys, now about to act as nippers attaching the anchor cable to lines coming from the capstan, lined up to take their turns, while some crew members put in place the capstan bars against which they would push to raise the anchor. Soon the clank of the capstan could be heard.

Giles felt the familiar anxiety tighten his chest that always occurred when he had to maneuver around a fleet. No doubt, every eye in the anchored warships would be looking at *Glaucus*, including the Admiral's own ones and those of all the captains he had dined with. So many things could go wrong when getting underway – not serious errors, but failures of seamanship that would invite pity from the watchers who had themselves had the same worries in getting underway, but who would not resist teasing any poor captain suffering a mishap when next they met. In a sense, the pride of the Royal Navy was at hazard.

The wind was from the west, strong enough to counteract the current so that *Glaucus* was pointing in the wrong direction. Soon the call came that the cable was up and down. It was quickly followed by the news that the anchor was aweigh. Even as the anchor was being raised and secured, *Glaucus* started to go astern until the rudder bit. The main topsails were released from their yards, and the frigate turned her bow away from the wind. A different string of orders was issued so that the jibs and the driver were raised, and all the square sails unfurled, the yards braced around, and all sails sheeted home. *Glaucus* gathered way on a larboard reach crossing the flagship's stern where Giles saw that both Admiral Stroganoff and his flag captain were watching. She then turned downwind, and Giles ordered the royals to be set. He knew that it was foolhardy to set all his sails while still in the anchorage, but he couldn't resist the show of bravado to demonstrate how a proper navy could handle its ships.

The wind was light, and the sky was clear so that the sun danced over the wavelets ahead as if they were sailing into a magic river whose surface was dotted with countless precious gems. Lieutenant Pirov called attention to passing sights. The most remarkable one was a huge palace in the baroque style built on an elevated site on the southern shore. It had a broad avenue leading down to the water. Lieutenant Pirov named the palace 'The Peterhof.' It was a summer residence of the Tsar, which Peter the Great had built to rival Europe's greatest palaces. Turning his telescope on the site, Giles was struck by the giant staircases descending from the palace, which had fountains between its two branches. When he asked the Russian lieutenant about them, he was told about the myriad of ponds and fountains that were a major feature of the palace's grounds, only a fraction of which could be seen from the ship. He added that one had to be careful in the grounds since there were trick fountains that could soak an unsuspecting viewer by coming on when he stepped on a particular stone. Apparently, the great tsar had liked practical jokes at the expense of his attendants. Giles determined that he must see this wonder while he was in St. Petersburg. He also wondered if it was possible to add fountains to the improvements he was undertaking at Dipton. He would have to discuss it with Daphne when he returned home.

As they sailed towards the city, Giles saw several rather large houses on the southern shore. Lieutenant Pirov said that they were dachas, which he explained were country homes where many of the wealthy and aristocratic families of St. Petersburg spent much of their summers. They could be reached by water in the summer and by sled during the winter.

As *Glaucus* glided eastward, it became evident that the way ahead seemed to be blocked by land. Consulting the chart, Giles realized that this was an island, and it soon became evident that they were also approaching the city. Lieutenant Pirov indicated that they should take the south channel where they would find the Imperial Dockyard and the Admiralty. They would moor in front of them where there was a quay.

As his ship moved towards the quay, Giles took a moment to look around. The island seemed to be joined to the mainland by a pontoon bridge beyond which the river broadened into an extensive basin. On the north shore, Giles could see a large fortress that would command and protect the Dockyard and Admiralty and effectively guard the end of the passage up which they were sailing. Rather strangely, there seemed to be a large church of rather exotic nature in the middle of the fortress. The waterfront on the south side was lined with baroque palaces in attractive pastel-colored stucco trimmed in glistening white. It was quite unlike any city Giles had ever seen.

Glaucus slid smoothly into her berth, deft sail-handling resulting in her losing all way just when they came to the correct spot so that her mooring lines could be handled with a minimum of effort. Giles took a moment to praise his officers and crew for a fine demonstration of seamanship from the start to finish of their short journey. Then he had to greet several officials who came on board the vessel. Lord Malthampton made the introductions. They seemed mainly to be there to establish links with Sir Walcott, who positively glowed at the attention. As they conversed loudly in French, Lord Malthampton drifted over to stand close to Giles.

"After we have left," the Ambassador began, "Lieutenant Pirov will suggest that you take a walk to see some of the city. Please go with him. Somewhere along the way, when he is sure you are not under surveillance, he will slip you into the Admiralty to meet with Count Smirnov, the naval minister. I am sorry about this subterfuge, but St. Petersburg is crawling with people who would love to tell Bonaparte or the Prussians all about your doings, and it would be best if as little was known about your real mission as possible."

"Aye, aye, my Lord."

"Oh, these are not orders, just suggestions to help you have a successful visit to St. Petersburg. There will be a reception at my house, which is also the British Embassy, this evening. Bring your officers and your midshipmen. Warn them about how strong vodka is."

"Very good, my Lord."

Further conversation was made impossible by Sir Walcott bellowing, "Captain Giles. I will be departing for the Embassy now. I shall require all my belongings to be removed from the hold and sent to the Embassy immediately. And I shall require my servants who have been helping you as sailors."

"I am afraid that the last part will be quite impossible, Sir Walcott. They volunteered to serve in His Majesty's Navy, and they cannot be released now. You were warned what would happen if you tried to be attended by more than two people."

"That is absurd. I cannot possibly do with only two servants. It was bad enough that you deprived me of their service on board, but it would be intolerable here in the Capital. Absolutely impossible! I demand that you release them immediately."

"I am afraid that I cannot."

"I must insist that they be released immediately. Otherwise, the Prince of Wales will hear about it, I can assure you, and the consequences for you will be dire."

"What an obnoxious fool," Lord Malthampton murmured. "I suppose you have had to put up with this all the way here." The Ambassador had clearly taken a strong dislike to Sir Walcott on their short voyage from Kronstadt.

"Sir Walcott," Lord Malthampton continued in a louder voice, "I should advise you not to threaten a captain on his own quarterdeck. He would have every right to throw you in irons. Now come along, I should be getting back to the Embassy. Captain Giles, thank you for the cruise. I will arrange for boats to take Sir Walcott's luggage to the Embassy. I look forward to seeing you again this evening. I hope that, in the interim, you will be able to find time to see some of the city. It is quite amazing."

As all the other visitors were leaving, with Sir Walcott jostling with Lord Malthampton about who would lead the way, Lieutenant Pirov approached Giles, "Captain," he said in a loud voice, "I understand that you would like to see something of St Petersburg. I can offer myself as a guide."

"I would indeed enjoy seeing this remarkable city. Thank you, Mr. Pirov."

"Then may I suggest that you wear a less ornate uniform. We don't want to call attention to ourselves."

Giles went below to put on civilian clothes. The suggestion seemed eminently reasonable to him. Naval officers in England usually did not wear their uniforms when ashore and not on immediate ship's business. While doing so, he asked Carstairs, who was assisting him, about Sir Walcott's former servants.

"How are they fitting in, Carstairs."

"Remarkably well, for the most part, sir. You know that many of the crew, indeed almost all of them, despise molly boys, though quite a few will bugger a shipmate or allow themselves to be buggered in the right circumstances. Most of Sir Walcott's men fit in quite well since they don't act like bum-boys all the time. Indeed, they claim that they only served Sir Walcott because the pay and food weres good, and they were not averse to some back-door play if it made life easier. Generally, they prefer women to men, but there is no return to that. Some of the lads still find Sir Walcott's entourage distasteful, but the new men are trying to pull their weight and so fit in pretty well. The worst of the catamites are those that Sir Walcott retained as servants on board, but one of the others, who claims he did not get buggered by Sir Walcott, a man called Hawkins, is a different kettle of fish. He is a bully and has already been dealt with a couple of times for trying to force himself on others."

"Do I need to take notice of his actions?"

"I don't think so. The crew are onto him and will continue to make it clear that he will pay for forcing his attentions on anyone or bullying them."

"Very good, Carstairs. Now I must go with Lieutenant Pirov."

The two officers set off along the quay going east and soon came to a junction of roads, including the one leading immediately to the pontoon bridge. The major street leading inland was called Nevsky Prospect, and Pirov turned into it. Giles was struck by how wide the street was. It made Piccadilly in London look like a narrow lane. He was also surprised by the number of canals that intersected the street and, looking along the waterways, how few other bridges there seemed to be, and how many boats were plying the waters.

"Most of the traffic in St. Petersburg is on the canals, boats in summer, sleighs in winter. The canals all freeze solid in the winter and provide good roads," explained Lieutenant Pirov. Giles wondered what happened in the fall and spring when the ice was too thin to take a sleigh, but the waterways were not yet navigable by boats. Lieutenant Pirov's explanation did not clear up his puzzlement.

Before going very far along the broad street, they came to a huge shopping emporium crowded with people examining a complete range of goods. Lieutenant Pirov named it 'Gostiny Dvor,' or so Giles thought, though he had trouble with the accent as the Lieutenant reverted to what struck Giles as a very thick Russian-type pronunciation when he gave place names.

Lieutenant Pirov insisted on wandering through the emporium, frequently stopping to examine various items on display. Suddenly he took Giles's arm and drew him behind one small stall and out through a narrow exit into some sort of lane that was not connected to the main street. They went a short distance along the passageway with the Lieutenant looking back frequently.

"Ah good, we are not being followed," he said.

"Followed?"

"Yes, Captain Giles. St Petersburg is a hotbed of spying, and the arrival of a special envoy on a British frigate will certainly have caught the attention of the French spies and their helpers and probably the Austrian and Prussian ones as well. Even the Turks will wonder why you are here. It is very easy to lose someone in Gostiny Dvor without the watchers being sure that shaking them off was our intention. Now we can go about the real business of our little stroll."

Lieutenant Pirov guided Giles to a landing stage on a nearby canal, where they boarded a boat. "We are going to the Admiralty. The Minister of the Navy wishes to see you and does not want others to know of your meeting."

The boat wound through several canals before stopping at another landing stage, closer to the heart of the city.

"We are actually very close to the Admiralty here," Giles's guide stated. Lieutenant Pirov led them to a nearby entrance to a garden, and ducked into it. A few steps took them to a modest door, possibly a servants' entrance, into a large building. Inside, they found themselves in an office building rather than a private residence. The office that Lieutenant Pirov sought was almost immediately at hand, and he showed Giles inside without their being seen by anyone else.

A short, slim, older man rose to greet them. He was fashionably dressed in an elaborately embroidered coat, cut away to reveal britches in a matching fabric, while silk stockings and shoes with two-inch heels sporting bejeweled buckles adorned his feet. He was displaying his own hair tied back in a queue, which was a light gray color without the aid of powder.

"Count Smirnov, let me introduce Captain Giles of His Britannic Majesty's Navy. Count Smirnov is our Minister of the Navy," Lieutenant Pirov said in English.

"Thank you, Lieutenant. You may leave us now. I'll call you when we are done," was the Count's reply. When the lieutenant had complied, the Count turned to Giles and said, in impeccable English, "I apologize for the clandestine nature of this meeting, Sir Richard. Rumors about a secret treaty with your country have been circulating. Sir Walcott is here to quash them, though I hope he doesn't realize it, so we don't want it known that you and I are meeting privately."

"I understand, my lord."

"Did you bring any documents with you?"

"Only this, which I was told to present to you."

Giles handed over the sealed letter that Sir David McDougall had given him. The Count broke the seal and looked at the letter. He laughed. "I see that your people are adept at discouraging spies or others into whose hands secret messages might fall."

"Sir?"

"See for yourself."

The Count handed over the letter. All it said was, "He speaks for me," followed by the Prime Minister's signature.

"Would you like a glass of wine, Captain? I find that it eases conversation at this hour."

"Gladly, my lord."

The Minister poured two glass of what turned out to be a very good claret, and they sat across from each other in comfortable chairs. Giles outlined the terms of the agreement he was authorized to offer and then went into various details, with Count Smirnov asking many questions. He seemed to be particularly interested in the pledge that the Skagerrak would be kept open no matter what France, Denmark, or Sweden did. Luckily, Giles had been given all the information needed to answer the Minister's questions.

After an hour of intense discussion, the Minister was satisfied. "Thank you, Captain Giles. Of course, I will have to present this to the Tsar, but I hope to give you his response shortly. Lord Malthampton is handling the land side of things, but that is really only a confirmation of what already exists. I do hope the special envoy you brought is up to his task. It would be nice to fool the French completely.

"There is the reception at the British Embassy this evening. I will be there, but we must pretend not to have met already. Lieutenant Pirov will take you back to your ship – what is she called again?"

"*Glaucus*, my lord."

"Strange name. Anyway, the lieutenant will make sure that it appears that you are concluding your sight-seeing trip around St. Petersburg."

Lieutenant Pirov was summoned. He and Giles returned to the boat by the same unobtrusive route, with the lieutenant making sure that the coast was clear before they snuck away from the building by the same door. Giles was then treated to an extensive trip through St. Petersburg's canals, finishing in the river where they returned to *Glaucus*, passing on the way a magnificent, green, baroque palace that the lieutenant identified as the Tsar's Winter Palace. Giles was quite overwhelmed by the baroque building. He idly wondered what Dipton Hall would look like if it were stuccoed over in a robin's egg blue with its main features and decorations outlined in white. He shook his head at this speculation. Dipton Hall was the wrong shape and built with the wrong type of material to be treated successfully in this way, and such a residence would look ridiculously out of place in the English countryside. He would just have to enjoy the architecture here fully, not then try to imitate it at home. However, he must see if he could find some colored etchings of St. Petersburg to take home to remind him of this unique city and to show to Daphne.

Before leaving the Embassy ship, Giles issued firm orders that none of the crew was to venture off the ship. He also assembled his seamen and pointed out that their host had requested that shore leave not be granted until they had returned to Kronstadt. This was to be taken seriously. Punishment for venturing ashore would be severe.

Giles took his barge to travel to the British Embassy by the canals. The Embassy was another fine palace on one of the canals. It was ablaze with light, as Lord Malthouse was sparing no expense to emphasize the importance of the special ambassador and to give the appearance that he still regarded himself as the number one representative of his King. The reception rooms were crowded with men in their best court clothes and ladies dressed in the height of fashion, clothes which undoubtedly came directly from France, even though none of them, Giles was sure, would endorse the subversive French ideas that had given rise to the new, looser styles.

The conversations were all in French, though most of the men spoke some sort of English when they were introduced to Giles. Lord Malthouse must have selected his guest list with that qualification in mind. Giles was chatting with a couple of men who had been introduced to him as merchants when he found himself somewhat isolated as everyone turned to observe the ruckus that Sir Walcott was creating. The special ambassador had been the center of a rather loud circle, and as other conversations developed, he kept raising his voice in an attempt to dominate the room. In this, he succeeded, as everyone stopped talking, wondering what the noise was all about. The baronet was exquisitely dressed, and his face had 'benefitted,' Giles thought, by the application of rouge and powder. He was now almost shouting in French. Giles was sure that he caught the phrase 'le Prince de Galles' many times. Sir Walcott must be boasting about his important connections.

"Your countryman seems to be very much in awe of himself, Captain," a light voice remarked behind him.

Giles turned to see a lady seated behind where he had been standing. "My apologies, madam, I didn't notice that I was blocking your view. You are?"

"Countess Maria Nicholaevna Donskaya. Lord Malthampton neglected to introduce us. I hope you are enjoying St. Petersburg."

"Immensely, my lady. I was taken on a most fascinating tour of the city today, not only through the streets, but mostly through the canals."

"Then you may have passed our palace. You must come and visit it. It is quite distinctive, and I would very much enjoy having your company."

"You speak remarkably good English, my lady. Have you visited England?"

"No. However, my father was of the opinion that England would become a more important country than France would, and the future lay in learning your language perfectly. My governess was English, and he encouraged her to make sure that I talked correctly. She was very strict, I must tell you, but it succeeded. Lord Malthampton says I speak perfect English though with somewhat of a Dorset accent."

"Does the Count share your excellent ability to speak English? I don't believe that I have been introduced to him either."

"No, he does not speak it at all, just French. He is not here tonight. In fact, he is away visiting his estates before the winter closes in. His holdings lie beyond Moscow, quite out in the country. Very boring. Very isolated. Very far away. He will be gone for several weeks, and I just rattle around in our palace as best I can.

"You may think my way of dressing is peculiar, Captain Giles," the Countess continued. "When I heard of the shocking murder of Queen, Marie Antoinette, I resolved never to dress in French fashions again, or at least not until the proper monarchy was restored. And I have kept to my resolve, even though most of the other ladies in St. Petersburg have succumbed to the revolutionary French fashions."

Giles, for the first time, examined the Countess closely. He had not been astonished by the way she was dressed, partly because he usually paid no attention to fashion and, he suddenly realized, his general impression was that she was just like he remembered his aunt having been as he was growing up. Now examining her, he became aware that she was only about his own age, certainly no older. She sat very stiffly on the edge of her chair, and he guessed that this must be the result of a tight corset, a garment that had passed almost completely from fashion, at least among younger women. In his opinion, it was a ridiculous garment, and he had been delighted with Daphne from the start because of her casual way of dressing. The top of the Countess's gown was cut to emphasize her plump breasts that were forced unnaturally up by her undergarment. Below her narrow waist, her skirts billowed out in what he realized was some sort of hoop skirt. Her face was very heavily rouged and powdered, giving no hint of what her skin might really be like, and he noticed that this continued down through her neck and her cleavage. However, this striking, but now that he examined it, very old-fashioned style was quite outdone by her headdress. It was formed by weaving her hair so that it stood straight up, elaborate, beribboned, and bejeweled. In the midshipmen's birth of his first ship, such arrangements had been the subject of intense conversation, as was every aspect of female dress, and how it was to be dealt with in amorous situations. He knew that such a complicated arrangement was meant to stay in place for weeks and would make sleeping awkward, not to mention many other activities in which his peers had been interested. The same was presumably true here.

His thoughts had slightly diverted him from the Countess's words, but he gathered that she had been discussing the contrasts between English houses and St. Petersburg's palaces. She was waxing eloquent about their differences, claiming that, though she had never seen the English ones, she was sure that the Russian ones in St. Petersburg, though not in the rest of Russia, were far superior. Giles diplomatically replied that it was very difficult to evaluate the differences properly when they could never be placed side by side. He was asserting that probably each should be considered well suited to their location. This the Countess disputed this and argued that they could compare them directly.

"Lord Malthampton has a display of engravings illustrating the contrast between Russian and English mansions. Let's go look at them to enlighten our discussion of the differences."

She rose gracefully to her feet and clamped her hand on Giles's arm. "It's this way," she announced, guiding them towards a passageway that appeared to be leading to a secluded part of the mansion.

"Is this wise, my lady? Won't it hurt your reputation?"

"Oh, puff to that! We won't be noticed," she replied, using her grip on his arm to draw Giles out of the room and down a hallway leading farther into the Embassy. Giles complied, not knowing what else to do and not wanting to protest in a way that would draw attention to his dilemma. After a short distance, the Countess opened a door and directed him into a small sitting room that was unoccupied. Along one wall, there were indeed pictures of various buildings, but instead of drawing Giles to them, the Countess spun him around so that he faced her.

"This is so much more private, isn't it?" she breathed and planted a kiss on his lips. Giles sprang back, horrified at what had happened, even though it fulfilled the start of many a fantasy he had had as a young officer. Those dreams had never included the foul odor that came from the Countess's lip as she kissed him. His revulsion was increased when he looked down to avoid her eyes and spotted a flea on her breast. He wondered if the heavy paint prevented it from biting her. Directing his gaze above her eyes, he spotted a mouse peek out from her elaborate headdress. Now totally flummoxed, he could only stammer, "My lady, we must not! Not here! Your reputation and my standing as a representative of my country are at peril! We must return to Lord Malthampton's reception."

Giles could hardly wait to flee from the room, but good manners intervened, and he again offered his arm to his companion. When she grabbed it once more, he sealed his link with her by placing his right hand over hers and dragged her back into the hallway.

"You are right, of course, Captain," the lady murmured. "But being near you quite overcame me. We must be discreet, but you can certainly visit me tomorrow at my palace. My servants are the height of discretion."

Giles was still afraid of causing a scene if he openly rejected her advances and was determined to avoid having anything to do with Countess Donskaya. "I shall look forward to visiting, my lady," he said. "Very much so provided that my duties on board my ship, or connected with her, will allow me the opportunity. Now that we are back in the reception hall, I find myself very thirsty. I must look for drinks."

Though he had seemed to imply that he was seeking refreshments for both of them, he was only concerned with being able to avoid the Countess completely. Sir Walcott must have spent the time during which Giles had been absent, imbibing some of Lord Malthampton's brandy, for his voice had become still louder even though the group around him had shrunk. Giles also noted that some of the officers from *Glaucus* had been drinking enthusiastically, while Midshipman Stewart seemed to be becoming enmeshed in the web of a young, matronly lady who seemed to be quite taken with the young man. Giles gathered his party together and approached Lord Malthampton to take his leave.

"Good of you to come, Captain Giles," said the Ambassador. "I trust you enjoyed yourself. I see you somehow avoided Maria Nicholaevna's clutches. Not many do."

The irony of this remark did not escape Giles, but he said nothing. He was simply glad to be returning to the safety of his ship after a very busy day and tortuous evening.

Chapter XVII

Captain Giles had the rare pleasure of sleeping beyond dawn the following morning. He arose at one bell of the forenoon watch to find that there had been a couple of developments while he slept. First, and pleasantly, there were invitations to a ball that the Tsar was holding that evening. Not so pleasantly, eight of his crew members had been forcibly returned to the ship with complaints that they had been involved in a fight in a tavern. The brawl had resulted in some damage to the establishment. The offenders had been escorted to the frigate in the early hours of the morning by some sort of municipal watch force. They were left there with strong requests that the perpetrators be punished and that such conduct not occur again. To emphasize the latter request, Giles saw that a group of soldiers was strung out along the quay. Mr. Stewart suspected that they were there to ensure that more members of his crew did not slip ashore and repeat the offense.

Giles was angry at this turn of events, for he had already told the crew that there would be no leave in St. Petersburg until he knew more about their plans. He had stressed that, when permission to go ashore was granted, each of them would be expected to conduct himself in an orderly fashion, showing respect for the country in which they were visitors. He even reminded them that they were as individuals and as groups representatives of their king and country and should make sure that they would continue to be welcome guests. Obviously, the offenders had not been impressed by his address. He should not have been surprised, however. It would usually take more than a lecture to keep sailors in port away from the grog and knocking shops. Still, he had hoped his crew was an exception. He did take comfort in the fact that the number of offenders who had been caught and returned to the ship was small. He wondered how many others had also gone ashore but had been more discreet in their peccadillos.

There was no point in delaying the punishment of the men whose behavior had caused the problem. Dealing with them promptly would allow the tension that he had felt on coming on deck to subside. The whole crew would be waiting to discover what would happen to the miscreants. He summoned them with their divisional officers to his cabin. They were, in fact, all in Mr. Correll's division. That fact surprised Giles since Mr. Correll had spent his time as a midshipman on Giles's vessels with mostly the same crew and was well-liked and trusted. He did note that two of the offenders were Sir Walcott's former servants, and they could not have been expected to have developed much loyalty to *Glaucus*.

Mr. Correll stated the offenses that had been committed: leaving the ship without permission, getting drunk in some tavern, and getting into a fight with Russian sailors in the same dive. That had led to the watch being summoned and the culprits being delivered unceremoniously to the boat. The miscreants had been unresponsive about what caused the fight though they claimed they were the innocent victims of Russian aggression.

Giles had no choice but to punish all the defaulters. He was not a flogging captain, and he had a painful feeling that he himself should have foreseen the problem better and that he should have tried to forestall it by stationing marine sentries along the quay. Not doing so had been a mistake even though he suspected that, if his sailors had wanted to defy him, they would have found a way past the sentries.

He did impose a punishment that he knew was likely to be the most effective in preventing a recurrence of the offense: he stopped their rum ration for the next three weeks. For most of the crew, the issuing of a tot of rum was the highlight of their day, and every one of the offenders would be reminded of how they had disappointed their commander and blemished the good name of their ship each time they had to watch the rest of their mates getting tots in the normal fashion while they could only look on with no solace.

Next, Giles ordered that the whole crew be assembled on deck. Speaking from the quarterdeck railing, he reminded them again that they were their country's representatives, but the meat of his lecture came when he announced what the penalties were for those who had ignored his first command. He forcefully promised that, in future, any man who left the ship without permission would have his rum suspended for one month and also would be flogged. His crew knew that he only resorted to the lash when offenses involved stealing from shipmates. This departure from the norm should indicate how very seriously he considered the matter. Giles, they knew, did not issue idle threats so that all of them should now be fully aware of how very seriously he regarded the matter.

The ball that evening was held in the Tsar's Winter Palace on the banks of the Neva River. It was not in honor of the British visitors but had some other reason for being held that Giles did not understand. They arrived at the watergate to the palace and were directed to the main staircase, a magnificent doubled structure that led to the ballroom, a vast hall brightly illuminated by elaborate chandeliers and featuring a most intricate parquet floor. Lieutenant Pirov gave their names to a richly liveried servant who, in turn, shouted them out. Lord Malthampton immediately came over to introduce them to many of the important dignitaries present, most of whom had not been at his own reception. Many of the men who had been introduced on the previous evening bowed to Giles politely even before he could acknowledge them while the women responded with curtsies to his bows. The one exception was Countess Maria Nicholaevna Donskaya, still wearing her outdated clothes and with the same elaborate headdress. She pointedly turned away, ignoring his bow. He was quite happy to be cut by her and wondered naughtily whether her mouse had given birth to more little rodents.

With Giles and his officers well supplied with people to talk with, Lord Malthampton drifted off towards a group where Sir Walcott was holding forth. Soon the orchestra was heard tuning up before launching into a stately minuet. Giles at the time had been talking with a lady to whom he had been introduced, although he had not quite caught her name. He had heard that she was a princess, so he could use her honorific title in polite conversation. She spoke impeccable, though highly accented, English.

Giles loved to dance, and seeing that the first place on the Princess's card had yet to be taken, he took the opportunity to ask her to join him in the stately dance. Unlike the Countess, the Princess was wearing a gown in the latest French style, in a light fabric, tied beneath her bust, but, otherwise, free-flowing. It left little to the imagination about what the dress concealed, and Giles noted that the Princess had a very attractive figure. She seemed to be flirting with him and brushing against him more than the dance required. Her conversation revealed that her husband was away and that her palace was magnificent. He would undoubtedly find it fascinating. When the minuet finished, Giles escorted the Princess back to her group, but he did secure another place on her dance card.

There was a great disparity between the numbers of men and women who were in the ballroom. A large number of the men had resorted to the card rooms, leaving their partners to fend for themselves. Giles had little interest in cards and less in gambling. Surprisingly for one who would take huge, aggressive risks when faced with an enemy ship, he found that he disliked losing more than he liked winning in a situation where skill played only a small role. He noted that the young girls or ladies were usually closely chaperoned and discovered that his invitations to dance were not welcomed by the chaperones. However, many of the other women, even quite young ones, were unchaperoned and were more than happy to dance with him. As he surmised, these were married ladies whose husbands were absent or were otherwise engaged in the card rooms. They were attractive, vivacious, and flirtatious. He was enjoying himself immensely.

A waltz was the dance that corresponded to his next entry on the Princess's dance card. In the more intimate dance, there was no mistaking her lascivious movements. Their meaning was confirmed when she whispered to him towards the end of the dance, "Let's find a private room. Better yet, why don't you come with me to my palace, where we can be completely alone?"

Giles was totally taken aback by this suggestion. "Your Highness … Princess … your reputation! Surely our absence will be noted."

"Pooh. Everyone does it. It is the French way, and French customs are still very much in fashion here despite France being taken over by that vulgar upstart, Bonaparte, who calls himself an emperor. A modicum of discretion is all that is required. Let us leave now, quietly."

Giles hardly knew what to do. As a midshipman or lieutenant, such an invitation was the stuff of ardent fantasies, but he had never before faced the actual opportunity. Much to his own surprise, when push came to shove, he found he did not want to be seduced by the Princess. This feeling was heightened when she leaned close to him, and he found that her breath reeked. He also noticed that her heavy application of perfume did not disguise more pungent odors. He would never have guessed it, but Daphne had clearly raised his requirements for romantic dalliance. Indeed, he realized that he really didn't seriously want to be involved with anyone but his wife. Was he getting old? A year ago, before he had met Daphne, he would have jumped at the chance of being alone with a lovely young woman. Surely, it couldn't be that, after Daphne, he would be settling for second best. Wasn't it Admiral Nelson who was said to have remarked that all men were bachelors east of Gibraltar? That did not correspond to what he was now feeling. How the old Giles would have laughed uproariously if he had been told about the foolishness of the new husband. The new Giles was happy to leave the old Giles behind, though with some pangs of regret.

"Ah, Madam … Princess … Your Highness," he stuttered, wondering how to refuse her offer without giving too great offense. After all, he had no idea how important and influential she or her husband might be. His mission called for diplomacy. "Madam … I cannot, regrettably."

"Of course, you can, Or are you like your countryman over there?" she inquired, nodding to where

Sir Walcott was holding forth surrounded by a set of men whose interest in the latest fashions was on display.

"No…no…no, Madam. Ugh …ugh," inspiration came to him then. "The problem is that I have to be available at a moment's notice. Last night, some of my crew caused a most regrettable disturbance. It should not happen tonight, but it may, and I must be available to deal with its consequences immediately if the problem does happen to repeat itself. I am afraid that being here as part of a diplomatic mission means that my time is not my own."

The waltz had ended. Giles was escorting a clearly, highly annoyed Princess to her chair when a servant approached him. As if the gods were hand in glove with him, the man said to him in a low voice, "Sir, there has been a disturbance involving your ship, and your presence is required urgently."

Giles gathered Lieutenant Pirov and some of his officers together and set off to find his barge. Lieutenant Hendricks had left with Countess Donskaya, and Midshipman Stewart had left with the same noblewoman as on the previous evening. He would just have to do without them for the moment.

On returning to *Glaucus*, Giles found a very angry Russian official and a dozen members of his crew huddled together, most of them showing signs of a very rough fight. He noted that the Russian guard on the quay had been doubled. The story emerged in steps. Lieutenant Correll, who had been taking the harbor watch, had no explanation as to how the culprits had been able to leave the ship and evade both *Glaucus*'s marines and the Russian guards. The first he knew of their absence was when the official, some sort of magistrate or captain of the city guard, had arrived with the miscreants. One of them had been bleeding from a knife wound. He was now being treated in the sick-bay. The civic official – his actual position being beyond Lieutenant Pirov's ability to translate – reported in the most aggressive tones that the gang from *Glaucus* had entered a tavern, already somewhat inebriated, and had assaulted both the barmaid and then the man who came to protect her. A general fight broke out, in which two Russians had been knifed, with serious wounds. It had required troops to subdue *Glaucus*'s men. The official expected the miscreants to receive severe punishment. He was not concerned apparently about recompense for the damage caused because the dive was a thorn in the civic authorities' sides.

Giles himself was seething with rage. The offenders had deliberately defied his orders and, in doing so, had besmirched the good name of his ship and of all their mess-mates. Clearly, stopping their rum ration had not been a sufficient deterrent. He would have to resort to more severe punishments. He might as well start now.

"Throw them in the brig – in irons," he said to the master-at-arms." I'll deal with them fully at two bells in the forenoon watch. Mr. Shearer, prepare the cats for use in their punishment."

That was such an unusual order coming from Giles that the bosun stared at his captain for a few moments before answering, "Aye, aye, sir."

Giles stepped close to the bosun. "Make them as light as you can, except for the one for Hawkins there." He said *sotto voce*. Hawkins was the former servant of Sir Walcott, who had been involved in the previous offense.

"Make his cat more severe, but not knotted at the ends – that is only for thieves no matter how angry I am."

Giles had trouble sleeping that night. He felt betrayed and was deeply disturbed that the crew, whom he had thought were behind him, had so blatantly flouted an order. Had he been naïve? Should he be like the other, "flogging" captains? He didn't believe in flogging. He did not like to rule by threat of severe physical damage. Besides, even a mild flogging made a man unfit for duty for a while, and a severe one rendered him useless for an extended period.

After tossing and turning for half an hour, Giles summoned Carstairs to his cabin.

"What is going on, Carstairs?"

"The ring leader is Hawkins, sir. The others are not very bright and are easily led astray. Hawkins told them that they could easily stay out of trouble if they drank quietly and didn't respond to any Russian slights. Soon after they entered the pub, Hawkins assaulted the barmaid, first trying to fondle her and then striking her when she resisted. When the barman tried to intervene, Hawkins punched him so hard that he knocked him out and may have broken his jaw. The other customers came to the barman's aid, and a general fight broke out. I am afraid our weak-minded crew-members thought that they had to stand up for their shipmate, even though he was clearly in the wrong. In the course of that, Hawkins pulled out a knife and stabbed one of the Russians. They also pulled knives, and it was getting very ugly when the watch intervened."

"I hate the mess that this Hawkins has got us into."

"Can't you get rid of him -- give him back to Sir Walcott or something?"

"No. We're stuck with him."

"Well, the rest of the crew do not like him. The other three we pressed from Sir Walcott are all right, but not Hawkins. All the officers know that he is bad news, but there isn't much that they can do about it."

"I'll be extra clear to the officers and the petty officers to be on the watch for any bullying or unnatural practices involving Hawkins, but it will have to be pretty decisively wrong to warrant hanging him. Make sure you let me know if there is more trouble."

"Aye, aye, sir."

Despite his broken night, Giles was up and dressed as usual before dawn. It was just as well that he was. At seven bells of the morning watch, a liveried messenger from the Admiralty arrived with a summons for Giles to appear for an audience with the Navy Minister at nine o'clock.

Giles dressed in his best uniform with his display sword; he used a cutlass when it came to boarding an enemy. He mounted the steps of the Admiralty at the appointed hour with Lieutenant Pirov, and they were shown directly into the Minister's room.

"Captain Giles," said the Minister, "welcome. Lieutenant, you may leave us. Captain Giles, I am very unhappy about the behavior of your crew. I had expected better of you."

This was said in a very loud voice before the door to his room was closed. Before Giles could reply, the minister winked at him and lowered his voice. "Most regrettable, though I suppose one cannot expect sailors not to get ashore if they can find a way. It does give me an excuse to see you in a way that would lead no one to surmise that our meeting is connected with secret negotiations. Before we get to that, I have to demand that your men, who did considerable damage and wounded several of our people, be punished. Visibly. I have heard that you are not a flogging captain, but seeing the culprits thrashed on your deck would go a long way to resolving things. A bit of blood would be good. You can expect that a crowd will gather behind our guards to witness the punishment.

"It would be a good idea, I think, if you returned to Kronstadt now. There is far less chance of your men getting into trouble when your ship is at anchor rather than moored to a quay. Furthermore, Kronstadt is better able to deal with sailors who have come ashore for a drink. You, of course, can still participate in social engagements here if you want to. It is not a long boat ride. I don't want to deprive society of your company. I have heard you have escaped the clutches of two of our sirens already, but I am sure that others would like to try their chance."

Giles had not appreciated how efficient was the gossip network at the Court. He was now doubly glad that he had not taken up the offers that had been made to him.

The two men then discussed the terms of the agreement that Giles had presented earlier. The minister wanted some clarification that Giles supplied and asked that His Majesty's Government consider a couple of additional provisions that he thought would be mutually beneficial, but the Tsar's Government was ready to enter into the secret treaty in any case.

With everything settled amicably, the Minister rose and accompanied Giles to the door of his room. As he opened it, he resumed his loud voice. "See that those punishments are carried out, Captain Giles! Then you must take your ship to Kronstadt and wait there for Sir Walcott to finish his business. Your crew's behavior has been totally despicable! Lieutenant Pirov will continue to accompany you." Since this declaration was accompanied by another big wink, hidden from the people in the outer room, Giles assumed a crest-fallen visage and apologized once more most humbly. Overall, he was very pleased with the meeting. His mission was accomplished, the punishment demanded was only the one he had already resolved to inflict on the offenders, and he was sure that Kronstadt would be a much more suitable place for *Glaucus*.

When he returned to his ship, Giles immediately ordered that the crew be assembled to witness punishment. The charge was read; the sentence was pronounced. The customary next step in the ceremony was interrupted by Hawkins, "You can't do this. Sir Walcott always protected me. He encouraged me to take my pleasures in taverns so that I could fulfill my duties better."

"Silence," roared Lieutenant Correll in whose division Hawkins had been placed.

"I won't. I have Sir Walcott's protection."

"No, you do not," said Giles coldly. "Mr. Shearer, gag this man so he cannot further disrupt these proceedings. Now rig the grating and let the cat out of the bag*."

As the Naval Minister had predicted, a large crowd had assembled on shore, waiting to witness the Royal Navy's version of punishment. The first culprit was lashed to a grating placed so that the crowd could not see the victim's back. The bosun himself administered the first half dozen strokes. From afar, they may have appeared to be very vicious blows, but, in fact, they only produced light pink welts on the miscreant's back. When the last stroke of the whip had landed, a bucket of water was thrown on the man's back, and he was cut down and taken from sight. Giles knew that the crew member's punishment came more from the embarrassment of being humbled before his peers rather than any actual pain being inflicted by this very light flogging.

The next ten offenders were treated in exactly the same way. When the last one was cut down, something happened to the grating so that it was rotated through a quarter circle. When Hawkins was tied to it, both his back and his face were visible to watchers on the quay. This change in what the spectators could see resulted in considerable shifting of places among them. Some seemed to prefer to witness the changes in the man's back produced by the whip while others wanted to concentrate on what was shown on his face as the searingly painful blows landed.

Mr. Shearer took the last cat from its baize bag. Those crew members who were close enough to distinguish its features clearly could see that the whip was made of a thicker, rougher, and stiffer rope than the preceding ones, and its tails were longer. It was also evident to the crew members that the bosun put much more energy into the blows and let the tails wrap farther around to the victim's side. That it hurt was exhibited by a loud shriek that followed the first blow and each one that followed. The thrashing soon produced moans and curses that filled the space between the lashes, though the curses lost their force by the eighth stroke and became whines begging that the punishment cease. After the twelfth strike, Mr. Shearer surrendered the cat to one of his mates, who continued with gusto to lay on the next two dozen. Hawkins' sounds died down to only soft mewling, and he was hanging loosely in his bindings by the time the punishment was finished. His back was bleeding freely from dozens of places where the cat's tails had broken his skin.

"Cut him down and take him to the surgeon," Giles commanded when the ordeal was finished. He turned away, sickened by the harm he had had inflicted. The man would likely be useless and in great pain for several days. However, he had had no choice, and he was sure that his crew realized that this was the case.

When the grating had been washed and returned to its place, and the deck had been swabbed to remove the evidence of what had taken place, Giles gave orders for the ship to get underway. He was surprised at how cheerfully the crew responded. It came to him that most of the sailors had welcomed the comeuppance of a very nasty character. They thought that the punishment, harsh as it had been, was fully justified. Indeed, they were quite happy to see that particular crew-mate reduced to a mewling lump of shattered nerves and skin. What he could not understand was how other captains could routinely inflict far harsher punishments or why mutinies against such brutal treatment were not much more common.

Before long, *Glaucus* was ready to cast off. Giles was pleased to see that the punishment parade had not reduced the crew's efficiency in any way and that they seemed as happy as he was to leave behind the quay in front of the Admiralty. He knew that his visits into society would be far less frequent and that carrying out his mission would be less fraught with the need to avoid seductive advances. However, reducing social hazards did not reduce his wish that he could sail for home right now. What in the world was happening at Dipton? Particularly, had Daphne given birth? Had the delivery gone smoothly? Did she regret that she had chosen a husband who could not be with her at such a crucial time?

Chapter XVIII

Daphne stretched out on a chaise longue near the blazing fire in her bedroom. She was indulging herself this morning. She had rolled over and gone back to sleep when Betsey woke her at the usual time and ordered breakfast in bed, something she usually did not want to have. She would dress later. For now, she was reading a novel and luxuriating in a guilty feeling that she really should be doing something useful.

It had been a busy couple of weeks since she and Lord David had returned from London. One way or another, she had been involved in her step-nieces' activities. Lydia was making quite heavy weather of her wedding plans, and Lady Marianne was not much help. Daphne's organizing ability was frequently called upon to smooth out tangles that her niece had produced.

Captain Bolton had had to go back to his ship, and Catherine had been moping about the house, convinced that her one chance at happiness had evaporated. Daphne had not been so sure since he had committed himself to coming to Lydia's wedding, provided that he had not been ordered to take his ship to sea on an urgent task. When the time did come, he had been able to return to Dipton on the day before the wedding.

Captain Bolton had asked to see Daphne almost as soon as he arrived at Dipton. In a rather stuttering but deliberate way, he had got down to his concerns. Daphne had to listen to a lengthy description of how much wealth he had already collected from prize money, what his prospects might be of gaining more and what his salary would be both on full pay and on half-pay. Daphne was finding this a bit tedious, though she did not show it. She already guessed what this catalog of finances was leading up to and had already evaluated what it suggested in terms of Captain Bolton's ability to support a wife. She was wondering whether he was intending to try to bargain over a dowry for Catherine.

Finally, the catalog ended. Captain Bolton summed up the situation. "Lady Ashton, I believe that my resources allow me to marry and to keep a wife in a comfortable style. I understand that Catherine is the ward of Captain Giles, and normally I would have directed all this recitation to him, but, of course, he is at sea. I understand that you have the authority to manage all his affairs."

"What is it you want to discuss?" asked Daphne, pretending that she did not know why he had inflicted his financial situation on her.

"Why, my lady, I am seeking permission to ask for Miss Crocker's hand in marriage. I believe that I can provide her with a secure future."

"Oh, dear," thought Daphne, "I hope he can be more romantic when he talks to Catherine. He hasn't struck me as such a cold fish before this."

What she said to Captain Bolton, however, was quite different. "Have you asked Miss Crocker to marry you, Captain?"

"No, of course not, Lady Ashton. I could see no point in doing that if she couldn't get permission to marry. I realize that my roots, though thoroughly respectable, are not on a level with hers."

Daphne almost choked on this statement. She knew that Captain Bolton's father was a rector in a rural parish in Norfolk. He certainly was a gentleman and well educated, though he was not rich. How far was that background from what she had been discovering about the status of Giles's half-brothers, his destitute half-sister, and his appalling father? They might be from the aristocracy and so automatically would be considered part of elevated society, but there was no question that Catherine was not part of that milieu. Anyone marrying her would not be acquiring any elevated social status to be derived from who her grandfather was. Indeed, Captain Bolton's claim to be a gentleman was stronger than her father's, and Daphne was fully aware that Giles did not think he had lost status by marrying her rather than some woman with a more aristocratically strong pedigree.

"I guess that I can give you permission to court Miss Crocker, Captain Bolton, but I will not pressure her to marry you. You will have to win her to your cause by yourself. I do, myself, consider it a very suitable match. First, though, I should inform you about the dowry provisions that Captain Giles has made for Catherine."

Daphne then laid out the terms that Richard had already specified and found that they were clearly more favorable than Captain Bolton had expected. They also discussed where the couple would live if Catherine accepted Captain Bolton's proposal. He had no true attachment to Norfolk, and he thought he should look for a place near Dipton since he would be away a great deal, and Catherine now had her family in Dipton and had some friends in the area. Daphne thought that was very sensible of the Captain and that it augured well for the couple's future. Being Daphne, she had at once started a list in her mind of potential properties that might become available.

Catherine accepted Captain Bolton's proposal immediately, and, much to Daphne's surprise, she blossomed into a quite radiant girl whose dearest hopes had been fulfilled. Daphne realized that her niece's apparent coolness to romance had been an armor worn to protect her from having to show disappointment and elicit pity. It must have been developed over a long time, but Captain Bolton had broken through it. Daphne hoped that, by allowing Catherine to express joy at happy occurrences, this development would not lead to her niece's experiencing more painful heartbreak if adversity struck in the future. Daphne herself preferred this less reserved Catherine to the girl to whom she had become accustomed. Her niece remained practical enough to realize that marrying a sailor, especially in time of war, had its own uncertainties and was certain to involve her husband being away for long periods in which his survival might be in question.

There was no hurry to arrange for Catherine's nuptials since Captain Bolton had left to take his command to sea immediately after Lydia's wedding. Mr. Dimster, Lydia's husband, had fitted easily into his duties as Dipton Hall's new steward and required no immediate guidance from Daphne. The harvest was in full swing, but her tenants and her own chief workers knew their jobs. There was little that might require her immediate attention in that area. Indeed, she could, for once, laze about, an activity that was quite new to her. It was a particularly attractive way to spend her time since her pregnancy was not so advanced that some regular activities had become somewhat awkward.

No sooner had Daphne realized fully that she did have some spare time to indulge herself than a spasm, a bit painful and not quite like anything she had ever experienced, rippled through her abdomen. She was puzzled by it, but she ignored it since it was not immediately followed by anything alarming. She would indeed try having breakfast in bed for once, and she summoned Betsey to arrange for it. As she returned to bed from the bell pull, she felt a gushing of water between her legs. She knew immediately what it was. Mr. Jackson, apothecary, surgeon, male midwife, and friend, had explained to her all the details of giving birth. Her water had broken! At last, she would cease to be 'with child.' Despite Mr. Jackson's careful instructions, she was afraid and unsure what to do next; except, she must have Betsey inform Mr. Jackson right away and have the cook start boiling water. She wasn't entirely sure of the reason for boiling water, but it seemed to be the first step required when a woman went into labor.

Betsey was dispatched to arrange for Mr. Jackson to be informed right away. Obviously, she had also told everyone else at Dipton Hall, for soon, Lady Clara and Catherine were at the door offering assistance. Luckily, Mr. Jackson arrived very quickly and found tasks for the women to perform other than hovering over Daphne looking concerned. He also arranged for her father to be notified, joking that it would do Mr. Moorhouse no harm to get quietly drunk while waiting for further news.

Mr. Jackson examined Daphne and proclaimed that everything was proceeding properly. His assistant, Mrs. Hales, arrived. She was an older woman from the village who often acted as a midwife to mothers who thought that a man, even a well-trained medical man, should have no part in births. She took charge of minor matters as Mr. Jackson concentrated on Daphne.

"You are opening up nicely, Daphne," said Mr. Jackson, poking his head up to look Daphne in the face.

"But it will still take time. Have a little bit of small beer. Birthing can be a thirsty business. Later you can have some of the water that Mrs. Darling is boiling. I've noticed that unboiled water may cause later complications. Now, tell me, have you arranged for a wet nurse?"

"I took your suggestion. Nancy from the dairy has agreed to take on the task."

"Good. Young Thomas is ready for weaning."

Daphne's reply was preempted by another spasm, something that Mr. Jackson had called a contraction. She gritted her teeth to keep from making any distressed sounds.

"Let it out," said Mr. Jackson. "Make a big noise if you feel like it. I know that doing so actually makes things easier. It may even encourage the baby to come faster."

"I could never do that. That would not be at all ladylike. Ooooch."

"Just let it out. It helps. There is nothing ladylike about giving birth. Bellow. Remember that cow when you helped me with the calving."

Daphne did not like being compared to a cow, but Mr. Jackson had a point. She didn't feel ladylike. Maybe giving birth was too elemental to be ladylike. She would try making a large noise when the next contraction arrived, just as the cow had. Not holding back her moans, nor trying to swallow them, did seem to help!

Giving birth seemed to Daphne to be taking forever. The process settled into a routine of Mr. Jackson shouting encouragement when he was not telling her "push," while she met the worst contractions, as Mr. Jackson named the spasms, with a shriek. Betsey seemed to be rushing around as if she was trying desperately to find something to do, even though Mr. Jackson seemed to have everything under control. Soon, although Daphne would not have described it as 'soon,' he was also calling out, 'The baby's coming. It won't be long now."

Then the male midwife's cries became more interesting. "It's almost here... Push... the head is out... almost there, Daphne... one more push... it's born, Daphne! Well done! It's a boy! Just relax now while I get him cleaned up." His patter was interrupted by the most joy-bringing sound Daphne had ever heard, a baby's cry. Mr. Jackson was still pattering on about how perfect the baby appeared to be and about what an easy delivery she had had.

"Here we go," the male midwife finally proclaimed. "Here is your son, Daphne."

Mr. Jackson placed the baby, well wrapped in a wool blanket, in Daphne's arms. Right in front of her was the sweetest little face she had ever seen. Cutely wrinkling its forehead and opening bright blue eyes to look at her before closing them tight again. She knew those eyes! They were the same as Richard's. Her son had hardly any hair yet. It looked rather dark, but she had heard that infant hair was not a good predictor of adult hair. Would he end up with her husband's blond locks?

Daphne had always thought that newborn babies were rather ugly, and she had been hard put to show the proper enthusiasm when their mothers had shown them proudly. But this one was different! He was beautiful!

Bernard David Horatio Giles. She and Giles had chosen the names before he had sailed, the first for her father, the second for his brother, and the third for Giles's great hero. What a lot of names for this little human bundle to live up to. However, for the time being, he was just himself and her very own. How she wished that Giles could have been here! Not that he would have been in the same room for the birth — that would never have occurred. However, he would have been with her now to share her joy and excitement.

Her reverie was broken by Mr. Jackson proclaiming, "There, that's all done. Daphne, do you want to see your father and Lord David for a moment now. They have been in the parlor all this time."

Daphne nodded her compliance.

"Mrs. Hales, Betsey, tidy Lady Ashton so that she can receive her guests. It will only be for a moment, Daphne. You need to rest."

Before the men could come upstairs, Daphne was visited by Lady Clara and Catherine. Daphne vaguely remembered that they had been in the room for the early parts of her labor. Mr. Jackson had then unceremoniously evicted them after Lady Clara had started to issue a string of irrelevant orders, and Catherine started fluttering around like a lost moth, trying to be helpful. Any annoyance they had felt by their treatment vanished when they saw the baby. They both cooed over him extravagantly. Lady Clara also claimed that Bernard's eyes looked exactly as had Richard's at the same age.

The male relatives were admitted immediately after the ladies. Both with the glassy-eyed look of men who might have consumed too much port or brandy while waiting for the ordeal to be over. Both showed less wonder at the new baby and somewhat more concern for how Daphne was feeling. Though it was only the early afternoon, her eyes were already closing as Mr. Jackson chased all the visitors from her room.

Daphne's first thought when she awoke in the morning was for her baby, and a host of questions arose. Was he still all right and healthy? Had the wet nurse fed him already? Had the nanny arrived? Would Giles really be pleased with a boy? He had said that he hoped for a girl, but she suspected that had been so that she would not be disappointed if the child were a girl. All the women she knew claimed that men always preferred sons, especially for the child born first. She must write to Richard immediately, even if only heaven knew when the letter might be delivered. Obviously, with all these questions, she must not just slack the day away. Before she could begin to fulfill her resolve, there was a knock on the door, and Mr. Jackson entered.

"How are you feeling, Daphne?"

"A bit tired and a bit sore. Nothing serious."

"Let me see." Mr. Jackson first checked for fever by touching Daphne's forehead and then held her wrist to judge her pulse. He followed this by an examination of her lower region. "Everything looks fine. You really should move about and resume normal life as soon as you feel able or even a little earlier. However, I don't want you going downstairs for at least another day. Otherwise, a reasonable amount of activity is the best way to return to normal, even if, in your case, 'normal' means an inordinate amount of activity. "

"Now, Lady Ashton, are you still intending to use a wet nurse?"

"Yes, I am. Nancy, my dairymaid, you know the one who just moved here with her son, Thomas, has agreed to serve. But why did you suddenly call me 'Lady Ashton'?"

"Because I suppose that I really should think of you that way and not as Daphne."

"Why in the world would you do that? Have I offended you in some way?"

"Not at all. However, the word is already out that Lady Ashton has had a successful confinement with me as the male midwife. I already have had two notes to call on ladies who, I know, are with child and who are being looked after by Dr. Verdour. They indicated that they might be interested in switching to me. I will be happy to displace him, but it will not happen if I refer to you as 'Daphne' because that is not elevated enough for them, and they will expect a suitable amount of respect. They certainly wouldn't have me if I called them by their Christian names as I told them what to do, and referring to you as I think of you would spoil the illusion. Quite beneath their dignity, even if preserving that priceless quality would kill them. So I was practicing trying to think of you as Lady Ashton."

"Well, I hope you will continue to think of me as the girl who used to follow you around to the dismay of her nanny and whom you taught so many wonderful things."

"Of course I will, but also the girl who has developed into a very remarkable woman, indeed a true lady in every respect."

"Then, in answer to your question, as I indicated earlier, I have engaged Nancy, my new dairymaid, to be Bernard's wet nurse. She can take him with her in a basket when she is going about her duties, or he can be looked after by Nanny Weaver."

"Nanny Weaver? Your old nanny?'

"Yes. Did you know that she married right after I came out and that her husband died last winter of consumption?"

"Of course."

"Well, she isn't really very old, and she is very good with children."

"I'm not too sure of that. She did allow you to follow me around, even into places that were not entirely suitable for young ladies."

"That didn't hurt me at all. After all, how else would I have found out how a cow gave birth to calves? Anyway, it was really my father's doing. Nanny Weaver wasn't always very happy about what I was doing going off on my own into the neighborhood, but my father usually took my side in such arguments."

"Very good, Lady Ashton. I imagine that I can look forward to introducing little Bernard to some aspects of life that are not part of a nobleman's usual education."

"I certainly hope so. Now you really should get on with stealing Dr. Verdour's patients. I know that there is nothing that pleases you more."

"Nonsense. Delivering healthy babies certainly gives more pleasure. In this case, my gladness is as much in improving the mothers' chances of a successful delivery as it is in showing up that old fraud Verdour. Now, let me examine Bernard, after which I will follow up on seducing Dr. Verdour's customers."

"Betsey, please ask Nanny Weaver to bring Bernard here."

Nanny Weaver must have been waiting for the summons and came immediately with the baby. He was awake, but looked sleepy. Daphne was even more convinced that she had never seen a lovelier infant. Mr. Jackson examined him quickly but thoroughly. "Nothing the matter with this little fellow. He's doing very well. Of course, with you looking after him, Nanny Weaver, he wouldn't dare do anything else, would he?"

Daphne remembered how often these two had had disputes about how much she should be allowed to do and see when she was allowed to follow the medical practitioner about. She hoped that before too long, they would have the same sorts of good-natured disputes, though, of course, young boys were not supposed to be as sheltered as young girls were.

Mr. Jackson took his leave, but not without first telling Daphne, "Don't spend all day in bed even if you want to, and Nanny Weaver encourages you to. You will recover much faster if you at least walk around a bit, but don't go downstairs until tomorrow or, even better, the day after tomorrow." That produced a glare from Nanny Weaver, who undoubtedly was of the view that new mothers should be coddled, exerting themselves at most to coo at their new offspring.

Daphne did spend several minutes adhering to Nanny Weaver's belief of a new mother's proper occupation, but then she realized that she did have other things that needed doing. Especially, she desperately wanted to write to Richard with the news of the birth of Bernard. It didn't matter that it would take weeks before the letter could be delivered. It had to be done now. Despite Nanny Weaver's frown and mutterings about how she had always been headstrong, she summoned Betsey to help her dress and then had her fetch writing materials to her table.

Words seemed to gush onto the page as she started her letter to Giles. They were all about what a wonderful boy had been born and how proud his father would be. She told only the bare facts about her own labor. No one reading the report would guess that there had been loud cries and frequent shrieks emerging from her room as the labor continued or that it had not been over in an instant. That was almost how Daphne now remembered the experience. After filling one side of the page, Daphne turned it over to give more prosaic news. She glanced out the window to see that the remaking of the grounds was still progressing well and had yet to be halted by heavy autumn rains. She would have to review plans to cease work when the grounds became too sodden. However, news of Dipton and the changes being made took up less than half a page, and she was back to writing on the topic of the baby. She finished with the hope that Giles would soon be home to see this marvel, though she was careful not to indicate that she blamed him for being away.

Two days later, Daphne was downstairs in her usual writing room, composing another letter to Giles when Mr. Moorhouse came bursting into the room, waving a sheet of paper.

"Daphne, look at this!"

"Father, what is the matter? And, yes, Bernard and his mother are doing well."

"Yes, of course, Daphne. I should have asked. Now, look at this."

Mr. Moorhouse laid a sheet of paper in front of Daphne. It was a notice of the by-election for the First Member of Parliament for the Borough of Dipton to be held at the Dipton Inn in six days' time at 2 P.M. The candidates were listed as the Honorable Mr. David Giles, vicar of Dipton, and Mr. Andrew Longshank, solicitor of London. The notice had been issued, it declared, in the name of Sir Thomas Dimster, Returning Officer for the Borough of Dipton. The notice was followed by a list of the eligible electors that ran on for several pages.

"Good heavens," Daphne declared, "that scoundrel Longshank is Lord David's opponent, and Sir Thomas is the returning officer. Well, Lord David will still win easily, will he not?"

"Not based on this notice. I don't know where the list of electors comes from, but it certainly does not correspond in any way to the list for the 1802 general election. I have that one here." Mr. Moorhouse produced a second piece of paper that listed twenty-three names, though, when examined, it actually listed twenty-three properties in Dipton, with their owners' names. Seven of the names were Bernard Moorhouse, Esq., while Charles Gramley, Esq. was on the list eleven times. The three remaining names were Mr. Jackson, Dr. Verdour, and Richard Goodacre, the owner of a small estate on the boundary of the parish of Dipton. "You see, the current list should simply have replaced Mr. Gramley's name with Captain Giles's. I don't know where Sir Thomas got these names on this new list. Some are our tenants, but only a very few of our people are listed. Most of the men on the list are casual laborers or tradesmen, but again most such people in Dipton have been excluded. Far more names are of men from Upper Dipton than from here. Even my own name is not on this new list. If I had to guess, the list was mainly chosen on the likelihood of getting people who could be easily bought for a half-crown and all the ale they could drink. If this travesty goes ahead, this Mr. Longshank will be elected, and, if that happens, it may be very difficult to get the election reversed."

"What can we do about it?"

"I just don't know. I do not know who would have authority over it. The principal magistrate for the area is Sir Thomas, and the other magistrates are his henchmen. I've never worried about that because I have never expected to have any business with them. I wonder if any of the men that you met in London might be able to intervene. We should do something. This is highway robbery!"

"I could ask Mr. Edwards, I suppose, if he has any ideas. No... that would take time, and time is of the essence if we are to prevent this from happening. I will write to Sir David McDougall. He was knowledgeable about the riding when he suggested that Richard become the member, and he is in a position to change things if he wants to. I'll write to him immediately."

Daphne turned again to her writing-table and started a letter to Sir David. "You know, father, I don't really understand how any of this works or why the two lists are so different. What should I say?"

"I think you should simply say that you cannot understand the radical difference in the voting list and that he had told Giles that your husband and father had control of the riding. Obviously, that is not now the case. I would add that you have no idea on what basis the new list was drawn up since it excludes many men with equal or better qualifications, in terms of rents paid or taxes contributed, to some who have been included."

Daphne penned the words embodying her father's suggestions. She then added that she was writing because the day-to-day management of her husband's affairs was in her hands. She added that she was sure that Sir David was interested in having Dipton properly represented and that his brother would be a far better member than would the alternative candidate.

She read the missive over before sealing it, using one of Giles's seals, though it did not indicate his new status as a Viscount. He had not had a chance to have any made with his new title and had refused to adopt the seals his half-brother had left. She summoned her chief groom, Geoffreys, a former cavalry trooper who had injured his knee while training and had been discharged from the army. His injury in no way affected his riding skills, and his limp did not prevent his working assiduously with horses.

"Geoffreys, take this letter to the Admiralty in Whitehall in London. Can you find it easily?"

"Yes, my lady. I have been in London many times."

"Good. It is for Sir David McDougall, the First Lord of the Admiralty, and he must receive it as soon as possible. If he is not actually in the Admiralty, find out where he is and take it to him as quickly as possible. If you can't do that, take it to the Prime Minister and insist that he read it. Ride post haste. Here is a purse to pay for changes of horses if they will not put the expense on Lord Ashton's account. If anyone in authority asks what the letter is about, you can reply that it is to prevent someone stealing a seat in the House of Commons."

"Very good, my lady. The fastest horse in our stables is Dark Paul, Lord Ashton's hunter. Can I take him for the first stage?"

"You know how he likes to get rid of his riders?"

"Oh, yes, my lady. He has tried it several times with me. We have come to an understanding."

"Then take him by all means. I will not let Sir Thomas Dimster have his own way."

Geoffreys knew better than to ask what Daphne was talking about. He left. Daphne and Mr. Moorhouse had just started talking about the implications of having a son who would someday become the Earl of Camshire when they heard the sounds of hoofs going from a trot to a gallop. They could do no more about the election mismanagement and were more than content to talk of other matters.

Their conversation did not last long. Nanny Weaver appeared at the door and insisted that Daphne must get some rest. Mr. Moorhouse noted with silent amusement that Nanny Weaver had reverted to treating Daphne as if she were still ten years old. He wondered to himself how long that would last. Daphne was now a mature, responsible, and self-assured woman. How long would it be before Nanny Weaver would be forced to recognize her changed status?

Chapter XIX

Kronstadt proved to be a far better place than St. Petersburg for *Glaucus* to moor while waiting for Sir Walcott to conclude his business. The local authorities and taverns were well accustomed to sailors' wants and habits, providing for their various desires and anticipating the problems they inevitably caused. Giles found that the company of Russian captains was far preferable to that of St. Petersburg aristocrats, especially since there had seemed to be far too many Russian ladies who were eager to seduce him.

Glaucus spent four days at anchor, during which each watch had been given two excursions ashore. Giles had been entertained on different Russian ships every evening, always returning to *Glaucus* in none too steady a state. He realized that, by staying at anchor so close to the dubious delights that Kronstadt had to offer his sailors, he might be encouraging the troubles that would follow from having an idle and bored crew while he and his officers would be better off with something to fill their time other than this hectic social pace.

The best thing to do would be to exercise the ship's company at sea. Giles informed the Admiral of his plans. Although the Russian commander seemed to be surprised that the English captain wanted to take his ship to sea so soon after a lengthy voyage, even if only for a day, he put no obstacle in Giles's way. As news of his intention spread through the Russian fleet, he received many requests by other captains to accompany him in order to observe the practices of the Royal Navy. Giles had to think a bit about the wisdom of granting these requests, but he realized that, since his mission was to encourage cooperation between the Russian and British navies, it would do no harm if the Russians learned from *Glaucus*'s practices.

The visiting captains arrived well before dawn, for, by now, the days were growing very short this far north. There was a fresh north breeze, and *Glaucus* raised her anchor as dawn was breaking. She made her way under only topsails to the Gulf of Finland to the west of Kotlin Island. Giles showed off a bit by having the crew spread all the courses and top gallants simultaneously. The wind was too strong for the royals to be used, and, indeed, Giles had had their masts sent down while in harbor. So with the ship nicely heeled on a reach, he had his crew send up the royal masts and yards and bend on the sails even though he did not intend to use them. Then he reversed the process by sending them all down again and stowing them. It was a splendid demonstration of seamanship with the frigate heeling under the pressure of the wind. When these maneuvers were completed, Giles sent the crew to dinner after they had been issued their daily tots of rum. He himself entertained the visitors in his cabin. Many of the Russians remarked on the table that the elder Mr. Stewart had presented to him. It was much better than what they would have expected to find in a frigate-captain's dining room. Giles made a mental note to make sure that Midshipman Stewart was told about their comments so that he could relay them to his father.

When everything was shipshape after their excursion, Giles allowed the starboard watch to go ashore with firm instructions to return by six bells of the first watch. The crew returned more or less on time, though some had had to be assisted to their boats by the watch. They followed the same routine the following day, though with a new group of Russian captains observing what was going on. When Giles relented and allowed the crew to follow their own pursuits on the following day instead of again practicing their skills while under sail, he found that he was invited once more for dinner aboard the flagship.

The party was another rowdy affair. Giles had figured out a way not to toss down the whole content of his glass when a toast was drunk. Instead, most of the liquor returned to the glass as he lowered his head while keeping a firm grip on the glass to hide how little had been consumed. As a result, his wits were far less impaired as the festivities wore on than they had been on previous occasions. The main topic of conversation was the performance of *Glaucus* that many of the captains present had witnessed. They had clearly been impressed both with the crew's performance and with the way that *Glaucus* sailed. They were telling the Admiral that Russian procedures and training should be improved so that they could emulate *Glaucus*. Giles was rather basking in the admiration he was receiving, as transmitted by Lieutenant Pirov's translation, when some other captains started to make different sorts of remarks, and a dispute broke out. Lieutenant Pirov now had no choice but to try to summarize the heated remarks rather than to translate them since they were often made simultaneously. Some of the younger captains were certain that their fellows were mistaken about how inferior their ships and crews were to what they had seen on *Glaucus*. Lieutenant Pirov whispered to Giles that one of the most adamant of the supporters of the excellence of the Russian Navy had recently been transferred from the Sea of Azov Fleet, which was not ice-bound for part of the year and had more reason to always be ready for action, in their case against the Turks.

The arguments became quite heated. When one side or the other scored a winning point, those of similar mind all joined in a toast. Luckily for Giles, he could abstain from these toasts, especially as Lieutenant Pirov's translating the dispute had tailed off as the claims were shouted more quickly and as the Russian officer himself became involved on the side claiming the superiority of *Glaucus*. Giles could sit back and ruminate on how common it was for ship's captains to have exaggerated opinions of the merits of their own vessels and crews. He had seen it often in the Royal Navy when officers of different ships got together.

Giles liked to think of himself as being above such disputes. This was partly because his previous ship had had some very serious defects, which had dimmed his enthusiasm for her. Her problems had given him a better understanding that there were some poor ships that could not be improved, no matter how proficient was her crew. Needless to say, he had no doubt that his own crew was the best in the Navy. The ship must be at fault for any poor performance of a vessel under *his* command. It was also obvious, in the present case, that *Glaucus* was among the finest frigates in the world. This evaluation was certainly not based on sentiment. His very objective evaluation of her performance was based on the trip from Portsmouth to Chatham, in which she had so clearly outperformed a French vessel, and on his experience during the long voyage to Saint Petersburg.

Admiral Stroganoff also was sitting back with a bemused look on his face as his captains disputed among themselves. In a lull in the heated discussion, he intervened. "There is no point arguing," he declared, in Russian, of course, which made Lieutenant Pirov suddenly remember his position as translator. "If Captain Giles will agree, I suggest that we hold a competition between Russian ships and Captain Giles's excellent frigate. In fact, I propose two competitions. The first would be on how quickly the ships can clear for action and fire three broadsides. After that, we can have a race between the ships."

This suggestion was welcomed enthusiastically by the Russian officers. A toast was proposed, as always, in this case to honor the Admiral's excellent suggestion. With all eyes upon him, Giles felt required to drain his glass completely on this occasion. He announced that he thought it was a splendid idea and that he and his crew would all welcome the idea of participating in a competition with their Russian equivalents.

The next step was to choose the Russian competitors, for there were many frigates attached to the Baltic Fleet, and only some of their captains were present. Most of those present seemed to believe that their ship should be chosen as representing the cream of the Russian fleet. In the end, Admiral Smirnov had to make the selection. One frigate was chosen, commanded by an officer who had served in the Sea of Azov fleet and had recently transferred to the Baltic fleet. A second selection came from among the captains at the dinner who had only served in the Baltic Fleet. The third was picked from among the frigates whose captains were not present.

This selection again led to heated discussions, particularly about the frigates chosen whose captains were present. Lieutenant Pirov was only able to summarize the points being made because various captains were simultaneously shouting their opinions. Giles noted that most of the disappointed captains were arguing that they should have been selected and that no one seemed to be suggesting that, if their own ship were not to be chosen, a ship other than the one the Admiral had selected should have been picked.

Admiral Stroganoff halted this discussion by announcing that he had made his selection and did not want any further comments. His Flag Captain then proposed a toast to the three choices. When discussion next broke out about exactly what rules should be adopted, the Admiral again intervened. The first lieutenants of the four frigates should establish the rules in a meeting with his Flag Captain, if that was acceptable to the English captain. Giles promptly agreed. Admiral Stroganoff then announced that the competition would be held in four days' time. The delay was occasioned by his belief that many of the elite of St. Petersburg would want to witness the competition, and waiting a few days would allow them time to arrange to attend. A final toast to the enterprise was proposed. Giles again felt that he had to toss the burning firewater down his gullet. Going on deck to return to *Glaucus* and, as a guest, being given the honor of being first to depart, he felt very proud that his progress to the entry port was more or less in a straight line.

The next few days were a time of waiting. Mr. Hendricks had gone to the flagship to set the rules for the competitions. They were simple, and Giles thought they seemed fair. The critical part was that each vessel would have an umpire aboard to ensure that everything was done according to the rules. For the Russian ships, several captains of British merchant ships agreed to serve as the umpires, while Captain Belosselsky, one of the captains who had been at the dinner where the competition was proposed, would serve on *Glaucus*.

If Giles had thought that he would be blessed with inactivity until the day of the match, he was sorely disappointed. At five bells of the forenoon watch, a small boat with a pair of portly, grizzled mariners on board approached *Glaucus*. Arriving on deck, they asked to speak with the captain. When Giles, who had been in his cabin dealing with the seemingly endless mounds of paper that the ship generated, came on deck, the men introduced themselves as representatives of the British ships in the merchant harbor, inviting him and his officers to dine with them and the captains of other British ships in Kronstadt. Since none of their ships had large cabins, they would meet in the dining room of an inn in Kronstadt.

It turned out to be a pleasant and, indeed, boisterous evening. The merchant captains were at pains to acquaint Giles with their problems with privateers sailing under French letters of marque out of various German ports. They had appealed to the Admiralty to provide escort vessels for convoys through the affected waters, but so far had had no reply to their petitions. Could Giles put in a good word for them?

Giles answered that he would indeed mention it and could sympathize with their having to run the gauntlet to pass from the Baltic Sea to the North Sea. It seemed to make the discussion less heated when he mentioned that, on his previous cruise, he had captured two French privateer brigs near the Skagen. He had thought that capture might alleviate the problem, but now he understood that the danger had not been eliminated. He would mention it to the First Lord when he next saw him.

The following day, Lieutenant Pirov returned from a visit to the flagship to report, with great excitement, that it seemed that all of Saint Petersburg's society would be descending on the area to watch the competition. Several prominent nobles had sent their servants to open their dachas and would be following soon. One of the wealthiest, Count Mikeladze, was also arranging a ball to follow the races. Giles and his officers would no doubt be invited. In addition, Admiral Stroganoff would be having a lavish party on the evening before the event. Giles, of course, would be expected to attend.

Giles wished that the festivities were already over. While he looked forward to pitting *Glaucus* against the Russian frigates, the social events surrounding the competitions inspired no pleasant anticipations in him. Indeed, he had had his fill of Russian celebrations, enough to last him a lifetime. He was still feeling the ill effects of the last several bouts of drinking. The prospect of more had no appeal whatsoever. Of course, he would also have to let his crew have more time ashore, especially if they won, and that would be good for neither their discipline nor their health. Dr. Maclean, *Glaucus*'s surgeon, had already reported several new cases of the clap and the pox. Clearly, a number of seamen had succeeded in getting ashore in St. Petersburg without its being discovered until the telltale maladies revealed themselves. Most distressful to him was that two of the patients were Midshipman Stewart and Lieutenant Hendricks. How was he going to explain Midshipman Stewart's problem to his family if he saw them on his return to England? Lieutenant Hendricks's illness made Giles all the more glad that he had refused the assignations with Countess Donskaya.

It was now too cold for the Admiral to hold a large reception on his quarterdeck the night before the competition, but with all the important people who had come to witness the encounter, he was bound to throw a lavish dinner, and Giles would be bound to attend. Hopefully, *Glaucus*'s officers would not be invited so that only he would have a fuzzy head when the trials began. Furthermore, he wished that his rival captains would also be invited. He was right on the first count, but not on the second. He was the only competitor present. To his dismay, he was seated next to the Princess, whose name he still had not mastered, on the one side, and to Countess Donskaya on the other. To make things even more awkward, the Princess's husband, whose name was just as indecipherable as was his wife's and strangely different from hers, was seated across the table from him.

It rapidly became evident that neither lady had lost interest in Giles. He couldn't help wondering how much of a danger to his health either one might be. In any case, the Countess, still corseted in the old-fashioned way, and still sporting a ridiculous headdress in which Giles suspected that the mice still nested, was far less attractive. Her peculiar appearance made it easier to follow up on realizing that even a mild flirtation with her might get him into a very awkward situation. He reckoned that it would be wiser to devote most of his attention to the Princess. It was pleasant flirting with a handsome woman when there was no danger of its going farther. However, both ladies were certainly prepared to go much farther than verbal sparring with him, as their conduct indicated, but he trusted that the Prince's presence would protect him from the Princess. It seemed that through at least half the dinner, one lady's hand or the other's was running up and down his thigh. At one point, he was afraid that their fingers might collide with each other as they both worked to arouse him, all too successfully.

As the party broke up, Giles found himself standing next to the Prince. "I understand that you brought Sir Walcott to St. Petersburg, Captain," the Prince remarked. He spoke excellent English with only a mild accent though he spoke with a slight lisp.

Giles replied in the positive, wondering where this conversation might be leading. Had Sir Walcott insulted the

Prince? From the many mentions of Sir Walcott that Giles had heard from other Russians, Giles was expecting a complaint. However, that was not the case here.

"That is true, Prince," Giles replied, suddenly realizing that his failure to capture the Prince's name might be an embarrassment. "Have you met Sir Walcott?"

"Yes, indeed. Splendid fellow! Did you know that he has left the Embassy and is now a guest at our palace? Such a fine man! If you need to contact him, that is where you will find him. Indeed, why don't you come to dinner next Thursday? We are easy to find. Everyone knows the palace of Prince Gruzinsky. Don't you agree, my dear?" the Prince continued, now addressing his wife.

"Alexander Georgovitch, that is an excellent suggestion, but you forget that we have commitments next Thursday. Maybe the following week. I will check my diary, Captain."

The following day dawned cloudy with a raw, high wind blowing from the north. To the west, ominous black clouds were towering. Though well protected, the ships in the anchorage were swaying jerkily, tugging on their anchor cables like dogs trying to shake off their leashes. It did not promise to be a comfortable day for the land-based nobles who were intent on viewing the competitions.

Admiral Stroganoff in the *Alexander Nevsky* led the way out of the anchorage, followed by *Glaucus* and the three Russian competitors. Most of the rest of the Russian warships that had been at anchor at Kronstadt trailed along behind, keen to have the boredom of harbor duty eased by the widely anticipated tournament.

The plans for the gunfire part of the day's activities called for the frigates to be anchored in line ahead by both fore and aft anchors to hold them steady. At the end of the line would be the flagship anchored at right angles to the frigates so that the many people crowded onto her decks could get a good view with no danger of being hit by an errant ball. All the other yachts and boats that had come to watch the fun would be on the safe side of the line.

At a signal from the flagship, a red flag breaking out at the mizzen cap, the broadside competition would begin. Each frigate would start with its guns bowsed* up tight to their sides and their powder in their magazines. Clearing for action had been abandoned as part of the competition when it was recognized how great were the differences in the amounts of material to be stowed on the various frigates. Umpires made sure that no one got started ahead of time. Admiral Stroganoff had warned all the competitors that he might send up other colored flags as a jest, so that they would have to wait for the flag to break out at the cap before proceeding. Indeed, he did send up a black flag before the red one. None of the ships was fooled.

Midshipman Stewart had the duty to watch the cap with a telescope and to shout out the minute that he could see the color. His shout of "red" set off a bustle of crew members going about their assigned tasks as quickly as possible. Giles's crew had no need of orders as they cast off the lashings on the cannon and ran them back so that they could be loaded. The powder monkeys exerted all their efforts to get the cartridges to the guns as quickly as they could. In went the cartridges, followed by the wads, followed by the balls, followed by another set of wads. The gunners pierced the cartridges and primed the gun; the crews jumped back as the gunners pulled the lanyard to make the sparks that would ignite the gunpowder. Giles had ordered each gun to fire as soon as it was ready.

It spoke volumes for the crew's training that the guns fired in the fusillade within seconds of each other as if a simultaneous broadside had been ordered. Even as each gun crew rushed to ready their weapon for the next shot, Giles looked at his competitors. None had fired a single gun when Giles's fastest gun crew started to haul their cannon into firing position. All of *Glaucus*'s second salvo had been fired before all the Russian frigates had completed their first rounds. His crew did not pause to see how their performance compared with their rivals. The third balls were all away before any of *Glaucus*'s rivals had fired their second. Shooting better than three salvos to a rival's two in actual combat was considered extremely good, and this performance was a bit better than that standard. There could be no doubt about who won the first trial.

Just as the smoke from the last broadside drifted downwind, the eighth bell of the forenoon watch rang, though no one heard it. A glance at the glass told Giles it was past the time for the crew to have their tots of rum followed by their dinner. The rum was much appreciated, but Giles was not about to let the sailors have a double portion, as he might have done had this been the only competition. The last thing he needed was inebriated men, and he knew that, with double tots, some of the more abstemious men would give their extra rum to their messmates. He had no desire to have any drunken crew members when it came to the race.

It would have been impossible to have the crew eat their usual dinner in the time available, especially as one of the requirements of the preparations for the cannon fire was that the cook-stove had to be doused*. Instead, Giles had ordered a large supply of Russian pies that were baked in Kronstadt. Lieutenant Pirov had introduced him to them, and he had arranged for enough pies to be delivered to the ship before she cast off that morning. Though he didn't really know the name of the confections, he did know that their first syllables sounded like 'Pirov,' so he was able to remember at least part of the name of the delicacy. The crew seemed to be very doubtful of this special dinner of pierogis, but after a few daring members had tried the pies and found them tasty, in a somewhat foreign way, they all tucked in with gusto.

The wind had been steadily rising as the morning had progressed. Now it was blowing a near gale. Giles had used the royals on his journey upstream to St. Petersburg, but he had ordered these sails, with their yards and masts struck below on the short trip from Kronstadt, after he had seen what sort of a day it promised to be. Now he even wished that he had struck the topgallants below as well. The rival Russian frigates still had the rigging for the royals in place. Giles knew that his caution would make *Glaucus* sail better in these conditions and suspected that the extra top-hamper would slow the others. As soon as the tricky sail handling that might be needed at the start of the race was over, he would have the topgallant sails and spars sent down.

The course had been laid out as a roughly diamond-shaped track with each side being about two miles in length. The race involved going around the course twice, staying outside the boats dispatched to mark the three outer corners. The starting line and finishing line was between the *Alexander Nevsky* and a brig that had anchored close to the Admiral's vessel. Too close, in Giles's opinion. He hung back to avoid being fouled by one of the Russian frigates, a precaution that was soon shown to be warranted. Two of the Russian ships did become entangled with each other. They rapidly drifted out of the way so that *Glaucus* could slip by close to the flagship. The frigate that had crossed the line first was laboring under having set too much sail, and Giles quickly got to windward of her. There was now no question of who was the faster ship. Tack by tack, *Glaucus* pulled away. If there was a race in progress for which there was any doubt of the outcome, it was the one for second place. The last two Russian ships had got loose of each other, and they seemed to be closing on the frigate that Giles had already passed.

The wind was backing and strengthening, and a nasty cold rain was starting to be blown into the face of everyone on deck. Giles had designated Mr. Brooks to deal with handling *Glaucus* since he was by all odds the best officer at getting the most from the frigate.

"Take another reef* in the mizzen topsail and douse* the fore staysail.* Quartermaster, steer for the marking ship. The wind's backing. Mr. Miller, adjust the sheets; we are now steering a course to the marker ship," the Master ordered. The ship was eased immediately from sailing as close-hauled as possible, and a noticeable gain in speed occurred. They sped forward with the second lieutenant giving a string of largely unnecessary orders since the crew already knew how to set the sails to maximize performance.

Glaucus raced around the first mark, but the backing of the wind meant that the next leg of the course was now a beat to windward, not the close reach that they had expected. As the ship tacked towards the next mark, the wind kept increasing so that it was now blowing a full gale. Mr. Brooks kept reducing sail as the wind continued to increase, and Giles noted that he did it in advance of the Russian frigates that seemed to be mistakenly thinking that waiting to reduce canvas would somehow speed their own progress.

Glaucus rounded the next mark and proceeded down the third leg of the course on a reach with the helmsman steering a course, and Mr. Miller constantly adjusting the sails. The increase in the wind and its backing had produced a nasty chop of waves, so they were not speeding along as fast as they would want. Nevertheless, they were rapidly pulling away from the closest Russian frigate, which was still making heavy weather of tacking up the second leg. If there was a close competition going on at all, it was between the last two frigates. The third one seemed to be using rather haphazard changes of course to prevent its rival from passing it. They were both carrying too much sail for the conditions. Their stability and ability to progress towards the next mark were thwarted by not having reduced their top-hamper when it would still have been easy to do so.

It was now blowing a full gale. As *Glaucus* approached the final mark, Giles noticed that most of the private boats had left the anchorage. The few that remained were straining at their anchor lines, as were the ships of the Russian fleet. The deck of the flagship was no longer jammed with onlookers. The fashionable crowd must have taken refuge below decks, and Giles idly wondered how many of them were being seasick. *Glaucus* was handling the blow without trouble, and his crew were used to keeping their stations in all weathers. They were not at all bothered by the increasing storm. The British frigate rounded the final mark, with Giles waving to the few people remaining on the flagship's deck and headed off towards the first mark again, now on a reach. The nearest

Russian frigate was only on the third leg, coming up towards the next marker, and the other two were battling it out and had yet to round the second mark. They would have to hurry, or else *Glaucus* might lap them.

Disaster struck as the trailing pair of Russian frigates came up to the second mark. The one that was slightly ahead and to windward of the other one had its main topmast break under the weight of canvas being carried. Giles had already noted that, for some unknown reason, her captain had been reefing his mainsail rather than his topsail, and the wind was such that both should have been heavily reefed already. If there was to be disparity, in Giles's view, it was the topsail that should have been reefed or even furled, as *Glaucus*'s now was. Having the main topmast go by the board meant that all control of the frigate was lost, and she swerved into her rival.

Giles could clearly see men falling from the yards of the Russian vessel due to the collapse of the rigging and the collision. He would not be surprised if many other men had been thrown overboard from the ships' decks and yards. The rule of the sea, which had been ingrained into him as a midshipman, took over. "Mr. Brooks, make a course to the two Russian ships now! We may be useful in the rescue attempts."

A string of orders had *Glaucus* on her new course immediately. Giles wondered whether there was much chance of survival for the men who had been flung into the frigid water, but he had to try his hardest to rescue them. The wind had backed a little more, and sailing close-hauled on the starboard tack meant that *Glaucus* could come to the spot from which the tangled frigates were now drifting without having to come about again. Nevertheless, it would be many, many long minutes before they could reach the relevant area where survivors might be found in the water. Mr. Brooks was ordering the sails trimmed even more carefully than when racing in order to squeeze every last knot out of *Glaucus*, and Mr. Correll was having a gang of seamen ready boats for launching as quickly as possible when they reached the relevant area. As they were undertaking that task and the sail-handlers labored to pull every extra foot from their ship, Giles and much of the crew could only stand idly by.

Giles turned his attention to the Russian frigate that had been in second place. He had presumed that she would also have ceased racing to come to the aid of her countrymen, but no, she was keeping to her course to reach the flagship, which would be her next mark. Giles was surprised, but it did not weaken his resolve to offer help.

Mr. Brooks was wringing every possible bit of speed out of *Glaucus*, but every wave breaking over the bow seemed to slow them. Finally, they reached the area where men had gone into the water. Despite the large, chaotic waves, all the boats were lowered to look for victims. The boats crisscrossed the area, and found in all thirty-one men. Unfortunately, four of those died even before they could be brought on board *Glaucus*. The others were rushed below, out of the wind, stripped of their clothes and wrapped in hot blankets that the cook had prepared. Dr. Maclean went from one case to another, and back again, instructing where the many eager helpers should rub to restore circulation in the shivering victims. It was some time before the surgeon could declare success in all cases and return on deck to report to the captain.

The two Russian frigates had succeeded in untangling themselves and needed no further assistance from *Glaucus*. Giles turned his attention to the race. To his surprise, the leading Russian frigate had continued along the race path. It was well into the second circumnavigation of the course. Giles was half inclined to head for the next marker his ship needed to round to continue the race. His fear that his rival now had too much of a head start turned out to be moot after he noticed that the race was finished. The *Alexander Nevsky* appeared to have dragged her anchor and was drifting down on the brig that had been anchored to form the other end of the starting and finishing line. Through his telescope, Giles could see that the smaller ship was raising its anchor. A burst of signals from the flagship told the other marker ships to up anchor and seek protection. It also, no doubt, ordered the frigate, which was still racing, to seek shelter. Giles concluded that he should do the same. He ordered Mr. Brooks to head downwind towards the southern passage between Kotlin Island and the mainland. Only when they were well into the passage did the waves moderate and the wind weaken a little. Even when they were safely anchored at the Kronstadt Naval Harbor, gusts still whistled through the rigging and caused *Glaucus* to pitch uncomfortably and tug erratically at her anchor rode.

Giles decided not to go to the flagship to report on the sailors he had rescued. Looking through his telescope at the decks of the ship of the line revealed that it was again crowded with the people who had that morning come eagerly to enjoy a day on the water with a competition to keep their interest. They now looked a bedraggled, fractious, and unhappy lot. They would, without doubt, make the lives of every one of the *Nevsky*'s officers from admiral to midshipmen miserable. Instead, Giles recruited Lieutenant Pirov's help in visiting the sickbay to try to cheer up the men who had been rescued. It was only when he had finished having a word with each of the survivors that he realized that the Russian sailors' main reaction to him, which was also Lieutenant Pirov's, was amazement that such a senior officer would even think about their well-being.

That evening, as Giles completed the day's addition to his ongoing letter to Daphne, he reflected on how unsatisfactory it was to communicate with her in this way. He had had no news of her since her coach had disappeared down the road in Chatham, and he had received none about the activities in Dipton or even of her report to Sir David MacDougall. Had the baby been born yet? If so, how had the birthing gone? Was it a boy or a girl? Even more importantly, had Daphne come through the ordeal unscathed? Perhaps he should take the seat in Parliament as Sir David had suggested. It would probably keep him in home waters and, even if he could visit Dipton only infrequently, he would receive news regularly. This thought made him wonder if the by-election had been called. He had expressed to Daphne his lack of interest in becoming an MP as he had to Sir David McDougall. She and her father would, no doubt, have taken him at his word and nominated someone else. Who might it be? How he longed for news! He almost regretted not standing for the seat.

Chapter XX

Geoffreys returned late in the afternoon two days after Daphne had given him his mission. He must have been in the saddle almost the whole time.

"Did you see Sir David?" Daphne asked as soon as the groom was shown in.

"Yes, my lady. I arrived at the Admiralty near noon yesterday. Sir David was not there, but his secretary thought that he was at Downing Street." Daphne was surprised that Geoffreys had not been left to kick his heels for hours in the standard Admiralty way. Perhaps they reserved that treatment for navy officers.

"I went to Downing Street immediately, but the clerks there said Sir David was with the Prime Minister. When I told them that the message was urgent and that you had required me to get it to Sir David as soon as possible, they relented and took it into him. I am afraid that I fell asleep while waiting for word of whether there would be a reply."

"What happened then?"

"I was woken up by Sir David himself. He gave me a letter for you. Here it is. And one for the commanding officer of the Army regiment, which is bivouacked near Ameschester. I am to deliver it immediately."

"Did he say anything else?"

"Not really, my lady. I did overhear the Prime Minister say to Sir David, 'This is serious, David, very serious. Can't just have chaps stealing seats in the House. Won't do! And it will be a lot easier to deal with if it can be stopped before this stooge is elected'."

"Thank you, Geoffreys. I think you should ride to Ameschester right away. Cook can give you something to eat as you go."

Daphne opened the letter as Geoffreys turned to go on the next part of his mission. The message was short.

Dear Lady Ashton,

Your letter has caused quite a bit of disturbance to the Prime Minister and myself. Thank you for bringing the matter to our attention.

We are taking the following steps to right the situation.

First, Mr. Justice Amery, of the Court of King's Bench, has agreed to become the electoral officer for Dipton. He has been given a warrant to hold the election using the proper list of electors.

Second, in his name, we have issued a new election notice with a revised list of electors. The list is the one you sent to me with the name of Lord Ashton substituted for Mr. Gramley's. Mr. Justice Amery will be bringing the revised list with him.

Third, Mr. Justice Amery will be traveling by post chaise and should arrive by the evening of the day before the election is to be held. He will be bringing with him his clerk and two specially commissioned bailiffs. I have taken the liberty of suggesting that they stay at Dipton Hall since the Inn may be a place of disturbance on Election Day. If this is inconvenient, I hope you will be able to make other arrangements.

Fourth, we are arranging for a company of the Ameshire Regiment of Foot to be at the election place to quell any disturbance that may arise as a result of the enforcement of the correct electoral procedures or the dubious nature of the voters' list that has been issued. We are enlisting your messenger to carry these orders to the officer in command at Ameschester.

Thank you again for your assistance.

I remain, madam, your humble servant

David MacDougall, KB

Daphne was surprised that Sir David had been able to move so quickly. It sounded as if the fraudulent election would not go forward in the way that Sir Thomas Dimster intended. Of course, she could accommodate the judge who would be overseeing the election, but propriety suggested that he would be better housed at her father's house, Dipton Manor. She would have to share the news about how the election was being changed with her father in any case, and she was sure that he would be happy to provide the needed accommodations. She sent him a note to tell him about the reply she had received from Sir David and the need to accommodate the judge. Mr. Moorhouse, however, soon came over to Dipton Hall, both to discuss the situation with Daphne and to welcome the judge.

Mr. Justice Amery did not arrive until late in the evening. He was a small man, slender and with graying hair that he wore tied back in a cue. He had a high pitched, soft voice. He had been traveling all day but was still alert because, he said, he had slept much of the way. He was hungry as were the men he had brought with him and was happy to enjoy a supper which Mrs. Darling had quickly prepared when he arrived, and which he shared with Daphne and her father. He had first made sure that his instructions to the soldiers had been conveyed,

Mr. Amery turned out to be a good conversationalist. He showed a genuine interest in Dipton, and he also regaled them with tales of amusing things he had observed while presiding in court. Daphne warmed to him. She had been afraid that Sir David was sending them a fierce and strongly opinionated man to enforce the true requirements of the electoral process. He did frustrate his listeners by steadfastly refusing to discuss what had happened to change how the Dipton election would be conducted. All Mr. Amery would say was that he had issued a new election notice and a new list of electors. He had told Geoffreys to post them wherever the original had been posted. It would supersede Sir Thomas's notice. All he would say about it was that it would be wise for Mr. Moorhouse to be present at the Inn at two o'clock.

The next morning Daphne really did not want to wait, as was proper, for some man to come and tell her what happened at the Dipton Inn when Mr. Justice Amery confronted Sir Thomas Dipton. She certainly could not mingle in the crowd that would be assembling in the inn-yard for the election. However, she could easily persuade her former lady's maid, Elsie, who was now the wife of the innkeeper, Carstairs, and was running the Inn in his absence, to let her watch from an upstairs window.

Daphne arrived at the Inn an hour and a half before the election was supposed to begin. That was none too early, for already some eager men had assembled in the inn-yard primarily to imbibe from the casks of ale and stout, which were available to those who would vote for Mr. Longshank. Some men were also gathered at the inn door, waiting for the proceedings to begin. Daphne hesitated as soon as she saw the gauntlet that she would have to run to reach the Dipton Arms.

"Come to see the fun, Daphne?" Mr. Jackson had come up from behind her as she waited.

"Yes. But I don't fancy forcing my way through that mob. I suppose that you are going to scold me for walking here so soon after giving birth."

"Why should I? It's good for you. But you may be wise not to plunge into that group by yourself in order to get to the door. Would you like me to escort you? There may be one or two catcalls, but nothing more this early in the proceedings. We can just wait until that lot goes into the inn-yard to get at the ale."

"That would be very good of you. How are your new and rich mothers-to-be doing?"

"As well as may be expected since they won't follow my advice. Strenuous exercise beyond a leisurely walk seems to be beyond the capabilities of most of them, at least as they perceive the situation. I warn them that having me as their midwife won't ease labor pains if they do nothing to get ready for the delivery except buy fancy clothes for the baby and themselves, but they just nod their heads and seem to think that hearing the advice is sufficient. At least they or their babies are somewhat less likely to die than they would with that butcher Verdour, and they haven't been confined in advance of the births. Now, I think the coast is clear. Let's go."

Mr. Jackson took Daphne's arm, and they walked unhurriedly to the door of the inn. Elsie welcomed them warmly, but rather distractedly. She was anticipating a brisk business as the crowd gathered. She had had dozens of pies baked, which were now ready to be served from tables already set up in the yard. Mr. Longshank's agent had ordered her to make the food ready just before the election was to start. Anyone who voted for his candidate was to be rewarded with a pie, as well as more of the ale or stout that the candidate was already providing to potential voters. So far, Lord David had ordered nothing though he was in the yard, as was Mr. Longshank. Her brother-in-law was busily greeting people, apparently quite unaware that the voters' list included very few people who were likely to support him, at least not without a better reward than what Mr. Longshank was providing. Both candidates seemed to be oblivious of their rather unpleasant earlier meeting.

"It is a pity," said Elsie. "Everyone in the bar the last few nights agreed that Lord David would make a very much better MP, but that strange list seems designed to prevent him from being elected. I, myself, don't like Mr. Longshank, but it hardly matters. I can't vote, and even Carstairs couldn't if he were here since his name is not on the list. It is very strange."

"It is that," Daphne responded, "but it is also not over, and everyone is in for some surprises. I cannot tell you what they are, but you can expect to lay out your pies, whatever the outcome, for if Mr. Longshank won't pay – and I won't be surprised if his agent breaks his commitment to you — I will pay for everyone to have one and to provide some more ale and stout. I think we will still have something to celebrate in Dipton. You should set your cook to making more pies as soon as she can and anything else that can be provided easily. They will be needed starting about two-thirty. Now I'd like to have a room facing the yard from which I can watch the proceedings."

"I'll be leaving now, Daphne," said Mr. Jackson. "Since I am not on the elector's list, I have no desire to be here for the election and see all these men become the worse for drink."

Daphne turned to him and said in a low voice, "I hope you will stay, Mr. Jackson. I think you will find that the list that is used is quite different from the one posted, and your name will be on it."

"What have you been plotting, Daphne?"

"I cannot say, because the man who is going to be in charge of the election told me to keep it secret. That is so that Sir Thomas and Mr. Longshanks will not be able to do anything about the planned surprise. I am sure you will find it amusing."

Elsie took Daphne to a room that overlooked the inn-yard and laid a table for a light luncheon that Daphne could eat as she watched the scene below her. The yard was filling up steadily, not only with men on the electors' list but also with others. There was a certain amount of bad feeling expressed as those who were without a vote found that they would be expected to pay for their ale. Daphne had thought it better not to tell him about the latest developments in case his conscience might lead him to warn the Longshank forces of what was afoot.

Just as the clock on the Church tower began to strike two o'clock, Sir Thomas, accompanied by a pair of large, tough-looking men and a clerk, entered the inn-yard heading towards a low platform he had had built in anticipation of conducting the election. At the same moment, from outside the yard, a bugle call sounded, followed by the rat-tat-tat of a drum. Then a band struck up a march. This was accompanied by the sound of marching feet. What was happening soon became evident to everyone in the inn-yard as a military band appeared at the entrance. It stood marking time as a company of soldiers marched past them and, entering the yard, proceeded along the sides of the square until they entirely encircled it. Each of the soldiers had a musket slung over his shoulder with a bayonet already affixed to it. When they were all in position, the cry came to first present arms and then to stand at ease. The effect was that the crowd in the inn-yard was now surrounded by armed men. They were standing at ease with their feet apart but with bayonetted muskets in their hands. The soldiers appeared to be fully alert. When they were in position, Mr. Justice Amery entered the yard. He was dressed in the robes of his office as a judge, including a full-bottomed wig. He was followed by two other men in antique and rather flamboyant uniforms, some clerks, and a platoon of soldiers.

On entering the inn-yard, the judge called out in a large voice, "Sir Thomas Dimster. In the name of the King, I hereby arrest you pursuant to a warrant on the charge of treason to the state and of fraudulently conspiring to misconduct the election for the First Member of Parliament for the Borough Constituency of Dipton. You will be bound over to face trial at the next assizes in Ameschester. Sheriffs, carry out the warrant and secure that man." He pointed directly to where Sir Thomas stood on his platform, and Mr. Justice Amery's two specially uniformed followers stepped forward with the soldiers to climb the platform. They took the baronet by his arms and marched him off the platform and out of the inn-yard. The crowd stood thunderstruck at this development. Before they could recover their voices, the judge mounted the platform, held up his hands for silence, rather unnecessarily, and addressed the crowd.

"Residents of Dipton. I must report that Sir Thomas Dimster, who was appointed returning officer for the election called by the House of Commons, has been arrested because he adopted a different method of choosing electors than that established both by the terms of the original creation of the Constituency and by the long tradition of how Members of Parliament are chosen by this riding. These actions constitute an act of treason for which Sir Thomas will stand trial in the next assizes in Ameschester. Despite this plot, the election will proceed today using the proper list of electors. Together with the revised notice of the election, that list has been posted in prominent places throughout the riding and supersedes all earlier notices and posted lists.

"The candidates for the First Seat in the House of Commons for the Borough of Dipton are the Honorable Mr. David Giles, vicar, of Dipton, and Mr. Andrew Longshank, solicitor, of London. As I call your name, please make yourself known and state your vote."

Daphne had been afraid at first that Mr. Amery's light tenor voice would not be able to command attention and respect. She had to acknowledge that she had been wrong. Though his voice was light, his measured delivery made his pronouncement more ominous and commanding than a full-throated baritone would have achieved.

Voting was rapidly completed with so few electors on the list even though Mr. Moorhouse had to repeat his vote based on each of his eligible properties, and, for each of Giles's holdings, it had to be established that Viscount Ashton was not present. Only Dr. Verdour cast a vote for Mr. Longshank. When every name on the list had been called, Mr. Justice Amery declared that the Honorable Mr. David Giles had been elected. Glancing at a note that had been handed to him, he continued by announcing that new casks of ale and stout had been opened and that pies and other confections were laid on tables outside the inn, all being a gift from Viscountess Ashton. As news of what was happening spread through the community, many men who had been excluded from the fake voters' list had drifted into the inn-yard. They were mostly people who would have voted for Lord David if they had had the chance, and they now quite clearly outnumbered the men who were to vote for Mr. Longshank. The latter, who had mainly attended due to the promise of free drink and food, accepted the outcome cheerfully. Since the free beer and food that were the main reason for their being there was being provided anyway, they were quite happy not to protest the election. Indeed, the scene in the inn-yard was so peaceful that the captain in charge of the army detail ordered his soldiers to stack their arms and enjoy the celebration. At that point, Daphne decided that she should leave. Mr. Moorhouse, Lord David, and Mr. Justice Amery all decided to follow her example before things became too rowdy. The latter did give his clerks permission to join in the festivities, but only after they had made sure that the records pertaining to the election were safe.

Dinner at Dipton Hall later in the day was a festive occasion, even though only Lord David and Mr. Justice Amery joined Daphne and her father. The judge turned out to have a lively curiosity about the community into which he had been thrust and a droll sense of humor. He kept them amused by a string of anecdotes about incidents in court that hardly met the dignity that was supposed to be reserved for formal judgment.

When the appropriate time came for Daphne to withdraw, Mr. Moorhouse intervened to say that, when she was the only female diner, she usually stayed to participate in the conversation that occurred over the port. So the cloth was withdrawn, the decanters of fortified wine were placed on the table together with plates of nuts and dried fruit, and the butler directed the footmen to place the glasses. The servants then all left while Daphne settled into her place at the table with the men gathered around her. Daphne's participation was probably most unusual in Mr. Justice Amery's experience, but he accepted the situation with equanimity.

Daphne asked whether Mr. Longshank would receive the same penalty as Sir Thomas.

"No," replied the judge, "I don't think so. Unless there is evidence that he colluded with Sir Thomas, the fact that the plot was for his benefit cannot be proven. That sort of conspiracy is not usually committed to writing. I do not doubt that Mr. Longshank is a despicable character. In fact, I am sure that he is, but that consideration is irrelevant. If being of despicable character were a bar to being a Member of Parliament, half the seats might have to be vacated.

"The latest gossip in London convinces me that Mr. Longshank would have been an entirely unsuitable member, but that would not be enough to link him to this particular conspiracy or any particular crime. Certainly, the stories being told in London about him indicate that he is a very shady character, but that also would not by itself send him to prison, let alone the noose."

Mr. Justice Amery then recounted some pieces of the gossip that was circulating in London society. It was the tale of how a titled lady and her crony, a vicar posing as a lawyer, had bluffed a bawd and her co-conspirators, including a baron, not only out of some sort of obligation to pay them a considerable sum, but the lady had also extracted a sizable sum from them by threatening to open a superior brothel in direct competition to theirs. The lever they had used was failures in legal documents that Mr. Longshank had prepared. His incompetence was the only reason that the bawd had been cheated out of her money, or so she proclaimed widely. It was only later that the shady whoremasters realized that they had been totally out-maneuvered and that the threat, which was being used to make them agree to forfeit their claims and pay the lady, must have been spurious. The most amazing part of the story was that it was the lady's husband who had inadvertently landed himself in the problem that the lady solved. He was away at the time, and it was doubtful that he even realized the nature of the problem. His absence was the reason why the lady undertook to hoodwink the madam. Mr. Amery speculated that if the husband had not been away, the whoremaster would never have been tricked.

Daphne was horrified to learn that her dealings with Mrs. Marsdon and Mrs. O'Brien had become well known. She strongly suspected that Mr. Amery was well aware of the name of the lady and probably of her 'lawyer' and was warning them that their adventure was not unknown. Daphne hurriedly changed the subject since she thought her father, who seemed to be fascinated by the judge's tale, was unaware of the problem she had had, and so, he was unaware that it was she who solved it. Daphne would rather he continue not to know about the business rather have him admire her adroitness.

"What will happen to Sir Thomas Dimster, now, Mr. Amery?" she asked. "Will he hang?"

"That is most unlikely. I expect some sort of settlement will be worked out before his case comes to trial. It will probably cost him a pretty penny in fines. Even if he did come to trial and was sentenced to hang, he would not likely be executed. Some sort of pardon would be arranged, I imagine. Again it will be expensive for him. In either case, he will likely lose any influence he has. His pawns will know that they, themselves, came too close to hanging to risk helping him again. For, if the government chooses to be harsh, they can hang Sir Thomas and his lackeys."

"Mr. Amery, I still don't understand why Dipton is a separate constituency with so few eligible voters," Daphne remarked, hoping that that topic would further divert interest from the goings-on in London.

"These borough ridings are very confusing and go a long way back," the judge replied. "From a very early date after the Norman Conquest, the House of Commons had shire constituencies and borough constituencies. The main purpose of the House of Commons was to approve taxes the King wanted to levy, frequently to pay for wars. Though the country was mainly rural and landowners played a dominant role in the affairs of state, much of the tax money had to come from the towns rather than from the shires in general, and they had quite different interests from their country cousins. So each major town was allowed to send one or more members to Parliament to represent the principal men of the town.

"That is still the case, though, over time, Parliament became much more important than the King and his council of barons. Some towns shrank, and others expanded, even ones that had not been recognized as boroughs. The ones that shrank remained constituencies returning the same number of members no matter what their size had become.

"However, new borough constituencies might be created, though in recent years they have not been. Some of the medieval kings created additional borough constituencies where the election of members would be controlled by one of their henchmen, and so, thereby, the king would get less opposition from the House of Commons. To make sure that their followers could control these new boroughs, their charters often had very restrictive limitations on who could vote. Dipton Borough is one of those ridings, I suspect. It was a small place even when King Henry VI made it a borough, and it has, of course, shrunk since then.

"Now, why do so few people get to vote in Dipton, for we saw that there are large numbers of men who would probably be allowed to vote if Dipton were not a borough with very restrictive rules? In the original boroughs, the requirements to be an elector were decided for each borough individually, I think, and so there was a hodge-podge of regulations. In some cases, almost anyone who has a house where he and his family live can vote. In others, the right to vote is much more limited. In extreme cases, being an elector is restricted to the owners – not the residents – of residences in certain specific locations. If the residence disappeared, the vote did too, but, otherwise, its owner has continued to be eligible to vote ever since, even if a different building has replaced the original dwelling or if it is vacant.

"I haven't had time to delve into what the basis for voting here in Dipton may be, but it seems that the vote is limited to houses on specific plots of land, and the vote is in the hands of the owner, not of the resident. Over time, I imagine that many of the original houses having a vote have been torn down and not replaced. Many of the remaining ones are owned by only a few people. That is why there are so few names on the list. Like a lot of these borough ridings, the elections here have not been contested regularly. I imagine that would have been the case again if Sir Thomas hadn't thought he could get away by holding the election on a false basis.

"I'd always wondered about why there are such differences between different places," Mr. Moorhouse broke in. "I grew up in Birmingham, where my father owned a factory. He could vote only for the member from the county, and most of the other people couldn't even do that, even though it was a very large town. It seemed strange when I came here to learn that one man, Mr. Gramley, essentially had been able to choose who the two members of Parliament would be. That did change when I arrived since I discovered that I had also bought enough votes that, in principle, the election could be contested meaningfully, but, in fact, Mr. Gramley could determine the outcome, so elections were not held. Except for Mr. Jackson, the apothecary, I would have been the only one casting an opposing vote."

"It is a very strange system," agreed Mr. Amery, "and I doubt that it will change soon. Too many powerful men benefit from the present arrangements. Now, it has been a very long day for me, and I must return to London tomorrow. So, if you will excuse me, my lady. I think I will get to bed."

That ended the dinner. However, as Daphne was leaving, Mr. Moorhouse said to her, "Sometime, my dear, you must tell me the full story of what you and Lord David did in London. No, no, the look on your face as the judge told the tale indicated that it was you and Lord David who had pulled off the feat. I'd have guessed anyway. How many ladies have a tame vicar to help their husbands out of scrapes when they are away? I think Captain Giles should be very proud of you."

As her coach took her back to Dipton Hall, Daphne reflected once more on how much she missed Giles. She had told him all about how she and Lord David had hoodwinked Mrs. Marsdon and Mrs. O'Brien in her letters to him, of course. But she wasn't at all sure that he would get them before he returned. She didn't want him to find out from idle teasing from Sir David or some of his acquaintances in London. Maybe he would come to Dipton directly from his ship while his reports were sent to the Admiralty. She knew that that was the standard practice, but then Giles was not on an ordinary mission, so he might have to report in person. How she wished that he were here!

Daphne did wonder how in the world she would explain the complicated rules that had led to the contretemps over the election, especially since she wasn't at all sure that she understood the subject at all. Giles was a young, intelligent and inquisitive young man. He would probably know all about the complicated matters of shires and boroughs and electors. If he didn't, how could she hope to explain them? She didn't want to appear ignorant to him, even if her ignorance would not, she was sure, bother him at all.

Chapter XXI

The weather turned colder following the fiasco of the frigate competition. Thick hoarfrost formed every night, and the decks and rigging became highly treacherous in the early morning. Sand was spread on the decks to prevent falls, but moving about the ship remained hazardous. Safety lines were rigged, but performing any duties on deck still slowed to a crawl. On one occasion, a rain shower turned to mushy snow before it ended, leaving the decks a hazardous obstacle course for anyone who had to leave the safety of the lifelines rigged to make movement easier. The need to depart from Russia before *Glaucus* might be iced in was becoming urgent.

Admiral Stroganoff had invited Giles to dine on the flagship on the day following the competition. While *Glaucus*'s captain had been expecting another raucous evening with a headache to follow in the morning, he found instead that there was only one other guest. The marine minister, Count Smirnoff, had come from St. Petersburg not only to confer with the Admiral about when the Baltic Fleet would be laid up for the winter but also to talk with the British captain. Giles received warm thanks from both men for his rescue efforts when crisis overwhelmed the race between the frigates. Furthermore, the Admiral apologized for the fact that one Russian frigate had not gone to the aid of the others but had kept on racing as if the mishap to another vessel were no concern of hers.

The serious business of the evening was then taken up. The Count had come to reiterate that the Tsar and his Council accepted gladly all the proposals Giles had carried in his head from London. The new part of what the minister had come to talk about was that the Tsar had thought it best to make the understanding a formal, though secret, treaty, and not just an oral agreement. Count Smirnoff had brought with him the necessary document. Giles was to bring it to London so that the British Government could ratify the agreement formally. The Tsar expected that a copy signed by the King would be sent to St. Petersburg in the spring, it being far safer to send it by sea than by land through countries alive with agents and sympathizers of the French.

Giles was delighted that his diplomatic efforts had succeeded, even though they had only involved reciting messages from his government. He would place the new document with the sensitive ship's materials. They would be sunk if there were any danger of *Glaucus* being taken by the enemy. Having concluded their business, the three turned to enjoying their dinner.

The men sat long after the cloth had been drawn, yarning away, with Giles finding out far more about Russia and its customs than he would ever have suspected would fascinate him. Their talk covered not only military or nautical matters but also politics and farming as well as the huge differences between the two countries. Giles, used to the fierce independence of much of the English aristocracy from the crown, was astonished to learn just how subservient their counterparts in Russia were to the Tsar. Furthermore, Russian nobles were expected to perform serious service as administrators in the government, not just because that was their inclination, but also as a requirement of holding their status. The notion that the Tsar could banish noblemen at any time to the far reaches of the Tsar's empire was quite alien to Giles's understanding of his own position in England. When the three naval figures decided at last to call it a night, Giles realized that his own horizons had been broadened immeasurably while he had no doubt that he had made two friends for life as a result of the long evening spent together. When he awoke the next morning,

Giles also realized how very thankful he was that they had been conversing over port, out of respect for the British custom, rather than taking glass after glass of vodka that the Russians drank more in gulps than in sips.

Giles had more very satisfying evenings and made various forays to Saint Petersburg for social occasions. His clear appeal to many flirtatious young women made him proud to have abstained from the offered pleasures without regret just by comparing them to Daphne. However, Giles was becoming more and more annoyed that he heard nothing from Sir Walcott about when the special envoy would complete his work. Finally, he had had enough. He would go to Saint Petersburg and give the baronet an ultimatum. If Sir Walcott did not return to *Glaucus* in the next two days, prepared to leave, Giles would sail without him. Hopefully, the prospect of spending the winter in snow-bound St. Petersburg, far from the delights of the Prince of Wales's circle in London, would make Sir Walcott realize that he must rejoin his ship. Accordingly, Giles set off in *Glaucus*'s cutter for the capital in the thin light of a Russian dawn, which promised that winter would soon arrive.

Stewart, who was in charge of the cutter, drew Giles's attention to a boat coming downstream towards them. In that boat's sternsheets huddled Lord Malthampton, appearing to be totally miserable about being on the water in the raw conditions that characterized the day. Giles directed Mr. Stewart to bring the cutter alongside the other boat and lower the sail so that they could find out why the British ambassador might be coming to Kronstadt.

"Well met, Captain Giles," Lord Malthampton announced when the boats came up with each other. "I was on my way to summon you to St. Petersburg."

"May I ask why, my lord?"

"It's that…that…that fool Lainey," sputtered the ambassador.

"What has he done now?"

"He has got himself declared *persona non grata* by the Tsar. Silly idiot! He has been given twenty-four hours to leave St. Petersburg. Unfortunately, he refuses to budge from Prince Gruzinsky's palace. I need you to bring some seamen to force him to leave on your frigate. Otherwise, the Tsar may well order his Cossacks to bundle the scoundrel into a coach and dump him at the Polish border."

Giles thought a moment. He could return to *Glaucus* to collect a file of marines to ensure that Sir Walcott returned to the ship, but that would take time, and he wasn't sure that it would be wise to have red-coated marines marching through a foreign capital. Though not dressed in fancy uniforms, the men in his cutter would be quite capable of ensuring that the baronet would accompany them, whether he liked it or not.

"My Lord, can you transfer to my boat so that we can go to the city to collect Sir Walcott? You can tell me the ins and outs of the matter on the way."

Lord Malthampton was assisted in clambering into *Glaucus*'s cutter. He sat in the sternsheets huddled in his greatcoat supplemented by a boat cloak. He clearly did not enjoy boating in frigid weather.

"Now tell me, my lord, what has Sir Walcott done to produce this drastic reaction from the Tsar?"

"I imagine that you know that he moved out of the Embassy to Prince Gruzinsky's palace. The Prince is well known for his lax morals and peculiar tastes, tastes that appear to be shared by Sir Walcott, I am sorry to say. Such behavior is strictly illegal here, but it is tolerated among the nobility if they are discreet about it. Prince Gruzinsky has not been. He and the Princess had a soiree to which people of the same ilk were invited. There is no question that unnatural acts took place, and not at all discreetly. A cousin of the Tsar was in attendance, though he is only fifteen years old. Not mature at all. According to reports, this youngster engaged in some very revolting practices, including allowing himself to be...ugh...to be...well... to be buggered, by all accounts very willingly, by Sir Walcott. It was all too public, and rumors are spreading like wildfire about the despicable goings-on at that soiree. The government simply cannot ignore it, especially as the Tsar himself was disgusted and furious at the perpetrators. He had to act, especially as he wanted it to be believed that his young relative was too young to know what he was doing, though the reports made it quite clear that he was an eager participant.

"Prince Gruzinsky has been banished to Siberia permanently. He is lucky to have escaped with his neck. Several other participants, including the Princess, have been banished to their estates. Sir Walcott has been declared *persona non grata* and must leave St. Petersburg within twenty-four hours.

"This is not good for either of your missions. The Tsar is so angry with Sir Walcott that he may well decide to cancel all the agreements between our two countries. That is, cancel them in reality rather than as a subterfuge to fool the French and the Prussians. He is furious that we sent that ...that... that faggot. Sir Walcott was supposed to be such an arrogant braggart that rumors would be spread that his behavior had soured relations between our countries, but this may make the play-acting all too real."

When the party, whose purpose now was to extract Sir Walcott from the capital, reached St. Petersburg, they took down the sails and unstepped* the mast so that the cutter could be rowed through the canals. Lord Malthampton directed them to the landing in front of the Palace Gruzinsky. A line of soldiers now guarded it. They, somewhat reluctantly, let the British through after Lord Malthampton firmly explained their mission. Carstairs pounded loudly on the ornate front door. A footman dressed in a rather gaudy livery opened it. Giles pushed by him and, in a loud voice, demanded that Sir Walcott Lainey be summoned immediately. Many minutes passed before the baronet appeared, wearing a silk dressing gown and looking as if he were recovering from a night of carousing. The Princess also appeared, in rather rumpled deshabille.

"Sir Walcott, I have come to take you to *Glaucus*. We will be leaving immediately," Giles announced firmly.

"I cannot possibly do that, Captain Giles. I have to recover from the shock of what occurred last night. Can you believe it? A troop of Cossacks – very handsome Cossacks they were too – came and took Sasha away. I fear for his backside. Such villainous, appealing men they were! Very upsetting. They also seized my two servants, can you believe it? How am I to get dressed properly?"

"Sir Walcott," announced Lord Malthampton. "You must accompany Captain Giles now! I am surprised that the Tsar didn't have you executed and then have his minister apologize profusely for not realizing that you have diplomatic immunity. My aides have been working to obtain the release of your servants, but I would not be overly hopeful."

"Carstairs, accompany Sir Walcott to his room and help him dress quickly," Giles ordered.

"Princess, please show us where Sir Walcott's luggage is kept. Captain, please send another man to help clean out Sir Walcott's room." Lord Malthampton was taking charge of getting Sir Walcott out of the country. Giles did as he was asked. The Princess had already sent several of her servants to get Sir Walcott's luggage and take it to the boat. She then turned to Giles.

"Captain, what will become of me? I am exiled to Sasha's estate a long, long way, even from Moscow. Not to one of his residences nearer to civilization, but one far away. What will I do? I cannot live there! Please help me. The boredom will kill me. Can't you take me to England on your frigate? After all, it is completely Sir Walcott's fault, and you brought him here. I told Sasha to be discreet, but he wouldn't listen, and that flaming … flaming … flaming I-don't-know-what to call him … pederast …has brought this upon me."

Lord Malthampton intervened, "I am sorry, your highness, but that is impossible. Captain Giles would be placing himself and the British government in a very precarious position if he were to thwart the Tsar's commands. There is nothing we can do for you."

That declaration did not halt the Princess, though she switched to French, probably to harangue Lord Malthampton more effectively. He seemed to be giving as good as he got. Giles left them to it so that he could make sure that the luggage would be loaded into the cutter and stowed properly. He noticed that Sir Walcott's possessions included several crates stenciled in Russian. Had the baronet acquired a taste for vodka while he was in St. Petersburg? Time would tell.

The boat was quickly loaded. Sir Walcott donned a splendid fur coat and hat in the Russian style, and Giles made sure that he did not dally any longer. Lord Malthampton gave up his argument with the Princess, rather unhappily it seemed to Giles, in order not to be left behind. At least the Princess had not pursued her pleadings outdoors, so they were able to depart quietly without attracting undue attention.

Giles wasted no time leaving Kronstadt. A courtesy visit to Admiral Stroganoff to thank him for his assistance and to bid him farewell was quickly completed, even though no less than four glasses of vodka had to be downed before Giles could leave the flagship. Then quick orders to Mr. Hendricks had the crew raising the anchor and setting the sails to depart from the harbor. Giles was eager to leave behind him the diplomatic subtleties that dealing with the Russians had required. So much so that, for once, he was not nervous about getting underway while being the focus of telescopes from the whole fleet. Possibly the vodka had removed his usual anxiety.

Soon *Glaucus* was passing the merchant harbor of Kronstadt. Mr. Brooks pointed out that all the British trading vessels had already left. His noting that the ships had certainly not tarried when there was a chance of early frost stranding them in the port emphasized how important was *Glaucus*'s departure from St. Petersburg. As Kotlin Island was left in their wake and the sails were trimmed to take them westward, Giles wondered if he would ever again see Russian shores. Would he regret it if he never returned, or would he be indifferent?

Glaucus's passage westward through the Baltic Sea was uneventful. The winds were favorable, varying from north-north-west to north-east so that the frigate did not have to beat to windward. Few squalls interrupted her smooth passage. Such squalls as they did encounter were invariably accompanied by sleet or snow and each day dawned colder than the one before it. Every night hoarfrost formed on the rigging, and the decks were icy and had to be sanded.

The slippery conditions could be blamed for the disappearance one cloudy night of Humphries, Sir Walcott's one-time servant. He was reported missing when the watch changed, and it was presumed that he had fallen overboard. There was no hope of finding him even if *Glaucus* stopped and lowered boats to search for him. Giles was suspicious. It had been a quiet night, and someone on deck should have heard him cry out when he went over the side and, anyway, the conditions were not so treacherous as to render falling over the side likely. His suspicions were confirmed when he asked Carstairs if he thought that Humphries might have been helped over the side. Carstairs looked wise and simply shrugged his shoulders. Some members of the crew must have decided that they should dispose of the troublemaker before he got more of them into hot water. Giles was thankful that the crew had removed a problem which he had known that he would have to deal with before long. He transmitted that feeling to Carstairs to relay to the crew, without a further word on the subject being spoken.

The crew did not seem at all bothered by the presumed drowning of Humphries. Not so, Sir Walcott. He was quite shaken up by the news. "That is terrible, Captain Giles, just awful. He was such a good servant. Very strong. Very determined. Bit on the rough side, but sometimes that is what is needed. Oh, I am quite heart-broken, Captain Giles. Heart-broken! And it's all your fault. If you hadn't been so petty about my servants, I would still be able to enjoy his services!"

Giles was quite taken aback. People of Sir Walcott's rank were not supposed to show any feeling for the death of a servant, let alone make such an effusive declamation. Luckily, he did not have to see much of Sir Walcott. The baronet dined alone, for Giles had become sufficiently disgusted by his behavior in St. Petersburg that he did not invite him to dine either with himself or in company with his officers. He did suspect that the special ambassador would have refused an invitation even if one had been extended.

Soon after the disappearance of Humphries, Sir Walcott resumed his practice of appearing on deck occasionally. He was now dressed in his luxurious fur coat and hat. He would have looked quite the Russian grandee had he strode confidently about the quarterdeck. Instead, after a few steps, he would huddle in a voluminous sea cloak clutched over his Russian coat and hat, looking totally miserable. The misery, Giles suspected, came more from his passenger feeling sorry for himself rather than from his mourning his despicable servant. Except for polite greetings, no one paid Sir Walcott any attention, and he would soon return to his cabin.

This routine continued until *Glaucus* came to the right turn leading into the Øresund. Ahead, a flock of merchant ships was gathered, not moving, pointing in all directions as if they were huddling together in the hope of escaping some undersea menace. One look through the telescope confirmed to Giles the lookout's identification of the ships as being some of the British merchant ships that had departed St. Petersburg ahead of them. As *Glaucus* approached the group of ships, she was greeted by various signals telling of distress and gestures that indicated that she should stop.

Giles backed the main topsail and came to a halt near the collection of merchant ships. Even before *Glaucus* stopped, small boats left the individual ships, obviously intending to meet with the representative of the Royal Navy. The merchant captains came aboard one by one, the time between their arrivals determined only by how swiftly one boat could move off to let the next one deliver its captain. Soon a babble of shipmasters was trying to get Giles's attention with their news. He remained polite but non-committal until all were aboard. Then he said in a stentorian voice, "Welcome all. What seems to be the problem?"

Babbling broke out once more until Giles held up his hands to quiet the noise. "One at a time, please, gentlemen. You, sir, I remember you from St. Petersburg. Captain Carruthers, I believe. You were one of the most vocal about the difficulties that you gentlemen encounter in leaving the Baltic."

"Yes, sir. I am afraid that the pirates have struck again, and they have taken one of our British vessels with a cargo bound for London."

"Tell me how it happened."

The story emerged with many an interruption from the various other officers to supplement Captain

Carruthers' account. The British ships had been sailing in convoy in the hope of being able to discourage the privateers. As they turned towards the entrance to the Øresund, they were faced with the problem of sailing into the wind and became scattered, possibly because this close to Copenhagen, they all felt safe. In any case, the leading ship, a vessel called *Judy's Luck,* whose master was called Captain John Carbuckle, had surged into the lead and had decided to go close to Swedish shore. This mariner, it seemed, had always been one of the captains who fretted most about the disadvantages of sailing in convoy since he had one of the fastest ships. As *Judy's Luck* cleared the end of a peninsula that hooked northwards, just after the passage to the North Sea itself turned north, she was close to the shore. Suddenly a schooner appeared from behind the headland. It was flying the French flag and was armed with four guns on each side. Captain Carruthers thought that they were twelve pounders. It was the work of minutes for the privateer to seize *Judy's Luck.* Both vessels disappeared behind the headland before any of the other ships could attempt a rescue even if they had been so inclined.

The seizure of *Judy's Luck* caused consternation among the other ships. A conference was held, and they decided that they dare not proceed since the schooner appeared to be more than a match for even a pair of their own ships, and the raid had happened so quickly that the privateer could easily capture another one or two before they could do anything about it. Some had argued for their gathering all their sailors on a couple of Trojan horse vessels in the hope of overwhelming the privateer when she tried to capture them, but no one would volunteer his ship, and most of the captains pointed out that none of their crew had signed on to engage in attacking enemies. They would wait for nightfall and then hope to sneak past the marauder.

Giles's inclination was certainly not to ignore the threat, even though *Glaucus* would be quite safe from the privateer's attack. However, he had to reckon on the repercussions of any action he took. The privateer was clearly using Swedish waters. Was she under Swedish protection? The Swedes must be aware of her presence. After all, the ancient town of Malmo was just a few miles up the coast. However, there would not be any naval ships stationed at that port, and it was a long way to Stockholm to call for help. In any case, the Swedish government would probably not be overly concerned about French privateers attacking vessels that were not Swedish. By the same token, Giles could hope that they would not be overly sensitive to *Glaucus* removing the threat to British shipping. It certainly wouldn't be enough to make them ally with Bonaparte.

Although it clearly exceeded his orders, Giles realized that he must capture this menace to shipping and rescue the British ship. Holding up his hand for silence, he first asked Mr. Brooks for a glance at his chart. As he had recalled from his previous examination of the map, it was shoal-water around and beyond the headland, and someone had written: "soundings* not reliable in this area." He couldn't use *Glaucus* to capture the schooner. The danger of grounding was too great. The capture of the schooner would have to be done using only his boats.

Giles took control of the gathering again. "I am going to capture this privateer and rescue your comrades. I will do it after nightfall. I suggest that you all stay together here, but be prepared to get underway a bit before sunset and follow me when I start as if I am leading you through the passage. I shall be close to the eastern shore, and you should all appear to be keeping together and moving farther to larboard. The signal that I have been successful will be a red lantern at the main topgallant truck. I would suggest that you then proceed together through the Øresund. I will be stopped for a considerable time, I imagine."

Turning to the Master, he asked, "When is moonrise tonight, Mr. Brooks."

It was no surprise that the answer came back immediately. "Shortly after three bells of the second dog-watch, sir. It will be a gibbous moon rising on a bearing of northeast by east."

"For those who do not understand naval time keeping, Mr. Brooks is telling us that the moon will be rising a bit after 7:30 p.m., so you can expect to proceed around eight o'clock. Good luck."

When the merchant-ship captains had left, Giles gathered his officers together. "We are going to have a cutting-out expedition against that sloop. She must be lurking somewhere beyond that headland. A bit before sunset, we will start sailing into the Øresund as if we have decided to lead the other ships through the passage. We will be trailing all our boats behind us. Just after sunset, while there is still enough light to see clearly, our jib sheet will part as we come about near the headland. It will somehow foul the staysail sheet. Mr. Brooks knows how to execute that trick. We will drop a sea anchor as if to hold Glaucus's head steady as we get the sheets untangled and a new jib sheet rigged. While that is happening, the boats will be brought in, presumably to prevent them from fouling each other. As soon as the boats are out of sight of the headland, our men will board them. Mr. Macauley, all your marines will take part in the assault. Divide them among the boats. Mr. Hendricks will be in command. The other two boats will be commanded by Mr. Miller and Mr.

Stewart. Mr. Hendricks, you may choose the seamen who will go with you. Your first job will be to take this schooner. Then secure the British ship that has been captured. Attack just as the moon is about to rise so you will have some light."

Giles was about to give even more detailed orders when he remembered that they would probably interfere with the efficient taking of the enemy. He couldn't anticipate exactly what problems his officers would face. Giving them too many instructions might inhibit them from acting in the best ways to overcome unforeseen difficulties. Instead, his next order was, "Right. You all know what to do. Get on with it."

Time bore heavily on all crew-members as they waited for sundown. Giles would have much preferred to begin a fight the minute it was decided to engage, but that was not the usual way in naval warfare. It was particularly difficult when all they could do was wait for the right time. Surely, there must be some more orders he could give to ensure success. He restrained himself. His officers knew their business and nagging at them would only produce unhelpful and distracting annoyance, which they would not be able to express to their commander.

Finally, the sun sank behind the Danish coast. Mr. Brooks had indeed done his job. *Glaucus* was in exactly the right position, close to the shore almost at the end of the point of land. With the light fading, they could only just be seen from the shore, and watchers ashore might have difficulty making out the details of their actions. *Glaucus* came about. The jib sheet was slashed by a seaman positioned so that there was no chance of anyone not on the frigate seeing his action. Men swarmed aloft to furl the sails while a sea anchor was thrown to keep the ship from falling back. Somehow, the boats that had been trailing behind the frigate were swept to the larboard side, the one away from the shore. No time was wasted pulling them up to the ship so that the raiding parties could board. With everything ready, they waited for another few minutes. A flurry of activity broke out after the jib sheet had been mended. The sails were unfurled, and the frigate gathered way on the starboard tack again. Hopefully, no one on shore would be able to see the three boats unship their oars and pull towards the headland.

Giles kept pulling out his pocket watch and holding it to the binnacle light to see how much time had passed since the boats had started towards the end of the headland. The hands of the timepiece seemed to be stuck. He even held the watch to his ear to make sure that it was still working. Finally, the time came to turn back towards the land. It was now full dark, though the land could just be made out as a blacker patch in the darkness off the starboard bow. Mr. Brooks, whose sang-froid in difficult circumstances was legendary, was having the log* dropped into the water almost as soon as it was recovered. He was also constantly ordering slight changes to the sails, even though he must have known that such frequent attention to their progress would have little effect on where *Glaucus* would end up when the moon rose. Finally, light could be seen through the trees to the northeast. Moments later, it was clear that the moon was rising. Soon the water to starboard was illuminated. They could make out a schooner at anchor half a mile to leeward and behind her what must be three merchant vessels, not just the one they had expected to find. Giles ordered that *Glaucus* heave to* until they could determine just what was happening. As the order was being executed, several flashes of light were seen from the deck of the schooner. They must be muskets or pistols being fired so that the cutting-out parties had succeeded in finding the schooner. A little later, boats could be seen heading from the schooner towards the anchored merchant ships. The schooner, after another pause in the action, could be seen to be raising her sails and to be moving. She must have anchored on a buoy to get underway so quickly. In moments, her head had turned to bring her onto the starboard tack. The merchant ships must have been anchored, for, while men could be seen on their yards ready to loose the sails, they remained head to the wind for some time. Then they too were underway. Giles wondered about the identity of the two extra ships.

The schooner was the first of the captured vessels that came up to *Glaucus*. Lieutenant. Hendricks returned to the frigate with a rather scruffy looking man who reeked of garlic.

"What have we here, Mr. Hendricks?" Giles inquired.

"This man seems to be the master of the schooner, sir, which is called the *Françoise Marie*. He has a French letter of marque, so she is a privateer. Mr. Macauley has secured the other officers and crew of the schooner. I have left Mr. Miller in charge. We have freed the three ships which were all captured by this ruffian. Two English vessels and one from the United States. Their captains will come on board as soon as they have raised their anchors. The *Françoise Marie* was on a buoy so we could get underway much faster."

Before long, the three merchant ships came out of the bay and hove to near *Glaucus*. Their captains came over to frigate. The first to arrive was the captain of the ship that had been snatched from right before the eyes of the other vessels that had been sailing together. He was genuinely grateful for having his ship returned to him. The second was the captain of a British vessel that had been captured earlier.

An American captain was the third ship's master. He named himself Nathanial Scrubbs. He drawled in the soft, southern manner as he expressed great thanks for being rescued. He had loaded a cargo of hemp and sail-linen in Kronstadt for transportation to Charleston, South Carolina, which was also his homeport. He thought that he would have no trouble as a neutral vessel sailing to a neutral port. That had not been the case. The commander of the French schooner had paid no attention to his loud protests about his ship being captured. He didn't seem to care that the American captain was pointing out that he was quite clearly sailing to a neutral port in a vessel that was American.

The privateer had not been impressed by his arguments. "You say you are American and not from England. That is nonsense. You come from a place called Charleston in somewhere called South Carolina. The first name clearly is in honor of King Charles of England. The second must honor some English queen. That cannot be a part of America. Their revolutionaries would have changed the name."

"His argument was nonsense. I have documents from the United States government that state that South Carolina is a state of the union, but he paid no attention," stated the American captain.

"You were quite correct in what you asserted," Giles agreed. "The privateer had no business taking your ship. He is nothing but a pirate. I will take him to England with me, where I expect that he will hang. I will need a full statement from you, please."

The ships all got underway again, sailing together. Giles was very happy with this accomplishment. He had been wondering whether his visit to St. Petersburg had really been worth the time and effort. Surely it could have been done just as well without the charade of the special ambassador, and he wasn't sure how necessary was his own part in keeping the Russian navy sympathetic to Great Britain. This recent action had been worthwhile. England needed the supplies which otherwise would have fallen to Bonaparte.

That night, Giles thought contentedly about how he should describe the action in his continuing letter to Daphne. He would tell her in detail of his accomplishment, but he had to be careful not to sound pompous or too boastful. He always found it difficult to describe success, but he knew that she would want to know every detail. He wondered if all the letters he had been writing to his wife on this trip would have to be delivered in person when he got home. So far, there had been no opportunity to send mail, and he himself might now be the best messenger. He had no wish to delay so that the mail could be delivered first.

Chapter XXII

Daphne realized after the excitement of the election had passed that she was recovered from giving birth. At least, she was happy to resume her usual routines. She found that she had added two new ones to the list. The new mother enjoyed holding Bernard and watching Nancy feed him. She made sure to allocate several periods a day to this pleasure.

What Daphne found tiresome was a ritual that followed the birth of a baby to a prominent family. Until she began to experience the custom, Daphne had not been fully aware of it. No one had ever suggested to her that she participate in it when she was just Miss Moorhouse, and somehow no one had told her about it after she married. The custom was for the ladies of good breeding to visit a new mother of their own elevated status to coo over the new child and gossip about other families of the same class. In the course of the gossip that inevitably accompanied such visits, Daphne learned that the Dipton election had split the community of would-be society leaders. Many thought that it was awful that Sir Thomas Dimster had even been charged with treason and faced the possibility of being executed. They thought that his actions were shrewd tactics of business, and it emerged that this group thought that Daphne had simply outmaneuvered him in a rather clumsy way, one not suitable for the wife of a leading member of the local aristocracy. Others thought that Sir Thomas's trying to take the election away from Lord David in favor of a lackey to serve his own ends was deplorable. In their opinion, he deserved to be punished severely, largely because it was so clearly not respectful of the Viscount who, due to his superior status in society, should naturally determine the outcome of the election.

Furthermore, social precedence aside, many of those who supported Daphne argued that, in buying Dipton Hall, Giles had also purchased the seat in Parliament that went with it. Sir Thomas was regarded by them as trying to steal something that belonged to Daphne's husband. The punishment, however, seemed to all the local gentry to be excessive.

The taking of sides over the secondary outcome of the election soon came closer to home. Thomas Dimster, although he was the oldest son of Sir Thomas Dimster, held firmly that his father was only getting what he well deserved. His wife, Lydia, Daphne's half sister-in-law, was quite of the opposite opinion. She thought it was terrible that the Dimster family should be pilloried because of a reasonable and shrewd move to enhance their influence. It was quite clear that she did not want to have her husband's eventual baronetcy tarnished by scandal or impoverished by the heavy fine that was widely believed to be necessary if Sir Thomas was to avoid the noose or banishment to the penal colonies of Australia.

Daphne had heard hints from her visitors that many thought she had outmaneuvered Sir Thomas simply to gain the influence that Sir Thomas had expected to derive from having an MP in his pocket. The baronet somehow thought that he deserved to get this advantage now that he could no longer act through Mr. Gramley, the former MP. Mr. Gramley's own seat had been the subject of the election. However, Sir Thomas's expectations from electing his man had gone farther than just swaying the MP in his own interest. Major Stoner, in his blunt way, had laid Sir Thomas's scheme out for Daphne one day when she had invited him to dinner in the hopes of furthering the romance with Lady Marianne.

"You certainly outfoxed that maggot, Sir Thomas Dimster, Lady Ashton," the Major declared. "The scoundrel feels that you have deliberately done him in. Apparently, he had had a good business going selling the influence of a member of parliament, namely Mr. Charles Gramley, to the highest bidder. He seems to think that it was his prerogative, by right of having done it in the past, to arrange things for a fee. He presumes that you will do the same thing using Lord David. Just shows how little he knows about you or the vicar. Can you believe it? He is even threatening to get back at you somehow for stealing his income. Never heard of such a thing! I don't know the ins and outs of the matter, but everyone is astonished how you got the better of the old scoundrel. Awful man! Disgrace to the nobility!

"Do you know," Major Stoner continued, "that that Dimster fella has been truly gleeful about not being in gaol? The judge from London somehow didn't realize that he would be committed for trial by our own magistrates and the other magistrates are all in Sir Thomas's pocket. As a result, they let him go off 'on his own recognizance' until the trial at the assizes. Can you believe it?"

"Is Sir Thomas still a magistrate?" asked Daphne.

"Yes, he is. Or so he thinks, anyway," replied Major Stoner. "He has also boasted that if any of your tenants or workers appear before him, he will have the book thrown at them. I think he is just hoping for a chance to get back at you and show that you cannot intervene in his plans without paying a high price."

"I don't see how he can do that," Daphne replied. "I don't have any business connections with him."

The conversation drifted off to other topics, and Daphne thought no more of Sir Thomas and his threats. Even when Major Stoner asked if he could call on her the next day, she presumed, correctly, that his request had nothing to do with the machinations of Sir Thomas Dimster.

The conversation that ensued when Mr. Stoner was announced into her writing room the next morning struck her as being very peculiar at the beginning. The Major started by stuttering a bit before getting down to any sort of coherent statement.

"You wanted to see me about something, Major Stoner?" Daphne interrupted a particularly convoluted sentence by the Major that was not getting to any point.

"Quite... Yes, Lady Ashton...Yes, of course...It's about ... It's about the Hunt." The look of relief on the Major's face made Daphne suspect that this was not at all what the man had come about but instead was a topic that did provide a convenient diversion while he worked up the courage to broach the real subject of his visit.

"Yes, Major? As you know, I have already agreed to have the Hunt Ball at the end of the season and to host a meeting of the Hunt itself."

"Yes, indeed, Lady Ashton. Very generous! Very generous, indeed! We are so lucky to have you! So lucky! ... But it is not about that that I wanted to talk to you. No, not at all. Not at all... It is, of course, very good that you support the Hunt with such generosity. Very good... "

The Major seemed about to get lost again in his convoluted speech without coming to the point.

"You had something more about the Hunt?" Daphne intervened.

"Yes, yes ... the Hunt ... yes, actually it's about the hounds."

"The hounds?"

"Yes. You see, old Colonel Redfern has been Master of the Hounds for years and years. Very good man, the colonel, though actually Charlie Maddox is the real master and trains the dogs. Excellent fellow, Charlie Maddox, excellent! We — the Hunt, that is, — we pay Colonel Redfern quite a large sum of money for housing the hounds, but it has been worth every penny. Best pack of hounds for miles around. Best pack! Without them, we wouldn't have such a pukka hunt. I suppose that I shouldn't say 'pukka.' Indian expression it is. Means very fine, just right, and… Anyway, no, we wouldn't have such good hunting. Certainly not. Couldn't do without Charlie, wouldn't be the same at all…"

Major Stoner seemed in danger of again getting lost, this time in the excellence of the hounds, and Daphne was afraid that he would not find a way out of this maze either. The Major wasn't usually this vague. There must be something else on his mind, Daphne thought and began to suspect what it was.

"So there is a problem with where the hounds can be kept, is there, Major?"

"Yes, indeed, Lady Ashton. That is the nub of the matter."

"And?"

"Well, Mr. Summers has been wringing his hands about it. He can think of no solution if Colonel Redfern really can't keep the hounds. I suggested that you be approached. That is, of course, that Captain Giles might be, but he is always away, and everyone knows you manage the estate when he is away. But Mr. Summers didn't like to ask … Good chap, Summers! Good chap! But not always straightforward. He thought that he couldn't just approach you, and no one knows when Captain Giles will return. And the Captain wouldn't have time probably to consider it before he was called away again. And anyway, why should he take it on when he is away for most of our meetings? Very delicate feelings has Mr. Summers. Wouldn't have done very well in India, I can assure you. Not a man for the John Company*. No, he wouldn't have done well out there, not well at all, I can assure you."

The Major was again losing the thread of his argument, so Daphne once more intervened to move him along, "So you were wondering if we would take on the hounds?"

"Yes, my lady. That's it exactly. Exactly! Summers didn't like to ask you, so I thought I would sound you out on my own. We all know that Captain Giles wouldn't take it on without consulting you first. Lucky man, your husband, very lucky! Unusual arrangement you seem to have. Wouldn't work for most people! Actually a bit shocking, but it seems to suit very well in your case."

Daphne had to step in again before the old curmudgeon reappeared, the man had a very low opinion of women's abilities. That had been the man whom she had first encountered on being introduced to Major Stoner. He had originally indicated to her quite clearly that having women riding to hounds was not at all appropriate. To give him credit, he had abandoned that opinion, at least in her own case, when she had demonstrated that she was a better rider than most of the existing members of the hunt. But his basic beliefs in the capabilities of women always threatened to emerge if they were not suppressed by his being diverted to a less offensive subject. Daphne was now quite fond of the Major and had learned how to steer him away from his most obnoxious comments.

"Well, I'll have to consider it, Major. Of course, it will be Captain Giles's decision completely. I will just do a bit of scouting out so that my husband can act more quickly when he returns. You can tell Mr. Summers that it was I who raised the possibility of moving the hounds to Dipton Hall when you told me about the problems with Colonel Redfern. It is really what happened."

"That is very good of you, my lady. Weight off my mind, I can tell you."

"Surely, the subject of the hounds was not the only reason you seemed so eager to see me this morning, Major."

"Well, ugh, well … no, it really isn't. I did want to sound you out about something else as well. Yes, something more personal, delicate, really. No, thinking it over, I realize that I shouldn't bother you with this matter. Not suitable. But still, I would like to raise it with you."

"Oh, spit it out, Major, spit it out! Don't beat about the bush. Better to be straightforward." Major Stoner's manner of speaking seemed to be catching. "I am not some delicate flower that needs to be protected from every change of weather. No, I am really quite robust." Daphne was starting to lose patience with the Major's fumbling around every topic.

"It's nothing like that. Lady Marianne…"

"Yes?"

"Well, her daughters now have very good futures. Miss Lydia with Mr. Dimster and Miss Crocker with Captain Bolter …"

"Yes?"

"Well, neither of her daughters will be in a good position to give her a home, and I know she feels that she would be a burden for them."

"I suppose that might be the case, Major Stoner. Lady Marianne is, of course, welcome to continue to reside at Dipton Hall." This was not exactly true. Daphne had never warmed to her half sister-in-law and would be more than happy to see her leave.

"Well, you see, Lady Ashton, especially in view of Captain Giles's absence, don't you know, that I think … I should talk to you … yes, definitely talk to you…about Lady Marianne," Major Stoner blurted out the lady's name in his final breath before his face turned an even more violent shade of red, even purple. Surely he wasn't about to suffer apoplexy from talking about Lady Marianne.

"About Lady Marianne, Major?"

"Yes… yes…yes! I want to marry her… There, I've actually said it! … I know that her two daughters had to get

Captain Giles's permission to wed, and I presume that it is the same with Lady Marianne."

"Good heavens, no. Major Stoner." Of all the things that might be on Major Stoner's mind, Daphne would never have guessed that he thought he had to ask Giles's permission to marry or that he would think that Daphne could stand in as a substitute for her husband. It must, indeed, have been very difficult for him to raise the subject with her, given his general opinion of women's place in the order of things.

"Lady Marianne needs no one's consent to marry," Daphne continued. "The situation of her under-age daughters was quite different. They were legally Captain Giles's wards. But Lady Marianne can make up her own mind. It must be different in India, maybe that is where you got the idea that mature women need a man's permission to do anything, but that is certainly not the case in England."

Daphne's statement, she knew, only applied to unmarried women, and only partially even then, but there was no point to go into the finer details of women's status. In Lady Marianne's case, maybe he was right that she needed to be guided by a man, even if it was not the law. Her half sister-in-law hadn't done very well on her own.

"Yes, I see," said the Major, rather taken aback by Daphne's certitude about the matter. The Major was becoming used to Daphne having a mind of her own and her willingness to express it in words and deeds, whatever convention might dictate. For a man who had been horrified about the idea of ladies really joining the hunt, he had come a long way. He had been won over to Daphne's position by her actions and her grace, but she wasn't sure whether he was not just making a single exception for her.

Still, if he could implicitly admit that mistake, he might be able to make many other changes to fit better into modern English society. It would certainly strengthen the chances of a happy marriage if Lady Marianne were to accept him.

"Do you think she might be interested in marrying me?" Major Stoner blurted out.

"Of course," thought Daphne. "The possibility of rejection when he was trying so hard to fit into society must be troubling him." She was almost inclined to give him a hug and tell him what he wanted to hear, though the first gesture would have terrified the poor man completely. So what she did say was, "You will have to ask her yourself."

"I could offer her a lot, you know," Major Stoner continued. "I made a great deal of money in India, a great deal. I have a really pukka estate here, really pukka. I know I am a diamond in the rough, or maybe I should admit to being a rough piece of quartz at best. Lady Marianne can smooth some of my rough edges off, I am sure, and make me more acceptable to society. She does have a suitably energetic side to her. That's not why I want her, of course. I think that, for the first time in my life, I am in love, can you believe it? But I am a bit too blunt for most people. I know it. In fact, yours is the only major house in the area to which I am welcomed as more than an appendage of Mr. Summers. Lady Marianne knows about how I have noticed these things and thinks that I can change and be more acceptable. You see, I have talked to her about my problem in getting accepted, but not about us getting married."

"Oh, dear," thought Daphne, "What have I let myself in for by encouraging this conversation?" She was well aware that her own first impression of the Major had not been favorable. What she said, however, was, "I think,

Major Stoner, that your best course of action is to talk with Lady Marianne directly. There is no point stewing about the matter any longer. I know you have given this step a lot of thought, so just get on with it. Here," she said, rising to go to the bell pull, "I'll ask Steves to tell Lady Marianne that you would like a word with her."

After the Major had left to see Lady Marianne, Daphne thought to herself that she hoped he could be a bit more direct with Lady Marianne than he had been with her. Otherwise, the poor woman might not even realize that she was receiving an offer of marriage.

Daphne decided that she would not wait around to hear the outcome of the meeting between Major Stoner and Lady Marianne. She would rather let Lady Marianne get used to the idea that she had been asked to marry rather than getting a minute-by-minute account of the Major's proposal. Instead, Daphne would start investigating what was involved in taking on the hounds for the Ameschester Hunt.

The person in the immediate neighborhood who would be most likely to be knowledgeable about hunting hounds was Mr. Griffiths, her stable master. He did, indeed, turn out to be conversant about what would be involved in taking on the hounds. It would be highly expensive, he pointed out. Furthermore, the dogs could be a noisy lot, and, so, they could be a great nuisance unless the kennels were located some distance from the Hall. However, after starting as the devil's advocate, it quickly became clear that he was really very enthusiastic about the idea. Training the hounds would mean that the fox population of Dipton's woods would be kept down, much more than would be the case if the foxes were being protected so that the hunt could find one easily. That would benefit the local hen coops.

That way of culling the foxes would be accomplished without drawing the approbation of the hunting neighbors. Having the kennels would also make training the hunting horses a lot easier and produce better results if they were already accustomed to following the dogs before they were sold. At Salton Masham, where Mr. Griffiths had previously been employed, there had been difficulty in training horses to ignore the hounds but still follow their cries when hunting. Having the hounds at hand would be much better than the artificial scenes he otherwise would have to use. There was, also, Mr. Griffiths proclaimed, a perfect place to situate the kennels, in a hollow in Dipton Wood, where the yapping of the dogs would not be heard from the Hall.

"There is one hitch about that site," Mr. Griffiths completed his discussion of the location for the kennels. 'Just,' Daphne thought, 'to show that he was being judicious and objective rather than enthusiastic.'

"What is that?" Daphne asked.

"It is very close to the track dividing Dipton Wood from Mr. Julius Wark's land. As you know, Mr. Wark won't let the Hunt onto his land, not even the dogs to start a fox running. That prohibition is no problem with the mature dogs. Charlie Maddox always has the hounds under control. Pups in training may be a different matter. I am not sure that he could prevent them from venturing into Mr. Wark's woods."

"I can see that that might be a problem. I'll have to think more about it."

Daphne did not know much about Mr. Wark. Although Dipton Wood adjoined his property, with a cart track separating them, she had seen very little of the man. His land was in the next parish, and it was also not in Dipton Borough, so he had not been involved in the recent election. She had heard that he was heavily involved with smuggling, providing a center for the trade, both as a place from which to dispense the smuggled goods to customers in the neighborhood and also as a staging ground for the transportation of contraband still farther inland. He was rumored to have several well-hidden storage places in the depths of his wood and was hostile to having neighbors drop in informally. It was widely presumed that the revenue officials did not harass him because of judiciously placed bribes and the general influence of men who appreciated the service Mr. Wark provided in facilitating the delivery of their foreign luxuries. He also had the reputation of treating trespassers and poachers very harshly, relying on the clubs of his gamekeepers rather than the magistrates' court to inhibit people from venturing onto his land.

Daphne returned from her conversation with Mr. Griffiths convinced of two things. First, taking on the hounds would not be a profitable venture. Second, this sort of activity might well attract Giles as a hobby. He had taken to the horse-farm with gusto, even though it had a long way to go before it might show a profit. Her husband would likely share Mr. Griffith's enthusiasm. So she should not reject the idea out of hand.

As Daphne had hoped, Major Stoner had actually succeeded in proposing to Lady Marianne. She had never seen her sister-in-law as excited as she was when Daphne returned from talking with Mr. Griffiths. Nothing would do than that she should sit down and receive a full account of how marvelous the Major was, though Lady Marianne did indicate that he had beaten around several bushes before getting to the point. He had sealed his commitment by giving her a betrothal ring, a large gold filigree ring with a prominent ruby as its central feature. It was of Indian origin, part of the loot that the Major had brought home from his time in India, and Daphne had to gush over it for some time to satisfy her sister-in-law. Giles had not given Daphne a betrothal ring, having had no chance to acquire one before proposing to her, but he had provided a very well crafted wedding ring that was now her most valued possession.

Daphne stated that, of course, Lady Marianne would be married from Dipton Hall and that Giles would provide the wedding breakfast. This was greeted with relief and enthusiasm, Lady Marianne's own allowance, of which she always spent every penny, would not have allowed any celebration that the Major did not fund.

"Oh, thank-you, thank-you." Lady Marianne declared. "Oh, don't you think that the Major is marvelous. He even stated that I wouldn't have to get married in my shift!"

"What?"

"You know. A widow has to come to her next husband naked, that is, in her shift, to make it clear that she is not bringing with her her dead husband's debts. But I don't have any debts that I know of, anyway."

"That is because Giles already paid all your debts and your husband's and has made sure you haven't run up any others since you came here," Daphne thought to herself. "I hope the Major knows that you and money are easily parted."

What she said, however, was, "I am sure that this is exactly what Captain Giles would want."

Daphne had not been overly concerned about Major Stoner's tales of threats from Sir Thomas Dimster to repay her for interfering in the Dipton election and for landing him with the likelihood of severe punishment for what he had tried to do. She had not seen her actions to stop the fraudulent election as being directed particularly at Sir Thomas, but simply as a way of ensuring a proper choice of the MP for Dipton Borough.

Daphne did, however, take umbrage at Sir Thomas's remaining a magistrate when he had shown such contempt for the law. She would write to Mr. Justice Amery about the matter. It did not occur to her that Sir Thomas still wanted revenge. The threats must have been issued in the heat of the moment, and the baronet would realize that taking action against her would simply land him deeper in trouble. In this belief, she was mistaken even though it took a while for his threats to materialize. Nothing happened for several weeks, and when he did move against Daphne, she did not realize immediately what he was doing.

Daphne awoke one morning to the news that Jacob Nester had been arrested for poaching in Mr. Julius Wark's wood. Jacob Nestor was one of her tenants, holding a small farm leased from Dipton Hall. He also worked from time to time in the fields of Dipton Hall. She was surprised. There had been no reason for Jacob Nester to poach in Mr. Wark's wood. It was Daphne's practice to allow her tenants and workers to take rabbits on her land since there were more than enough to satisfy the wants of Dipton Hall and of Dipton Manor. Indeed, at present, she had a surfeit of rabbits and hares in her woods and they were making a nuisance of themselves in the various farmsteads over which she had control. Jacob would have had no problem getting his catch in Dipton Wood. If he had been doing so, it would have been natural for him to use the track that separated her land from Mr. Wark's, so Daphne believed that the charge might have been fabricated. This was especially so since it was not Mr. Wark's custom to deliver offenders for judgment by the magistrates. He thought direct action by his lackeys served as a better way to protect his game and his privacy.

Mr. Wark was a known ally of Sir Thomas. Could this be the fulfillment of Sir Thomas's threat? It started to seem more likely when one of Daphne's morning visitors mentioned that Mr. Wark had been heard to say that he and Sir Thomas thought it was time to teach poachers from Dipton a lesson by hanging some of them.

The hearing before the magistrates for the poaching offense was to be held in Ameschester at ten o'clock in two days' time. Daphne knew that she would have to be present, even if it was unlikely that the magistrates would allow her to speak because she was a woman. Unfortunately, Lord David was in London on some business to do with his assuming his seat in Parliament, and her father was sick with a stomach malady that Mr. Jackson said was not serious, but would confine him to Dipton Manor for several days. She realized that she had no other man to call on to take her place in defending her tenant.

Daphne would have to go herself to the hearing in the hope that she could be heard. She would stay the night at the Fox and Hounds in Ameschester so that she would not be rushed getting to the hearing. Possibly, she should also speak to her solicitor to arrange that he could speak for her to the tribunal. Mr. Snodgravel was adequately skilled as a man to handle routine contracts and tenancy agreements, but he was not an impressive or an assertive one. He was, however, the only one she could call on who might make an impression on the magistrates. He might even be up to challenging Sir Thomas's right to continue to act as a magistrate when he was under indictment for treason. She had received a letter from Mr. Justice Amery to the effect that Sir Thomas could not possibly sit as a magistrate until his trial had been heard, but she had no hope that she herself would be allowed to present it.

How she wished Giles were here! He would know how to deal with the situation. When would he be coming home? His presence would allow her to be less preoccupied with this wretched affair and more with her maternal responsibilities. It was very difficult sometimes to have to wear his hat as well as her own, even though she recognized that the present problem was all the result of her own actions. She was sure that he would be quite pleased about the future marital status of Lady Marianne, but she wouldn't take any credit for bringing it about.

362

Chapter XXIII

Giles's little flotilla made its way up the east side of the Øresund without seeing any other ships. They slipped past Copenhagen and continued up to the end of the sea passage in the dark. If Danish ships were patrolling the area, they were not close enough for *Glaucus*'s crew to see them by moonlight, especially as the sky had clouded over near midnight. The wind was light, and it took the ships more than two full days to approach the end of the Skagerrak.

They were sailing easily on a north-west breeze as they passed the Skagen soon after dawn. Ahead, the fog banks that typified the North Sea were starting to break up. Suddenly in one of those banks, flashes were seen, followed quickly by the sound of cannon firing. Some sort of naval action was happening in front of them. There seemed to be three or maybe even four sources of the gunfire though they were all so close together that this impression was largely guesswork as long as they were shrouded in fog.

"Clear for action," Giles roared. "Mr. Brooks, we should get over there as quickly as possible to see what is going on. Use all sails to get the maximum speed out of *Glaucus*."

The placid deck erupted into frenzied action. In a remarkably short time, Mr. Hendricks was able to announce, "Cleared for action, sir."

"Very good, Mr. Hendricks. You have shaved thirty seconds off your previous best time." Giles had been timing how long the exercise took. He knew that that sort of behavior by the captain, acting as if this were just a routine drill, would calm nerves as battle approached.

"Mr. Hendricks, load, and run out."

Just then, the fog bank broke up and exposed three frigates. Judging by the smoke that was slowly dissipating, a very hectic battle was being fought. The center ship was firing her broadsides on both sides while the outer two were replying from their sides nearer the middle ship. They would soon be able to grapple and attempt to board their victim.

"The center frigate is *Perseus*, Captain Bush's ship," Midshipman Stewart announced with great excitement. "The other two appear to be French frigates, somewhat bigger than *Perseus*. They might be thirty-sixes or maybe even thirty-eights."

"Mr. Brooks, keep all sails filled and furl them only as we go into action," Giles ordered. "*Perseus* may even have an advantage in a broadside duel since she is firing more quickly than either of her opponents and can use both sides. Bush must have a nearly full crew to be able to fight both sides simultaneously. However, if the other ships grapple with her and try to board, he will have a hard time holding off their combined crews."

Giles's thoughts were interrupted by the presence of Sir Walcott, who had apparently just realized that *Glaucus* was not steering to avoid the battle of the ships ahead. "Captain Giles, what are you doing? You simply cannot think of getting involved with those ships. Remember your orders! I am still the special envoy to the Court of the Tsar of Russia! You cannot put my life in jeopardy! I forbid it."

"I am afraid that you cannot forbid anything, Sir Walcott. Your mission is over. Even if you do not return to London, the Ambassador will no doubt make a report on your performance."

"But, Captain, it is too dangerous. I might be killed!"

"If that is your worry, I suggest that you go to the orlop now. You will be quite safe there."

"But...but...I cannot possibly go there. Isn't that where all those horribly wounded sailors will end up?"

"Yes. Maybe you can help Dr. Maclean. In any case, get off my deck."

Giles roared the last sentence at the ambassadorial pest. Sir Walcott looked startled and even terrified at the tone of the Captain and scurried to the companionway leading below. Giles knew he should feel ashamed at how he had terrified his passenger, but, instead, just now, he was feeling a guilty glee at even slightly venting his real feelings about Sir Walcott.

Time crept forward terribly slowly. The men on *Glaucus* could only stare at the battle. As Giles had pointed out, *Perseus* seemed to be giving as good as she got, firing almost three broadsides to her enemies' two. However, it was only a matter of minutes before the French frigates would come alongside her, and then the situation might become hopeless. *Glaucus* must get to the battle as quickly as she could.

The frigate to starboard of *Perseus* had crept closer and closer to the British frigate and looked as if she should be ready to grapple. The other one had fallen slightly behind but was pointed towards the English frigate as if she intended to slide up *Perseus*'s larboard side to board. The second frigate's guns had fallen silent as they could no longer target the British frigate, but *Perseus* could still fire into her. The guns, however, would not stop the French ship. Giles's friend, Toby Bush, was about to be required to repel boarders on each side, likely an impossible task.

Then the battle took a surprising turn. A cannonball from *Perseus*'s starboard battery, aimed high for no apparent reason, had skimmed over her opponent's bulwark without striking anything until it slammed full force into the mizzenmast. Giles saw what had happened. It was a lucky shot, and probably a mistaken one. With the enemy about to grapple, Giles would have expected Bush to be ordering his deck guns to load with grapeshot* or canister*, not with round shot. However, whether fired deliberately or by mistake, that one ball had a major impact on the fight. It had broken the enemy's mizzenmast. The mast seemed to waver, and then a roll of the French frigate to larboard made the mast slowly fall towards *Perseus*. Down it came, taking with it some of *Perseus*'s rigging, until it was almost, but not quite, lying on *Perseus*'s deck. It's fighting top* and the mizzen topmast had struck the other French frigate and pinned that ship in a position where its bow was pointing a bit towards *Perseus,* and its stern was moving away so that most of the enemy's starboard guns could still not be brought to bear.

The balance of the fight had changed dramatically with the French frigate's mizzenmast going by the board. That ship was now held at close range to *Perseus*. The British frigate's quicker handling of her guns had already put many of her enemy's cannon out of service. Now her more rapid fire was silencing more and more of the remaining guns while also pounding the French frigate's larboard side to splinters. The continuing bombardment must be wounding a huge percentage of the French ship's gun crews. Things were not much better for the rest of the French crew. *Perseus*'s carronades*, having put the corresponding French guns out of service, had switched to grapeshot, which plowed horrible swaths of wounded and dead sailors across her decks.

The French on the first frigate were massing near the fallen mast to try to somehow storm aboard *Perseus*, but the only bridge to their opponent's deck was the fallen mast. It was rounded. While that fact would have presented no problem to any of her crew who were used to working aloft, it did mean that the French sailors could only cross the gap between the vessels one-by-one. The chances of their not being picked off by *Perseus*'s muskets were non-existent. Of course, the problem of using the fallen mast as a bridge worked both ways: *Perseus*'s crew were equally unable to board their opponent. The two ships seemed like two chained dogs, close enough to bark and snarl at each other but unable to bite.

The situation was equally fraught with danger on *Perseus*'s larboard side. Here, the topmast of the starboard frigate held the opponents apart. The top was between the ships, and the mizzen topmast and especially its rigging was holding the ships apart. Their bows were closer together than their sterns, and if the French crew could cut away the rigging of the mast, their bow might be brought up to *Perseus*'s side. Captain Bush's crew might be able to withstand an attack from that quarter. However, the severe pounding from her opponents' guns, which *Perseus* had already taken, and the numerous musket exchanges between the ships must have wounded many of *Perseus*'s crew. Her captain, his friend Bush, might well not have enough men to hold back the larboard boarding party while still keeping the crew of the frigate to starboard from crossing the downed mast to fall upon *Perseus*'s defenders.

Giles was debating which French frigate to engage when the wind took the decision out of his hands. It had been blowing from the northwest so that *Glaucus* could sail towards the combat on a close reach. Now the wind backed in such a way that *Glaucus* could only just come up to the frigate on *Perseus*'s starboard side without having to tack. There was no time to tack and tack again to reach the other enemy ship. He ordered Mr. Brooks to bring the ship to the starboard side of the southern enemy ship as quickly as possible but to be sure to take enough way off her so that they could grapple and hold the ships together side to side. He ordered the deck guns to load with grape and fire as they bore. This would at least create chaos among their opponent's crew members who had already moved from the larboard side of their ship in order to repel *Glaucus*'s boarders.

Mr. Brooks had judged the timing of backing the main topsail and the ordering that the others be furled to perfection. *Glaucus* slid close to the French frigate's side. Grapnels* were thrown, and their lines belayed. This was done just when there was enough way on her to resist the influence of the recoil from her own first broadside and the impact of the French reply so that Giles's ship came to rest against the other frigate's side. *Glaucus*'s crew immediately lashed the two ships together. Another blast of grapeshot from *Glaucus* preceded Giles roaring, "Boarders away."

Giles led one boarding party and Lieutenant Hendricks another. The two forces overcame the French opposition in minutes. The French captain roared, "Je me rends." Giles took a moment to accept the French surrender and delegate Mr. Correll, his third lieutenant, to take charge of the captive. However, he could not take any time to enjoy his victory.

Giles's next step was to race to the mast-bridge that connected this frigate to *Perseus*. Bush had left only a small guard to prevent Frenchmen from crossing. That had been sufficient so that now, with the surrender, there was no one to prevent *Glaucus*'s crew from crossing via the fallen mast to their countrymen. Giles scrambled onto the mast, took a moment to get his balance, and then led the way for his force to aid *Perseus*. In the strange super-clarity of battle, when everything seemed to slow down, and his immediate position became clearer even though the overall situation remained chaotic, he still found time to reflect on the foolishness of racing along a rounded surface, that of the fallen mast, when it was years since he had last walked along a ship's yards to show off. Nevertheless, he made it across without stumbling, and he was quickly followed by most of *Glaucus*'s crew.

A moment's pause allowed him to realize that the other French frigate had at last been able to get its bow alongside *Perseus*'s. Bush was now leading his own crew members to thwart a French attempt to board, but he was being pushed back by the greater number of French sailors. Giles was rushing to lend his crew-members' support to the actions of his friend when he received a blow to his shoulder. It knocked him off his feet, and, in falling, his head struck something solid. He lost all consciousness.

When Giles came to, he found himself propped up against something substantial, probably *Perseus*'s mast. His head hurt abominably, and it was considerably more painful than his shoulder. Captain Bush was hovering over him, looking concerned as well as exhausted.

"Wha' 'appened?" Giles mumbled. Why couldn't he talk clearly? How ashamed his old nanny would have been if she could hear him. She never let him talk in a sloppy way.

"You have taken a ball in your shoulder — from one of their marines in their fighting top — and you have hit your head," Bush informed him.

"And the ba''le?"

"Your arrival turned the tide completely. Just after you fell, your first lieutenant led the way onto the French frigate, and she surrendered in short order. It was just a pity that one of the marksmen in her fighting top hit your shoulder before that occurred. The butcher's bill was very high on *Perseus*, as you can imagine, but it was even higher on the French ships. Now rest easy, Richard; your surgeon is about to come to treat you properly."

Giles blanked out again, and some time must have passed before he revived to find Dr. Maclean busy cutting off the shoulder of his coat and his shirt.

"Oww! That hurts!"

"I bet it does. And it will get a lot worse before I am finished. Here, drink this. It will take the pain away and make you even woozier. It's laudanum."

After that, Giles again relapsed into unconsciousness. He only awoke after he had been carried to *Glaucus's* deck, where he was sitting in a chair. He felt disoriented but was aware that both his shoulder and his head hurt terribly.

"Ah, you're awake again," said Dr. Maclean. "I got the bullet out, and a couple of bits of bone it had splintered off. I hope I got all the cloth the ball carried with it into you. If I did, it should heal without any problems. If I didn't, you may have some serious problems with the wound. I left a drain in because there will undoubtedly be some puss. There is nothing I can do for your head. It should get better over time, but try not to over-exert yourself for the time being. I know that you won't follow that advice until everything is squared away after the battle, but I have to give it anyway."

"What is our butcher's bill?"

"Four seamen dead, eight wounded, three very seriously who may not live, and you, of course."

"That is very light."

"Aye, sir. The story is quite different on *Perseus* and the two French ships. *Perseus* lost more than half her crew, dead or seriously wounded. Two lieutenants and a midshipman were killed. Even Captain Bush took a musket ball in his arm, his good arm. Just a scratch, really. And a bullet grazed his head."

"Thank you, Dr. Maclean. I hope that Sir Walcott didn't make too much trouble."

"That one! I still can't believe it. Do you know, he started by trying to get me to declare you incompetent for putting him in danger and for not taking him to England directly. I was about to order one of the loblolly-boys* to restrain him when the first of the wounded was brought below. That subdued him. He was almost sick, and then he recovered. He was horrified by what he saw and offered to help. Incidentally, his two servants were in the orlop too, and they pitched in to help as well. All three of them are now helping on *Perseus,* where the situation is much grimmer than here. I don't think that Sir Walcott had really thought about what happens in battle and that it is not all glorious action and bugle calls. Incidentally, one of the servants asked me if I thought there was any chance of their being accepted as volunteers into your crew. I told them to ask you. Apparently, it had never occurred to them that you might be approachable. Now I have to go. Lieutenant Hendricks is waiting to see you."

The first thing that Giles noticed when Lieutenant Hendricks entered was that his arm was in a sling.

"You are wounded, Mr. Hendricks."

"Yes, sir. A cutlass slash as I was boarding the *Reine Audu.* That is the name of the second French frigate, sir. The cut is not nearly as serious as your own wounds, Dr. Maclean tells me."

"And *Glaucus* herself?"

"We got off fairly lightly, sir. Some damage to the topsides and the gun deck, but nothing that the carpenter cannot repair in short order. However, there is one major problem. One of the last balls from *Jeanne Manon Roland* - - that's the name of the frigate that we engaged – hit the mainmast. It tore out a large portion of the mast where it struck and also cracked what was left. It is a wonder that the mast continued standing. Mr. Evans believes that, by lashing three timbers around it tightly and by not spreading too much sail on it, the jury rig will take us safely to England. The carpenter is engaged in that work right now, but he isn't making any guarantees. But you know how Mr.

Evans is. He would only guarantee that it would hold up if he was sure that you could take it round the Horn. The *Roland* suffered a great deal of damage on her larboard side, and her gun deck is a shambles with her side badly damaged and many of her guns dismounted with their carriages ruined. I have Mr. Stewart and a file of marines overseeing some of the French prisoners in setting things to rights so that she can proceed, but she will also require a visit to the shipyard before she can truly sail again. We will be hard put to get her to the shipyard.

"*Perseus* is in no better shape. Her gun decks are a shambles, and she took four shots between wind and water on her starboard side at close range. She is leaking very badly. *Perseus*'s pumps are barely keeping up with the water coming in. I have lent her some men to help and our portable pump. Captain Bush is preparing sails right now to fother* over the holes to reduce the intake. Hopefully, that will lessen the inflow enough so that his carpenter can make some sort of repairs.

"*Reine Audu* suffered a great deal less though more than we did on *Glaucus*, except for our mast. Since Captain Bush lost two lieutenants in the fight, I have ordered Mr. Correll to take charge there with a small number of our sailors. He is effecting repairs. Her officers have given their parole, as have those of the *Roland*. I have most of her crew working on *Perseus* with Lieutenant Macauley and the rest of his marines overseeing the prisoners. They are also lending a hand where they can. We did get that fallen mast removed finally so that all four ships are rafted* together properly. That should help make sure that *Perseus* doesn't sink before the worst of the leaks is covered by the sail."

"Very good, Mr. Hendricks. Carry on. I think I shall have to sit here a minute or two more before I can oversee the work more actively."

"Aye, aye, sir. But sir, I think you would be better in your bed. Dr. Maclean said so."

"Damn your insolence, Hendricks! I am in command, and I must stay on deck!"

Giles felt guilty about snapping at his first lieutenant, but not enough to do anything about it right away. Instead, he soon found his head nodding as his mind became more blurry, and he was fast asleep in minutes.

Giles awoke to find himself in his own bed. The motion of the ship told him that *Glaucus* was still rafted up with the other frigates. The light coming through the stern windows indicated that it was shortly after dawn. His headache was still there, but he was thinking more clearly. He looked about to find his servant, Ferguson, asleep in a chair.

"Ferguson, you lazy creature, get me some coffee."

The servant shook his head as he roused himself. "Can't, sir. Dr. Maclean said to give you nothing but water when you woke up. He also told me that I should summon him the minute that happened, so that is what I am going to do now."

Giles was reflecting that maybe he shouldn't have appointed one of the stupidest and laziest men on board to be his servant. His choice had been based on the consideration that Ferguson would simply be in the way with any other assignment. At least, he didn't do any harm as a servant and could follow simple orders. But maybe Giles should look out for his own comfort for once and not just consider the good of his ship.

Dr. Maclean came bustling in. "I see you are awake, sir. How is the head?"

"It hurts like crazy."

"Are you disoriented?"

"No, it is not as bad as the last time I got hit on the head."

"Good. And your shoulder?"

"Very sore. And throbbing a bit."

"Let's have a look."

Dr. Maclean removed the bandages over Giles's shoulder carefully, doing his best not to make easing the dried discharge from the wound cause more agony. The area around where the bullet had entered was inflamed, and it was obvious that there had been a significant amount of discharge of greenish-yellow fluid. "Not as good as I hoped, I am afraid, but it is early days. I will put a poultice on it and keep it immobile. I hope that it will heal. It is likely to be sore for some time. You also have a slight fever. You can certainly get up, but don't let yourself get chilled. If you are tired, rest."

Dr. Maclean helped Giles from his hanging cot before leaving. Dressing with Ferguson's help was a problem. Giles had never realized what a large part his left arm and shoulder played in daily life. He had real difficulty adjusting his breeches so that he could button them at the waist, and fastening the flap one-handed was almost impossible. Maneuvering his shirt over his shoulder was an agony, and he ended with his coat thrown over his shoulders like a cloak. Doing all this was not easy, and he had to sit down for a few minutes before he had the strength to go on deck.

There he found an overcast sky with the wind blowing lightly from the north-north-west. Most of the signs of the recent battle had been removed on *Glaucus,* and the only hint of the real damage she had suffered was in the extra stays* that were supporting the main mast and the timbers that were lashed to it. Only a small watch was evident on deck, and the officer of the day appeared to be young Mr. Fisher.

"The rest of the crew are on the other frigates, sir, as are the other officers. There is a terrible lot of damage to them. Much worse than us," the midshipman squeaked. His voice had only recently started to change, and what came out of his mouth could still be surprisingly shrill. "I think the other ships may be ready to sail soon, sir. Mr. Brooks is concerned that we will be caught by a much stronger wind soon, and we don't want to be all tied together if that happens."

Looking across, Giles saw that the ship next to him – what had Hendricks called her? The *Roland* or something like that – had obviously been in a fight, but the main evidence that revealed this was a very jury-rigged, cut-down mizzenmast. From the next ship, *Perseus,* he could hear the clank of the pumps. He wondered if the water was still gaining or if Bush had stemmed the tide. He couldn't see enough of the fourth ship to determine her state of readiness.

"I'd better see how the other ships are getting on myself. Just keep a close watch here, Mr. Fisher."

"Aye, aye, sir."

Giles had to be assisted to cross over to the *Roland*. His shoulder certainly was hurting very severely for a small wound, and it prevented him from doing many ordinary things. Mr. Evens had fashioned a jury mizzenmast using the main topgallant mast and the main royal mast. It should suffice to get them to a shipyard where proper repairs could be made. Her larboard side had been badly chewed up by *Perseus*'s broadsides, but the proper repair was also the job of the dockyard.

The news was also good when Giles crossed to *Perseus*. Captain Bush welcomed him aboard, though he omitted the elaborate ritual used when a captain came aboard another ship. He had also been wounded, though in his case, the evidence was a bandage wrapped around his head, caused, Bush told Giles, by a splinter. Three of the shot holes below the waterline had been plugged, and the fourth would soon follow suit. The pumps were now gaining steadily on the leaks. In doing so, they were also reducing the pressures on the repairs. *Perseus* also would soon be ready to sail. Giles avoided having to cross to the fourth frigate. From *Perseus*'s deck, he could ascertain that she was ready to proceed. He could expect that all the ships would be able to set off for England within the hour.

A flotilla of four frigates! Giles wryly thought that such a force might be a commodore's command if the ships were all healthy. Of course, they were not, and nor was their commodore. Daphne would appreciate the irony of a banged-up captain being the commodore of a banged-up flotilla, though he might first have to explain to her what a commodore was. He knew that she would be much more dismayed by his injuries than she would be amused by his wit. He had so much to tell her, and he did so want news of her.

Simply put, he missed her. Now, at least, he was headed towards her. Lord, how his shoulder hurt! And his head. He might just take to his bed for a while until his flotilla was ready to resume their journey home. Maybe he would dream of a peaceful life with Daphne and their baby at Dipton Hall.

Chapter XXIV

Daphne was taking her breakfast in the parlor of the Fox and Hounds in Ameschester when she saw the overnight post-coach from London dash into the inn yard. Idly observing the coach, she first saw a man with a peg leg and a bandage around his head awkwardly exit the vehicle. When he turned around, she realized that it was Captain Bush. She was already rising from her chair, hoping that he might help her with the trial when another man appeared. He had his arm in a sling, and he had stepped out of the coach in such a way that all that Daphne could see of him was his back. However, there was no mistaking that back! Giles had arrived! Any thought of consulting Mr. Snodgravel immediately vanished from her mind.

Daphne jumped up from her table, upsetting it with a great crash of crockery, which she ignored. She ran out of the parlor, through the inn door and straight across to where the coach stood. Luckily, Giles had turned and seen her coming, for she flung herself at him in a way that would have knocked him down if he had not braced himself. With Daphne safely nestling in his arms, they gave each other a huge hug and a lasting, warm kiss. It was an absolutely improper manner for gentlefolk to behave, but they didn't care. People could think what they liked!

"You are home!" Daphne exclaimed. "It's wonderful! But you are hurt. How did that happen?"

"Rifle bullet while we were taking the French frigates. I'll tell you all about it. But first, what brings you to Ameschester?"

Daphne explained briefly, finishing by saying, "It doesn't matter really, now. Not with you home and wounded."

"No. It is important. We are responsible for our people. We will have lots of time after the hearing to catch up on all the news. Let's go into the inn and you can tell me all about the problem. There is one bit of news I do have to know right away, however. About the baby."

"Oh, of course. You haven't heard? We have a boy. He is just the most wonderful baby! He is called Bernard, as we agreed before you left. Berns for short. He's perfect! Oh, I have so much to tell you! Did you get any of my letters?"

"No, and I have lots of news to tell you, also. But let's deal with Jacob Nestor's difficulties first."

The inn staff had righted the table that Daphne had knocked over and cleaned up the mess she had made. She was mortified to realize what she had done, but she was greeted again by kind smiles and polite service. It would never have occurred to her that all the local people took pride in the fact that the very unconventional Daphne Moorhouse had become a great lady by marrying Captain Giles and had remained as spontaneously unpredictable a person as she had always been.

Daphne had observed before this occasion how Giles assembled facts and arguments methodically before making a decision on important matters. She had never before seen him operate with a time constraint. Without rushing her, he got the essence of the charge against Nestor from her, why she thought the allegation might be spurious, and why she felt so helpless in the face of the malice of Sir

Thomas Dimster. Within half an hour, Giles had extracted and evaluated every bit of information she had about the situation and was ready to proceed. For the first time, Daphne felt some strong hope that poor Jacob Nestor would not be hanged or even convicted.

The magistrates' court was to be held in a room of the Fox and Hounds. Giles and Daphne made their way to it, accompanied by Captain Bush, Carstairs, and Captain Bush's coxswain, a man called Tramorgen. Giles surveyed the room as they entered, deciding whether he would be more effective speaking from the back of the room or the front. He chose the front and led his party to seats in the front row.

The magistrates appeared and took their seats on a slightly elevated platform behind a long table. Sir Thomas Dimster occupied the center chair, flanked by two other men whom Daphne did not recognize, but she presumed that they were the other two justices of the peace.

Sir Thomas took up a gavel, banged it on the table in front of him, and announced, "We are now in session. Constable, bring in the cretin so that we can get him hanged properly."

As the chairman sat back to await his order to be obeyed, Giles rose to his feet. In a voice that was not overbearing, he addressed the clerk who was seated at the end of the table, "Note my words carefully, clerk."

Then, in a voice that could reach the fore-topgallant cap in a gale, he continued. "Sir Thomas, you have no authority to sit as a magistrate. Your appointment has been canceled, as you well know. I demand that you excuse yourself immediately."

"I will do as I please," replied Sir Thomas. "My appointment was revoked by mistake, so we will pay no attention to that contention. You, sir, cannot interrupt our proceedings this way. Constables, arrest this man and hold him in the gaol until we have time to deal with him. It will do him good to cool his heels there for a couple of days until we decide his fate."

Both constables looked a bit nervous at the order. Giles unquestionably had the look of a man who was used to command, far more than did Sir Thomas. However, they didn't have much choice, especially if they wanted to keep their positions. As they stepped towards Giles, Carstairs and Tramorgen rose from their chairs. The constables hesitated, looking very unhappy about the prospect of taking on the two menacing sailors.

Giles took advantage of the pause. "Constables, arrest Sir Thomas Dimster and convey him to the gaol," he said. Then addressing the whole room, he announced, "I am Captain Sir Richard Giles, an officer in His Majesty's Navy and, as such, I am an officer of the crown with full authority to put down sedition wherever I find it." Giles had no idea if his claim to authority had any validity, but, if not, he would cross that bridge when he came to it. It never occurred to him that he might be guilty of much the same type of offense as was Sir Thomas. Since Sir Thomas was rendered temporarily speechless by the effrontery of this man, and knowing that, in fact, he should not be presiding over the court, Giles was able to continue without being interrupted.

"I have here a letter from Mr. Justice Amery stating that, in view of the charges pending against Sir Thomas Dimster, his commission as a Justice of the Peace has been revoked. As a result, he has no authority to sit on this court, let alone to preside over it. I suggest that you other magistrates have Sir Thomas held for the assizes both on the original charge and on the charge of knowingly impersonating an officer of the crown."

If Giles had no real idea of what the law was, the same was true of the two remaining magistrates. They were landowners in the area and only served as magistrates because of the prestige that the position offered. They had no training of any sort to do their jobs. After a hasty consultation between themselves, in which they concluded that Sir Thomas seemed to have landed himself in very hot water, which they did not want to spill over onto themselves, they told the clerk to prepare the necessary document needed to have Sir Thomas taken to the jail and kept there.

"Now, gentlemen," said Giles, since the two magistrates seemed to be in some doubt about what to do next, "you should hear the case that brought us here – the alleged poaching on Mr. Wark's land."

"Quite right," proclaimed one of the two remaining magistrates. "Let's get the miscreant in here so that we can hang him properly."

Jacob Nestor was brought in, looking very disheveled and grubby after spending some time in gaol.

"Right," said the magistrate who had decided to act as chairman. "What do you have to say for yourself before we sentence you to hang?"

Giles was on his feet again, "I would call to your attention, your worships, that, for at least the past forty years, magistrates do not have the power to order capital punishment. All you can do is bind him over for the assizes, but, first, you have to establish that there is a case against him."

Giles had no idea where he had picked up these pieces of information, or even if they were true, but it should be enough to make these incompetents think twice about ordering any hangings. "You have not done that yet. Don't you think that you should call witnesses to present evidence of the crime?"

The magistrates' immediate response to this was to huddle together. The silent one seemed to be a good deal less happy with what was happening than the vocal one. As the conversation continued, he seemed to be getting angry, and his final remark could be heard clearly by everyone in the room, "Sir Thomas got us into this, and he isn't about to get us out of it. We may be on thin ice, so we had better do everything according to the book. Captain Giles seems to know what the book says, so we had better do what he suggests."

"Mr. Wark," said the magistrate who had assumed the chair, "is your witness here?"

"Yes, your honor, it is Mr. Jenks, my gamekeeper. He is sitting beside me."

"Mr. Jenks, come up here so that we can all hear you clearly. Now tell us what happened."

"Yes, sir," replied the gamekeeper. "It was night time, about ten o'clock, I'd say. I found this man here with a brace of rabbits, fresh-killed, don't you know? So I held him at gunpoint while my assistant, Georgie, tied his hands behind him. Then I marched him to Mr. Wark's barn, where we kept him until morning and then brought him here. Can't have poaching, can we, sir? Or so Mr. Wark said."

"I see," commented the magistrate. "That seems cut and dried. Let's get on with the sentencing."

Giles was on his feet again. "As Nestor's master, I demand my right to question this witness."

"What? Oh … well, just go ahead, if you must."

"Now, Jenks, where and when did you find Nestor?" Giles took over the questioning.

"On the track between Mr. Wark's wood and Dipton Hall's. It was just at dusk. He had a brace of rabbits in his bag."

"What made you think he was poaching?"

"Well, he had the rabbits."

"Are Mr. Wark's rabbits different from my rabbits?'

"No, sir."

"So Nestor could have caught them in Dipton Hall Wood."

"I suppose so."

"What made you think they were Mr. Wark's rabbits?"

"Mr. Wark told me to seize any of Lady Giles' tenants or workers who had rabbits and take them to gaol for poaching. He said that Sir Thomas Dimster had asked him to do so to teach Lady Giles not to meddle in his affairs. He said that Sir Thomas would make sure that he hung the offender and would let Lady Giles know why it had happened."

"So, to sum up, you are saying that Mr. Wark conspired with Sir Thomas Dimster to murder one of my people?"

"I suppose. But Mr. Wark was very firm about teaching people a lesson to stay well away from his wood. He don't like people going there – they might find out where he hides the smugglers' goods."

That got an audible gasp from the other watchers in the room. Everyone knew about the smuggling, of course, but stating it so blatantly in open court was sure to make the revenue officers descend on the wood with their troops and quite possibly dry up the supplies of brandy, wine, tobacco, and other luxury goods in the area.

"Thank you, Jenks,' said Giles. "Your worships, I suggest that it is now clear that there is no case for Nestor to answer. You may want to have Mr. Wark arrested on charges of conspiring to commit murder, or whatever the offense really is, and add that charge to those against Sir Thomas as well."

"Yes, Captain Giles. Quite right. Constable, arrest Mr. Wark. He is over there."

"And Nestor?"

"Yes, yes. Jacob Nestor, you are free to go."

Daphne couldn't resist her impulse to hug Giles as the court concluded. It was totally inappropriate to show such affection in public, but she was far too glad to have him back and acting so strongly for her not to show how she felt. It immediately bothered her that he winced at her embrace, not from embarrassment, as first she thought, but from the pain in his shoulder. She had forgotten that he was wounded!

Captain Bush refused their invitation to ride in their carriage to Dipton. "You will want to talk and talk without me present. I'll just get a coach to take me home."

Both Giles and Daphne were glad. They had so much to tell each other, and it simply could not wait. Daphne immediately asked Giles about his injury, but he fobbed her off by saying, "It is nothing. Just a minor wound I received when Bush and I captured two French frigates. His wound is more serious, especially as he took a ball in the thigh as well."

Before Daphne could ask more details about both the battle and the wounds, Giles said, "Now you must tell me about the baby."

It took quite a while for Daphne to tell Giles about his son, especially when one of her remarks diverted the conversation temporarily onto other matters. Mentioning that she wasn't nursing young Bernard led to the question of who was his wet-nurse. Revealing the name led to the question of how Giles's illegitimate half-nephew, Thomas, and his mother, Nancy, were doing. Then, the discussion came back to the topic of the nanny. Daphne explained how Nanny Weaver had brought her up and had agreed to play the same role for young Berns. Luckily, from Daphne's point of view, Giles had no opportunity to ask about how the matter of the London lease had been resolved.

The carriage was turning through the gateway marking the start of the drive to Dipton Hall before Daphne could ask a question about Giles's voyage. She got no reply since, instead, he asked. "Has it suddenly become very cold in here?"

Daphne looked at him. He was shivering as if he were in a blizzard without clothes, even though it was quite warm in the carriage, and he had on a great coat. Before she could do anything, the shivering stopped, but Giles was now slumped in the corner of the carriage, not like himself at all. Daphne yelled to the coachman to get to the Hall as quickly as possible. Something was clearly wrong, but she couldn't think of anything to do about it immediately. Had taking over the hearing been too much for him? What had she been thinking when he arrived, clearly wounded and tired, to ask him to help Jacob Nestor?

The carriage pulled up to the portico of Dipton Hall, and a footman opened the door. "Assist Captain Giles out of the carriage, Justin," Daphne ordered the footman, "and take him upstairs immediately. Steves, send for Mr. Jackson, at once. Captain Giles is critically ill. Have him come right away."

Daphne trailed Giles and the two footmen who were almost carrying him upstairs.

"Take him into my bedroom," she ordered. "Undress him and help him into his nightshirt and into bed. Steves, have the fire in the bedroom built up again. I want it warm, really warm."

Daphne supervised the servants assisting Giles to undress and to get into a nightshirt and then helped him into bed. While this was going on, she noticed that his wound in the shoulder was looking red and swollen and that blood and other discharges were marring the outside of the dressing over the wound. She immediately ordered that the cook should start boiling water and for someone to find some clean material to use for bandages. She knew that Mr. Jackson always seemed to need boiled water and clean bandages when he had wounds to deal with. It was still a little chilly in the room, and Giles had started shivering again. Daphne didn't hesitate. She stripped off her dress, not waiting for Betsey's help, with buttons popping out all over the place, and crawled under the covers with Giles and held him tight. Her husband needed warmth, so she would provide it!

It took endless minutes for Mr. Jackson to arrive.

"Daphne, you can let go of him now. In fact, you can get out of bed so that you can help me. Captain Giles, what is the problem?"

"I feel cold and sometimes too hot and very weak. My shoulder is hurting abominably."

"Let's have a look."

Mr. Jackson placed his hand on Giles's forehead for several moments and then took his pulse. He looked more and more perturbed at what he was discovering.

"I am afraid that your wound has become infected and has caused blood poisoning. I'll have to have a look at it. But first, I need a clean glass."

Betsey handed the apothecary-surgeon a clean glass. One of Daphne's peculiarities was that she insisted that the glass on the nightstand be washed every day. Mr. Jackson took a small bottle from the bag he always carried when attending a patient. He poured a small measure of some gray liquid into the glass. "Drink this, please, Captain. It has horrible taste, I am afraid."

"What is it?" Daphne asked.

"A tincture of mold, a special mold, that seems to help cases like this. I don't know why. Daphne, you can get dressed while I look at the injury. You others," Mr. Jackson addressed the servants who were in the room, dithering about not knowing what to do. "I need some sheets or other covering to protect the bed."

Without waiting for an answer, Mr. Jackson started to remove the dressing from Giles's shoulder. "As I suspected. I don't think your surgeon succeeded in getting all the debris out of the wound before sewing it up. It is not healing at all properly. I am going to have to open it up again. Daphne, you are the best person here to help me. Get into your oldest clothes. They are likely to be ruined."

As Daphne signaled to Betsey to find her least valuable dress, some of the servants looked at her in astonishment. It was not the proper role for the lady of the house to assist a surgeon in his tasks. That was up to a servant. They were slowly getting used to Lady Ashton's eccentric ways, but this went beyond anything they would have expected. The servants who had been with her longer, and had known her as a young woman before she had even met Giles, recalled how she had assisted Mr. Jackson more than once when everyone else around had seemed likely to faint or be sick when faced with the reality of severe wounds. Doing the unexpected could almost be expected of Lady Ashton when faced with a crisis.

"This is going to be extremely painful," Mr. Jackson warned Giles. "Drink this, it will help a bit."

"What is it?" Daphne asked.

"Laudanum. It should help the pain and maybe reduce the dangers from my having to open up the wound again."

In a few moments, Giles seemed to retreat into himself. Mr. Jackson tested his pulse again and then began working on the wound. He removed the stitches and eased his fingers into the cut that Dr. MacLean had made on *Glaucus*. Mr. Jackson would have to open up the wound to see what had been left in it.

"As I thought," he muttered. "It is not healing."

Soon the surgeon was deep into the wound. Daphne helped by passing instruments and, at times, by helping to hold the wound open or to wipe away blood that was obscuring the inside of the cut so that Mr. Jackson could work better. Despite the laudanum, Giles was clearly in pain that he was trying to bear stoically, but some groans did escape his lips. These diminished as Giles seemed to withdraw into himself.

"Thank Heavens," Mr. Jackson said after a while." I have found some strands of cloth that may be causing the problem."

The surgeon continued to probe the wound and found some more small bits of cloth. He also discovered some tiny fragments of lead, which he also removed, and also some small splinters of bone. The search for foreign objects in the wound seemed to go on forever. At last, Mr. Jackson was satisfied.

"I think I have all of it," he said to Daphne. "The bullet hit his shoulder bone. It cracked the bone, and, in doing so, it must have broken off some pieces. Nothing special needs to be done about that. It will heal on its own if we can get the blood poisoning under control. The bullet carried pieces of his coat and shirt right into the wound, and that is what produced the problems. The ship's surgeon must have removed most of the material brought into the wound, but he didn't find it all or every bit of the bullet that must have broken up when it hit the bone. Not surprising in the middle of a battle that he couldn't find everything. The things that were brought into the wound are likely the source of the problem. Now, I will just pour some more of this tincture into the wound and some rum. And then we can close it up."

When Mr. Jackson had finished, Giles was comatose, possibly simply as a result of the laudanum, but also probably from the pain the drug had not fully suppressed. The patient had borne the operation stoically, but it must have exhausted him. Despite all the other people still in the room, Daphne stripped off her now soiled gown and again slipped into bed to try to keep Giles warm.

"That is all I can do," Mr. Jackson said, regretfully. "Keep him warm. If he awakes, give him water – boiled water – and another measure of the tincture. I have another pair of patients I must see. One of them is Captain Bush, who also is wounded. Then I shall be back."

For the next forty-eight hours, Giles's condition bounced up and down. Sometimes his pulse would race, and he seemed to be burning up; sometimes, the symptoms retreated, offering hope of recovery only to be dashed by the next onset of fever. Sometimes, he slept calmly or even talked coherently to Daphne; sometimes, he thrashed about, and Daphne had to hold him tightly to try to calm him. Sometimes he muttered phrases that indicated that, in his mind, he was reliving some aspects of his life. On one occasion, what he shouted sounded like, "That damned sodomite. I should flog him, not my sailors. Damn the man." On another, he muttered, to Daphne's great distress, "God, the way she moves, I could bed her easily." Yet, again, this time to Daphne's amazement, "I must ask Miss Moorhead, I must. Even if she doesn't want to marry anyone at all and especially not me, I must try to persuade her. I need her. Oh, I need her."

Giles's illness seemed to be like a battle, waves of soldiers attacking the bastion that was his life, only to be turned back by the defenders, at what cost to them still to be determined. Could the attackers be overcome? No one knew, but Daphne was determined that she would do anything that might help.

After two days, the situation changed. Giles's feverish mutterings stopped, and his temperature seemed lower and more stable. His pulse strengthened and became more regular. His sleep was calmer, and it seemed deeper. Daphne took these developments as promising signs, but she tried not to hope too much. She, herself, was exhausted even though she had been in bed with Giles the whole time. She shifted her position in the bed and promptly fell into a deep sleep herself.

Low, thin, late-autumn sunshine was coming through the window when Giles awoke. He felt weak, but he was no longer light-headed. He was starving. He sat up in bed and announced, "I'm hungry."

Betsey, who had been keeping vigil while her mistress slept, came forward with the broth, which, at Mr. Jackson's orders, they had been feeding him whenever they could.

"Not that slop. Real food!" Giles ordered testily.

Daphne had woken up and observed the change in Giles. "You are back. Oh, that is wonderful!"

She hugged her husband.

"Owwwuch, not so hard! My shoulder!"

Daphne let go immediately. "Sorry. I didn't mean to hurt you. It's just so good that you are a bit better!

"Betsey, Mr. Jackson told Cook what to prepare for Captain Giles to be ready for when he can eat. She will have something ready for him. Get it."

In a few minutes, Betsey returned with some rich lamb stew that Daphne spooned into Giles's mouth. He ate only a small amount before he leaned back, exhausted. Mr. Jackson arrived at that point. He again felt Giles's forehead and took his pulse.

"I think the crisis is past. With luck – and good nursing – he should recover. He should sleep again now. I'll be back later to change the dressing."

Daphne was filled with enormous relief. Giles had come through the worst, it seemed, and was on the way to recovery. She wouldn't lose him. Bernard would have a father. There was so much to tell her husband, and now she would be able to do so. What a mess she was after the ordeal of doing what little she could to keep him alive! She must have a bath and get clean clothes. Right now, before he woke up again. She knew he would have to go to sea again sometime, but for now, he was here and deserved the best of everything.

She told Betsey to have a fire lit in one of the other rooms and to have Cook heat water for a bath. She was off to the nursery. She had not seen her son since the crisis in Giles's health had come upon them. Bernard hadn't even met his father. Now she would have lots of time for him, starting right this minute. After a refreshing soaking and fresh clothes, she was going to bring Bernard, her little bundle of joy, to meet his father.

With any luck, before long, life could return to normal. As normal as it could be when her husband might well be called away to put his life on the line again. She would have to make the most of whatever time she would have with him before he received another assignment.

Giles also reveled in being able to enjoy the home Daphne had made and in being able to discover everything that had happened in his absence. Damn Napoleon! If it were not for the threat that he posed, Giles would happily give up his commission for the life of a country gentleman. This was not to be.

Author's Note

This is a work of fiction set in an historical context. None of the events detailed happened, and none of the main characters existed. It is, if you like, an alternative history, or what might have happened if reality had split off from Giles's world sometime in his recent past but had not got too far away. Many positions, such as the First Lord of the Admiralty, are real but are occupied by fictional characters. Of course, many prominent people mentioned were real, such as the Prince of Wales or the Tsar of Russia. On the other hand, the diplomatic matters that took Giles to Russia are entirely fictional.

While most places are entirely fictitious, this could not be the case of London and St. Petersburg. While some commercial enterprises mentioned are fictional, others actually existed. Examples are Nerot's Hotel, Hatchard's, Fortnum and Mason, and the Haymarket Theatre. The last three are still there. The house at 11 Arlington Street is fictitious. The site is occupied by quite a different building; I have no reason to believe that, in earlier times, a house at that address, if there were one, was used for anything but the most proper of activities. *Gostiny Dvor* is still a feature of St. Petersburg, though it has changed vastly in two centuries.

The sex trade flourished in London at the turn of the eighteenth century as it always had. High-class brothels flourished cheek by jowl with the London homes of most respectable pillars of society, some of whom were not above profiting anonymously from the activities they might publically deplore. The particular incidents in this tale are, however, imaginary.

Readers who are interested in reaching me can email me at jgcragg@telus.net. I always enjoy hearing from readers, both those who liked the yarn – they are always very encouraging – as well as from those who do not – whose criticism suggests ways to improve the next attempt. I might add that reviews given on Amazon are appreciated. Incidentally, reviews on one Amazon site are not usually transferred to another. For instance, Amazon.com often has different reviews from Amazon.co.uk. This is a point worth considering, not only when buying books, but also when considering the many other things that Amazon sells that may have useful reviews

Glossary

Belay (v.) Tie down. Regularly used by mariners to also mean stop.

Bowse Haul in place by a tackle.

Brace (1) (Nautical) A line attached to the end of a yard by which the yard (and its sail) may be rotated to best catch the wind.

(2) (Game-hunting) A pair.

Brail up Furl a square sail by drawing it up to the yard from which it hangs.

Brig (1) A two-masted ship square-rigged.

(2) Slang for the prison on board a ship.

Brideswell The prison where prostitutes were usually confined. How Daphne, in her innocence, might have known of it remains a mystery.

Bumper Very large drinking vessel.

Canister (shot) A tin can (canister) filled with small lead pellets of other bits of metal used as an anti-personnel weapon. It differed from grapeshot primarily in that grapeshot was loaded into a cannon in a canvas bag.

Cat The cat was the whip used to flog seamen. It was made by the bosun from rope. It was customary for a new one to be made for each flogging.

Carronade   A short gun, frequently mounted on a slider rather than a wheeled gun carriage, only used for close-in work. They were not usually counted in the number of guns by which a ship was rated.

Cloth (drawn)   Refers to the stage of a meal when the final dish had been consumed. The tablecloth was then removed, and the men in attendance drew together to imbibe liquor stronger than wine, usually accompanied by nut and fruit. When ladies were present, they withdrew to the drawing-room just before the cloth was drawn. It was usually a time of more general conversation than occurred during the meal.

Consol   A bond issued by the British Government with no stated redemption date, paying to the holder a specified amount per annum in perpetuity. Only recently were the last of them purchased and canceled by the government.

Douse   (1) Take down.

  (2) Put out.

Driver   A Gaff rigged sail on the mizzenmast. It was a fore and aft sail with the leading edge attached to the mast rather than a square sail whose center would be at the mast.

Entail   A provision that the inheritance of real property would go to specified members of a family (or other specified groups), usually to the closest male relatives. Usually implied that the present owner could not leave it to someone else and was usually put on a property to prevent the immediate heir from dissipating the inheritance but would pass it intact (more or less) to the next generation.

Fighting top   A Platform on the mast where the main part met the topmast from which marines could fire their muskets on to the deck of an opposing ship.

Fother (a sail) Pull a sail treated with oakum under the bottom of a ship to slow leaks.

Georgie   Name used by Sir Walcott to indicate familiarity with the Prince of Wales, whose name was George. It is believed to be the origin of the name in the nursery rhyme 'Georgie, Porgie, pudding, and pie…'

Grape (shot)   Musket balls, or sometimes small scrap metal, used to fill bags, which were then inserted in cannot as if they were cannot balls.

Grapnel   A metal hook or set of hooks attached to a line that could be thrown and hook on to the edge of another ship or a wall.

Harris's List (of Covent Garden Ladies)   A   booklet published annually in the late 18th-century listing prostitutes in London, often with their specialties.

Heave to   Stopping the forward motion of a ship by turning one sail to work in opposition to the others.

Helm alee   Turn a ship into the wind. (It sounds backwards but originates from the time when ships had tillers, which were pushed in the direction opposite to the desired turn.)

Jobbing Captain   A post-captain who has not been appointed to a ship and is employed to temporarily captain another captain's ship.

John Company   Nickname for the East India Company.

Jolly boat   A small boat, usually the smallest on a ship.

King's shilling   Volunteers were paid a shilling for joining; pressed men were not.

Larboard   The left-hand side of the ship looking forward. Opposite of starboard. Now usually called "port."

Larboard watch   Crews were usually divided into two watches, who alternated the times when they were on duty with each other. The other one was called the starboard watch.

Lead line   A line in which knots have been tied at fixed distances, with a large piece of lead at the end, was used to measure the depth of water.

League   Three nautical miles.

Lee way   The speed with which a boat is blown straight downwind when trying to sail upwind.

Let the cat out of the bag   Traditionally, when the cat (q.v.) had been made by the bosun, it was stowed in a baize bag until needed; hence the expression, which has evolved into a somewhat different meaning over time.

Loblolly boy   A medical assistant in the Navy.

Log   (1) Record of events.

(2) Measurement of the speed of a ship, obtained by throwing a piece of wood overboard attached to a knotted line and counting how many knots are pulled out over a fixed time period.

Miss stays   When tacking, failing to have a turn that switches the direction from which the wind is coming so that the ship is stuck and unable to complete the turn.

Mrs. Fitzherbert   The wife (though the marriage was not officially recognized) of the Prince of Wales.

Muster Roll   List of all men serving on a ship.

The Nore   Anchorage in the Thames estuary off the mouth of the Medway River. A major anchorage for the Royal Navy in the Age of Sail.

Nosegay   A small bunch of flowers held in or attached to the hand to be placed near the nose to disguise the presence of unpleasant odors.

Oakum   Fibrous material got from unraveling old ropes used with tar to caulk wooden ships.

Orlop (deck)   The lowest deck of the ship, below the waterline.

Painter   The mooring line at the bow of a small boat.

Pocket Borough   (later usually called a rotten borough.) A formerly well-populated town that still returned two members to parliament even though the population had fallen so low that one or a few landowners could select the next MP certain that they could control the election.

Quarter day   The days on which traditionally rents were due, tenancies expired or began and other matters settled. They were Lady Day (March 25), Midsummer Day (June 24), Michaelmas (Sept. 29), and Christmas (Dec. 25).

Quarter deck   The outside deck of a ship at the stern.

Rafted   Ships or boats are rafted together when they are tied to each other while at anchor.

Redoubt: A minor or subsidiary fort. Here referring to a gun platform made level with guns firing over a parapet.

Reef	Reducing the amount of sail exposed to the wind by gather and then tying part of it to a spar.
Remove(s)	(Applied to dinners) Separate dishes at dinner. There usually weren't courses as we know them, at least not after the soup. Instead, a variety of different dishes would be served in turn.
Revenuers	Agents of the Customs and Excise authorities whose job was to find and seize smuggled goods and arrest the offenders.
Rout	A large, formal evening gathering. It had a slightly risqué connotation.
Sack	A (cheap) fortified Spanish wine. At this time, decent sherry was referred to by this name, but the older meaning of the term still remained in occasional use for lesser types as well.
Salvage	Fee paid by a boat's owner to rescuers of a ship in danger but not abandoned.
Shrouds	A rope ladder formed by short lengths of rope tied tightly between the stays of a mast.
Sheet	A line controlling how much a sail is pulled in.
Skagen	Northern most cape in Denmark
Skagerrak	The passage (strait) between Norway and Denmark.

Slow match   A fuse in the form of a rope which burned at a premeasured speed used to blow up barrels of gunpowder or other bombs while allowing the persons lighting it to escape.

Sounding   Taking the depth of water with a lead line.

Spring line (or just spring)   A rope attached to the anchor cable, which, by being pulled in or let out, could be used to change the direction in which the bow of the ship (or its broadside) was pointing when at anchor.

Spotted Dick   A pudding made with dried fruit, usually served with custard. Lighter than a plum pudding.

St. Stephen's Day   The day after Christmas. The term Boxing Day now used in the United Kingdom and some of the Commonwealth countries to refer to this day did not come into common use until the middle of the nineteenth century.

Standing Rigging   All the lines that hold the masts up and other ones that do not move as the ship is sailed.

Stay(s)   (1) A line used to prevent a mast from falling over or being broken in the wind.

(2) Corsets.

Step   (1) Promotion from lieutenant to commander.

(2) Place a mast in a vertical position, usually on a small boat.

Sternsheets The sitting area in the stern of a small boat.

Strakes Planks used for the hull of a ship.

Strike Lower the flag of a ship to indicate surrender.

Struck below Clearing out the partitions and furnishings on the fighting decks of a ship, including especially the captain's cabin, and stowing them out of harms' way.

Studding sails Additional square sails used to extend the width of the usual sails on a square-rigged ship.

Tack Change the direction in which a ship is sailing and the side of the ship from which the wind is blowing by turning towards the direction from which the wind is blowing.

Taffrail Railing at the stern of the quarter deck.

Third rate Naval ships were rated by the number of guns they carried. A third rate would have somewhere between 64 and 80 guns nominally.

Ton That part of London society most interested in adhering to the latest fashions.

Twelfth Night The evening of the Twelfth Day of Christmas, January 6, which is twelve evenings after Christmas Eve. Oddly enough, this is also the date of "Old Christmas," the date to which the revision of the calendar assigned December 25, according to the unrevised calendar. Traditionally it was the time when roles between servants and master were reversed. By the early nineteenth century, it had been much toned down, and when celebrated, it often was a party for the servants at which their masters would make a brief appearance. Often not celebrated at all.

Unstep   Take a mast from its vertical position on a boat, usually to lay it horizontally.

Walmer Castle, A shore defense castle, dating from the sixteenth century. The residence of the Warden of the Cinque Ports.

Wardroom   The part of a ship used by the senior officers of a ship.

Warden of the Cinque Ports. A largely ceremonial title by the 19th century, though some holders did take their possible duties of defending the coast seriously.

Watch   (1) Time: A ship's day was divided into four-hour watches, with one further divided into two. The watches were

         First watch: 8 p.m.- 12 midnight

Middle watch: 12 midnight -
4 a.m.

Morning watch: 4 a.m. – 8 a.m.

Forenoon watch: 8 a.m. – 12
noon

Afternoon watch   12 noon – 4
p.m.

First dog watch   4 p.m. – 6
p.m.

Second dog watch   6 p.m. – 8
p.m.

In each watch, time was marked off in half-
hour segments, so the one bell of the First
watch would be 8:30 p.m., two bells would
be 9:00 p.m., and so on.

(2) Division of the crew. The crew was
divided (usually) into two watches, the
starboard watch and the larboard watch,
which alternated when they worked (in
normal circumstances) and when they were
at leisure or asleep.

(3) Time when officers were on duty.
Referred to as "being on watch" or "watch."

(4) Police force on land

Wear (referring to a ship)   The opposite of tack where the maneuver of changing which side of a ship the wind is coming from is accomplished by turning away from the wind.

Wedding portion   A dowry, so called because it was regarded as the portion of her father's estate that an unmarried daughter might expect to have.

Wherry   A rowboat used as a water taxi.

Writ   The document authorizing the holding of a by-election. It's being issued had to be moved and passed in the House of Commons first.

Yellow admiral   Someone who has been promoted to the rank of Admiral without being given a command. Largely created to allow the promotion of a captain with less seniority.

Printed in Great Britain
by Amazon